April's hand went to his,

partially covering its hard, leather-like surface. Her fingers stroked his, seeking their warmth, compulsively needing to touch some part of him. She turned his hand over until his palm was toward her and studied its callused strength with her fingers. Bringing it to her face, she pressed it against her cheek in a gesture of complete surrender, of intimate tenderness, and felt the wild desire rushing through her veins.

MacKenzie grew rigid as her soft caress ignited blazes more painful than that of the knife days earlier. The gentleness of her touch, and all it represented, filled him with a desolation greater than the barrenness of the desert. He knew he should take his hand away before he was lost, but the velvet feel of her cheek transfixed him. He had no will as she moved his hand to her lips and he felt their soft touch. Without words, she was proclaiming her love for him, offering him everything she had without condition or expectation.

Dear Reader:

Harlequin offers you historical romances with a difference: novels with all the passion and excitement of a five-hundred-page historical in three hundred pages, stories that focus on people—a hero and heroine you really care about, who take you back and make you part of their time.

This summer we'll be publishing books by some of your favorite authors. We have a new book by Bronwyn Williams entitled *Dandelion*. It continues the story of Kinnahauk and Bridget and their grandson, Cabel. Brooke Hastings makes her historical debut with *So Sweet a Sin*, a gripping story of passion and treachery in the years leading up to the American Revolution. *Seize the Fire* is an exciting new Western by Patricia Potter. Caryn Cameron's latest, *Silver Swords*, is an adventurous tale of piracy set in Florida in the early 1800s. You won't want to miss these or any of the other exciting selections coming soon from Harlequin Historicals.

We appreciate your comments and suggestions. Our goal is to publish the kinds of books you want to read. So please keep your letters coming. You can write to us at the address below.

Karen Solem
Editorial Director
Harlequin Historicals
P.O. Box 7372
Grand Central Station
New York, New York 10017

Seize the Fire

Patricia Potter

Harlequin Books

TORONTO • NEW YORK • LONDON
AMSTERDAM • PARIS • SYDNEY • HAMBURG
STOCKHOLM • ATHENS • TOKYO • MILAN

Harlequin Historical first edition July 1989

ISBN 0-373-28626-0

Books by Patricia Potter

Harlequin Historicals

Swampfire #6
Between the Thunder #15
Samara #20
Seize the Fire #26

PATRICIA POTTER

is a former award-winning journalist with a passion for history and books. As a reporter with the *Atlanta Journal* she met and reported on three presidents and covered southern news stories as varied as the space launches and the civil rights movement.

This resident of Atlanta, Georgia, has her own public relations and advertising agency. Her interests in animals and travel are not especially compatible, but she does manage to fit them both into her busy schedule. Her reading runs the gamit from biographies to espionage, and she is currently the president of the Georgia Romance Writers of America.

Tyger! Tyger! burning bright
In the forests of the night
What immortal hand or eye
Could frame thy fearful symmetry?

In what distant deeps or skies
Burnt the fire of thine eyes?
Oh what wings dare he aspire?
What the hand dare seize the fire?

William Blake
"The Tyger"

Prologue

The mournful wail of bagpipes wafted plaintively through the forest. There were few to hear, only a solitary Indian hunter seeking food, and he lifted his head in puzzlement at the strangely discordant but compelling sounds. The rest were animals, which scattered in fear—all except the gray wolf, which lay at the feet of the man breaking the forest peace.

The alien music grew louder as the old Scottish hymn came alive in highlands much like, but so very far from, its original home. The keening notes reflected struggle and sorrow, man's loneliness and, lastly, in a great surge of power—final victory.

The musician took the pipe from his mouth, listening to the echoes of the closing notes reverberating through the trees, his proud head tilted as they faded slowly into silence. There was a moment of complete stillness, then the forest creatures once more found their voices, each one a part of an ancient symphony that beggared any of man's creations.

Or so MacKenzie thought as he listened intently to the forest music. It would be a long time before he heard its alluring sound again on this mountain.

He looked at the platform he had built, the platform that bore the body—if no longer the soul—of his father. There was no sorrow in the gesture, only a measure of duty toward a man who had lived true to his own values. That those values had not included love was something MacKenzie had accepted many years ago. Like the wolf at his feet, MacKenzie was a lean, cautious, forest-wise creature raised merely to survive. He had never known love and he did not miss it.

He felt comfortable in the Scottish clothes he had donned this day—the wool shirt and kilt, the thick leather belt and the red and black tartan. They had belonged to—and long been revered by—Rob MacKenzie, and now his son recognized that heritage for one last time.

But it would end here—with the death of his father and this last concession to his father's obsession with the past—with injustices real and imagined. For MacKenzie knew that he was the last. There would be no more of the line to follow. He would not pass on a legacy of hate, the stigma of "half-breed." He had learned to be a man alone, and thus he would stay— needing no one, trusting none, except perhaps the wolf at his feet.

His hands busied themselves with the kindling under the platform, and he watched without expression as the fire took hold and the flames shot upward, beginning their hungry attack on the platform. His father had requested this—a Norseman's funeral. Rob MacKenzie had always taken pride in that part of his ancestry, in the wild and free plunderers who had explored the world. Past glories. They had been his father's life. That and the lonely solitude of the mountains, which he had craved as most men craved love. It seemed only fitting now that his ashes be spread by the wind among the peaks and valleys he had known better than any man.

MacKenzie looked on impassively as the platform was consumed by fire. He wondered, briefly, at his lack of feeling. But then there had never been much between Rob MacKenzie and the bastard half-breed son known by whites and Indians alike only as MacKenzie.

His mother had been a Shoshone Indian, bought as a convenience from another tribe, which had captured and brutalized her. She had suffered her lot as concubine and slave to the older MacKenzie in dumb, embittered silence until her death years earlier. MacKenzie had never known a tender gesture or word from either of his parents—indeed he had never expected any. It was an alien notion—love. He knew the word from the Bible—and the worn battered volume of Robert Burns poetry his father had brought with him from Scotland so many years earlier—but it had no real meaning to him. It was like the Burns stories, something faraway and fanciful.

His father had, grudgingly, taught his son to read—"'Tis no' so easy ta cheat a mon who can read"—as he taught him to hunt and live high in the often snow-covered mountains.

MacKenzie had been eager to learn, for the escape into words, and he had memorized much of the Burns poetry as well as long passages of the Bible, although he knew that enjoyment had not been his father's purpose. Rob MacKenzie had sought to instill in his son his own obsession with Scotland, with the past, and had dressed him in kilts and taught him the pipes. It had been the one way in which MacKenzie had pleased his father—the pipes—for he had a natural aptitude for music, for hearing a tune and remembering it.

Sometimes when Rob MacKenzie was very drunk, he would tell his son he must one day return to Scotland and reclaim the title of lord, forgetting that it was lost nearly a hundred years earlier. At other times he would get violent, and the child would escape to the woods. It was there, among the animals, that he found some measure of pleasure and peace. They were his playmates, his companions, and he had a special kind of understanding with them. They seemed to sense that he meant them no harm, that he was, in so many ways, like them. He had the same silent grace, the same watchful eyes, the same instinct for danger.

He had left the mountains occasionally, first to trade pelts for his father, then to find his own way, and each time he encountered a hostile world. His thick, raven-black hair and bronze skin proclaimed an Indian heritage that brought him scorn and trouble in a white world. He fared little better in the red one, which distrusted anyone with white blood. MacKenzie had learned long ago that he belonged nowhere, not to his father's Scottish past, nor to his mother's tortured Indian present. And he had schooled himself not to care. His own abilities, his own strength were all that mattered. He would have turned his back on all men, Indian and white, except for the dream that carried him time and again into a world he despised.

He had to walk among white men to achieve it, so he did . . . reluctantly, cautiously, emotionlessly. He steeled himself to rise above the insults and distrust, to silently return the scorn while he worked toward his goal.

He had been employed these past nine years as an Indian scout for General Ira Wakefield, one of only two white men he had ever respected. He had left several times for reasons he would rather forget, but had been lured back by promises of autonomy and money. This would be the last time. The next assignment would earn him enough money for a beginning...the realization of his long-nurtured plans.

MacKenzie undressed and changed into his familiar worn buckskins. He looked around at the spartan cabin once again before gathering the familiar Bible and his father's cherished copy of Burns's poetry. In a tanned buffalo hide he wrapped them carefully, along with the bagpipes, the Scottish dress and a purse of coins and bills—the remnants of his past and the hope of his future—and buried the bundle under a towering evergreen. He would be back to fetch them, and Wolf, after this one last tour with the Army.

He would leave his father's other sparse belongings—clothes, some worn blankets and skins and a few remaining food goods—where they were. Few knew of the isolated cabin, only a mountain man or two and several Utes, and they would be welcome to what was left.

MacKenzie waited until the fire died down to a bank of dull red coals and then crumbled into ashes. He would risk no chance of fire to *his* forest, his home. He said a terse farewell to Wolf, mounted his horse in one lithe leap and rode slowly from the clearing into the deep forest.

He didn't look back. The only sound in the evening silence was the quiet hoofbeats of his horse...and the long, mournful cry of the wolf. MacKenzie's hands tightened on the reins for he understood, and knew, the same lonely anguish.

Chapter One

Freedom. The last warning blasts of the train whistle seemed to scream the word to April Manning. Freedom, it repeated. Freedom from darkness, from mourning, from blacks and grays. Freedom to once more see the colors of life: a gurgling blue stream, a golden sun, the fresh vivid green of a forest. They had been there, of course, for the past four years, but they had been veiled by somber disapproval.

Freedom. How wonderful the word sounded. Freedom to wear a bright dress, to smile, to laugh and, most of all, freedom to see her too-solemn young son grin, and play, and be a child.

April felt the first lurching of wheels under the train car and her heart made similar jerky movements as she looked at Davon...no, Davey. Davey now. A name for a boy. She had always thought Davon too heavy, but her husband's family would call him nothing else and she, too, had finally bent to their will. As she had, to her everlasting shame, to so many other things.

She would not look, now, at *their* stiff, accusing figures standing on the platform. The four of them were there, she knew. They wanted her to know of their violent disapproval to the very end. But she wouldn't give them that satisfaction. Besides, she could see them only too clearly in her mind. Mrs. Manning, her late husband's mother, and his sisters—Emily, Dorothy and Margaret. All would be clad in the same heavy, ugly black they had worn for four years. Their mouths would be pursed in tight, grim expressions, each so alike in her fear of life, in her tight hold on grief.

Freedom from gloom. The last whistle accompanied the quickening chugs of the train. April's hand reached over to Davey, who sat so quietly across from her. Childhood, and what should have been its joy, had been drained from him in that house of sorrow. Laughter and play had been banned . . . mischief discouraged by scolding tirades. She had wanted to leave for months, for years, but David, her husband, was missing in the war, and she felt it her duty to wait where he had left her, to be there when he returned . . . she and David's son.

But he didn't return, and months turned into years. Long, agonizing years of waiting for some word. Word that never came. Not until the war ended, and one of his sergeants was released from Andersonville Prison. It had been a miracle that the man survived four years of Southern imprisonment, but he had, and his first action after healing was to visit Captain David Manning's family and tell them about David's last hours. The sergeant and Captain Manning had been the only survivors of a Confederate ambush. But the captain had been mortally wounded, and the sergeant stayed with him, and buried him, before his own capture. He had reported Captain Manning's death to Confederate authorities, but somehow the news had never reached federal headquarters.

April had felt pain, but it had been dulled by years of waiting, of secretly knowing. Otherwise there would have been some word. She had been a ghost for those four years, haunted by an aching loneliness. Every moment knowing but not knowing. Living in a netherworld where smiles and laughter were unknown, where hope lingered painfully, then died. The confirmation of what she had come to believe had been both torturous and freeing. The contradiction did not elude her. Never again, she told herself silently. Never again would she subject herself to such agony. She had had her love, and she would treasure it, but she wouldn't subject herself—or her child—to such hurt again.

"Come over here," April told her son, and Davey moved to her side, letting her hug him to her, not wriggling under the increased pressure as he sensed her need with his five-year-old instinct. He was such a good little boy. Too good, too solemn. Too wise, April thought as tiny tears clouded her cerulean blue eyes. Her arm tightened around him. He would have a chance now, a chance to run and ride, to get into mischief, to tease and grin. Her father would see to it. Doughty General Wakefield, fierce and proud, was but clay in a child's hands, she knew that well. He fought and loved with the same intensity. The thought of him filled April with warmth.

It was a warmth she badly needed after the years of coldness. But she had loved David, loved him as only a young, inexperienced girl could love. And they had had so little time together—barely time to get to know each other.

Her father had disapproved of the marriage—not because of David, who was one of his finest young officers, but because of the rush. April and David, who had courted only a month, decided to marry when David was transferred east. Already the clouds of war were on the horizon, and Wakefield knew David would soon be in the middle of the hostilities, but April had always been stubborn, and now she was unmovable. So they had married at her father's post in Arizona, then taken stages and a train to Charleston, where David was stationed at Fort Sumter. They had nearly a year and a half together, a happy time, particularly when Davey was born, before Southern enmity persuaded David to send his wife and son to his family in Boston. She never saw him again. The war started, and he was lost in one of the first engagements.

April had tried, for David's sake, to adjust. But Mrs. Manning was still mourning for a husband dead ten years past. Two of April's sisters-in-law were in their late twenties, plain and unmarried. The third was married, also to an army officer, but he was killed early in the war, and she moved back into the Manning house, a bitter figure in black.

All had doted on David and disapproved of April. Her laughter offended them; her gaiety horrified them, and she felt more and more stifled until she feared becoming one of *them*. Still she worked desperately to please them, even after the news came that David was missing in the first few months of the war.

The train had reached the outskirts of Boston, and April looked toward the neat, tended fields with resurgent hope.

Spaces. Spaces to roam. Spaces to see. No more hot, closed, black-draped rooms. No more bitter words about the one activity that had so incensed the Manning family and that had given her purpose and satisfaction.

"You desecrate your marriage," Mrs. Manning had angrily told her, absolutely forbidding her to tend the Confederate wounded in the prison hospital in Boston.

Emily gave her the usual malevolent glare. "You never loved David, or you wouldn't do this."

But April did. It had been her first rebellion but not her last. In those moments, she had learned she could stand up for herself and fight for what she believed.

She had not, at first, meant to so infuriate her husband's family. She had merely wanted to help...someone. Anyone. Feeling trapped and useless, she at first volunteered at one Union hospital, but it had more volunteers than it needed. One of the doctors recognized her fierce need and told April of the wretched conditions at Fort Warren, which held Confederate prisoners of war. April had known many Southern officers on her father's staff; they had always been unfailingly gallant and, no matter what, she couldn't hate them for doing what they felt was right. Always the defender of the weak, April received permission to help at the hospital and went several times a week, taking what little food she could scrounge, writing letters, trying to spread a little comfort. She suffered for it because hate was as much a resident in the Manning house as grief. And she was afraid Davey suffered for it, too, but something within her compelled her actions. She tried to explain once.

"If David's in a Confederate prison, I would hope some Southern woman would try to help him."

"You're a fool," her mother-in-law said. "Not one of those traitors would lift a finger, and now you're giving comfort to our enemies...perhaps to the very Rebel who killed David."

But April couldn't blame the soldiers she saw and tended. So many of them were merely boys—starved, war-sick, mutilated boys who wanted only to go home...

Home. Arizona now. Arizona with its strange, stark beauty. Arizona was a beacon to her, a place of sun and warmth, and it was a shimmering glow that had remained in her memory during the frigid wet winters of an inhospitable north.

She was going home. It was her most difficult rebellion, as the Manning women had used every ounce of guilt in their formidable arsenal. David would have wanted Davey to stay in Boston and be raised by his family. How could she think of taking him? How could she so betray her husband?

But she persisted, knowing in her heart that her husband would want Davey to be raised happily, not weighed down by the bitterness that had already made its mark.

Could it really be over? The waiting, the hoping, the praying, the endless lectures, the hateful looks and wounding words? Would she and Davey, at long last, have their own life, to mold as they wished?

She would miss David, her husband of so few months. She would always miss him. He had been handsome and tender and, unlike the rest of his family, joyous. She had often wondered how that inherent gladness of spirit had survived the deep gloom of his family. But perhaps he had once given it a light, and that light had been quenched when he left. She had been nineteen the last time she saw him, and now she was twenty-three. It had been nearly five years, and sometimes she couldn't quite remember what he looked like. It frightened her, because she knew she should. At least, that way, she could keep part of him alive.

But he had left her a wondrous gift—Davey. Wonderful, serious, responsible Davey, with his father's green eyes and dark hair.

April looked down at him. He was sleeping, his head resting against her side. She leaned down and kissed his tousled head. Now, she promised silently, now you will know laughter.

April's optimism and hope faded slightly as the train moved west. It was late August, and the heat was oppressive. It strained the tempers of the passengers. Cinders and dust made it almost mandatory that windows remain closed.

April was the only woman in the car, and Davey the only child. The war was now more than four months over, but still most of the men were in uniform, or parts of uniforms—living reminders of the country's recent agonies. There was still turmoil as soldiers were slowly mustered out of the army and started for home or for a new life elsewhere. Everyone seemed to be on the move. Despite victory, a feeling of dissatisfaction hovered in the air. Four years of bitter fighting had changed so many, had made it impossible for them to settle into old jobs. The west beckoned now as never before.

Sprinkled among the travelers were two men clad in gray Confederate trousers, evidently ex-prisoners finally released and making their way home. They endured the constant taunts and challenges in silence. April studied them carefully, wondering at their forbearance, noting the way one visibly swallowed a fierce urge to retaliate. She couldn't help but wonder why they were just now traveling. Surely they would have been released months ago. Or why they hadn't worn something less likely to invite trouble?

After one particularly ugly verbal attack, intended, she knew, to incite a fight the Southerners could not possible win, April told Davey to stay in his seat, and she rose, moving to where a growing number of men joined to bait the two ex-Rebs. The men parted as April reached the two victims. The passengers had been together for two days in the hot railroad car, and they all knew her story of a missing husband just recently known dead. They had played with Davey and shared food with them . . . all but the Rebs, who had stayed to themselves.

April ignored the stares of the men and completed her journey toward the two men who sat alone in the back. She saw the knotted hands of one; the second seemed oddly indifferent. She looked at the seat opposite them, a seat that had remained empty despite the overcrowded train.

"May I sit with you?" she asked softly.

Surprise darted over the face of the older Southerner. He, too, had overheard the young widow's story. He rose. "We would be pleasured, ma'am," he said, in a pleasant but wary drawl, his eyes never leaving his antagonists.

April looked around at the faces—some angered, some abashed, some puzzled. "The war's over," she said, her voice shaking slightly. "There's been enough violence, enough hate, enough death..." Her voice faltered on the last word, and that, more than anything, sent the Union veterans back to their seats.

April leaned back in the seat, closed her eyes for a moment, opening them only when she felt Davey's small hand on hers.

"Mama?"

April looked at his earnest face and patted the seat next to her, inviting him to sit. "Everything's fine, Davey," she said comfortingly. She knew he must have felt the tension in the car; his face was puzzled and his little body stiff.

When he settled in the security of her arms, April's eyes met the quizzical ones of the Southerner who had risen. The other's remained curiously blank.

"Thank you, ma'am," the older man said with an almost imperceptible smile. "I'm Blake Farrar, formerly a lieutenant with the Texas First Cavalry. This is my brother, Dan." His mouth tightened, and bitterness clouded dark brown eyes. His hand touched his brother's sleeve, but there was no response, not even a flicker, from the man next to him.

"He's been injured?" April questioned gently.

Farrar sighed. "In ways you can't see. In ways I'm afraid you can't heal."

April's eyes misted at his anguished words, surprising the Southerner once more. "So many," she whispered. "So many wounds and hurts ... so many dead ... "

A compassion Blake Farrar thought long destroyed surfaced. His voice was very low. "You, too, I've heard. Sometimes ... we forget ... the pain back home." His hand started to reach out, then dropped. His voice grew stronger. "Where are you going, ma'am?"

April straightened. "Home. Arizona."

"You have family there?"

"My father," April said with a slight smile, the thought of him reviving her. "And you?"

"Dan and I are for Texas. I have a wife. Two children." His hard look softened. "I haven't seen them in four years."

"You've been at ... " April hesitated at the word.

"Fort Warren," Farrar confirmed, once more with deep bitterness. "Two years. Two long, miserable, hungry years."

Davey had been listening and at the familiar words, he spoke up. "Mama went there," he said. "Grandmother didn't want her to. They fought about it all the time."

Farrar's eyes widened. "I thought your husband ... "

"Was Union?" April answered. "He was. But I hoped...had hoped—someone down South would try to help *him*."

The Reb's eyes gentled for the first time. "I didn't think anyone cared," he said slowly. "It was hell there, begging your pardon, ma'am."

"There were others," April said, embarrassed.

"Not many, I think," he replied.

"I didn't see your brother in the hospital," April said, anxious to change the subject.

"He didn't have the kind of wound they treated there," Blake said. "You see, Dan couldn't stand the killing. We were at Shiloh, and he shot a Yank...turned out to be nothing more than a boy. It destroyed something in him. He just walked away, right into a Union patrol, and I had to go with him. He hasn't spoken since."

"You've just been released?"

"Three months ago. I met a doctor, hoped he could help Dan." Farrar shrugged. "He helped me get a job at the docks, but that quickly ended when so many Union soldiers came home. And Dan wasn't getting any better. I thought going home might help, but we didn't have any money. The doctor, God bless him, loaned us enough money for the trip, but it wasn't enough for clothes, too." He looked wryly at his ragged Confederate trousers. "I thought the war was over. Now I wonder if it ever will be."

April looked at her son. He would grow up without a father because of the war. She squeezed Davey's arm.

"My boy's about his age," Blake said wistfully, his eyes intent on the small figure across from him. "He's very good."

"Too good," April replied. "We've been living with my husband's family, and I'm afraid they didn't know much about small boys. Sometimes I wish he would get into mischief like other children."

"I doubt it will take him long to learn," the Texan said with a real smile. His hand reached over to Davey. He touched the small face with gentleness and wonder. "If only we could all be so innocent..."

April and Davey spent the next several days with the Farrar brothers, Davey finding an instant friend in the silent one. Although Dan Farrar still kept his silence, his eyes warmed when Davey's sleepy head sometimes dropped into his lap. And

Davey listened with fascinated interest to Blake's tales of Texas and the Alamo.

They separated at St. Louis, April and Davey changing to a train that would travel over newly completed tracks to Kansas City. The Farrars caught a Butterfield stage headed south to Texas.

Blake bid April and Davey goodbye with gratitude and real regret. "If ever you need anything, need anyone, please remember us," he said, giving her the name of the town nearest his ranch. "Your Davey has helped Dan more than anything else could, I think... Perhaps my own children can do the rest. Thank you." He took her hands in his. "I hope you and Davey find the happiness you deserve." With that, he turned abruptly, and he and his brother climbed onto the stage.

At Kansas City, April and Davey also transferred to a coach. They would go to Fort Atkinson, then Santa Fe, and finally across the New Mexico territory to Arizona...

Would it never end? April did not remember the journey as being so long, but then the first time she had been a new bride, and everything had been so gloriously wonderful. She and David had never stopped talking, and it had all seemed such an adventure.

Even Davey was squirming restlessly in the Concord coach. There were another four passengers squeezed into its confines, and piles of mail were stacked in every corner. April felt she would never want to sit again after the constant jolting along the primitive roads. The only relief came when the horses were changed every twenty miles or so. Then she and Davey could stretch and walk during the few moments it took to change horses and drivers. Sometimes there would be a hot meal available, though it was usually little more than rancid bacon, bread and coffee that tasted like dishwater. It was still better than the hardtack and jerky that most passengers, including April and Davey, carried. The heat prevented any variety.

The other passengers were mostly a silent lot, all of them men headed for the California gold fields. Of the four, two drank constantly, to April's quiet dismay. The smell of liquor and sweat made her want to gag, and only the approaching journey's end made it tolerable. She greeted the first sight of desert with joy, particularly at sunrise when the bright glimmering sands caught the serene beauty of a rising sun. Where others thought the desert stark and ugly, April had always found a quiet radiance in it. She had hungered for it for five years, and now not even her drunken companions could quiet the triumph growing within her.

At Santa Fe, she and Davey gratefully left the coach and rested in the frontier town for several days before continuing. There was a stage heading west, and a small army encampment on the border of the New Mexico-Arizona territories. She knew from her father's letter that she could get transportation from there to his headquarters. He had warned her about marauding Apaches, and made it clear she and Davey were not to travel into Arizona without adequate escort.

Already Davey was changing, his green eyes glistening with eagerness and curiosity. He was full of questions about this strange barren land, so different from the bright greens of the northeast.

Most intriguing to him was the thought of a horse. For his very own, April promised. And a dog. He should finally have a dog, his dearest desire for the past year. But the Mannings had been horrified at the thought of a "filthy beast" in their home. But now he would have both, and more.

April told him stories of her own childhood and pets. She had moved often as a child. Her father had been a career army officer, serving in a number of posts from Kansas to the northwest to Arizona. He had been assigned to Arizona as a colonel in 1858, and it was here that April's mother died, and where April's heart, for some reason, stayed. Wakefield was one of the few officers not called east during the war, although he did fight the Confederates when they crossed into New Mexico during the first year of the war. His real expertise was with the Indians, and he finally won his general's star at the war's end. April had not seen him in the past five years, but they had written frequently to each other. She knew he would adore Davey and give him the masculine influence and love the boy seemed to crave.

Only a few days now, perhaps a week at most, depending on the Army's schedule. Arizona. Home. Father. April shivered with anticipation as she and Davey boarded their last coach.

Chapter Two

MacKenzie, his eyes wary and his right hand taking the rifle from its scabbard, slid from his horse.

He stooped, studying the pony tracks carefully. They were from an unshod pony... and recent. And many. Too many. There had been several small groups of Apache renegades killing and burning in the southeast corner of the Arizona Territory. It appeared now that they might have joined forces, and that boded ill for both the settlers and the Army. And himself.

It meant he would have to stop by the small garrison on the Chaco River and give warning before heading back to Wakefield's headquarters. Not, he thought wryly, that his advice would be heeded. Not by Sergeant Peters, nor by Peters's friend, Terrell. And their shavetail lieutenant didn't have the sense God gave a chicken. But distasteful as it was, dealing with the two men who regarded Indian blood with bitter hatred was his job.

MacKenzie remounted his Appaloosa. He had selected the horse for its toughness and speed, but it was deceptively ugly and ungainly. It had often invited taunts, but MacKenzie knew the horse's endurance had saved his life more than once. He eased back in the saddle, wiping the sweat from his brow and taking one last sweeping look across the mesas. He pressed his knees against the horse's sides, urging it to a gallop. The sooner he reached the Chaco River, the sooner he would rid himself of a disagreeable duty.

Seven hours later, as dusk approached, MacKenzie reached the small cluster of buildings that comprised the Chaco post. Because of recent hostile outbreaks, it had been reinforced and should have had a commander of higher rank than Lieutenant Evan Pickering. But the captain who was in command had been abruptly recalled to Washington, and no replacement had yet arrived. So MacKenzie had to deal with a damn fool, a cocky West Point graduate who knew little about the West and less about Indians. And who depended almost entirely on his two top sergeants, both of whom hated MacKenzie and deeply suspected any and all of the Army's Indian scouts.

MacKenzie paused before riding in. He was bone tired and filthy. He had been in the saddle for two weeks, scouting alone. It was the way he wanted it. He didn't like depending on anyone else, nor did he enjoy being responsible for other scouts. He had repeatedly turned down Wakefield's offer to be named chief of the scouts. Besides, he had argued, some of the officers and enlisted men refused to listen to him because he was a 'breed. 'Breed. God, he hated that word. But he could expect to hear it repeatedly in the next few hours. He shifted in his saddle, his buckskin trousers straining against his muscular thighs. Because of the heat, he had replaced his usual buckskin shirt with a more comfortable cotton one, its sleeves rolled up and the neck open where a sweat-stained bandanna ringed bronze skin glistening now with beads of perspiration.

A hand went across his face, feeling the bristling beard. He would be eyed with disdainful disapproval by Pickering, who was always dressed like a rooster, flaunting his carefully pressed uniform like tail feathers. MacKenzie sighed. He would spend the night here, find a bath and hit the trail again early in the morning. The deserted mesas always held special appeal after the prejudice and hate at Chaco. He steeled himself for the coming confrontations and rode into the encampment.

"I don't believe it," the heavy, blue-coated figure blustered. "Those damned Apaches hate each other too much to band together."

"They may hate you more," MacKenzie replied coolly, eyeing Sergeant Peters with his usual contempt.

"Does that include you?" Peters sneered, his lips twisted with loathing.

"I don't think about you one way or another, sergeant," MacKenzie said with the small burr he had learned from his father and which was noticeable only when he was angry.

The implication that the sergeant merited no thought at all caused the man's face to go even redder. "You arrogant red bastard." He practically spit the words.

Only an almost imperceptible movement of a cheek muscle indicated MacKenzie had heard the words. He turned his back on the burly sergeant and once again faced the young lieutenant.

"Do as you will. I gave you the information. I'll be giving the same to General Wakefield. There could be a large uprisin' brewing and the ranchers should be brought in."

Lieutenant Pickering looked from the tall, lean scout to his sergeant. When he had first been assigned this post, he had been told to listen to his top sergeant. He did not like Sergeant Peters, but neither did he like the insolent half-breed who showed no respect for rank or, for that matter, the army. And the man's person was disgraceful. Unshaven. Dirty. Pickering didn't consider the fact the scout had been in the saddle nearly nineteen hours a day for the past fortnight or more. His nose twitched as he wondered, once more, why this particular man seemed to hold Wakefield's trust so firmly. *He* wouldn't trust him any farther than he could throw him. Which, he realized, looking at the animal power of MacKenzie, was exactly no distance at all. The thought added to his feeling of inadequacy, and he vented his frustration on the scout.

"I won't order the settlers in on your guess," he said. "They could lose everything."

"Not their lives," MacKenzie said very quietly, the soft burr even more pronounced as he emphasized the last words. *Damn their stupidity.*

"I'm in command here," the lieutenant said. "Not you."

"No," MacKenzie said in a low but openly contemptuous tone that infuriated both Peters and Pickering. "And it's on your shoulders, not mine. If I'm right, and they die, it'll be you the general blames.'' The implied accusation was his last weapon, and it was a measure of his concern that the burr had become very pronounced. It was the only indication of any emotion, and only he knew what it represented.

"You just want those ranchers to leave everything to your friends," Peters blustered.

"My friends?"

"Your Indian friends, MacKenzie. That way, they can take everything without a fight."

MacKenzie shook his head in disgust and turned to leave. "You're naught but a fool, Peters." He turned to Pickering. "And you're a bigger one if you don't do something. I'll be leaving at dawn."

Peters caught MacKenzie's shoulder. "You don't call me a fool, injun, and get away with it."

MacKenzie looked at him calmly, then looked at Pickering. "You're a witness, Lieutenant. I'm not fighting him. Not now, not ever. He's not worth it. I'm going to take a bath and leave." He turned to Peters. "Now take your hand off me."

"Sergeant Peters!" For once, Pickering's voice carried authority. He didn't understand it, but he knew General Wakefield valued this particular scout, and he wasn't going to jeopardize his career by seeing the man killed or badly hurt by one of his own men. Nor did he want Peters dead. He knew how Peters fought. And he knew MacKenzie's reputation.

"Damn it, sir," Peters said. "He needs a lesson in manners."

Pickering silently agreed as he saw MacKenzie's thin smile, which was really no smile at all. "Let him go," he ordered, and Peters reluctantly took his arm away.

Without another word, MacKenzie disappeared out the door and headed toward the bathhouse.

In answer to the sergeant's fury, Pickering tried to pacify him. "You can teach him a lesson someplace else, Sergeant. Not here."

"I'll kill that half-breed bastard," Peters promised before turning and leaving for his family quarters. His anger continued to mount, and he transferred part of it to his daughter, Ellen, when he reached the stark living area. Where in the hell was she this time, when his dinner should be ready? Fooling around again, he supposed. With one of the enlisted men? Officers? Was any man so plagued as he? Ellen couldn't seem to keep away from men . . . any man. He lifted a bottle from the messy table and took a long pull from it. If she wasn't home after a few drinks, he would go look for her. And then he would beat her within an inch of her life.

MacKenzie washed the grime from his body, taking brief satisfaction in being the solitary occupant of the small bathhouse. Exhausted from days of riding and nearly sleepless nights, he had paid one of the Indian women to fetch and heat some water. He sank in the tub, letting the hot water soothe his aching muscles.

He had planned to spend the night here, but now he would not. It meant trouble, and trouble was something he was trying to avoid. He cursed his own tongue. He shouldn't have let Peters get to him like that, but damn, they were fools. Dangerous fools. The only thing to do now was to get to Wakefield, and perhaps the general would order the area evacuated. MacKenzie could only hope it wouldn't be too late. There could be a bloodbath. He closed his eyes. God, he was tired. He dreaded the thought of remounting.

MacKenzie was so exhausted, so physically drained that his usually sharp ears didn't hear the slight noise as the door opened or the almost soundless footsteps that approached him. He was nearly asleep, all his warning instincts dulled. His first indication that someone was with him was the touch of a hand on his chest.

His eyes flew open. Ellen Peters was kneeling beside the tub, her fingers trailing across his wet chest, caressing it with knowledgeable intent.

MacKenzie shot up in the copper tub. "What in the hell are you doing here?" He shoved away the girl's probing hand.

Ellen's strangely colored eyes consumed him, and her mouth twisted into an inviting smile. Her hand sought his rock-hard bronze chest again, which she had coveted for so long.

"No one saw me," she whispered, an intense gleam in her eye. "It's just you and me."

MacKenzie glared at her. Ellen Peters, like her father, had been nothing but trouble since he'd first stopped at Chaco. She was pretty enough, but there was something not quite right about her. He had often found her staring at him with an intensity that made him uneasy. He had overheard talk that she was easily available, but the combination of her possessiveness and her father's rage had kept most of her liaisons very short indeed. In his brief stops at Chaco, he had not missed the ardent invitation in her eyes, and he had avoided her. No woman was worth the trouble he knew she represented. Once more, he shoved her hands away, and he rose, wrapping a towel around his waist.

"You have no business here, Miss Peters," he said, hoping the reserve in his voice might do what anger would not. "Your father will be angry." Anger, he swore silently, would be the least of it.

"To hell with my father," Ellen said. "All he wants is a servant." Her hands reached for the towel and before MacKenzie could react, it was on the floor, and her hands were on his manhood. "I want you," she whispered softly.

MacKenzie felt himself instinctively harden under her touch, and he moved swiftly away, grabbing his buckskin trousers.

As one of her hands reached for him once more, he caught it. "No," he said succinctly. "Now get out of here."

"You're refusing me?" Ellen said with disbelief, her eyes narrowing and a strange glowing light invading them. "You...a half-breed...refusing me..." Her voice rose. "You should be grateful someone's willing to even touch you, you dirty..." A long flow of filth followed.

MacKenzie ignored her and continued dressing, his dismissal fueling the rage in her voice. He felt trapped as her words got louder and louder. He strode over and put his hand over her mouth. "Quiet," he warned softly, but the girl was beyond reason, and he felt her teeth on his hand. His other hand instinctively tightened around her shoulder, and he heard her scream.

MacKenzie sensed rather than heard the menacing presence of Peters, and he whirled toward the door, one arm still on Ellen. He heard the girl's shrill voice. "He's trying to rape me, Papa."

His arm propelled the girl away from him as he faced Peters. "That's a lie."

But Peters's face was frenzied, and his hand was reaching for the revolver at his side.

MacKenzie was too far away to reach him, but his knife was lying on a table next to him. With lightning speed, his hand reached for it and let it fly with one deceptively easy motion. It reached its target just as the pistol discharged.

Everything became a blur. MacKenzie could hear Ellen Peters screaming, and then the room was full of blue uniforms. He fought, but there were too many. He took a blow to the head, then his stomach, and he was on the floor, his body twisting in agony as one boot after another found its mark in his chest, his buttocks, his stomach, his groin, his legs. And then red—the color of pain—turned black as he slipped from consciousness.

Even the slightest movement was agonizing. Through a fiery haze of pain, MacKenzie slowly regained consciousness, his senses reviving one by one. There was not one part of him that didn't feel intense hurt. He tried to move to explore the wounds and their severity, but his hands were bound tightly together. So were, he knew instantly, his ankles. And not kindly. The ropes bit into his flesh, and the slightest struggle against them seemed only to make them tighter. The ropes around his wrists and ankles were apparently joined by another rope. If he tried to stretch, he only increased the pressure on both.

His eyes adjusted to the darkness until black became gray, and he could decipher shapes and forms. There was no guardhouse at Chaco, and he had been imprisoned in one of the several storerooms. There were boxes piled along the walls, and his allotted space was small. He could not straighten his body—if he had wanted to. And, at the moment, he didn't think he did. Not when a stabbing pain traveled through his chest as he struggled to relieve the pressure on his wrists.

There was silence. Complete silence. Only his own broken breathing echoed in the room. He couldn't hear movement outside, and didn't know if it was night or day. If he could feel his cheeks, he would know from his beard how long he had been here; he had shaved just before his bath. Was it four hours? Eight? More than that? And Peters. Was he dead? He must be. MacKenzie remembered those last few minutes with complete clarity. He seldom missed with a gun. Never with a knife.

He could smell blood and sweat. That told him something. He had been here, like this, more than several hours.

He could feel the dryness in his mouth. His throat was parched, and his body yearned for liquid.

Forget the thirst and the pain. He had killed a sergeant in the U.S. Army. He remembered Ellen Peters ... the way she had screamed rape. Even Wakefield couldn't help him now. Not that he would expect him to, not that he even wanted him to. MacKenzie had always taken care of himself. He would this time, too.

Ignoring the torture of his torn wrists and the severe bruises that covered his body, he struggled to bring his bound hands up to his mouth, twisting his body to do so. Pushing his knees up to his chest, he started to chew on the knots.

Pickering could almost see his short career come to an abrupt halt. A murder and rape in his command! Committed by one of his general's top scouts. And now Sergeant Terrell was demanding the scout's death.

"He should hang ... now," Terrell said. Peters had been his friend, his best friend. "Slowly," he added with relish.

Pickering paced the floor. There was no question of MacKenzie's guilt. Her face awash with tears, Ellen Peters had told the whole wretched story ... how she had gone to fetch some soap, not knowing anyone was in the washhouse ... how the 'breed had grabbed her and was forcing her to submit ... how her father had attempted to rescue her and was callously knifed to death in front of her horrified eyes. She showed the dark bruises on her arm as proof. Despite her reputation, or lack of one, no one doubted her story. A white girl would never be attracted to a savage like MacKenzie.

But lynching?

At least, Pickering thought, General Wakefield would come to realize the true nature of the scout he had trusted so completely. In fact, Pickering would like to see the general's face when the charges were lodged.

"Lieutenant?" the sergeant probed. He already had a group of soldiers ready and willing to proceed. Many of them had seen the remains of tortured comrades, and it made little difference to them whether MacKenzie's Indian blood was Shoshone or Apache. Indian was Indian.

"No," Pickering said. "I'm sending him to Fort Defiance for a trial."

An ugly look came over Terrell's face. "Why can't we save ourselves the trouble, b'God? We all know he done it."

"There will be no lynchings under my command," the lieutenant reiterated. "You can take charge of him, if you want," he added, seeking to calm his now highest-ranking sergeant. "Just make sure he gets there alive."

"Barely?" Terrell said as if seeking approval.

Pickering shrugged. "You're in charge."

"And if he tries to escape?"

"Alive, sergeant. I said alive. I don't want any questions or investigations by General Wakefield."

"He'll wish to hell he was dead before I get through with him," Terrell said.

Pickering stared at him. "Handle it your way."

The sergeant saluted, making ready to leave when the lieutenant added as an afterthought, "Perhaps I'll go with you. Sergeant O'Hara can take care of matters here. Pick thirty men. Just in the event MacKenzie's right about the Apaches. We'll leave the day after tomorrow."

Terrell could feel his face flush. He would rather have had MacKenzie to himself. Regardless of what Pickering ordered, he had planned to hang the half-breed along the way and, as he had said earlier, slowly. Not the way the Army would do it, a clean break. No, MacKenzie would strangle to death, dancing to Terrell's music. Terrell had already selected the men who would keep their mouths shut. Now he would have to rethink the plan. But, he vowed, MacKenzie would die before he reached Fort Defiance, before Wakefield could interfere. Damned injun-lovin' general.

Pickering did not miss the fleeting disappointment on the sergeant's face. It strengthened his resolve. "That's all, Sergeant," he said curtly. Still, he would not wish to be MacKenzie in the coming days. The whole affair just proved you could never tame an Indian.

Thinking bleakly about the next miserably hot days on the trail, he sat down at his desk, fingering the charges he had prepared against the scout. Anger boiled up inside him. As if he didn't already have enough problems in this godforsaken country. With the exception of MacKenzie's death, he would allow Terrell a free hand. A small smile played around his mouth as he anticipated MacKenzie's humbling.

The door to the small storeroom opened, and MacKenzie flinched against the sudden light.

Terrell stood there, flanked by two men, one of whom held a gun. As MacKenzie's eyes adjusted to the streaming light, he saw the other was the post blacksmith, and he was holding a length of chain. Damn his luck. He was almost through the rope. Only a few more moments, and his hands would have been free.

Terrell stooped and investigated the chewed ropes, his mouth straightening into a tight, cruel smile. "Damned injuns will eat anything," he said. "We'll see about chain." He nodded to the smithy. "Bind his wrists tightly," he said.

MacKenzie struggled to sit up and maintain a shred of dignity despite the stabbing pain that violated every part of his body. He felt the rough rope fall from his wrists, then the chain links once more binding them together. The blacksmith used his tools to close them with an iron link that could be broken easily only by another blacksmith. Through the haze of pain, MacKenzie remembered an old trick he had once been shown, and turned his wrists in such a fashion that the chains would be looser than the blacksmith intended. Not loose enough that they would fall away, but sufficient, at least, to present the faint possibility of working out of them when the time was right. The rest of the length of chain dangled from his wrists, and he watched with an air of careless indifference as the blacksmith bolted a ring in the storeroom wall.

The bonds around his ankles were cut, and he was hoisted roughly to his feet.

"Take him to the latrine," Sergeant Terrell said. "Then chain him to the wall." He looked at MacKenzie with a small, malevolent smile. "Thirsty, 'breed?"

MacKenzie stood, swaying slightly as he fought against weakness. He would not give Terrell the pleasure of seeing him fall. In response to the sergeant's question, he merely stared impassively ahead, nothing in his face giving indication of need or desire.

His detachment infuriated Terrell. "You will be on your knees begging before I finish with you," he threatened. "We're taking you to Fort Defiance day after tomorrow, and you will walk every step of the way."

Still receiving no reaction, he angrily turned to the man with the gun. "Give him just enough water to wet his lips. I heard injuns can go days without water. We'll find out."

April stared at Lieutenant Pickering with puzzlement. She had not expected to be greeted with open arms, but neither had she expected to be regarded as something akin to a contagious disease.

She carried papers her father had arranged, which were signed by a major general in Washington, requesting that Mrs. Manning and her son receive every consideration and assistance from the army to reach Fort Defiance. They did not carry her maiden name, Wakefield. She had always felt awkward with the fawning and exaggerated courtesy the name produced. It was enough to let them think she was just an army widow, travelling home. For, after all, that was what she was. But she had not considered the possibility of resistance, particularly from the young lieutenant.

"It's too dangerous," he was saying for the fourth time.

"Not," April said succinctly, "with the company of an army troop." She had heard there would be a detail leaving on the morrow for her father's headquarters.

Pickering looked at her with real dismay. She was obviously a person of some importance; she had extraordinary papers with her. He did not care for her to learn what had so recently transpired on *his* post. But now he had no choice.

"We're taking a dangerous prisoner to trial," he explained. "It will be no place for a lady... such as yourself," he tried, hope in his eyes. God knew he needed no more problems.

But April merely looked at him with grim determination. "Surely," she pressed, "a troop of American soldiers is a match for one prisoner...and protection for myself and my son. Or," she challenged, "am I wrong?"

Pickering silently cursed her. At any other time, he would have flirted with her. Though she wore a high-necked, long-sleeved dark blue dress, which showed the effects of long travel, and her rich, chestnut-colored hair was pulled back in a severe knot at the nape of her neck, she was pretty enough. There was a glimmer of gold in her hair, and her eyes were a deep, rich blue. They were, he thought uncomfortably, uncommonly direct for a woman.

"All right," he finally surrendered. "You and your son can ride in the wagon with Miss Peters...she's going to testify."

"Perhaps," April said softly, "I can be of some assistance." Despite the lieutenant's reticence, she had already heard of the young girl who had almost been raped and who had lost her father. Her heart had contracted with sympathy when she learned the details. She remembered her own grief when she lost her mother, and how much it would hurt if she now lost her father. She would do what she could for Ellen Peters. As for the murderer, he would be well-guarded. She couldn't understand Pickering's concern.

It ended there. Pickering had no choice but to allow her to accompany them. His sallow face reflected his displeasure.

She and Davey were given use of one of the nicer officer's quarters. Both fresh water and food appeared, and Davey, particularly, ate the stew with a hearty appetite. Their recent diet had been austere, to say the least, and it was bound to get bad again on the trail. After eating, he clamored to go exploring. Pleased at his excitement and interest, April readily consented. Hand and hand, they left the hot, airless quarters and walked toward the river. The temperature was rapidly cooling as the sun disappeared. It was a strange time in the Southwest, a time of blistering days and cool nights. Davey had skipped on ahead when April stopped suddenly. Just in front of her, two blue-coated soldiers led a man in buckskin trousers and torn cotton shirt. His hands were bound by a chain in front of him, and the end was being jerked first one way, then another by his captors as they laughed. One vicious shove sent him sprawling at her feet.

April stepped back. But she couldn't take her eyes from the man as he struggled to rise. His eyes met hers . . . so briefly she was stunned by the impact.

She had never seen such eyes. They were a deep, dark gray, and completely impenetrable. Not that they were empty. She had a fleeting impression of depth upon depth. Of currents swirling, a bottomless vortex of complexity. But she blinked, and when she looked again they were hooded. Calm. Emotionless.

She heard the laughter once more from the soldiers, and she suddenly hated them, although the reason escaped her. This must be the man who tried to rape an innocent young girl, who had killed a sergeant in cold blood. She stepped back, and her eyes swept him coldly.

His mouth twisted into a slight grim smile as he recognized her evident repugnance. Back on his feet, he turned away from her and, if she didn't know better, she would say it was pride that held his shoulders so stiffly. But it couldn't be that. Not a murderer and rapist. She watched as he was led to a shed and pushed inside, the two guards still with him. They reappeared a moment later and carefully locked the door.

April didn't understand the chill that suddenly ran up her back or the deep feeling of disquiet that swamped her. She bit her lip in confusion, then called for Davey and thoughtfully walked back to their temporary quarters.

An hour later, when Davey was asleep, April went several doors down the long building, which served as family quarters, to see Ellen Peters. She wanted to offer her sympathy and meet her travelling companion.

Something about the girl immediately rang false. April had started to put her arms around the young girl in sympathy, but Ellen had flinched and stepped back. To be expected, April thought, after a man had touched her with violence. Until Sergeant Terrell entered, and the girl flung herself into his arms. Again not unusual, April pondered. The sergeant was evidently a family friend. But then April saw the girl's glistening eyes. And they held neither grief nor fear.

The longer she stayed, the more uncomfortable April became. There was an atmosphere she remembered only too well from the Manning home—unadulterated hate. In the north, it was directed against Southerners. Now it was aimed at Indians—all Indians.

She was glad she had put Davey to bed. It didn't take long for her stomach to knot at the conversation. Hate. Vengeance. Murder. She remembered the calm gray eyes of the accused renegade and compared them, in her mind's eye, with the sly, malicious ones of the victim.

Don't do this, she told herself. Don't make a martyr out of a killer. There is no question of his guilt. Perhaps it was only the girl. She had seldom disliked a person on sight. Especially one who had been through what Ellen Peters had apparently endured. But the girl repulsed her as no one else ever had.

Sergeant Terrell, apparently assuming that April shared his prejudices, was telling the girl that he intended to make the half-breed suffer on the trip, that he had withheld water from the man to see how long he could go without it. The soldier apparently didn't see the distaste in April's eyes, for he laughed as he told Ellen how he intended to make his prisoner beg before reaching Fort Defiance. "If he doesn't die first!"

April could not stand their presence another moment. The trip ahead of them looked longer and longer, and she hated to think that Davey would be exposed to such cruelty. She would talk to Lieutenant Pickering in the morning. And, if she must, she would tell them exactly who she was.

She couldn't sleep that night. She kept seeing the man in buckskin trousers, and his eyes haunted the darkness. She recalled his battered face, the blood on his clothes and, most of all, the pride in his bearing. And the eyes. So fathomless.

You're romanticizing, April, she scolded herself. He's nothing but a rapist and a murderer, and he's bound for a hangman.

He's also a human being, a voice within her persisted. And they have no right to treat him, or anyone, like a mad dog.

But what if he is? What if he is no more than a rabid animal?

No! April knew. She knew with all the instincts she valued that he was not a merciless killer. Her father had always told her she was a good judge of character, like himself. He took great pride in the fact; he was seldom disappointed in the men he chose for leadership. He could quickly separate the weak from the strong, the judicious from the foolish. And this man, she had heard, was one of his personally selected scouts.

MacKenzie. She had heard the man's name during the evening, and it rang a bell somewhere in her mind. Now she searched for it, only slowly recalling a letter in which her father mentioned the name. "He's a strange man," she remembered him writing, "a man without loyalties. But once he gives his word, nothing deters him. I'm glad to have him back."

MacKenzie. She remembered now. She remembered being fascinated with her father's short portrait of a lone and independent mountain man who, he said, was the most savvy scout in the Southwest.

That man and the one described earlier in the evening didn't match. Didn't match at all. Something was wrong, very wrong. April shivered in the cool night. Her natural affinity for an underdog surfaced. She would not allow the sergeant to kill the man before her father could sort it all out. She didn't know how she would stop it, but stop it she would. Somehow she would.

Chapter Three

April couldn't take her eyes off the man walking behind the wagon. No matter how hard she concentrated or how many times she tried to turn her attention to Davey or to the stark beauty around her, her eyes continually wandered back to the man called MacKenzie.

She, Davey and Ellen Peters had already been settled in the back of a supply wagon when he had been led out. She hadn't missed the smug satisfaction in Ellen's eyes as the chain attached to MacKenzie's wrists was padlocked to another chain at the back of the wagon.

Once more, April was startled at his composure, his seeming indifference to his own discomfort. No emotion at all showed in those remarkable eyes as the punishing, humiliating chain was secured. His eyes locked with hers for just a second, a flicker of recognition crossing them quickly before going blank again. He didn't acknowledge her presence in any other way. He simply stood there, waiting stoically for the wagon to start moving.

His clothes were the same as the night before, still blood-stained and torn. He wore knee-high moccasins on his feet, and she flinched as she thought of the terrain they would be travelling.

Before the wagon started, she had a chance to study his face. It had none of the usual handsomeness, but was, instead, like a hewn piece of oak with strong, striking features that caught and held one's attention. Those deep-set gray eyes again continued to dominate her thoughts, but she also noted the high cheekbones, strong chin and firm mouth. His hair was midnight black, and straight. At the moment one tuft fell over his forehead, between his eyes. He seemed not to notice.

She couldn't decide if the rich oak color of his skin was due to his Indian blood or the fact that he had apparently lived his life out-of-doors. Black bristles covered his lower face but somehow they merely made him look more intriguing. Dangerous without being frightening. She knew her rapt attention was only too obvious to him, but again he bore her scrutiny with what seemed to be supreme indifference. Even when his eyes touched Ellen Peters, there was no emotion. April didn't understand that at all. There should have been something: anger, lust, shame. Something.

She had meant to talk to Lieutenant Pickering about Sergeant Terrell's intentions, but the lieutenant had ridden ahead before she was called, and April had had no opportunity to do so. She would, she decided, when they stopped. In the meantime, she watched MacKenzie walk behind the wagon, showing no strain or weariness. He was lean and tall and as graceful as a mountain lion, his steps light as they kept pace with the wagon, always keeping some slack in the chain so he wouldn't be thrown off balance by a sudden lurch. Despite the slimness of his hips, she could see muscles bunch under his shirt and the cloth of his trousers. She sensed an enormous amount of leashed power simmering under his calm exterior, and couldn't help but wonder what would happen when he exploded. April knew, from Sergeant Terrell's words, that he had probably had little or no water last night and this morning, and the sun was a bright ball of red fire. The coolness of the night had disappeared under its blistering rays, and she wondered how long the man could continue without water or rest.

Unfortunately, Davey, too, was watching with fascination. Unable to withhold his curiosity, he finally asked the question. "Why is that man chained?"

"He's being taken for trial, love."

"Is he a bad man?" Davey's green eyes were bright with interest. "He doesn't look bad."

April was startled at the boy's observation. She glanced at Ellen Peters. "That's yet to be decided," she said calmly, noting Ellen's face flushing with anger under the words. April did not hide her growing doubt.

The reply satisfied Davey, who went on to other questions, which April answered with half her attention. The other half was still focused on the enigmatic prisoner. She was suffering every step with him, probably more than he if his unchanging expression was any indication.

Noon came, and the sun glared like a shield of red-hot brass, its rays scorching the earth. Familiar with the heat and unwilling to suffer through stays and petticoats, April had donned a split riding skirt and cotton shirt she had owned before her marriage. But even with the lighter clothes, she felt the sweat trickling down her neck and between her breasts, and Davey was squirming with discomfort. Yet MacKenzie still showed little effect, although April knew each step must be torture. She and the other passengers, at least, had several canteens of water, all of which were nearing empty. She herself had declined the last offer of water, unable to tilt the canteen in front of MacKenzie's eyes, although she noticed Ellen took great delight in doing so, as well as in letting water drip onto a handkerchief and wiping her face with it. April had wanted to slap her.

At last, a halt was called, and the wagon rolled to a stop.

April had expected the Indian scout to drop when the wagon stilled, but he did not. He stood there defiantly, as if mocking Terrell's best efforts.

His relentless eyes fastened on hers, and she felt something tighten inside. She sensed he was measuring her against the background of his experience, and she was found wanting. She was surprised at how much the thought hurt. *He's a murderer, April.* Regardless of whether Ellen Peters told the truth, he had killed a sergeant. With a knife. No civilized man would do that.

And he was definitely not civilized. How could he radiate such danger, such mastery in his position? But he did. Even in chains, he seemed to dominate the group by his open contempt. His refusal to allow thirst or exhaustion to affect him taunted his captors and made him stronger than they. She could tell by Terrell's flushed face that he recognized the arrogant mockery.

April and Davey left the wagon to stretch their legs, but April kept one eye on MacKenzie as she searched for the lieutenant. She saw the horses being watered and fed, the men eating, and she and Davey were given water, bread and dried beef. She noticed the prisoner was given nothing.

Having made his point, MacKenzie settled on the ground, his long body folding into a sitting position. The chain was barely long enough to permit his wrists to reach the ground but, as always, he seemed to consider it merely inconvenient. Those hooded eyes, however, moved constantly, and she knew they missed little. His lips were cracked, and yet his tongue never tried to moisten them.

April watched as the large sergeant eyed the prisoner thoughtfully, then busied his hands with a rope. In minutes, he had fashioned a noose, and he approached MacKenzie.

"You can wear this the rest of the way, 'Breed. To remind you that every step you take brings you closer to the hangman." He dropped the circle around the scout's neck and tightened it, but MacKenzie didn't flinch or change his expression by so much as a blink as the rough rope cut and bruised his neck and the rope's end fell to the ground in front of him. If anything, April thought she caught a flash of victory in the man's eyes. His silence had goaded his enemy into action. He intended to goad him into mistakes. She didn't know how she knew that. But she did. MacKenzie had not given up... he was merely waiting. Waiting for what? Despite the heat, April felt shivers run up and down her spine.

Once more, her eyes met his, and she wondered at the depth, at the secrets in them. Something in her reached out to him, and she saw startled perception in his face. But like everything concerning him, it was gone so quickly she thought she'd only imagined it.

April could wait no longer. The soldiers were preparing to mount again, and still there was no lieutenant. She was at least going to see that MacKenzie received some water. Lieutenant or no lieutenant, she could stand his torture no longer.

Very resolutely, she took a cup and filled it with water from one of the barrels on the wagon and approached the prisoner. She saw his eyes watch every movement, saw their sudden warning as she felt a rough hand on her arm.

"He's not to have no water," Terrell said roughly.

April whirled around to face him. "He can't go any farther without it."

A grin broke out on Terrell's face. "I don't know. He seems fine to me. They say injuns don't need water, not much, no ways. They ain't human, you see, missy. More like dogs than men. He seems right natural down there with a collar round his neck. Anyway this ain't none of yer business. He killed my friend, tried to rape his baby girl..." His eyes narrowed as he looked at her. "Perhaps that's what you're after..."

April's hand went back and struck his face with all her force. Just as swiftly, his fist hit her, knocking her to the ground. April heard Davey cry out, along with a low vicious growl from the direction of the prisoner. She saw Davey attack the burly sergeant with all the small fury he possessed, only to be easily swatted aside. She grabbed him up, trying to protect him from another blow, heedless of the cut on her mouth. She clutched Davey to her, her whole body trembling with rage. When she finally looked up, the sergeant was standing, red-faced and unrepentant.

She heard him bluster, "You shouldn't go messing in Army business." She could only glare helplessly at him. She was no match for his strength.

"What in the hell is going on?"

April turned and saw Pickering riding up, his face white with anger.

"Your sergeant," April said tightly as she rubbed the growing bruise on her cheek, "seems to enjoy tormenting those who can't fight back. I wonder if he fights men as well as he does women and children."

Pickering looked at Terrell with horror. "You hit this lady? Her son?"

"I didn't mean to, sir. It was an accident. She was interfering with the pris'ner," Terrell said defensively. He didn't know exactly who the lady was, only that she was the widow of an Army captain, but he suddenly felt fear. "You know we can't let anyone near the prisoner...he's too dangerous. She just didn't understand that." He turned to April, hastening to make amends of some kind. "You understand that, don't you, missy? I was just trying to protect you."

April straightened. "*You're* the one I need protection from, Sergeant." She turned back to Pickering. "I want to lodge charges against this man."

Pickering looked at the angry, defiant woman in front of him, a line of blood now trickling down her cheek, and felt the tight ball in his stomach grow larger. This whole trip was a nightmare. His eyes moved to the Indian scout who had caused it all. The man was standing again, his fists knotted together in tight balls, his legs braced as if ready to pounce. There was something very menacing in his face.

"He hasn't given that man any water," April said. "It's inhuman."

Pickering, at the moment, was feeling none too lenient toward the man who had started it all. "Sergeant Terrell knows best," he said soothingly. "You can see he doesn't seem to be suffering. He's an Indian," he added as if that explained everything.

The statement only served to fuel April's anger. "If I hear that once more..." She didn't know how to finish the sentence. She didn't know what she would do. Damn them.

She tried again. "He's a human being," April said quietly now, "and I'll not stand by and watch this...this bully of yours torture him. Look at that rope around his neck. How can you permit such a thing?"

Pickering flinched at the raw contempt in her voice. "Now, Mrs. Manning. There's only one way to deal with these murdering savages...wear them out. It's like the sergeant said, he's very dangerous." There was a note of finality in the lieutenant's voice.

April used her trump card with some reluctance. "Would your general agree with you? Would he condone the abuse of prisoners?"

"General Wakefield?" the lieutenant said. "He gives no quarter in the field."

"That's in the field," April said coldly. "Not against helpless prisoners. And I have occasion to know. I'm General Wakefield's daughter."

Both Pickering and Terrell went white. April glanced over at MacKenzie and saw what might have been amusement. She wasn't sure. She didn't know if anyone could ever be sure of what the man thought.

Pickering was the first to speak. "But why...didn't you say anything?"

"I didn't think I needed to," April replied with a sharp edge to her words. "I assumed, quite incorrectly as it turned out, that an army widow would be given the same respect as a general's daughter." Her glance went back to Terrell's now livid face. She wondered idly how one's complexion could go from stark white to bright red in a matter of seconds.

"And I assure you, Lieutenant, that my father would never tolerate . . . this." She looked at MacKenzie, who was lounging against the back of the wagon, the hideous rope falling almost to the ground. It occurred to her that he wore it as nonchalantly as most men would wear a scarf.

She leaned down and picked up the cup and returned to the water barrel, refilling it as the officer and sergeant, along with a score of other soldiers, watched her warily. When it was filled, she walked to MacKenzie and pressed it into his bound hands. She watched as he raised it carefully, awkwardly, and took slow sips. When the water was gone, he gave the cup back to her, one eyebrow raised quizzically.

"That wasn't necessary, Mrs. Manning," he said.

It was the first time she had heard his voice, and April was surprised at the soft, pleasant baritone sound and the small, but distinctive, Scottish burr that distinguished the words. It was gently, courteously said, but quite without thanks. Mesmerized by his steady gray gaze, she knew by the use of her name that he must have heard the full exchange.

"But it was," she said just as softly. "If not for you, then for myself . . . and Davey."

He merely nodded, understanding, as she stood there, thoroughly disconcerted by his insouciance. She eyed his wrists, torn open by the chain links, and turned her attention back to the rope around his neck. It had been cruelly tightened, and she could see it eat into his flesh. She winced.

"Do not let it worry you, Mrs. Manning," he said. "It doesn't me. You've done enough."

"No," she said. "Not nearly enough. You need food and more water."

He shrugged. "Leave it be," he said. "I don't need your help."

"I wouldn't let anyone treat a dog like this," she said without thinking. For the first time, she saw emotion flicker across his face. Pure rage. And she suddenly remembered Terrell's earlier words. She knew he must have heard them, and she had just compounded the injury.

The burr was very heavy when he finally spoke. "I'm nay a dog . . . not an object for your pity." He turned his back to her.

Mortified that her words were so misunderstood, she stared at his back helplessly before turning to Pickering, who had watched the exchange with a satisfied smile. "You see, Mrs. Manning, you can't be decent to them."

"Take that rope from his neck," April said furiously, then took Davey's hand and returned to the wagon, knowing that a few ill-considered words had probably done more damage to MacKenzie than all the torment planned by Sergeant Terrell.

Step by step. Just think about the next step, not the one after that. MacKenzie fought to keep the spring in his walk, to show every one of them that they could never, never defeat him.

But the pain was terrible. He knew his feet were bloody inside the moccasins. He could feel the wash of blood as each foot touched the ground. The soft hide had not been designed for the punishment inflicted by the hard, rocky terrain. He wondered how long he could continue.

He had to keep pace with the wagon, or he would be jerked from his feet and dragged. That was what Terrell wanted, what he was waiting for. Well, Terrell would wait until he reached hell, and MacKenzie hoped to speed that journey.

Think about something else. Wakefield's daughter. That was a surprise. He knew the general had a married daughter somewhere east. The man had mentioned her once in a rare terse conversation. She had probably even been on a post when he had been there. But he never approached the living quarters and rarely stayed overnight. He usually came late and left early. His eyes went to the wagon. She was like her father—determined and combative. There had been no lack of courage, and his anger grew once more as he remembered the blow she took on his behalf. But he had not asked it, had not even wanted it, he assured himself. He had seen her watching him several times, and had wondered about it, for, unlike so many other women, she had not averted her gaze when caught by his own eyes. Nor had she looked at him with distaste or loathing. Just interest, and something close to sympathy. He should not have snapped at her. She had meant well, and he remembered the stricken look in her face at his cruel reply.

He could see her now, leaning over to talk with the cub. He liked the way she did it. As if the boy was a friend. There was a closeness about the two that brought forth a pang of regret. What would it have been like, he wondered, to have had that kind of a mother?

He was jerked by the chain. His thoughts had changed the rhythm of his feet, and the slack had run out. He had to brace himself to keep from falling, to hurry his movement to keep nearly abreast of the wagon.

Keep going. Tonight. Tonight, he hoped, Terrell would believe him too tired to require heavy guard. And he would soon start faltering to encourage that belief. He hated to give Terrell that satisfaction, but it could mean his freedom. And that meant everything!

He had thought about General Wakefield at Fort Defiance, about the possibility that the general might listen, and believe. But he soon discarded the idea. Terrell meant to see him dead before they reached Wakefield. And, even if he lived to reach the fort, who would believe a half-breed's words against a white girl's? Even Wakefield couldn't help him now . . . even if he could trust the man. And he didn't. Not entirely. He didn't trust anyone. It was a lesson he had learned early, and he had never found reason to doubt its wisdom.

Rape. Murder. He would surely hang. He remembered the feel of the rope around his neck before Pickering ordered it removed. It had taken all his strength, all his will, not to fight it. But the time wasn't right, and it would only have meant satisfaction for Terrell. Let Terrell think he was winning the battle between them.

The sun was going down, and some of the heat was receding. Before many more minutes, the cold air would hit him, chilling the sweat that caked his body in layers. They would call a halt before long. Lieutenant Pickering was never one for much effort.

One step . . . then another. And another.

He was right. Within the next hour, Pickering ordered a dry camp. MacKenzie had stumbled those last minutes, one time even being dragged several feet before catching his balance. It was planned, but it hadn't been difficult to do. God, but he hurt. All over. The long walk had done nothing to alleviate his other injuries.

With satisfaction, he noticed Terrell's malicious grin. Give him a few more hours of pleasure; it would be gone in the morning. One way or another, he would be free...or dead...by first light.

He was surprised when a private cautiously offered him both food and water—and a blanket. The blanket was greater appreciated because under its folds he could work his hands free. He glanced at the Manning woman, positive it was her doing, and was further convinced when he saw her arguing heatedly with Lieutenant Pickering. She apparently wasn't the type to quit, even after his bitter words. A most unusual female.

But that was the least of his interest now. His eyes scanned the camp as guards were posted. He was taken several yards away to attend to his private needs—apparently a courtesy offered only because of the women present. He was rechained to the wagon, his leash offering only one position in which to lie. His ankles were bound tightly with rope, but that didn't matter. They had not rechecked the chain around his wrists. Terrell, in his confidence, did not post a separate guard at the prisoner's side, a fact for which MacKenzie was supremely thankful. He studied the position of each of the pickets, the terrain he would have to crawl to reach them . . . and finally the horses. They had brought his own Appaloosa with them. Another unexpected gift.

Pickering was an idiot. There were not nearly sufficient guards in a country crawling with Apaches. And many of his men were not Indian-wise soldiers. Most of them were new to the West, recently arrived from an entirely different war in the East. One in which, MacKenzie understood, men stood up in waves and marched into cannon fire. He had thought that immensely stupid. But then the same had happened in Scotland so many years ago. He had heard the tales from his father.

The camp was finally silent. He didn't know where the Manning woman and her boy were sleeping. He had not been able to see them from his limited view. Not that it mattered. He knew every step he would take. But first his bonds. He moved

his wrists, refusing to acknowledge the agony the struggle cost
him. His wrists turned, and the chain slackened. He tested
them. His hands almost, but not quite, found freedom. He
needed moisture, something slippery, to help them slide loose.
Without a moment's hesitation, he looked cautiously around
him and then sat up, drawing his wrists to his mouth. They were
already slightly bloody, with red lines going deep into the skin.
But not enough. He bit hard into his left wrist, tasting blood,
feeling it flow freely. He washed both wrists in it, and then he
tried the chain again. It was slippery with the wetness, and he
worked his wrists first this way, then another, until he felt one
go free, then the second. He placed the chain quietly on the
ground and started working on the ropes around his ankles.

He was free!

April stared at the silver moon in the black sky. There were
wisps of clouds playing among the field of stars. She studied
one that she fancied was winking at her; it was a particularly
bright gem that seemed to hold some kind of promise. But
what? She suddenly felt tired and depressed. Something special
had left her life . . . the part of her that had always been so op-
timistic. More than four years of war had done its part in killing it. But today . . . today was even worse. She was seeing a
meanness of spirit, an unreasoning hatred, a deliberate desire
to inflict pain. It couldn't help but dull the world for her.

Her arm went tighter around Davey. She wished she could
protect him from it. She had seen his confusion several times,
and his small burst of fury when she had been hit. Poor Davey.
He had known so little real happiness. She had wanted it so
badly for him, particularly on this journey. But her interfer-
ence on behalf of MacKenzie had completely isolated them
from their companions. Ellen and Terrell looked at her with
complete loathing, Pickering avoided her with deftness, and the
other soldiers eyed her warily. Not only was she the general's
daughter now, but she was an Indian lover.

She sighed, listening to the lonely howl of a coyote somewhere in the distance. Through eyes grown accustomed to the
darkness, she saw the prairie grasses sway with the growing
wind and the dwarfed pines standing like sentinels against the
sky. She shivered in the cold night air, even with the three

blankets she and Davey shared. And she wondered once more about MacKenzie. She had again joined battle to see he had some covering. She had also fought Pickering about tomorrow's trek. The prisoner should not be forced to walk, she insisted, but on this subject the lieutenant was adamant. There was no way, he told her, he would permit MacKenzie in the same wagon as his victim. Nor would he allow the man to ride. MacKenzie, he explained, was a superb horseman, the best he had ever seen and, even bound, might be able to escape on horseback. "He's half Indian," he repeated again as if that explained everything. "He's all Indian in heart."

April didn't even try to explain that she had been around Indians most of her life, much longer, in any case, than Lieutenant Pickering. She had grown up in frontier posts where Indians had often been employed in some capacity or another, or had come to trade goods, or even in surrender after some conflict. She had found them much like whites. Some good, some bad. Some kind, some cruel. She had even, on occasion, played with Indian children as a child, had known some of the scouts. She wondered now why she had never encountered MacKenzie. He apparently had been a scout for her father for some time. MacKenzie. He must have another name. Why did she care? Why did he so dominate her thoughts? No man had done that before. Except David. Damn MacKenzie. Damn him for ruining this trip, for invading her mind. She closed her eyes and willed herself to sleep. But it didn't work. She felt Davey wriggle beside her, and she recognized the symptoms. Sighing once more, she shook off the blankets and rose, gathering one around her son. She looked around. The camp was completely still. She didn't even see the sentries she knew had been posted earlier. But April wasn't worried. They were probably patrolling the area around the camp. Hand in hand, April and Davey walked to a small stand of trees in back of the picket line where the horses had been tethered for the night, and she turned her back, giving him some privacy. Her eyes once more swept the camp.

"Mama..."

She looked down on the small but sturdy figure.

"Cold, love?" she asked, feeling his fingers tighten in hers in agreement. April leaned down, pulling the blanket tighter

around him. Her eyes still on her son, she started walking back
to where they had bedded down for the night. They were pass-
ing the horses when she was startled by a sudden movement.
She looked up.

It was a shadow. A tall, graceful shadow at the picket line,
just three feet away from her. She had seen enough of Mac-
Kenzie that day to identify the shape immediately. A small cry
of surprise escaped her mouth, and she felt a strong hand go
over it, felt her body held closely by an arm that could have
been steel.

"Quiet." She heard the whisper and stopped struggling. And
then she was free, but Davey was in his arms, MacKenzie's hand
now over her son's mouth. "Quiet," she heard him say again,
"and you and the cub will not be hurt."

Her hand went to his arm. "Let him go. Please."

In that small gleam of moonlight, she saw pain flicker over
his face. Deep reluctance. But also determination. "You will
both go with me," he said, and his voice held none of its earlier softness.

"I won't say anything . . . just let us go."

He looked at her, and dark gray eyes seemed cold and merciless in the dim light. "I wouldn't trust anyone that much," he
said in a tone laced with iron. "Can you saddle a horse?"

She nodded, then stared at him. "The sentries?"

"Unconscious," he said. "But probably not for long." He
had already untied an Appaloosa on the string and he swung
easily up on it, Davey securely in his arms. "You can come. Or
you can stay," he said shortly, growing impatient. "But the boy
goes with me till I'm sure of safety. If I hear you cry out, he'll
die." MacKenzie detested his words, but he knew of no other
way to insure her silence. It would take too long to tie them, and
even then it would be risky.

April hated him in that moment, and her expression must
have indicated it, for he said again, "You'll not be hurt, you
and the boy, if you do as I say. I didn't want this, but now
there's nothing for it. I cannot leave you here."

April knew nothing would change his mind, and she quickly
saddled a horse. "Take that bedroll," he demanded, pointing
to one near the picket line. She lifted it, feeling its weight, and
placed it across the saddle. He also had one, she noticed, as well

as a rifle slung across his shoulders and a gun belt around his waist.

"Quietly," he warned, and they walked the horses out of the silent camp. She saw one still form at the edge, and another not far from it. Again, she shivered. She didn't know if they were unconscious, as he claimed, or dead. How ruthless was he? Had she been so wrong? As they distanced themselves from the camp, MacKenzie finally spurred his horse into a gallop without saying a word.

He knew she would follow.

Chapter Four

Dawn was deceptively peaceful. Silver and pink tinged the earth in layers. The moon lagged behind in an azure sky as the sun rose above the craggy horizon. It was benevolent in these first few minutes of morning, drawing the chill from the air but not yet beating the earth with relentless rays.

April felt anger and outrage simmer inside her. Both emotions had burgeoned through the long night, overwhelming the body-numbing weariness. She now hated the man who rode so tirelessly in front of her, but strangely felt little fear of him. Instead, she knew a deep sense of helplessness, of being completely at the mercy of another person. She had thought herself free of such bonds, and now she was trapped deeper than ever before. April sensed that the man, MacKenzie, would not harm Davey, but she couldn't forget his harsh words or take the slightest chance with Davey's life.

She had followed him mindlessly through the cold night lit only by the slice of a new moon. She repeatedly blessed the fact that she had dressed warmly for the night with several layers of clothing, including a wool coat. But even then she was chilled to the bone. At one point she had urged her horse next to MacKenzie's and was slightly comforted by the fact that the man had wrapped Davey warmly in a blanket. Davey was sleeping easily in his arms.

April had asked to take her son, and MacKenzie merely shook his head in denial, his eyes impenetrable in the night.

She fell behind him, uncomfortable with his intense scrutiny and unwilling to indicate any sense of companionship. She was a prisoner now, as he had been hours earlier. He kept a steady pace, maintaining a fast walk for several miles, then a trot, then a walk again. She knew he was husbanding the strength of their horses and recognized the discipline such caution required in light of the urgency she knew he felt.

Every muscle in her body hurt. She had been an excellent rider years earlier, but she had not ridden astride in five years, and her body was protesting the brutal punishment. She kept praying MacKenzie would stop for a rest, but he showed no signs of weariness or pain, though she knew he must be feeling both. She had seen the livid bruises on his arms and chest, and his wrists, when he had seized her, had been scarlet with blood. He rode without stirrups, having sliced them from the saddle shortly after leaving camp. She supposed he used a saddle only because it was then easier to carry the extra rifle, saddlebags and bedroll that he had stolen from the camp.

Pickering had said he was a superb horseman, and April now knew the words were no exaggeration. He was beautiful on a horse, so much a part of the Appaloosa's easy gait that the two were one continuous fluid movement. He looked relaxed, but April could almost feel his taut wariness. She wondered if he ever relaxed. She doubted it.

What was he like? Did he feel even a twinge of guilt about taking Davey? He had seemed oddly gentle hours earlier with her son asleep in his arms. Or was she just trying to reassure herself?

She heard Davey's voice. "Mama?"

April's knees tightened against the horse's side, and she increased the pace until, once more, she was beside MacKenzie.

"I'm here, Davey," she said calmly, seeing his frantic searching look. He was wriggling, trying to free himself from MacKenzie's firm grip. "It's all right, I'm fine."

She looked up at MacKenzie's face, her eyes pleading, asking for confirmation, as she continued, "We'll be stopping soon for a rest."

The scout merely nodded, but his quick appraising look approved of her, and April, unwillingly, felt some of her quiet anger replaced by an unfamiliar tingling sensation. Why, she wondered, should she care whether she had his approval? But she knew the answer instantly, knew that it was probably very rare, and she felt a surge of pride in receiving it.

Don't, April. He's ruthless. He's threatened to kill Davey, and he will do anything...anything to get free. He's an outlaw. A renegade. He's killed a man, and probably won't hesitate to kill again—even Davey. How can you even think about pleasing him? You should be thinking about escaping.

But how? She didn't know where she was. There were hostile Indians in the area. Their safety—Davey's and her own—now lay completely in the hands of their kidnapper.

They stopped by a small stream. MacKenzie lifted Davey and leaned over the saddle, gently settling him on the ground. He again nodded to April, giving her permission to dismount. Once she was down, he, too, dismounted, taking the reins of both horses in his hand and leading them down to the water.

It took April several minutes to even try to walk. Her muscles complained in new ways, and she almost fell. But she straightened and grabbed Davey in her arms, hugging him to her until he protested.

"I'm thirsty," he complained, and April suddenly realized that she, too, was parched. She and Davey went to the stream, and leaned down to drink, savoring the water still cold from the night. She tore a piece of cloth from her skirt and washed his face with it, then her own. She marveled at how much better she felt. She had another need, and realized Davey did, too. He was contorting uncomfortably again. April looked up and found MacKenzie's eyes on them. He was standing some twenty feet away, pacing the horses' intake of water. His head inclined toward a small clump of trees, and April flushed as she realized he understood her necessity. Damn the man. It was as if he read her mind. But need overrode modesty, and she hurried over to the designated spot, waiting first for Davey before knowing relief of her own.

When her clothes were replaced, she took Davey's hand and returned to the stream. The horses were now hobbled, and MacKenzie was at the edge of the stream, washing feet that were torn and bleeding. When he finished, he took off what was left of his shirt and tore it into strips. April flinched as she thought of the dirty, sweat-soaked shirt binding the raw wounds.

Seized by a sudden compulsion she didn't understand, she went over to him and regarded him hesitantly. She had tried to help before and been rebuffed. April saw the sudden wariness in his eyes as she approached. He obviously didn't trust anyone, not even someone so completely in his control.

"You'll just get infection," she said bluntly.

MacKenzie only raised an eyebrow in question, his eyes cool and appraising.

April winced. Did the man ever speak? She had only heard him twice—first when she had offered him water, and his voice had been soft and attractive with the intriguing burr, and later when he threatened Davey, and it had been harsh and uncompromising. Which would it be now?

She steadily returned his gaze, shedding her jacket, then one of the extra shirts she had donned last night as protection against the cold. It was almost clean, worn only last night over another one. She handed it to him without a word.

His expression didn't change, but he took it and, with a knife, cut the garment into bandages and deftly wrapped them around his shredded feet. When he finished, he washed his wrists and tried to bandage the one he had bitten; it was still bleeding slightly.

April watched him struggle for several seconds as he tried to use his teeth to tie a knot. Finally, without a word, she stooped and took the bandage from his hand and, ignoring his now slightly perplexed look, she neatly wrapped it with experienced hands. When she had finished, she continued to stand there, searching his face for a sign of something.

"Where are you taking us?" she asked finally.

She was surprised when he actually replied. "There's a Navaho village a day's ride. I know them, and you and the boy will be safe there until Pickering arrives. I don't think," he added with a slight trace of irony, "he'll be too far behind...not with the general's daughter gone." Every word seemed carefully weighed but still held that soft, distinctive burr that, under other circumstances, would have completely charmed her.

April nodded, glancing at Davey. Apparently quite content with his new adventure, her son was exploring the bank, oblivious to the tense atmosphere between the two adults. Her attention turned back to the scout and his intriguing face.

She had never seen such strong features. It was as if they had been sculptured in stone. Or perhaps they seemed stronger because of his cryptic expression. April couldn't help but wonder if he ever smiled and, if he did, how it would affect a face so marbled in gravity. His watchful eyes were regarding her with the same intensity that she had focused on him, and there seemed a question in his look.

Her eyes fell to his naked chest. She had never thought a man's body could be such a thing of perfection. Corded muscles rippled with his slightest move, and his deeply tanned skin was the color of rich, glowing bronze. The only flaw were the large, ugly purple bruises that covered nearly every part of his upper body, and April recoiled as she thought of the pain he must have endured, both when he received them and on the long walk yesterday.

When her gaze traveled upward again, she noticed MacKenzie's eyes had not moved from her. She inwardly flinched, knowing that she had probably never looked worse in her life. During the long night, her hair had come loose from its usual neat coil, and it fell in undisciplined curls down her back. Her face was probably dirty, and she needed only to look to see the wretched state of her torn and stained clothes. *I don't care,* she tried to tell herself. *I don't care at all.* But she did. Terribly.

Suddenly angered by MacKenzie's close scrutiny and embarrassed by her own obvious examination of the man who held her and her son captive, she turned to leave. She stopped when she heard his low voice.

"I would not have harmed the boy."

She turned and stared at him, knowing it was probably as much of an apology or explanation as he was capable of offering.

Not wanting Davey to hear, April's reply was just as soft. "I didn't think you would."

"Then why...?"

"I couldn't take even the slightest chance with Davey's life." She met his eyes directly, not faltering.

He merely nodded. That seemed to be his response to most everything.

"It wasn't necessary," she couldn't help but add. "I wouldn't have warned anyone." And she knew she wouldn't have. She had, in spirit, been on his side since the moment he was chained to the wagon. Or perhaps even when she had first seen his eyes. They were not the eyes of a murderer.

"I didn't think so," he surprised her by saying. There was the smallest twitch of his lips. "But I couldn't take the slightest chance." April couldn't quite believe the hint of roguish mischief in his voice as he turned her own words around.

But such a thought died quickly as his face once more was shuttered, as if he regretted the brief confidence. He rose lightly despite the fact that his feet must be terribly painful. Yet there was no limp, no hesitation as he went to the horses.

She watched him check the contents of the bedrolls. She suspected they belonged to the pickets he had attacked. Each had the required hundred rounds of ammunition for the Spencer carbines he had stolen, along with several days' rations. She saw quiet satisfaction dart across his face as he found a blue uniform shirt in one and a razor-sharp knife in the other.

He pulled the shirt over his heavily muscled back and chest, and April could see the cloth strain against the supple, hard body. He stooped down and with a piece of his old shirt quickly tied the knife to his ankle. Without a glance at her, MacKenzie took the canteens from the saddles and filled them. There was no wasted motion in his actions. Each sleek movement was precise and confident. April thought she had never seen such a self-assured man. Warmth flooded her with unexpected impact. And she fought it. Bitterly. She could not allow herself to feel anything for a man whose life span appeared anything but long, who had taken herself and her son hostage and forced them on this exhausting trek. But as hard as she tried, she couldn't shake a certain excitement as she watched him move like a graceful, dangerous forest animal.

MacKenzie took the hobbles from the horses and turned toward her. "It's time to go," he said, interrupting her wayward thoughts.

April wanted to protest. A few more moments. But one look at his face dissuaded her. She knew he felt they had already stayed too long.

"Can Davey ride with me?" April questioned instead.

"He's safer with me," he replied shortly, and she knew it would do no good to protest. Davey seemed to have no objec-

tions as he was once more lifted in MacKenzie's arms and
swung onto the Appaloosa.

As they rode side by side from the stream, she thought she
saw a look of sympathy, and even admiration, before Mac-
Kenzie's face settled into its usual implacable lines.

MacKenzie pushed as hard as he thought the horses—and
April Manning—could endure. He wasn't overly worried now
about immediate pursuit. Pickering would be far behind and
probably falling farther. Most of his troopers were unused to
the heat and lack of water in the southwest, and they had no
good trackers. It would take them time to find the trail over
rocky terrain. As long as he kept moving, he would be safe.

He wanted to maintain that distance, but he also wanted to
see Mrs. Manning and her son safely settled with the Navahos.
It was a small camp of several families MacKenzie had been
able to save from the forced march of Navahos to Bosque Re-
dona in eastern New Mexico. MacKenzie had more than a few
regrets about his role as a scout for Kit Carson last year when
the colorful colonel virtually starved the proud Navaho nation
into submission. The subsequent march by the reluctant participants across New Mexico to barren lands had been a nightmare MacKenzie wanted to forget. But he had, through
Wakefield, won exception for several families that had once
sheltered him.

He looked at Mrs. Manning. She was doggedly keeping pace.
Her grim expression, however, told him it was costing her
much. He felt an unaccustomed guilt as her straight back and
set features spoke of pride and determination—and of a courage unusual for a woman. She had not complained once during the journey, nor had she displayed any fear. There had
been, at first, open anger, but even that had seemed to fade
during the last hours. Or perhaps it had been dulled by weariness. She had every reason to detest him.

She had surprised him at the stream when once again she had
tried to help. Even after he had threatened her son and forced
them both to endure such discomfort, she had unselfishly offered her own clothing and quiet assistance. He had been too
startled to refuse it, and had not known how to respond. Until
he tried to tell her he had meant Davey no harm, and even that

was offered awkwardly. No harm? He was dragging them through Indian country, scarcely allowing them enough water and food and rest. He had never consciously caused hurt to women or children before, and yet he was doing it now. To survive. There had been one other time when he had been responsible...but he had not known then what his actions would sow...

He did not welcome the reminder. He had tried to lock those moments from his mind. Except in the deep of night when they battered at his consciousness and kept him from resting.

But he had known exactly what he was doing when he took the boy...Davey. And he knew he would do it again—-given the same circumstances. For that reason, he could not apologize. Words would mean little.

How had things gone so wrong? Everything was gone now. Everything he had worked for and longed for. He had been foolish from the beginning to believe things could be otherwise, that he could create and build something fine, something solely his. He would be hunted for the rest of his life now. And he would probably do as his father did...find an isolated spot on some mountain and live alone.

His hand felt good, resting on the boy. He had never known that something like this—the small body snuggling trustingly into his large one—could spark such confusing feelings. Feelings of tenderness and protectiveness that warmed the cold place inside. He didn't deserve them. He had subjected them—the boy and his mother—to hardship and danger.

But he couldn't be retaken. He would not let the bastards win. Not men like Peters and Terrell and Pickering. He would not die at the end of a rope or be caged like an animal. No matter what he had to do! But he would, somehow, see that the Mannings were safe.

He looked at April again. She looked untamed herself with the wild chestnut hair streaked with gold and the indomitable head arched stiffly. She was different. He had known that the moment he stumbled at her feet and had seen the anger that flickered across her face so fleetingly and realized it was not aimed at him, but at his guards. And later, when she defied Terrell. He had not wanted her hurt for him...so he had snapped at her like a trapped animal might. Now he was put-

ting her through pain much worse than that quick blow of
Terrell's.

She is so very pretty, even now, after a night and half a day
in the saddle, MacKenzie thought. Brave and pretty and very
desirable. He felt a craving in his loins, a ravenous hunger
combined with a slow, pulsating warmth that spread throughout his body. He wondered how it would feel—touching her. He
had known few "good" women, and bedded none. His physical needs had been satisfied by whores or curious saloon
women. Don't even think about it, MacKenzie told himself.
Don't torture yourself. You've done enough harm to someone
who doesn't deserve it. With supreme discipline, he tried to
erase the thoughts from his mind, but his body wouldn't obey.
To rid himself of the demons that were torturing him with
burning, stinging stabs of desire, he tightened his hold on the
boy and once more urged his horse into a trot.

MacKenzie's idea of a day's ride was not like anyone else's,
April realized along about midafternoon. They had stopped
several times but had not dismounted. He had merely offered
her water and some hardtack, then pushed on again. She was
pitiably grateful when he finally called a halt at a small water
hole surrounded by several trees. She was beginning to think he
would never stop. She had never known such weariness, such
pain from harshly used muscles and bones. They had continued through the morning, sometimes at a walk, sometimes a
trot. Davey had been uncomplaining, seemingly content in
MacKenzie's arms. Only once had she heard a small whimper.
She had kicked her horse forward, having lagged behind, but
as she neared she heard a low, crooning sound. Pacing herself
several lengths behind, she listened in amazement to an uncommonly rich voice. She didn't understand the words, but the
unusual melody hung in the air like a gentle morning mist,
softening the heat, gentling the landscape. And then he seemed
to sense her nearness and the voice stopped, breaking the magic
and hurtling her back into reality, into fatigue and pain and
anger.

For the anger was still there. It was mixed with numerous
other emotions, many of which she didn't understand. There
was pity when she saw his wounds, a warm, inexplicable tingling when she watched his quick, sure movements, resent-

ment as he moved tirelessly ahead while she grew numb with exhaustion. He had disrupted all her plans, but even more than that he had awakened something inside her, something she had tried hard to bury. Something she couldn't define, but which she knew was dangerous.

When the horses stopped, MacKenzie once again motioned to her to dismount first. As if, she thought bitterly, she could even think about escaping him. He was always so wary, so cautious.

She started to slide gratefully from her horse, but she kept going down. Her legs simply refused to hold her. Almost in a fog, she saw MacKenzie move, move so swiftly that he seemed almost a blur. She felt his hand at her elbow, gently guiding her to her feet and steadying her. The touch seemed to burn her, to spread from her arm to the inner core of her body. It was so strong, so confident, so *protective*. But when she looked at his face, it showed no emotion, and the eyes were hooded, and she knew she must have been mistaken. She was sure when she heard his words. They seemed as indifferent as his expression.

"Are you all right, ma'am?"

All her anger, frustration and hurt exploded at the insane question. She had had no sleep in two days. She was hungry and thirsty, and every bone in her body felt as if it had been on a rack in some ancient torture chamber. Her son had been threatened, she had been forced to ride through some of the roughest terrain this side of Hades, and he wanted to know if she was all right. She started to laugh, but there was no humor in it.

MacKenzie reached out for her again, and this time when she felt his touch, she recognized its gentleness, and she resented it, resented it with all her being. Instinctively, her hand went out and, with all her remaining strength, she slapped him, leaving a new red welt against the already battered face. The sound seemed to reverberate in the air, leaving a deafening stillness in its wake.

His hand dropped from her arm, and he stood back. There was complete silence and, for the first time, April felt fear of MacKenzie, and she was afraid to look at him. There was a palpable aura of violence and danger always around him, and she was deathly afraid she might have unleashed it.

"You're a brave woman, Mrs. Manning," he finally said, and despite herself she felt a spinning sensation that had nothing to do with weariness. There was no hint of anger in his voice or the slightest touch of reproach. There was, instead, a certain note of satisfaction.

She looked up at him. His mouth had softened ever so slightly, and he was regarding her with respect. "I was wondering when that was comin'." His expression was suddenly wry. "But I didn't think you had that much strength."

April stared with horror at the red splash of color that remained on his stubbled cheek. Before she had hit Terrell, she had never struck anyone in anger in her life. Now twice in as many days she had responded in a manner she'd always thought barbaric. And her blow must have been doubly painful against the bruised skin. Her deep blue eyes clouded with regret. "I'm sorry," she whispered.

"Don't," MacKenzie said in that deep voice she thought could charm birds from a tree. Foolish birds. Like her.

That strange Scottish inflection was more evident as he continued. "You had every right . . . and more."

There was something hesitant in that hard face, made harder now by the black beard that covered his jaw and cheeks. But the dark gray eyes were as unreadable as always.

Again MacKenzie broke the silence. "Get some rest, Mrs. Manning. I'll look after the boy."

April looked around and saw Davey standing there, regarding them both solemnly. He had seen his mother hit the tall man who had held him so comfortably. Why was she angry?

April leaned down and held out her arms. When Davey walked into them, she whispered, "I'm just tired, Davey."

"Don't you like him, Mama? I do."

April hesitated, then looked at MacKenzie standing there, a strange expression on his face.

"Yes, love. I like him."

Davey brightened, feeling his world right again. "I'm hungry."

April's smile was brilliant. She had been blessed with this child. Did MacKenzie have anyone? Her father had said he was a loner. But he had such a way with Davey. She had never seen her son respond so readily to someone . . . unless perhaps the silent Confederate on the train. And that had been a sort of magic. A need they both had. Perhaps that was all it was now. Davey seemed to need a father so badly. Maybe it wasn't MacKenzie after all. But even as the thought flickered through her mind, she dismissed it. There was already something special between MacKenzie and her son. She sensed it.

April tried to stand, but once more her legs balked. She felt herself being lifted into strong, masculine arms, smelled the scent of him and heard the strong beat of his heart. The weakness in her legs seemed slight to the weakness that swept her body at his closeness. Weakness and yearning and a sweet aching. She closed her eyes and partially understood Davey's own contentment in this man's hold. She didn't know whether it was the sure confidence of his arms or the feeling of shelter or the unexpected gentleness of his hands. They were all there and, like Davey, she had seldom felt so safe, so protected. Even here in this tiny oasis in the middle of nowhere, surrounded, perhaps, by hostile Indians; kidnapped; and, by now, followed by angry troopers.

She felt herself being lowered under a tree where there was a trace of shade. MacKenzie surprisingly knelt next to her and, without asking permission, took off her boots and drew her riding skirt about her knees. Before she could protest, his strong hands were kneading her legs, moving surely from one set of aching muscles to another, and she started to feel wonderful relief even as his touch left searing brands on her skin and consciousness. She watched wonderingly at his deftness as gentle but sure fingers eased away the pain.

Too soon, the fingers left her. He was standing. "Get some rest," he said again. "I'll watch Davey."

Despite herself, April closed her eyes at the soft command, and almost immediately she was asleep. She had only a moment to wonder that she was so willingly leaving Davey in the care of an accused murderer.

Chapter Five

MacKenzie watched as April's eyes closed and her body relaxed. She should sleep well, now that some of her sore muscles were soothed. God knows she needed it.

He had been amazed at her uncomplaining endurance and more than a little chastened at her apology after she had struck him. He winced as he thought how much he deserved it—that and more.

She was indescribably beautiful to him now. Great golden-brown lashes shuttered her sometimes compassionate, sometimes fiery eyes, and her long hair fell in curls around her face. The face had strength and character, qualities made more apparent, he thought, by the smudges of dirt. She had withstood hardship without complaint and, after all he had done, still considered her son and even himself before her own needs and comfort. It was something he had never before encountered, and he didn't understand.

It struck him with sudden pain as he realized, for the first time, just a little of what he had missed and would continue to miss. He had relished the feel of Davey's small, trusting body against his, Mrs. Manning's odd concern, her touch this morning when she had bandaged his wrist. He had been oddly pleased when Davey told his mother he liked him, had heard Mrs. Manning's reluctant reply—even knowing, as he did, that it was for Davey's sake.

But he couldn't think about such things. They would reach the Navaho camp sometime early this evening, and these few fleeting pleasures would become only memories.

His eyes moved from Mrs. Manning to Davey, who had sat and was watching him seriously.

"Would you like to help me?" he asked abruptly.

The boy's face brightened, and he nodded.

"Come, then, and we'll take care of the horses together." He started to walk away, but he felt a small hand on his, and he hesitated, then took it. Once more he felt an unusual twinge as the boy's hand rested comfortably in his large one.

He let Davey lead his Appaloosa to the water while he led the black gelding. He knew his own horse was steady; he wasn't as sure about the other. MacKenzie watched carefully, explaining to Davey that he must not let the horse drink too fast or he would have a bellyache. Davey's quick understanding and eagerness to help moved him once more. The boy was like his mother.

"Am I doing it right?" Davey asked, his face earnest and eager for approval.

"Aye," MacKenzie said. "You're a natural horseman. Both you and your mama." He was rewarded with a dazzling smile, the first he had seen on the boy's face. It was like sunshine after a storm.

When they were through, he asked Davey if he would like to help once more, and Davey eagerly agreed. MacKenzie went to one of the bedrolls and undid it, taking out some dried beef strips and hardtack, and a small mirror he had discovered.

He went to the stream, Davey at his heels, and sat cross-legged at the water's edge, watching as the boy imitated his every move. Using strips of his old shirt, MacKenzie washed his face and handed Davey the small mirror.

"Can you hold this very still?" he questioned, his lips smiling slightly at Davey's energetic nod.

MacKenzie slipped the knife from the band around his ankle and started shaving, watching the mirror intently. He had the Indian's contempt for facial hair even though his father's had grown long and unkempt. When he was through, he felt better than he had in several days. He also trimmed his hair around the sides and back. For convenience, his hair was short, shorter than that of most whites. If he didn't keep it short, it would fall in long shanks over his eyes, and he needed no distraction. Long hair was also easier to grab in a hand-to-hand fight. He had done it himself during several battles and was not willing to give his opponents that advantage.

God, he was tired. He didn't know when he had had more than a few moments of sleep, and that was fitful snatches in the storeroom. Pain had then kept him from more than an hour's release. But he couldn't sleep yet. Not until he delivered Mrs. Manning and Davey safely to the Navaho village. The horses' droppings would direct Pickering . . . slowly . . . to that destination, and then MacKenzie would disappear into the mountains.

He watched as Davey's head began to droop, and he reached down and picked up the boy. Carrying him to April's side, MacKenzie settled him down next to her. He then searched for green wood to carve a bow. He would not have time to prepare it properly, but it would have to do. For the next several days, he would not use a firearm, and he intended to leave most of the rations they had with Mrs. Manning and the Navahos. They needed them more than he; he was heading toward the high country, where game was plentiful. His hands moved knowledgeably over the wood.

He woke April as the sun was beginning its drop from the sky's apex. A slight breeze was cooling the air. Startled from a deep sleep, she was confused at first, then immediately awake as she remembered where she was. Her eyes frantically searched for Davey and found him curved beside her, a contented smile on his face.

"It's near time to go on, Mrs. Manning," MacKenzie announced.

She looked up at him, startled. He was clean-shaven, the first time she had seen him without the dark bristles that had made his face appear so hard. It was still hard: the chin set and determined, the lips locked in a tight, grim line, the eyes still shuttered against invasion. But it seemed to have lost some of the savagery that marked it earlier.

He handed her a canteen and some food and watched as she slowly ate the poor fare. It was prepared for convenience, not for taste, and April had to force herself to eat. But she knew she needed her strength . . . both for herself and Davey. She didn't know how long she would be expected to continue today.

It was as if he read her mind. "We will reach the Navahos by nightfall," he said slowly. "Pickering should be there by noon tomorrow. Even he should manage that." He didn't try to hide his scorn.

"And then," April said with sudden insight, "he'll have to take us home...he won't be able to follow you."

The wariness in his face told her she was right.

"You had more than one reason for taking us," she accused him.

MacKenzie cursed her quickness. It had not been the main reason, but it had been in the back of his mind from the beginning. His lips tightened even more, but he nodded. He would not lie to her.

He saw a cloud gather in her eyes. For some reason, she was disappointed in him, and he was surprised at how much the thought troubled him. When he spoke, however, his voice was curt and indifferent. "There's no more time to waste. Wake the boy."

April watched as he filled the canteens, leaving one with her for Davey, along with some food. She woke her son and gently teased him into chewing some beef and drinking some water as her eyes continued to study MacKenzie's quick movements. He went to the horses and resaddled them. They, too, had needed a brief respite, and he had relieved them of the saddles and blankets after watering them. After taking off the hobbles, he stood impatiently, reins in his hands.

April rose painfully. MacKenzie's ministrations had helped some, but she was still stiff and sore. She thought MacKenzie's mouth softened at her obvious discomfort but, as ever, any flicker of emotion was quickly gone. Unlike the other times, however, he did not mount first, but offered his hand for her foot and helped her into the saddle.

"You've decided I'm not going to run away?" she challenged, and was gratified at his brief wry look.

"Not without the boy," he replied.

"Why don't you let me have Davey? You could easily overtake me with your horse."

Again she surprised him. She was a better judge of horseflesh than most men. Although he had not spurred his horse to full speed, she had obviously seen its capabilities. Not many did, and his respect for her rose.

But he couldn't let her see it. She might use it against him. Instead, his words were curt. "I couldn't spare the time."

"Damn you," she said, and felt a certain satisfaction when she saw a muscle flex in his cheek. But he didn't say anything. He merely turned away, reached down, picked Davey up and placed him on the Appaloosa. With one easy movement, MacKenzie jumped behind Davey and nudged the horse into a trot. April followed, wondering whether she had only dreamed his gentleness earlier in the day.

MacKenzie's concentration was impeded by the woman. He knew he shouldn't be affected by her sudden disappointment in him. He was doing what he had to do. And he couldn't quite understand why she could accept that he had to take her and the boy to keep them from crying out at the camp, yet was upset over the other obvious benefit of their presence. It didn't make sense to him.

But he didn't have time to brood about it. An hour from the stream, they intersected pony tracks, dozens of them, and MacKenzie's entire attention was immediately riveted on them. His mind quickly ran through the possibilities. He doubted it would be the Navahos. They had given up hunting this far away from camp and were raising their own crops and animals now.

Apaches? They usually didn't come this far north. But they were on the warpath and might be ranging north in hopes of finding horses, food and slaves. They often took young men and women and even children from other tribes and sold them to Mexican ranchers. It was one way to raise money for rifles. MacKenzie involuntarily shivered. It would be worse than death to the freedom-loving Navaho.

Or it could be the Utes, reaching down from Colorado on a hunt or raid. They, too, took slaves and sold them.

But whoever and whatever made the tracks, they could mean trouble for his Navahos, for himself and for the Mannings. It was the last thing he needed now.

His hand tightened around Davey's waist, and he slowed his horse until Mrs. Manning caught up. He didn't want to frighten her, but he knew she should be aware of the danger.

When she was by his side, he pointed to the tracks. "It could be Apaches or it could be Utes. The Utes won't bother us. The Apaches..."

He didn't need to say more. April immediately understood. The Utes sometimes raided neighboring tribes and quarreled frequently among themselves, but they had worked with Kit Carson against the Navaho. They had no current grudge with the whites. Her father had kept her posted, in letters, of action in the area.

April paled a little at the thought of Apaches, but that was her only sign of concern. She looked at him questioningly.

"Stay close by my side," he said. "If I yell, ride like the devil's behind you. I won't leave you." He paused. "Can you shoot?"

She nodded. "I grew up on army posts, and my father thought I should learn... It's been a while, but I don't think it's something you forget."

He took the rifle from his back and started to hand it to her. He couldn't let himself think she might turn it on him. He wouldn't leave her undefended if anything happened to him.

"I'm better with a pistol," she said quietly and watched as he slung the rifle around his shoulders and, without a word, handed her the Colt from the gun belt around his waist. She felt it for a moment, trying to familiarize herself. She had forgotten how heavy it was, how ugly. It was an instrument of death, and while she had once mastered it she had never liked its purpose. Her father had insisted, however, since she often went riding by herself. She put it in one of the saddlebags, leaving the top of the bag unbuckled.

She kept pace with him now, often turning to study his face for clues. It was watchful, and she saw his eyes darting rapidly over the horizon. It was ideal ground for an ambush: large, craggy rocks, hills, heavy underbrush. They were entering the mountain area, and there were thousands of hiding places.

April wondered why she didn't feel more fear. And why she had such a sense of security with this man. The feeling scared her more than the Apaches. It suddenly came to her how much she was trusting MacKenzie, how much faith she had in him. He might protect her physically, but emotionally he was doing things to her she'd never thought possible.

I have to get away from him. The thought hammered at her consciousness. She and Davey. She looked at Davey in his arms. Her son looked as if he belonged there. She remembered MacKenzie's warm touch earlier in the day and understood. MacKenzie, she reminded herself, is an accused murderer. He'll most certainly hang once they find him. And they *will* find him. They always do. And what will that do to Davey? And me? Pain curled inside her at the thought. She had never witnessed a hanging, but she had heard about them. She knew it wasn't a pleasant way to die, even when it was properly done, which didn't always happen. April's hand touched the saddlebag as she resolved to get away from her kidnapper . . . after this danger. If he didn't leave her and Davey with the Navahos as he promised, she would *make* him leave them there. Now that she had a gun, she could protect both herself and the boy until the soldiers came. And then she could forget MacKenzie. She *would* forget him.

MacKenzie's pace had slowed. If he had been cautious before, he was doubly so now. He rode alone to each rise, mounting it carefully, eyes searching for movement. It was dusk before they reached the outer edges of the Navaho land, much later than he'd anticipated arriving.

He knew immediately something was wrong. There were always sentries at this point. And there were masses of tracks, all made within the past twenty-four hours. Then his nostrils caught the smell.

His hand went up in silent command. One finger pointed to a hill at their left, and April obediently followed, understanding instantly that speech was not wise. MacKenzie studied the landscape, finally finding what he sought. With gentle pressure, MacKenzie covered Davey's mouth and slid from his horse with the boy in his arms. April followed his lead silently, taking the reins of her horse and almost soundlessly following MacKenzie's footsteps up a slight rise.

He pointed to a place surrounded on three sides by sheer rock. The front was covered by underbrush. His hand urged her down, and he placed Davey in her arms. "I want you to stay here," he said in a whisper. "No matter what happens, what you hear, stay here unless you hear my voice. Will you do that?"

She nodded. Her faith in his judgment—in this matter, anyway—was complete.

He looked at her black horse. At least the color was a blessing. But he was afraid to leave it with them. A whinny or the stamp of a hoof might lead an Apache right to them. Yet if anything happened to him, she needed to be able to find the horse quickly. "I'm taking your horse just around the side of the hill," he said. "There are a few trees there. I'll stake him out."

April did not want the horse to go. "Then why can't we hide there, too."

He sighed. "You're safer here among the rocks...with some protection. The horses would stand out. Please do as I say."

It was the "please" that decided her. She knew he wouldn't have said it if he weren't desperate. She nodded her assent.

"If I'm not back by morning, and you've heard no noises during the night, get the horse and try to follow our trail back. You should run into Pickering." He handed her a couple of canteens and some beef jerky and finally, after a brief hesitation, his gun belt with its ammunition.

He looked at her as if he would like to say something else, but didn't. She wanted to ask him not to leave her. But couldn't. His face was frozen with determination. Something was very wrong. She knew that, and she also knew he wasn't going to tell her what. He had made his decision, and he wasn't going to change it. She would not humiliate herself by asking.

In the growing darkness, he took one last look at her and marveled at her control, although he saw the fear in her eyes and the confusion in Davey's face. He felt something clutching at him in his gut, and he almost bent over with the pain. He didn't want to leave them. But something very bad had happened over the ridge, and for their sake he had to know what. He couldn't make any decisions until he did. Nor could he subject them to what he was afraid he was going to see.

His hand reached out to Davey's shoulder and, involuntarily, moved up to touch April's face. He withdrew it instantly. He had no right. Then he saw the slight reassuring gesture had relaxed both of them, and he felt somehow comforted. He had needed that touch. MacKenzie reluctantly left, his moccasins making no noise as he disappeared.

* * *

It was worse then he had feared. The stench came from dead bodies, now bloated by the heat and sun. Men. Women. Young children. Only the young men and women were gone, taken, he knew, as slaves. The huts had been burned, the dogs killed. All the livestock was gone. Crops had been trampled. MacKenzie felt sick. He had done these Navahos no favor a year ago when he had won them a reprieve. Apaches. He recognized the lances and arrows. And the mutilations. Apaches believed they gained strength from cutting their enemies. One of those so butchered had once saved MacKenzie's life.

He fell on his knees as he viewed the carnage. He wanted to beat the earth at the waste. He had seen it before—too many times. And each time it had taken a little more of his soul. The first time had been the worst, because then it had been his fault. He had led the soldiers to a small, peaceful village of mainly women and children. He had not known the lieutenant was a bloody bastard with a hunger for glory. When he saw what was intended, he had attacked the lieutenant, had been subdued by a score of soldiers and tied to a tree where he had watched the rape of an innocent village. It all came back now, every terrible minute. It had not helped that the lieutenant had been court-martialed, that a major named Bennett Morgan had seen the man dishonorably discharged. The memory still haunted him; he doubted that it would ever leave him. He had resigned then and disappeared into the mountains for several years until General Wakefield had found him once more. He had wanted to say no, but Wakefield knew him only too well, knew his dream, and he had offered it. And a certain freedom of action. So he had reluctantly agreed. He had had only a few months left . . .

"Damn," he whispered to the dead. "God damn this world." MacKenzie didn't know how long he remained there on his knees, nor did he know that wetness formed in his eyes and traveled down his cheeks.

It was dark when he rose. There was one hut left partially standing, and he dragged and carried the bodies into it. He would not let the animals have them. When he was finally finished, he placed wood around the hut, and twigs and dry pine needles. He lit the pile, remembering only too well the same ritual nearly a year earlier.

MacKenzie mounted his horse, knowing it would take time for the tiny flame to kindle and light the dark night. He had to get the Mannings and move fast, although he believed the Apaches had probably gone south with their newly gained slaves and livestock. Some might have lingered. He couldn't take the chance he was wrong, not with the woman and boy.

Only fleetingly did he think about leaving them here in case Pickering was closer than he believed. The blaze in the sky would certainly speed them. But curious Apaches or other renegades might also be drawn to the scene of death, and he would not risk that. Immediately, he thought of an alternative. Between here and the high mountains, there were several ranches and a Ute Village. In the meantime they would have to ride tonight, and ride hard.

He tried to think of ways to soften the news for the woman. He knew she was going on grit alone, and part of her strength, he thought, was because she knew the ordeal was soon to end. Now he could promise nothing, only more uncertainty, more discomfort, more pain. And yet, deep inside a place he wouldn't recognize, there was a sudden gladness that he wouldn't lose them yet.

The time seemed endless to April as she huddled in her tiny hiding place. Davey had gone to sleep, and as she listened to the night sounds, the least noise became magnified. The whispering breeze among the pines was a roar, the call of a faraway coyote seemed only yards away. She had never been so frightened. Perhaps she should have been, these past several days? She had wondered frequently why she was not. But MacKenzie's absence terrified her much more than his presence had.

MacKenzie. How could one man so shake her entire being in such a short time? Make her question everything she had planned? Make her feel shivery and wanting and tender at the same time? He had left her here. Alone. He had treated her indifferently from the beginning, unmindful of her discomfort and pain and hurt. He had been intent only on his own escape. So why should she give a care? Except to see him captured, and she and Davey returned safely. She should be glad to see him in irons, in jail. So why was the thought so completely abhorrent? And why could she think of nothing but his proud, lean grace and his striking eyes—and those few seconds in his arms?

April felt the pistol growing heavier, and she grasped it anew, steadying it. Where was MacKenzie? What was he doing? Why had he told her so little? Perhaps he planned to leave them here alone while he made his escape north. Terror struck her anew. She had thought several times that she would use the gun against him, force him to take her and Davey someplace safe, regardless whether it fit into *his* plans. And now, in her anger at him she started to consider the idea once more. If he *did* come back. God, please make him come back. She leaned against the rock and waited, her hand locked on the gun, her finger on the trigger.

The moon was still a sliver, but bright stars lit an unclouded night, and MacKenzie had no trouble adjusting his eyes. He often traveled at night, and seemed to have extraordinary vision during those hours. Whether it was practice or training or something else he did not question.

He had no trouble finding April and Davey Manning. In order not to frighten them, he called out softly, then approached. The rifle was in his hands but held carelessly now. He had scouted well before returning, and there was no sign of human life—or trouble—within miles.

Tired and still sickened by the recent violence, he did not anticipate trouble from another direction. He went easily into the place he had prepared for April Manning, only to find her hand firmly on the Colt and her finger taut on the trigger. And the gun was pointing straight at his heart.

Chapter Six

April's hand didn't waver, and through the very dim light MacKenzie saw the determined set of her chin. He stood absolutely still.

"Drop the rifle." The command came clear and loud in the quiet night. There was no hesitation or weakness in it.

Only the slight throbbing of a muscle in MacKenzie's cheek indicated he heard as he considered the order. He was in no hurry to obey.

He shifted the rifle in his hand—not toward her or in any threatening manner, but not toward the ground, either. He knew she wouldn't shoot unless he made a move. But he wasn't quite sure whether she might shoot if he reached for her gun. He simply didn't know to what lengths of desperation he had driven her.

MacKenzie realized he had been gone for hours, hours that must have terrified her. The fact that he had had no choice made little difference. It did not help his conscience that those hours had come after the kidnapping of her son, a bone-wrenching day of riding and uncertainty about his intentions despite his poor assurances. Why, after all, should she trust him at all? A man accused of murder and rape who had grabbed a small boy. His terrible weariness was swallowed by an aching hurt as he watched the strong, courageous face just feet away from him. In minutes she would crumble. He could tell from the too stiff posture, the almost desperate cast of her chin. And he didn't want that to happen. She needed that pride to keep her going.

She had told him she could shoot, and she certainly held the Colt as if it were familiar. Her finger was on the trigger just tight enough to prevent him from trying to jump her, but not tight enough so the pistol would go off without intent.

"You don't want to fire that gun now," he finally said quietly. "There's Apaches not long gone."

"The Navaho camp?" There was the first hint of uncertainty in her voice. He had told her that was their destination.

The silence answered her question.

"I want to go home. I want to go to Fort Defiance."

"I know," he said in a gentle voice.

"I can wait here for the soldiers. You said they wouldn't be far behind."

"It's too dangerous... I couldn't leave you and the boy alone. And I can't stay."

"Then where?" It was a cry of desperation, and MacKenzie's hand tightened around the rifle. What in God's name was he doing to her? But there was no alternative. None at all.

"I will see you safe." It was all he could say.

"No," she said. "Davey and I will stay here."

"I can't let you do that."

Her hand tightened on the gun. "I said, drop the rifle!"

"No, Mrs. Manning." The voice was soft and regretful, but absolute, and April knew she had lost. She slowly lowered the gun.

"Damn you," she whispered.

MacKenzie stood, wanting fiercely to reassure her, to comfort her, to touch her, but he had no right, and he knew she would reject it now. His mouth, always grim, tightened into an even firmer line. His hand balled into a fist as he fought the desire to take her into his arms.

Davey was mercifully asleep and had been spared the tense scene. MacKenzie's eyes went from the boy to his mother, and he saw the defeat and confusion, and it pierced him to the depths of his being. He turned abruptly.

"I'll be getting the horses," he said, forcing the words, hoping they didn't reveal his own uncertainty.

April made a move to hand him the gun, but he shook his head. "Keep it," he said, his voice once more oddly gentle. As he disappeared, April leaned against the rock, trembling. She had been able to hold it in check while he was there in front of her, but now it rocked her body.

She had known, from the start, that she would not be able to shoot him. Her only chance was a bluff, and he had seen right through it. And now they would go on, and on, and on, and part of her was angry, and part terribly tired and part . . . relieved. She really had not wanted to stay alone, and she couldn't deny the feeling of safety she had with Mac-Kenzie. But she feared that feeling as much as she feared the Indians out there.

In the distance, she saw a glow, a golden halo reaching into the sky. It was in the direction from which MacKenzie had come, but she had no time to ponder its source, for she saw him approach, the two horses in tow. He silently handed the reins to her and helped her mount, his hand resting on hers a moment longer than necessary. She felt his warmth and strength, and she straightened her back.

MacKenzie picked up Davey, careful not to wake him, and swung up on his Appaloosa. Without any more words, they moved silently out, the golden glow behind them flaring in one last gasp, then slowly fading into nothingness.

April's fear during the long hours alone had dulled her to the biting cold, but now it attacked with ferocity. She shivered and tried to gather her jacket tighter around her. She was emotionally and physically drained, and she wondered if life would ever return to any kind of normalcy. She looked at MacKenzie's straight, unyielding back, and envied him his endurance. At least she had had several hours of sleep yesterday afternoon and could catnap on the horse. He had had none in two days, perhaps longer. How could he keep going? He would surely have to stop soon. No one could continue to maintain this pace.

April wondered what had happened during the hours he had been gone during the night. He was always grim-faced, but there had been something more when he returned. A stark bitterness. And, perhaps, sorrow. It was hard to tell with him. He guarded his feelings as most men guarded gold. If, that is, he had any. She was beginning to wonder about that. And with each step of her horse, she wondered more. Where was he taking her and Davey now? Where would it end?

The first hint of dawn broke the darkness, and black faded into a dull gray as clouds swarmed the sky, blocking even a hint of a warming sun.

MacKenzie stopped at another small stream. April didn't even puzzle any more at his uncanny ability to find water in this dry country but, instead, she slid gratefully from the horse, dropping where she landed. She didn't have the strength to take even one step.

Davey, now awake and bright-eyed, went to her, and MacKenzie followed. His eyes swept over her, missing nothing—not the droop in her shoulders or the infinite exhaustion in her face. He sighed. She had been stronger than he had any right to expect, but she couldn't go much farther. He looked at the threatening thunderheads beginning to form in the sky, and knew they had to find shelter. The rain would erase any trace of their trail, and he suspected Pickering would not pursue them much beyond the Navaho camp. The lieutenant would probably have to report to Fort Defiance, where they would send out additional search parties. He smiled wryly. He would not like to be in Pickering's boots when the lieutenant faced Wakefield. He could almost hear the roar now. Pickering's career had ended the moment MacKenzie took Mrs. Manning and Davey. But what in the hell was he going to do with them now?

There were several ranches between here and the high mountains that were now his goal. And if worse came to worst, there was a Ute village where the woman and boy would be safe while word was sent. The Utes had a strong treaty with the United States because of the leadership of Chief Ouray. And a daughter of a general would be well treated and protected.

But now he needed to find shelter. He saw April shiver in the cold morning air, and he took a blanket, slitting a hole in the middle. He offered his hand to her, and she took it, once more feeling its remarkable warm strength, which seemed to flow into her. She stood, swaying just a little as he settled the blanket around her. With another quick movement, he cut a piece of rope and tied it around her waist.

"That should help some," he said tersely as he felt her blue eyes on him. They seemed enormous now in a face pinched by exhaustion.

April didn't answer. She was simply too tired.

"An hour more," he said, and there was more than the usual softness in his speech. "An hour more and you can sleep as long as you wish."

April barely comprehended the words. An hour seemed a lifetime to legs screaming in agony, a mind crying for sleep. But she knew she could not fight him. There was a magnetic power in him that lured something inside her to obey, to go beyond what she thought she could do. She nodded and received a fleeting reward—a small, rueful smile that held an engaging hint of admiration. It disappeared quickly, but for a moment it eased his face, and she thought how attractive it was. If only he would do it more often.

She watched as once again he carefully tended the horses and filled their canteens. All too quickly, he was back. She felt his sure, confident hands around her waist, and she was being lifted effortlessly into the saddle. How assured those arms felt. She wondered, briefly, if she imagined a slight hesitation before his hands left her. Then she pondered the warm glow that started to burn within her at the thought. Foolish April. He was thinking of nothing but escape.

Then they were moving again, and she could only clutch the saddle horn and pray for a quick end to this. One hour. Sixty minutes. She started to count to keep her mind from absorbing the punishment. She never considered the fact he might have lied. One hour. Then fifty-nine minutes.

Half drugged with exhaustion, she didn't realize he had taken her reins, or that he was leading them through the middle of a small stream to hide their tracks. He was watching carefully for horse droppings and stopped once to disperse a pile near the edge of the stream. He didn't know how far he would have to take her, or how long they would have to rest, and he didn't want the cavalry on his tail now. He again doubted whether Pickering would continue this far, but he couldn't be sure. The threat of losing the general's daughter might just spur him on.

He looked at April, her head nodding, her hands clutched tightly to the saddle, as if locked there. The blanket made her shapeless, and her hair was a curly mass falling down her back, the rich chestnut brown streaked with hints of gold and red. She was a valiant one. And so was her boy. He never thought a small lad could be so good, so quiet, so completely trusting of a stranger. But Davey had burrowed a hole in MacKenzie's chest and seemed content. He was awake now, and watching everything, occasionally holding out a hand to point at something unfamiliar. MacKenzie would try to explain, at first simplifying his words, but then he realized it was not necessary. The boy was uncommonly bright and absorbed everything.

As they continued to climb the streambed, the clouds grew heavier and more ominous. MacKenzie knew exactly where he was going—a cave he had occasionally used on scouting trips. He finally saw the rocky face of the foothill he was seeking and left the streambed, carefully guiding the horses through tangled underbrush to an opening in the rock. He dismounted and went to April, noting her almost glazed eyes as she made no effort to move.

"We can rest here," he said, offering his hand, but she made no move to take it. He went around to her other side and released her foot from the stirrup and returned to the left side. His hands reached up to her waist and once more she was in his arms. Like Davey, she seemed to snuggle there for a moment, unaware of the sudden tautness of his body as it came in contact with hers. He carried her inside, Davey at his side, and he set her on the floor of the cave. It was deep, and he looked back into the dark interior. He doubted they had any animal companions; he would have heard or smelled them by now. But with the boy, he would take no chance. He lit a match and told Davey to stay with his mother while he searched the cave. There was nothing but some old animal bones and a few mostly broken pieces of ancient pottery. One jar, however, was virtually intact, and he brought it back with him.

The cave was cold, and MacKenzie saw Mrs. Manning shiver. He left and was back within minutes with an armful of firewood, and his hands quickly had a blaze going. He left once more and tended the horses, taking off the saddles, rubbing the backs where sores were beginning to show from the hard riding. He hobbled them, then returned to the cave, bringing the bedrolls with him. He fashioned one into a pillow for Mrs. Manning and took a blanket from the second, pulling it up around her.

"I'll watch the boy," he said as he had the day before. "You sleep."

"What about you?" April was barely able to mutter, but the thought nagged at her. He must be much more tired than she . . . if that were possible.

"I can rest with one eye open," he said with a slight smile. "I'm used to it."

April believed him. Her eyes closed and she was asleep almost instantly.

When she woke, Davey and MacKenzie were gone. She felt a moment's panic and forced herself to think. There was still light filtering into the cave, so she had not slept the entire day away. And the fire had obviously been frequently tended; the pile of ashes was substantial, and there was a stack of firewood against the wall of the cave. Once more, she was struck by conflicting feelings. She still couldn't quite comprehend that indefatigable energy that kept him going when most men would have fallen. It frustrated her that he could do so much, and she must appear so weak. And once more, there was that strange, warm feeling of protection, of knowing that she and Davey were in good hands.

But where were they—MacKenzie and her son?

She rose slowly, every muscle screaming in protest as she made her way to the cave's entrance. Clouds were boiling in the sky, large black and purple splotches reshaping themselves as they crossed overhead in great, hurrying masses. The wind was blowing hard, and her hair whipped around her face, and the leaves and limbs of nearby trees groaned and whistled as gusts bullied their way through them. There was an expectancy in the air because of the approaching storm, and April wondered why she wasn't frightened. She had always liked storms, but then she had always been well-protected by sturdy structures, not out in the middle of an untamed wilderness with only a cave for shelter. But now the elemental electricity excited her, and she felt a small flame start deep inside at the thought of sharing it with MacKenzie, even though she knew she shouldn't.

April saw a movement in the brush, and MacKenzie's rangy, graceful form appeared first. Davey was tagging behind, a large fish in his hands and a huge smile on his face. MacKenzie was carrying several fish on a thin piece of rope, a satisfied gleam in his eyes.

His eyes swept April, and she thought for a moment how much they resembled the gray, frothing sky. If only she could read them. But she could only see the complexity, as she had that first night. Nothing more.

"Dinner," MacKenzie proclaimed. And April thought to herself it was the only unnecessary word she had ever heard him utter.

"I caught a fish," Davey said with great pride as he showed his treasure. "MacKenzie taught me how."

April's eyebrows lifted. "MacKenzie?"

"He said I could call him that. It's all right, isn't it, Mama?"

Once more, April looked at the man who had so radically changed her life in the past few days.

There was a tiny, almost indefinable glint of amusement in his expression. "I didn't think Mr. MacKenzie sounded quite right. Everyone just calls me MacKenzie."

"No other name?" April couldn't help but ask.

The brief amusement disappeared, and tiny bitter lines formed at the corners of his mouth. "Many," he said, "but none I would say in front of the boy."

April was stunned at the intensity of his words. They held a deep, savage bitterness he had kept well-hidden until now. She recalled Terrell's brutal treatment and wondered how MacKenzie had held his temper. It must have taken superb willpower to have endured what he had with so little show of emotion or concern. She could sense the suppressed violence in him.

MacKenzie turned away abruptly, obviously regretting that brief lapse of control. "I'll clean them," he said shortly, taking the one fish from Davey and adding it to his own. He went some twenty yards from the cave and sat, cross-legged, his back stiff and hostile, the sharpening wind ruffling his thick black hair.

April hesitated, wanting to say something. It was almost as if she could feel the jagged wounds within him. He had revealed them for only the briefest of seconds, but she knew they ran deep. She moved toward him, then took measure once more of the tense, hard body and knew he wouldn't appreciate sympathy. And yet there was such a deep longing in her to comfort, to share, to soothe…her kidnapper? Davey's kidnapper?

The man who had put her through such physical agony? It didn't make sense, but as she looked at him, his very strength and reserve seemed to magnify that brief image of vulnerability.

One fist clenched her side in an effort to keep her distance. She stood there for a moment, then retreated into the cave with Davey, who was chattering eagerly about the fish. He had never gone fishing before, and he was filled with enthusiasm. MacKenzie, he said, caught *his* fish with a spear he had made from his knife and a piece of wood.

"But I caught one all by myself with the pole. MacKenzie just helped a wee bit."

Every time Davey said "MacKenzie," his eyes shone with adoration, and April was flooded with new fear. She had never seen Davey so open, so flushed with excitement. Her son was already imitating MacKenzie's slight burr. What would happen when MacKenzie disappeared from their lives? As he undoubtedly would, and soon. Davey had adopted MacKenzie without reservation, without question.

And MacKenzie? He had been uncommonly patient with the boy. She had seen him whispering to her son on the long ride, and she remembered the haunting song that had filled the air with a misty loveliness of its own. Would he miss Davey? Or her? The last question sent a stab of warm longing coursing through her, leaving a bittersweet aftermath of anticipation and fear. She had thought herself immune to these kinds of feelings after four years of a purgatory of waiting. She thought she had successfully schooled herself against them, and now they frightened her with their raw intensity.

April fed the fire, welcoming the chance to busy her hands and take her mind away from the renegade scout. She *had* to think of him that way. The flames grabbed the new fodder and danced upward, sending a wave of warmth across the cave, but April didn't feel it. Instead, a sudden chill ran through her body, a fear so deep she felt her body shiver. But she couldn't identify it.

She tried to shake the feeling, taking Davey's hand and leading him to the blankets where she wrapped herself and him, listening all the time to his eager, happy words of his new adventures with MacKenzie. After what seemed hours, he quieted and went to sleep in her arms, and she searched the small face with a love so great it hurt. It was still flushed from the outdoors, and the fire, and memories of a happy day. There was a contented smile in place of the old, apprehensive look so often in place at the Manning home. April felt a surging tenderness for Davey and gratefulness to MacKenzie for the gift of joy he had given Davey this afternoon. Even as she knew it would end soon. And she and Davey would be going home. She tried to think happily about the prospect, about the moment she and Davey would be free, but she could only feel a deep emptiness at the prospect. Curled up with Davey, it was her last thought before she drifted into a troubled sleep.

April woke to the rumbling roar of thunder, the lonely sound of rain hitting earth and the savory smell of cooking fish. She opened her eyes slowly and knew it was evening. The cave was dark, lit only by the occasional spurt of flame from the fire. MacKenzie had let it almost die, apparently to cook the fish, which were skewered on a stick. It rested over two piles of rocks on each side of the fire. April felt Davey warm against her, and she didn't move as she adjusted her eyes to the darkness.

She saw the lithe, sinewy outline of MacKenzie's body, and wondered once more at the primal grace of it. Every movement was so sure, so confident. He seemed like one of the dancing shadows created by the flares of flame. She heard a new roll of thunder as it gained power and fury and crashed in great waves of tumultuous sound, followed by an immense flash of light, which illuminated the cave. It seemed to focus on MacKenzie's face, framing the hard, angular planes and his compelling masculinity, resting for a split second on eyes that looked like a storm-tossed ocean, restless and tormented. April felt a stab of longing that was becoming painfully familiar. She had never so wanted to touch someone . . . not even with David. She had loved David, but it had been a gentle, dreaming young love; she had never felt this overpowering need for contact, this aching in her body that stretched from its core to every nerve end. She shivered with her own need and drew her arm tighter around Davey.

"Mrs. Manning." His voice was so soft it was almost a whisper, but it was audible through the noise of hard, driving rain. She wondered how such a large man, such a strong man could have such a quiet voice. She also wondered how he knew she was awake. She was in the shadows, and she had not moved. He was uncanny about sensing things. He left her with few thoughts of her own. She could only hope that at least one of them was safe.

"Mrs. Manning," he said again. This time there was a command in it.

April reluctantly sat up, carefully unwrapping Davey from her arms without waking him. She knew MacKenzie must be conscious of the fact she had been watching him, studying him. She eased her son to the ground, saw that he was well covered and moved to where MacKenzie knelt before the fire.

"Yes?" she said coolly, willing reserve in her voice, even disdain. As befitting captive to captor, she thought. *I can't forget that! Please God, don't let me forget that.*

His gray eyes pierced her with the electric intensity that was so much a part of him. His body was tense, almost, April fancied, like a cougar's before striking. And that is what he reminded her of . . . a fascinating, dangerous mountain cat. Free and untamed and beautiful with its sleek sureness and power. But the image was suddenly broken when his hand went up to his hair and raked it in a gesture that denoted the first uncertainty she had seen in him. It was an almost boyish movement, and once more April detected the vulnerability that he tried so hard to hide.

"Yes?" she said again, this time in a softer tone.

MacKenzie hesitated, obviously trying to find words. "We'll stay here a day or two . . . so you and the boy can get rested."

April knelt beside him so she could meet his eyes. He was struggling to say more. She waited.

"You do not need to worry," he said finally, his face set as granite. "I'll not touch you."

April's face must have reflected her surprise for he continued. "I didn't hurt that girl back there."

MacKenzie's jaw was rigid, and April understood how difficult the words must have been. He was not a man who explained or apologized or justified. Yet he was trying, awkwardly, to reassure her. What small hostility she had tried to summon melted altogether.

"I know," she said, and there was so much conviction in her voice MacKenzie's mask broke and she saw open astonishment in his face.

"Davey's a very good judge of character," April continued. "And so is my father."

"Your father?" He couldn't hide his confusion.

"He wrote me about you. He trusts you."

"He *did*," MacKenzie said wryly. "I don't think so anymore."

April bit her lip, then summoned all her courage. "Go back with me," she said passionately. "Go to Defiance with me. You know my father. He'll see you get justice, that Ellen was lying."

There was no mistaking the pain in MacKenzie's face now. "I've also killed a sergeant."

"Self-defense," April guessed. "It was self-defense, wasn't it?"

He looked at her steadily, scarcely understanding that she believed him, that she trusted him after all he had done to her and the boy.

"You don't understand," he said finally. "It makes no difference. The word of a half-breed would mean nothing against a white girl or Terrell or the others. I wouldn't stand a chance." His voice was once more bitter.

"But I could tell them what Terrell did..."

"Do you really think anyone cares...that it would matter? Then you're a fool." His face once more froze, and his eyes were like cold steel. It was as if he had placed a stone wall between them.

April couldn't let it go. "My father..."

"Your father would probably happily see me hang now." There was regret in his voice but no yielding. "I'll not go back."

Davey stirred then, and both MacKenzie and April quieted their voices although their eyes still battled.

It was MacKenzie who finally spoke. "The fish are cooked...and there's hardtack." A suspicion of a smile appeared at April's grimace. But she didn't say anything.

"You are a very unusual woman, Mrs. Manning. Do you never complain?"

"If I think it will do any good," she replied, her eyes lighting with mischief. "And you might call me April. After spending several nights together, I think it would be appropriate."

The cold reserve dropped from MacKenzie's face, and once more he seemed, for a second, at a loss. "April," he said, his senses savoring the sound, "It fits you well." But then he turned away from her, and April sensed the withdrawal, and she knew the wall was still there.

Chapter Seven

Daylight crept into the cave, moving slowly to encompass the entrance, then where the fire still burned, and finally to where April Manning and her son slept.

MacKenzie had been awake for hours. He had caught naps through the night, but was aware of the need to feed the fire, to keep his charges warm in the cold, damp air. He had lived for years on scattered pieces of sleep, knowing well the penalty in both the animal and human world for unawareness. He would wake at the slightest sound, or the cooling of a fire, or the rustle of an oncoming storm. His senses never slept, not even when he was totally exhausted.

The rain had stopped, but the air was still cold, unusually so for this time of the year. He shifted his gaze from the fire to the sleeping pair on the other side of the cave.

Mrs. Manning—he wouldn't let himself think of her as April, he couldn't—was still sleeping soundly. She had tamed her wild hair into a braid, which fell over her right breast, and one hand cradled Davey. Long lashes covered the blue eyes that hovered in his mind, and her wide, generous mouth was curved into a small smile. How gently she slept.

His prisoners. He did not think of them that way although he knew she must. He had listened to her plea the night before, when she suggested he return them to Defiance. He had even considered it for a moment, but he had had enough of "justice," and contempt and humiliation.

If he thought there would be the slightest chance...but there wasn't and never would be.

When he had taken the boy, he thought it would only be a matter of hours, but it had been days, and it might well be many more. He had not meant to hurt either of them, and now he was responsible for both, and he was astonished and dismayed at how quickly each had grabbed a piece of a heart he had thought hardened. Something happened when Davey stuck his hand in MacKenzie's and eyed him with such trust. He had never known what it meant to touch another's life and give it the bright happiness that glowed in the boy's face.

And April Manning. She warmed him as no other person had. She challenged him with her courage and endurance, eased him with her bewildering trust. He had sought to comfort her last night, and it was he who was comforted. Even if he couldn't show it.

He couldn't let her know how much he wanted to touch her, to hold her, to feel her warmth. For then, they would both be lost. He sensed in her a passion that, when fully awakened, would be all-consuming. And he could give her nothing. Less than nothing. Only hiding, and fear, and death.

With no little disgust at his self-indulgence, he quickly rose to his feet. They would stay half of the day to let Mrs. Manning's sore muscles adjust, then continue on to the Ute village. He and Davey would do some more fishing this morning, and perhaps he would even try to hunt with the rough bow and arrows he had fashioned. He knew he would have little range; the bow had none of the suppleness of a properly prepared one, but perhaps... They needed fresh meat, and such gifts would make them doubly welcomed by the Utes. He added enough wood to the fire to keep it going for another hour or two. He would not be gone any longer.

April felt Davey tugging on her. His face was gloomy. "MacKenzie's gone," he announced.

She felt a sudden apprehension, then studied the cave. The fire had been recently fueled, and both saddles and bedrolls were still there. His one blanket was neatly folded near the wall. He had given three to April and Davey. Everything else was neat. The fish bones from the night before were gone. She smiled at the thought of MacKenzie cleaning the cave as carefully as any Boston housewife.

She stood and stretched and felt better than she had in days. Some of the pain in her bones and muscles was fading, and she felt well rested. She felt more alive than she had in years as she wondered which of the several MacKenzies she would encounter today. He had, unwillingly enough, showed them all yesterday: the terse, quiet loner, the gentle man who taught her son to fish, the intense, attractive man who said her name fit her. There had been something in the way he said it . . . something warm and approving.

In the meantime, she and Davey needed to make good use of the time. She had been far too tired in the past several days to do anything about their appearance. Now she would find the stream and try to remedy that. She wished desperately that she had a comb. Her hair was never easy to control and now it was a messy web of snarls.

April quickly looked through the saddlebags and MacKenzie's bedroll, where she found a bar of soap and a comb. She took two of the blankets to use as covering while she washed hers and Davey's clothes. Taking Davey's hand, she let him lead her to the stream where he and MacKenzie had fished the day before.

It was a beautiful rain-washed morning, even though there was a sharp bite to the wind. The sky was as deep and pure a blue as she remembered seeing, and the sun was spraying the water with freckles of gold. The mountains rose up in purple splendor in front of them, and even this stark, rocky hill country was colorful with an occasional wildflower. Against all common sense, April felt shivers of joy run up and down her spine. It was so incredibly peaceful, so lovely in its own lonely way. It seemed a place apart from violence and death, as if she and Davey and MacKenzie were the only people on earth and they were in harmony. MacKenzie. Her thoughts seldom strayed from him now, and her eyes anxiously searched for him. While fearing to find him.

Was it just because she and Davey were so dependent on him? She had no idea where they were, nor was she even sure they were in as much danger from Apaches as MacKenzie had indicated. Perhaps it was just his way to keep her from trying to run away. But why? He had made no move to hurt her, and she knew she and Davey were a burden to him. They slowed him down, and she sometimes fancied she sensed his impatience even though his face never showed the slightest anger or disapproval.

MacKenzie mystified her, taunted her with his apparent indifference to her as a woman. He had been kind enough that day when he had rubbed her sore muscles but that, she knew, was only so she could continue. She tried to convince herself that his gentleness with Davey came from that same concern . . .

Don't think about it. It's a short episode, a small adventure in your life, April told herself. Don't think about it as anything more. Still, she couldn't keep her eyes from searching for him, or quiet the expectation that hovered inside her. Davey, now convinced that MacKenzie would soon be back, squirmed free from her hand and tripped from one discovery to another. He beamed as he told April the name of a cactus MacKenzie had pointed out. "You can get water from that," he explained proudly. "MacKenzie said so."

April worried at the awe in Davey's voice. What would he do when MacKenzie was gone? Would he understand?

April stripped down to her chemise and pantalets, shivering a little in the cold. She washed both Davey and herself quickly, then her hair and finally their clothes. When she was through scrubbing them, she lay them out on rocks and bushes to dry in the sun and wrapped the two of them in the blankets as she told Davey a story about a prince and princess in a faraway country.

Only once did Davey interrupt. "Did he look like Mac-Kenzie?" he asked. "And did the princess look like you?"

April smiled at the thought of MacKenzie in armor, but not at all at the thought of him slaying a dragon.

"Yes, love," she whispered. "I think he might."

So absorbed were both of them that they didn't hear MacKenzie's soft footsteps, nor sense his presence as his longing eyes moved with fierce protectiveness from the slender blanket-clad woman to the child. He listened silently, hands knotted in fists and eyes filled with immeasurable pain. At the story's end, he moved away soundlessly.

When Davey and April returned to the cave, April smelled coffee and cooking meat. She wondered how long MacKenzie had been back. She felt self-conscious at her appearance. Her thick hair was still a little wet and curling in all directions. Her clothes were also damp and clung to her slender form. But at least she was clean.

She met his eyes when she entered and, almost shyly, held out the soap. "I borrowed your soap... I hope it's all right."

MacKenzie couldn't take his gaze from her. There was an uncertainty in her face that made him want to take her in his arms and quiet the questions and doubts in her eyes. Instead, he turned away. "Use anything you need."

April stared at his back, feeling the palpable tension between them. Despite his rough words, she knew he felt the surge of electricity between them, the flash of desire that burned her as nothing else had. It had been growing between them, day by day, and now she knew it frightened him as much as her.

"MacKenzie," she said softly. When he turned she knew she was right. His eyes were tormented in that one second before the protective shield was back in place.

His voice was cool when he finally replied, "Mrs. Manning?"

"April," she insisted.

"Mrs. Manning," he said in a tone that allowed no argument. It was obvious he was trying to keep distance between them. As if a name could do it, she thought with dry amusement. The electric current was even stronger now, and she felt her body tingling in reaction.

And his. She could see it stiffening, visibly see the control he was exercising over it. The expectancy in the air was several times greater than yesterday when the storm was whipping itself to a fever pitch. She felt it start in the core of her being and spread until all she wanted was to touch him, to feel his arms around her.

April was sinking in a quagmire of want and need. MacKenzie's eyes had lost their shield and reflected the same burning, aching agony she felt. She had never known anything like it before, this craving that made her forget everything else, every piece of respectability, her father, everything... everything but Davey.

Davey. She felt his hand pull on hers. "Mama?"

She heard his voice from a distance, and tore her eyes from MacKenzie's rigid form. She knew she had been holding her breath, and now she released it slowly, trying to find some sanity in the effort.

MacKenzie watched as tears formed at the corner of April's eyes and their usual clear color turned a misty violet that tore at his soul. He closed his own eyes, forcing himself to regain control, to steel himself against the growing vulnerability these two were creating within him. He could not afford it. He could not make mistakes now—for his sake or theirs. He had no future. He must make certain they did. If anything happened to them, he would be damned forever.

With the greatest effort he had ever made, MacKenzie swallowed and walked several steps away. He turned, his eyes avoiding April's. "You and the boy eat. I have things to do. We leave in a few hours." He spun around and left the cave without another word.

MacKenzie took the hobbles from his Appaloosa and adjusted the bit. He slipped his rifle over his shoulders and vaulted to the horse's back, tightening his knees against its side. He felt free without the saddle, more a part of the horse's fluid gait. His heels dug into the horse's flank and sent it into a gallop.

The tension inside him seethed and boiled, constricting his stomach into a ball, attacking his gut. He had come so close, so very close to reaching out to her, to taking her.

"Aah . . ." The anguished war cry tore from his mouth as he sought release from a hunger he had never known existed until now. The horse under him stretched its legs in even greater strides, sensing its rider's need and responding to it. MacKenzie was at one with the animal, his lithe form riding high on the neck, a portrait of grace and power.

He didn't know how far they went before he slowed the horse, feeling its lathered heat under him, seeing its foam-flecked mouth. He pulled up and dismounted, sliding his hand down the Appaloosa's neck in apology. The horse and Wolf . . . his friends. He needed no others. MacKenzie walked the Appaloosa, letting the horse cool slowly, letting his own fevered thoughts bathe in the cold, cleansing air.

There was a ranch not far away. He had ignored that possibility because, he admitted, he had not really wanted to relinquish Mrs. Manning and Davey. Not yet. But this morning showed how very important it was that he do so. He had had need of a woman before, but it had never been this sweet aching that overshadowed everything else. Perhaps it was because he had never really *liked* a woman before. And he liked April Manning. Very much.

And because he did, he was becoming careless. He should have been scouting the area rather than listening to nonsensical tales of princes and fairies. Or making coffee from their very limited supply. But he had wanted, in some way, to please her, to see the smile again.

MacKenzie swung back up on his horse and set his mind to the tasks at hand. He would check out the Ebert ranch, then make a wide arc south to see whether there were any signs of army or Indians. April Manning would be safe. He had left his pistol with her and, as far as he knew, no one knew of the cave. No one alive, anyway.

The sun was directly overhead, but still it was cold. An early winter, perhaps. He needed to get up into the mountains before the first snowfall. The passes, once swallowed by snow, were impassible, even to one who knew them well.

Wary and watchful, MacKenzie retraced his steps down the streambed they had climbed the day before. After an hour, he cut away and went west, setting a fast but not wearing pace. There were still no recent tracks, but he felt an unease, an edge that he had come to respect. It usually meant trouble. He didn't want to think it was there because of the woman and child, because they had, somehow, destroyed instinct, which had kept him alive this long.

He was five miles from the Ebert ranch when he saw the first signs. Numerous pony tracks, again from unshod ponies. Heading south from the ranch. The familiar sickness started in his stomach. The Eberts had two young children—a girl and a boy. He had warned them to leave several months ago, when the Apache raids moved farther north, but Tom Ebert had felt they were far enough away from the trouble. They had scratched out a living with a small corn crop and a few horses. It had been

Ebert's plan, as it was MacKenzie's, to raise horses. It had been a small bond between two taciturn men.

Knowing it was too late, MacKenzie nonetheless pushed his horse into a gallop, seeking the bluff that overlooked the ranch. He dismounted half way up and crawled until he could see over its top.

MacKenzie closed his eyes when he saw the scene below. The ranch house was gone, burned to the ground. Bodies, including several in blue uniforms, lay scattered like broken dolls. He could pick out Mrs. Ebert because of the dress.

So some of Pickering's men did get this far. It was probably Corporal Patterson. Patterson was the most savvy and conscientious soldier in the small command. MacKenzie felt a wave of regret. For Patterson. For the others. Most of all for the Eberts. He studied the terrain, seeing nothing move. It must have happened fairly recently. He supposed that the troops had heard the shots and come to assist the settlers.

It had been another misjudgment on his part. Patterson had followed his trail faster than he thought possible. The corporal had probably lost it someplace along the creek bed and cut over to the Ebert ranch. MacKenzie realized he had been a fool not to start out early this morning, but he knew his charges had badly needed rest, and so did he. It didn't matter now, he thought darkly. Pickering would have to go back now.

MacKenzie considered the alternative of going down to the killing ground. Apaches were thorough. There would be no one left alive, and there was really nothing he could do. He certainly couldn't take the time to bury them, and he supposed Patterson's absence would soon bring additional troops. He cursed roundly. He simply couldn't leave without checking. Grimly, he half walked, half stumbled down to his horse and mounted again, reluctantly turning his Appaloosa toward the Ebert place.

He had been right. There was no one left alive, not even the little Ebert girl. The boy was gone, taken, probably, to be raised as an Apache brave. It *was* Patterson, and he had been tortured before dying. It hadn't been more than several hours earlier.

MacKenzie didn't even think about burying them. It would take too long and now every minute was dangerous. He and the

Mannings were no longer safe in the cave, either. It was too close to both the soldiers and the Apaches. He had misjudged Pickering's tenacity...or was it desperation? MacKenzie briefly considered the possibility of leaving Mrs. Manning and the boy to await the troops, but quickly dismissed it. He could not leave them in this valley of death, nor could he risk the possibility that Pickering might just give up the chase when Patterson didn't return. The Ute village was still his best choice.

MacKenzie went down the hill to the Appaloosa and, moving cautiously over rocks that would not leave a trail, headed for the cave.

April paced the cave, which was quickly becoming a prison. Davey was asleep, and she dared not leave him alone. They had eaten part of the rabbit MacKenzie had prepared, but his abrupt departure and curt words had taken away her appetite, and she had merely picked at the food. The coffee, boiled in tin cups found in the bedrolls, was black and bitter, too bitter for her taste. She supposed MacKenzie was used to it so strong. It would keep him awake, alert. If it didn't kill him first, she thought wryly. Yet she knew he had made it for her. It would have been a small gesture for anyone else, but a large one for him. She suspected he was not used to doing things for others.

His presence haunted the cave. He was such a contradiction: harsh and gentle, strong and yet oddly vulnerable. A man accused of the worst possible crimes yet able to sing a lullaby to a child. *Where are you, MacKenzie? And who are you? Who are you really?*

MacKenzie was wondering that same question. The whole fabric of his life was changing. In only four days, he had discovered wants and needs he had scorned all his life. He was feeling real fear for someone else, realizing the richness of trust, the elusive joy of affection Davey gave so freely, the quiet pleasure of friendship offered by April Manning, the promise of rapture that shone so innocently in her eyes. He greedily wanted to seize them all, to seize the fire...

But he would not be the one burned. It would be the woman and child. And he would never, never let that happen.

Feelings of futility and bitterness swept over him, almost blinding him. He wiped his eyes with the dust-covered sleeve of his shirt, wishing for the old oblivion where survival was his only concern. The glimpse and the promise of something more were heavier chains to bear than any man could devise. And now he would wear them forever.

April's joy at seeing MacKenzie dimmed quickly at his almost savage expression. Even Davey drew back, sensing that something was very wrong.

"We're leaving now," he said abruptly, his gray eyes as cold and merciless as a winter sea.

"But you said..." April started, then stopped. It obviously no longer mattered what he *had* said. "What's happened?" she asked, searching his face, which revealed little.

MacKenzie stooped down until his face was level with Davey's. "My horse is just outside," he told the boy. "Can you start rubbing down his legs... like I showed you?"

"Just like you showed me," the boy affirmed.

"Go, off with you, then," MacKenzie said, "but no farther than the horses."

He turned to April, his gaze serious and hesitant, as if weighing how much he should tell her.

"What's happened?" she asked again. As the silence lengthened, anger crept into her voice. "I'm not a child."

"No," he agreed, somewhat to her surprise. "You're not. And you have a right to know." His eyes bored into hers. "I should never have taken Davey... and you." He sighed, then continued. "The night before last... when I left you... the Apaches had raided the Navaho camp and slaughtered everyone. Today... it was a ranch. Not far from here." The words came slow as if forced by sheer determination. "They're dead... along with an army patrol from Pickering's troop."

"Looking for us?" April whispered.

MacKenzie nodded. "I tried to warn them... I tried to tell them the Apaches were banding together. But they wouldn't believe a half-breed." His voice was low and bitter. "I didn't want this, none of it."

"What are you going to do now?" April asked quietly.

"I never thought the Apache would come this far north," he replied. "I thought I could find someplace safe for you." His words were tinged with a kind of pain, and April felt his quiet desperation. "I would take you back now, but you wouldn't be safe, even with Pickering's troop. There's hundreds of Apaches south of us now, and if Pickering has any sense he'll make for Defiance before they find him."

"You would take us back?" April repeated with a sort of wonder. He had said repeatedly he would not.

He gave her the slightest suggestion of a smile. "Not quite all the way," he amended. "Just far enough that they could find you and protect you. But I won't trust you and Davey to Pickering. They'll be damned lucky if they live through this."

"Then..."

"The Utes have a treaty with your father. They respect him. There's a village four days from here. Four hard days," he added, eying her speculatively. "They can get a message to Defiance."

Four days. Four more days with MacKenzie. Her clouded blue eyes met his, and she thought for the briefest moment that he, too, was savoring the idea. But no. She and Davey were nothing but burdens to him.

"I'll get ready," she said stiffly.

His hand reached out and touched her shoulder, and she felt seared by his touch. Seized by a sudden impulse to walk into his arms and be comforted, she did the opposite and jerked away, bewildered by her own action. His hand fell, and his eyes grew icy before he nodded and turned away.

MacKenzie understood her repugnance. He had promised her rest, and he was breaking that promise. He had promised her safety, and that, at the moment, was questionable. He had brought her and her son into terrible danger and subjected them to exhaustion, thirst and danger. She had every reason to despise him. But it hurt. God, it hurt.

By late afternoon, they were back on the trail, climbing up and up. April noticed the increased number of pines, no longer dwarfed but reaching for the sky. The streams were deeper and the temperature cooler. Afternoon became dusk, and the sky changed to a deep velvet blue that framed violet peaks haloed by moonlight and an infinite number of bright stars.

April rode with more confidence now, all the old assurance flooding back. Her muscles were adjusting themselves, and she felt a quiet joy, even in this dangerous country, in the loveliness of early night.

She looked at MacKenzie, who rode alongside her, one of his arms cradling a sleeping Davey. His body seemed relaxed although she knew his eyes were constantly moving, studying every tree, every rock. He never really rested. She was beginning to wonder if he ever slept. He had said he had last night, but she still had not seen him do so. She wondered what he would look like...asleep. Would some of that taut energy, that aura of barely leashed violence seep away? No. It was a part of him, as much as those finely honed muscles and suspicious eyes and casual elegance as he rode. April thought she had never seen anything quite as splendid as MacKenzie on a horse. There was a oneness about them, a fluidness that was very beautiful.

He turned suddenly, and his eyes met hers. The dim light made them impossible to read, but she felt them assess her, and she squared her shoulders and straightened in the saddle. She saw his mouth curve with a tenderness he usually reserved for Davey.

And she knew she would do anything for him, go any place he said. With frightening realization, she knew she didn't want the four days to end.

Chapter Eight

MacKenzie stared at the abandoned Ute campsite with something close to desperation. There was nothing remaining of the thriving camp of several months ago. He knew that the Utes were nomadic and seldom stayed in one place long, but this clan had seemed more settled than most, and when he was here five months earlier there had been no plans to follow the buffalo to the central plains.

He looked around hopelessly. They had not been gone long. The ground still showed signs of camp fires, and barren spots on the earth showed clearly where teepees recently stood. Just long enough, MacKenzie thought bitterly.

MacKenzie cursed silently to himself. It was as if fate itself was his opponent. Everything had gone wrong from the moment he had first entered the Chaco army camp. In total frustration, his right hand raked his hair before he turned and looked at Mrs. Manning and saw the question in her eyes.

He didn't have an answer. For the first time in his life, he was at a total loss. Behind him lay hostile Apaches and an army anxious to hang him. In front were the San Juan Mountains, a haven for him...but the Mannings? The mountains were treacherous even for one who knew them well; a mistake, even a minor one, could be fatal. They couldn't go back; they couldn't go forward. *The devil's playing with you for sure,* MacKenzie thought.

He dismounted. Davey had been riding with his mother this morning. MacKenzie had wanted all his senses alert, and he had often spurred his horse ahead, making circles, checking for tracks. Nothing was as it should be. The Apaches had never come this far north before, not in his experience, anyway, and now he was beginning to wonder whether there could be some sort of alliance with the Utes. They had been allies years ago against the Comanches, but MacKenzie dismissed the idea almost immediately. The Utes had decided long before that their small number was no match for the might of the United States. They had negotiated repeatedly with military leaders, gaining concessions and land that no other tribe had been able to win. They wouldn't risk that now.

MacKenzie knew the Utes well. His mother had been Shoshone, and the Shoshone had ancient ties with the Ute. The Utes, the best horsemen of all the area tribes, respected MacKenzie's many skills. They had a common love of horseflesh, a common interest in crossbreeding. MacKenzie had, in fact, won his Appaloosa in a contest of horsemanship. It was the first time a Ute had been defeated in such a test, and the loser had challenged MacKenzie again. It was then that MacKenzie won possession of a small, lovely valley—the heart of his dream. His now dead dream.

The remainder of his hopes, now gone, sent a sudden shadow across his face and deepened his frown.

"MacKenzie?"

April's tentative question stung him back into reality. He looked up at her as she sat restlessly. His eyes were bleak as they noted her tired face, now furrowed with concern. The last four days had been torture for her, pure and simple. He had driven them relentlessly, pursued as he was by his own internal devils. It had been the only way he could keep from touching her, from quieting the want that plagued him constantly. And it had never been stronger than this minute, despite the new obstacles. Sitting on her horse now with ease, she was, to him, all that was proud and spirited and beautiful. Her back was straight, as it always was when he watched her. Her golden brown hair was twisted into one long braid that fell halfway down her back. But, as always, it was her eyes that held him. The deep clear blue of a mountain lake. Unafraid. Direct. Tired now... there were lines at the corners, but no blame or accusation clouded them. She seemed to face every hardship, ever obstacle with an uncomplaining acceptance that constantly astonished him. Yet there was fire there. He had seen it the night she pointed a gun at him, the day she defied Terrell, the afternoon she had slapped him despite her fear and exhaustion. And he had seen it constantly in her relationship with the boy. She laughed with Davey, teased him, challenged him as MacKenzie looked on with lonely, hungry eyes.

He saw something similar in the looks she furtively cast his way. He recognized the warmth in her eyes, the awakening desire, even as she tried to hide it, and it made everything more painful. He knew the mistreatment he'd suffered at Terrell's hands was nothing compared to what he was experiencing now. For he had never wanted anything as badly as April Manning, and his personal code, as well as his sanity, would not allow it. For her sake, for the boy's sake, for his own sake.

He felt a surging tenderness as he watched uncertainty wash across her face as her question went unanswered. His hands reached up for Davey. "We'll rest here a while," he said, setting the boy on his feet. With one hand holding the bridle, he reached for her with the other hand. MacKenzie felt warmth flood him at her touch, and he treasured the trust inherent in it. When her feet touched the ground, his left hand left the bridle and settled on her arm, steadying her. At least that's what he told himself as his hands lingered there, unwilling to let go.

Their eyes locked, clouded, troubled gray searching blue ones suddenly alive with the electricity that sizzled between them. His hands tightened against her jacket with a need that had a life of its own. It deepened as MacKenzie saw her eager response and felt her hands on his chest, burning and searing through the shirt he wore. This was a magic he had never known before, and it made him lose the control that he had honed to an art. There was no meaning to anything but her touch, the look in her eyes and the tender smile on her lips. No one had ever looked at him like this, and he held it in his mind and locked it in his heart.

He slowly dropped his arms and backed away, his face twisting with the effort. At her look of painful confusion, his right hand went up and touched her cheek with such gentleness that April wanted to cry. It moved to cup her chin, and he lifted it until she gazed directly into his swirling thundercloud eyes.

"It cannot be," he said in a voice so low and sad that it pierced April's soul with its raw agony. "It cannot be," he repeated, as if trying to convince himself. His hand left her face, and he whirled around. He stood there alone for a moment, his hands knotting and unknotting, the muscles in his cheek throbbing as he sought to restore his self-discipline.

Tense and frightened at the sudden passion that had flamed between them, April watched as his stiff back slowly relaxed and his hands stopped their compulsive movements. She wondered at the mental strength that allowed it, for she felt caught like a butterfly on a pin by her own emotions. There was such a deep, sweet yearning inside her that she no longer cared about the consequences. She wanted only to touch him, to wipe away that loneliness she sensed in him, to feel that hard body against hers...

April closed her eyes. It was ridiculous. She had vowed not to love again, and now she was trembling like a lovesick schoolgirl over a man who had kidnapped her and her son, who was wanted for murder. *But it didn't matter. God help her, it didn't matter.* Something had happened to her in the past several days, had awakened senses dulled for so very long. Not only awakened them, but brought something new. She had loved David, but she had never felt this wild wanting that made her feel so alive.

April watched as MacKenzie took the two horses and walked away, and she slowly, reluctantly turned toward Davey, who was happily exploring the clearing. They had climbed steadily for the past four days, and this place was nestled between the foothills and the high mountains, which seemed to reach in green and blue splendor to the sky. They had stopped just long enough to sleep and eat, MacKenzie always impatient to continue. She knew he only tolerated the pauses because of her and Davey, but he never said anything. His shortness of speech and constant tenseness said it for him.

His eyes had been as unreadable as always. Sometimes she had caught a brief change in his expression when she found him looking at her. But those times had been rare. He was, more often than not, looking any place else. She smiled now, knowing that it was not indifference that made him look away... as she first had thought.

A setting sun sent streams of gold shimmering through the trees, flooding the clearing with diffused light. The leaves of the oak and mountain mahogany were just now turning into muted shades of red and yellow and orange. April could smell the rich, spicy scent of the pine and juniper. She drank in every sight and smell, relishing them. Despite her deep weariness, she wanted to dance and sing with the simple, uncomplicated beauty of it and the wonderful, astonishing stirring of life within her. MacKenzie, in some way, had heightened all her senses, making them greedy for more.

"Davey," she called. "Let's go find MacKenzie." She was finding his name easier to say. Her lips seem to savor the sound.

They followed his path through the trees, to a deep, clear stream where he was watering the horses. She had learned the horses always came first when they established camp. Once the animals were tended, MacKenzie would then turn his efforts to a fire, or hunting, or the distribution of food.

He watched April and Davey warily as they approached. He felt as if he had given part of himself away earlier when he allowed April a glimpse of his need. But the bright joy in her face made indifference impossible, and he couldn't prevent a smile as he saw the woman and boy together, their feet barely touching the earth as they skipped over to him, their faces creased with laughter and their eyes filled with mischief and light.

"Can we stay here?" April asked with hope. "Just a little while. It's so lovely."

If all the demons in hell were after him, and MacKenzie was half convinced they were, he could not have said no. They should be safe enough here for several days. The Apache would not come this far into Ute territory, nor, he knew, would Pickering be tempted this far north, not with men dead four days back. And God knew they all needed more than the little rest they had had at the cave. He could hunt while trying to decide what next to do. Which reminded him of the impossible choices. But he would not let that spoil April's happy mood. Once more, he thought how like her name she was. Fresh and pretty and bursting with life and hope. He wondered about her husband . . . Davey's father. What had he been like? What had happened to him?

Like a child, April took off her boots and gingerly tried the water. She abruptly did a tiny, involuntary dance as the stream sent pinpricks of icy pain through her tired feet.

Amusement lit MacKenzie's eyes as Davey, ever curious, did the same. "It comes directly from the snow above," MacKenzie explained. "And it's deep enough not to be warmed much by the sun."

"Can we go fishing?" Davey asked hopefully. Fishing had become his joy, a private time together with MacKenzie, who made him feel very grown up.

"Aye. There should be some trout there, fat and just waiting for you. But first you can help with the horses."

"And me?" April asked. "What can I do?"

He eyed her speculatively. She must be bone tired, but she had the same eagerness to help as Davey. His breath came quickly, and he felt a lump setting in his throat. He tried, without success, to swallow and seemed, for a moment, to be suspended in time.

He could barely manage the next words, but he couldn't let her see how she affected him. "You can gather some wood for a fire and find us a good place to sleep tonight."

"Here," April said. "Right here, next to the stream." The streambed fell sharply just feet away, and she could hear the rush of water, the happy gurgling as it sped between the rocks and tumbled downward in a small fall.

Once again she saw a hint of a smile break the angular planes and hard lines of MacKenzie's face. Perhaps it was its rarity that gave it such enchantment. But everything in her warmed at the sight.

He nodded and went back to unsaddling the horses, hobbling them and rubbing them down with Davey happily assisting as far as his small size allowed. April looked at them both, her heart beating faster as she watched them work in tandem, a silent harmony between them. She watched until it hurt too much, and then she went to find wood. Even then he was still with her as MacKenzie's rich baritone voice hummed that haunting melody she had heard the first day of their strange journey.

* * *

Flames reached upward, casting eerie shadows over Mac-Kenzie's freshly shaven face. His eyes were darker, more mysterious than ever to April, who couldn't take her eyes from him.

Davey had long ago succumbed to sleep after a day he had proclaimed the best in his whole life. He had caught several fish, with MacKenzie's assistance, and had helped clean and cook them. Pride was evident in his broad smile and tilted chin, and he hadn't stopped talking about it as the sun dipped behind a mountain in a spectacular sunset that left a warm pink glow bathing the valley. Nothing, April mused, was as pretty as a mountain sunset or sunrise. The mountains themselves changed colors as the golds and oranges and reds took their turns in framing them with first soft, then vivid tints, each more hauntingly lovely than the last.

From MacKenzie's expression, April knew he felt the same awe, although he said nothing. Their eyes met in silent appreciation, and it made her feel closer to him than ever.

She moved to the fire, seeking its heat. With the darkness came cold, and Davey was wrapped in two blankets settled on a pile of pine boughs MacKenzie had gathered for them. It would give protection from the cold ground, he explained, painstakingly working them so they would not scratch. He only shrugged when April asked why he did not do the same for himself. She guessed that he did not want to be too comfortable . . . that it would dull his natural wariness.

April's move toward the fire put her within inches of MacKenzie, who was staring into the flames, his face set as if carved in stone.

She reached out and touched his arm, and he drew back as if burned, his eyes meeting hers with hot intensity.

"I . . . I . . ." April said hesitantly as she met his glowering visage. "I just wanted to thank you for being so kind to Davey."

MacKenzie released a long breath, as if he had been holding it. "He's a good lad. You have reason to be proud."

It was unusual praise from MacKenzie, and April felt a wave of warm pleasure flooding her. She said nothing, not wanting to destroy the moment.

It was MacKenzie who finally spoke, and April was surprised at the quiet intensity of the question.

"His father...?" It was a question that had been plaguing him these past few days. Where was April Manning's husband? What happened to him? She had never mentioned him, yet there was a sadness in her eyes at times. He had known Wakefield's daughter had gone east, but he knew nothing else. He and the general had never indulged in a discussion of personal matters. Their contact had always been all business. It was the way MacKenzie had wanted it.

April bit her lip, and her eyes clouded. "He was killed in one of the first battles of the war...but we didn't know...not until the months after the surrender. He was just...missing. Davey never knew him."

MacKenzie felt a stab of pain, one of the few he had ever felt for another person. To have a husband killed outright was one thing, but not to know for years...

He couldn't stop the next question. "Did you love him?" Once it was out, he inwardly cursed himself. It was none of his business.

But all he saw on April Manning's face was a small, wistful smile. Her eyes met his directly. "Yes," she said softly. "I was eighteen and he was twenty-six and already a captain. He was kind and gentle and..." Her voice fell off. She was going to say strong, but now she hesitated. She had once thought so, but now she realized how dominated he had been by his family. Strange that she hadn't really understood before. Somehow MacKenzie's total self-reliance made her husband seem weak. "Yes," she said again, reassuring herself. "I loved him."

MacKenzie noted the hesitation, heard the tiny note of doubt and was surprisingly glad.

"You're just coming home now?" he questioned, once again startling himself with the need to know.

"I was," she said with that smile of mischief he had seen before. "Before I was waylaid." Her eyes twinkled with something like amusement, and he felt his heart lurch in an unfamiliar way. How very badly he wanted to explore the sweet promise that seemed to hover around her, to taste the gentleness she lavished on Davey.

As if it had a will of its own, his hard, callused hand moved toward April, touching her hand with feather lightness. He half expected her to jerk away, but she didn't, and his hand turned hers over, exploring its contours, relishing its feel. Until he felt the blisters. He drew it closer to the fire where he could see. His eyes moved to her face, and he noticed the raw red where her skin had peeled from exposure. Once again, he cursed, this time out loud.

"Why in the devil didn't you say something?" As always when he was angry, the burr was more noticeable. April had come to recognize those moments; it was usually the only way she knew something was bothering him. His facial muscles never seemed to change; nor did the tight grim line of his mouth.

"Why?" she answered simply. "We couldn't stop."

He closed his eyes. How could he have been so blind? In his headlong flight, he had completely ignored her discomfort. He thought of the several times she had inquired about his wounds . . . his feet, which had almost healed now, his wrists, which she had wrapped so carefully, not once but twice on this trip. He had looked, but he had not seen. Because he had not wanted to. Because it would have slowed him down.

"We could have bound them," he said, still fingering her hand as anger deepened his voice. Anger at himself, but April didn't know that. She just knew that the brief shining moment was gone, and she felt desolate. What was it about him that made her heart act in such totally unpredictable ways? She looked at his fierce expression and felt shivers run up and down her spine. Tingling, expectant shivers.

"I'm sorry," she said finally, seeking a way, any way, to break the silence.

There was complete quiet, like the stillness before a storm. His words, when they came, were as low and fierce as the first roll of thunder. "Don't ever, ever say you're sorry . . . not to me . . . never to me." He continued slowly. "My God, what I've done to you . . . you and the boy . . ." His voice faded, but like the thunder it left an echo. "Not ever," he repeated. He unwound his long-lean body and stood, his eyes for once revealing open wounds. "Not ever," he said once more, and April thought she heard a slight tremor in the sound as he swung around and disappeared into the trees.

April waited for him to return. She added wood several times to the fire, watching it flame anew and studying the different shades of gold and red as the bright glow seemed to play and tease. There were only a few wisps of clouds in the sky and they laced the moon, whose crescent had increased in size. A week? Had it been only a week since her life and Davey's had become so intertwined with that of an outlaw? She watched as the clouds played hide-and-seek with the moon and the myriad stars that jeweled the heavens.

She remembered that first night, the night that had started it all, when one particular star seemed to wink at her with promise. She didn't know then the danger of losing her heart to a man who had no future, who wanted no attachments, who shied away from any emotion.

But those few moments together at the fire—his soft touch and his anger at her hurts—showed, if only briefly, another facet. He was not as unaffected as she thought. She had glimpsed a want and need as deep as her own, and she was determined to break the shell he had built around himself. So she waited. Even as her eyes tried to close and her head drooped, she waited. She finally lay beside the fire, still waiting until, unwillingly, her eyes closed.

MacKenzie had a purpose in leaving. Several, in fact. There was a plant, yarrow, which held a healing substance. He planned to gather enough tonight to soothe her hands, her burned face. But he would do it tomorrow. He didn't think he could be alone with her again. Not tonight. Not after seeing the warmth and desire flare in her face and feeling the responsive craving in the depth of his being. It had taken every ounce of control he had to keep from enfolding her in his arms, to keep his lips from reaching for hers.

Damn! What was happening to him? He should be thinking of flight, of how to rid himself of her instead of thinking how much he wanted her with him. With him, the outlaw. With him, the hunted.

He had never really recognized loneliness before. He had been comfortable with his own company, with the wild things around him. He had never needed people, at least he had never believed he did. He had never wanted to depend on anyone, nor have anyone dependent on him. But now he had two, and he couldn't deny the satisfaction in providing for them, even when he did it poorly. As he had with April Manning.

Her blistered hands and burned face came back to haunt him. Why had she said nothing? Why had she not cried and pleaded like other women would have done? That, he knew, he could deal with. This stoic courage was something else altogether. And her eyes. The eyes that trusted, that searched, that . . . sought something he didn't have the right to give.

MacKenzie felt the chill of the wind and heard its lonely wail as it swept down from the high mountains through the trees. It would be an early winter. He could smell it. He could see it in the thickness of the animals' fur. The earlier the better. For him. But what about April? *He had to think about her in some other way. Not April. Mrs. Manning. The woman. A stranger.*

But she was that no longer. And neither was the boy. They had, in little more than a week, become part of him, and he didn't know how he could survive the rest of his life without them, without the radiance they seemed to carry with them. It had been better not knowing. For he could see hell clearly now, and it was not the fire and brimstone his father delved from the Bible. It was knowing affection and being denied it. It was feeling tenderness and having to stifle it. It was lighting a fire only to have it quenched as its first burst of warmth stretched toward him. He had devised his own hell when he had taken Davey, and now he would have to live in it.

MacKenzie was gone when April woke. He had been there. She knew that. His blanket had been spread carefully over her, and the pile of wood was substantially lower than when she had last fueled the fire. Damn him. He was like a ghost, a protective, elusive ghost.

Dawn was coloring the eastern sky with a golden haze, and a bright fiery orange sun lay close to the earth. Even so, she shivered in the cold air, despite the blanket, her jacket and riding skirt and several other layers of clothing. She wondered about MacKenzie. As far as she knew, he had only the one stolen shirt. They would need more covering if the air continued to get colder. If they stayed together. If....

Davey threw off his blankets, his hands rubbing his sleep-filled eyes. Then he searched the clearing, and April knew he sought MacKenzie. Always MacKenzie now. The Appaloosa was gone, so were the bow and arrows, but the rifle was there, leaning against a tree, and so were his saddlebags and the contents of the stolen bedroll. Protection? Had he left the rifle here for protection? She already had the pistol, tucked away in one of her own saddlebags. *He* should have it. One or the other. She felt sudden fear for him, even knowing he was the most capable, cautious man she had ever met.

She took some of the hardtack from MacKenzie's small hoard, and she and Davey chewed on it. There were several fish remaining on a string in the stream, and she supposed MacKenzie would cook them later. She suddenly wished she knew how to clean a fish, but she didn't. It was a chore always performed by her father's striker, an enlisted man paid extra to serve as a servant to officers, or, in Boston, by the cook. She had never realized quite how useless she was, not until now. She could take some pride in her riding ability, and even perhaps a few nursing skills, but that, she thought sadly, was about the extent of her accomplishments.

Davey was full of energy and eager for a walk. April shrugged off her feeling of inadequacy. MacKenzie would make anyone feel inadequate. They followed the stream for a brief time until they reached a pool shaded by mountain oaks. April sat, drinking in its cool perfection while Davey explored. His curiosity was boundless, and April enjoyed the endless chatter, thinking how much he had changed since leaving Boston, how much he had opened up. Part of it, she knew, was simply leaving Boston and its dreadful morbidity. But a larger part was due to MacKenzie. Davey had found someone to imitate, to look up to, and April was glad it was the quiet, aloof man who was so frustratingly competent at everything.

She closed her eyes but kept her ears open, listening to Davey and his little-boy sounds until they suddenly stopped. April could sense his fear even before her eyes opened, sense the menace that so completely shattered the peace.

Davey was twenty yards away, near the pool, and just feet away from him lumbered a huge brown bear, its teeth bared as it moved closer to her son, who was now frozen with fear.

The Colt. Why on earth had she left it in camp? But there was no time to think about it. "Davey," she called out softly. "Davey, move back, slowly." But he didn't hear, or couldn't obey. He just stood there, stiff, as the bear reared on his back legs and pawed the air with huge clawed feet and continued toward the boy.

April looked frantically around, her eyes finally resting on a large broken branch on the ground. She had to distract the animal, drive him away from Davey or attract him in her direction. She screamed, hoping MacKenzie would hear, hoping that the bear would turn her way, but it ignored her, all of its attention fixed on the boy.

April grabbed the branch and ran toward the great animal, all the time knowing she wasn't close enough, or strong enough, to do anything.

She didn't know what part of her recognized the hoofbeats, or how she knew instantly that it was MacKenzie. It all happened so fast, it was a blur of motion, of senses. She saw MacKenzie propel himself from the nervous, shying Appaloosa onto the bear, a knife glistening like silver in his hand. She saw the huge paws wrap around him in fury, and the knife go up, then down, and up again, no longer silver but a deep red. Suddenly everything was red. She saw the spurts of blood that washed the ground and didn't know its source . . . the bear or MacKenzie. *Please God, not MacKenzie.* And then the bear fell, MacKenzie with it, and with horror she saw the animal twitch in death throes while MacKenzie lay still, his body covered by one enormous paw as blood began to seep from the dozen small wounds on his body, and the huge jagged tear in his side.

Chapter Nine

April knew she had to do something, but the enormous animal was still twitching, a giant claw once more reaching mindlessly for MacKenzie, as Davey stood by in stunned terror.

She waited no longer. She reached where the two lay intertwined—the man and the bear—and with strength and determination she didn't know she had, she lifted the huge leg, crying in frustration as it landed once more on the still form beside it. She tried again, tears almost blinding her as she tugged and lifted and pulled until finally MacKenzie was free.

April went to his feet, grabbed them and pulled him away from the bear. But his weight was more than she could handle, and she could move him only inches, knowing that she was probably causing him to bleed more. But she had to get him away from the still moving animal. "Help me, damn it," she whispered desperately to him. "Help me."

MacKenzie's eyes flickered open, and the iron gray was glazed with pain. "Davey?" he said, his mouth contorting with the effort.

"He's safe." She leaned down, and tears washed her face. "Thank you. Thank you for my son."

MacKenzie relaxed, his eyes closing for a moment. "The bear?"

"Dead...dying." She didn't know exactly what; its legs were still twitching, but the eyes were empty. She paused, looking at MacKenzie's paling skin, the blood that was puddling under him. She pulled off her jacket, then her shirt and stuffed them against the wound; they were instantly soaked. "I have to stop the bleeding." Fear made her voice shaky.

His eyes remained shut, and for a moment she thought he had lost consciousness again, but then they opened, and they were clear. "You'll have to sear it."

"Cauterize?" she said with horror. She had worked in a hospital and had seen many unpleasant things. It was the reason now she could bear to see his blood. But to press white-hot metal against his torn flesh? She trembled.

"You must," he said relentlessly.

"I don't know if I can."

"You can do anything," he answered, and she knew she could. For him.

"What must I do?"

A muscle throbbed in his cheek as a new spasm of pain attacked him. "The knife... get the knife."

April shuddered. The knife was embedded in the bear. There was blood everywhere, but one look at MacKenzie's clenched teeth steeled her. Biting her lip, she approached the animal; his movement was slowing, and she had no doubt now he was dead. She saw the hilt of the knife in the region of his heart. April closed her eyes for a moment, praying for strength.

"You can do it."

She heard MacKenzie's words, and the confidence in them shamed her. It was her fault this had happened. She should not have taken her eyes from Davey. And MacKenzie would bleed to death if she didn't do something now. Her teeth piercing her lower lip, she leaned down, placing her fist around the slippery red hilt of the knife. *You can do it.* His words echoed in her mind. She pulled, and her hand slipped. She seized the knife again, this time with both hands, and pulled with all her strength, feeling it tear through muscles and tissue that didn't want to release it. And then it was free.

"Mrs. Manning!" She heard the weakening voice and realized she was still standing there, the knife in her hand, paralyzed by the horror of it.

"Mrs. Manning... my horse. Get my horse. Bring him over here."

Grateful for another order, April shook off the numbness and hurried to do his bidding. The Appaloosa was standing in the trees, half wild with the smell of bear and blood but too well trained to leave its master. Its fear was palpable, but it finally obeyed her insistent tugs. When they reached MacKenzie's side, she leaned down and gave him her hand. It seemed so fragile to her, so inadequate. But he took it, and rose shakily until his hand found his horse's neck and his arm went around it. April could feel the enormous effort it took him to move, to grasp the horse's mane.

"Go, boy," he whispered to the horse. "Help me. Back," he murmured to April. "Help me get back to the camp, to the fire..."

April pressed her shirt tightly against his side as MacKenzie let the horse's strength guide him along, his feet stumbling over the uneven ground, his face going whiter with each step. She could feel his skin growing clammy, and she grew cold at the realization. She knew what it meant. She turned around and saw Davey following, his face awash with tears and filled with guilt. Her heart died a little for him, but she couldn't comfort him now. MacKenzie needed her more.

Somehow they got back. April never really knew how, just that it was his tremendous willpower. As they neared the fire that was now little more than embers, he let go of the horse and fell to the ground, his face twisting in agony.

"The knife," he muttered. "Heat the knife."

April didn't even think now. She was caught in his urgency. She would not let him die.

She piled more wood on the fire and stuck the knife blade in the new flames, wincing at the sweet, cloying smell of burning blood. She wished she could have washed the knife first, but the fire would purify it.

April went over to MacKenzie. Davey was standing at his side, looking lost and scared. "Bring me a blanket," she told him, knowing that he also needed something to do. When Davey returned, she folded it and put it under MacKenzie's head. MacKenzie was holding the shirt close to his wound with his right hand, and Davey put his hand into the scout's left one.

MacKenzie suddenly knew a new fear, that he might crush the tiny fingers when the pain flared anew. He tried to smile at Davey, but it was more a grimace. He deciphered the boy's guilt-ridden face.

"It wasn't your fault," he whispered. "You can do something for me."

Davey's smudged, tear-stained face looked questioning.

"Find me a stone…a big, round, smooth stone. Can you do that?"

The boy nodded, releasing MacKenzie's hand as he ran to find the perfect stone. He didn't know why MacKenzie wanted a stone, but Davey was determined his friend would have the best there was.

MacKenzie saw April watching him as she waited for the knife to heat, and he met her gaze directly. He didn't want her to see his weakness; she needed what strength he could give her. He knew she could do what had to be done, but he also knew how difficult it would be for her. Her heart was too gentle for the agony she would be forced to inflict, but there was no choice. He had seen a core of iron in her that he doubted she yet totally realized. She was so much stronger than she knew.

"A piece of wood . . . I need a piece of wood to bite on."

April searched the ground with her eyes, glad of the momentary diversion. She found a branch, an inch in thickness, and broke off a piece. She handed it to MacKenzie wordlessly.

"The knife should be ready." His voice was expressionless, and April trembled, wondering how on God's good earth she could do what he was asking.

"You must." It was as if he were reading her doubts. "I'll bleed to death if you don't." He could feel the blood leaking from him, saturating the cloth that held the wound together.

April forced herself back to the fire. The steel was glowing white hot in the flames. She tore a piece of cloth from her riding skirt and reached down to pick up the handle, feeling it scorch her skin even through the layer of cloth. But the pain was minor next to what she knew was coming.

Davey was back, pressing something into MacKenzie's hand. She heard MacKenzie's weakening voice. "Help me hold it, Davey. Help me hold it, and close your eyes with me."

In that moment, she knew she loved MacKenzie. Even seconds away from a torment she knew would be terrible, he was more concerned about her son and his feelings than his own coming ordeal. It made her stronger, and she approached him with determination. She kneeled beside him, on the opposite side of Davey, and took the cloth from the deep, jagged tear, flinching as she saw torn muscle and tissue.

His gray eyes met hers, and he nodded, ready, his teeth now clamped on the piece of wood, his hand, with Davey's small one tightly covering it, clutching the stone.

She willed her shaking hands to be firm as she pressed the knife to the raw, gaping opening, feeling his compulsive jerk and hearing his soft, low moan as if it were a scream. She held the knife steady, searing the wound, shivering at the sound of sizzling skin and the stench of burning flesh. There was another jerk of his body, and then he fell back, and she blessed the unconsciousness that relieved him of pain. For now. When he woke again, it would be bad, very bad.

"Live, MacKenzie," she ordered. "Live."

Then she was aware of Davey again. His eyes were still closed, as MacKenzie had asked, but his face was pinched with misery and hurt.

April pried his fingers from MacKenzie's still hand. "Take the cups, Davey, and get some water for me. And this . . ." She unwrapped the torn cloth from her hand and gave it to him. "Wet this, so we can wash him."

Davey stood still before her. "Will MacKenzie be all right?" His lower lip quivered, and his eyes were swimming with tears.

"Yes, love, he'll be all right."

Davey wanted to believe. He looked at the pale face of the man. "It's my fault."

April took him in her arms, her hands stroking his dark hair, comforting. "No, love. It wasn't your fault. It was nothing you did. And he *will* be all right. I promise you."

The tears fell then, in huge torrents, and April felt the wetness in her own. She didn't even think it strange that she and Davey felt so strongly about this aloof man they had known little more than a week. It seemed a lifetime now. When Davey's tears were spent, she straightened. "Some water, Davey. He'll need some when he wakes."

Entrusted with doing something for MacKenzie, Davey obeyed, and April sat and stared at the scout while keeping one eye on her son.

It was the first time she had seen MacKenzie still. Thick black lashes shielded his eyes, and a lock of midnight black hair fell over his forehead. Tight lines of pain still controlled his face, and she wondered if she would ever see it relaxed. If she would ever see him smiling. Her hand went to his face, exploring its strong lean contours, trying to smooth the hard, uncompromising lines. His usually bronze skin was almost pale. His brow was clammy to the touch and wet with sweat. How could anyone lose so much blood and live? She knew a fierce protectiveness. "You have to live," she whispered. "There's so much for you to discover. Laughter and love, and peace. I know you don't believe it now. But there is. And I'll help you find it. We'll find it together."

When the knife touched his skin, MacKenzie felt his whole body arch with an agony so fierce he felt he was being torn apart. He was alive with fire, with pain greater than any he had ever felt. His fingers squeezed the stone until they were white; the fingers on the other hand dug into the earth with a frantic clawing movement. His teeth clamped down on the wood, stopping a scream that came from deep within him. Shadows came and went, a blessed darkness hovering just beyond them, but while part of him called out for oblivion, another part fought it. He needed his senses about him, the woman and boy needed them. But as he struggled to remain conscious, fought desperately against the weakness, he felt himself slipping irretrievably into a blurred haziness, then blackness. He carried with him the whisper of a soft voice, a promise buried some place deep inside him . . .

When he struggled to the surface of consciousness, MacKenzie thought he was again being consumed by fire. He fought against the heat that beaded his body in sweat and struggled against hands that tried to keep him still. His side was a torment where great swells of agony competed, each one greater than the one before. When his eyes finally opened, he saw April's weary, worried face.

"How long . . . ?"

"Several hours," she said, and she flinched as she saw the ravages of pain in his face.

"I've got to . . ." MacKenzie tried to move, but fell back.

"You've got to do nothing but rest. We need you too badly to have you die on us." The last was accompanied by a small, tired smile. She sensed it was the only reason that would mean anything to him.

MacKenzie fell back, recognizing the sense of her words. Besides, he was too weak to do anything else. The heat turned into cold. Shivers shook his body, and he silently raged against his helplessness as the woman covered him with all their blankets and fueled the fire. He could only lie there, too weak to help, to make even a minor protest. Her clothing was still covered with blood, and her face was lined with worry. Yet there was a new strength and confidence about her that made her truly beautiful. Another wave of pain attacked him, starting in his side and forking throughout his body. And the heat came back, terrible, racking waves of heat that sucked the moisture from his body. He threw off the blankets, unable to bear their suffocating weight. The movement stoked the pain until he was drowning in it. Until, once more, he was falling, falling into a dark abyss of nothingness.

MacKenzie drifted in and out of consciousness, going from bouts of fever to racking shivers, never quite gaining complete rationality. April kept Davey going back and forth to the stream, filling their coffee cups with water as she sponged the scout's fevered body, then covered it with blankets when the icy cold attacked him. Day disappeared into evening, and still he seemed no better. If anything, he seemed even paler and more disoriented.

April's fear grew as the hours sped by and he grew worse. They were running low on food; the stolen rations were enough for perhaps one or two days longer. She had the rifle and pistol, but she had never tried to shoot game, only stationary targets. And even then she wouldn't know how to clean them. Once again, she cursed her own ignorance of the most rudimentary skills of survival.

And she couldn't leave the man on the ground. Not even for a few moments. Several times he had thrashed around in pain and fever, and she had to use her whole body to restrain him before he reopened the wound. He mumbled frequently but rarely could she understand him. The burr was now so thick as to make his words incomprehensible.

As she washed his face once more, she realized how very little she knew about him, how tightly he kept to himself. She didn't know where he came from, or what he wanted, or why he was with the army he seemed to despise and distrust. She didn't know what had carved those hard lines in his face, or what happiness he had had. Or if he had loved. Especially if he had loved.

Only once did she comprehend his words, and then they were filled with a pain not born of his wounds. "It's women and children . . . only women and children . . . God damn you to hell . . . let me go, damn you. Let me go . . ."

Once more, he moved violently, as if trying to escape bonds. April tried to quiet him, her hands forcing him to the ground, her desperation making her strong enough to pin him down, her soft, soothing words somehow quieting him. When he stilled, April found his face wet once more, but this time from her own tears. There was so much pain in him. For all his strength and outward impassivity, there was so much pain . . .

MacKenzie woke to the first tenderness he had ever known.

He felt her hand against his cheek, and he didn't want it to leave, so his eyes remained shut as he carved the sensation in his mind.

And then he cursed himself for the weakness—even as he continued to hesitate to move and lose that precious contact.

His head pounded and his side throbbed, and he felt as weak as a newborn babe. But something wonderful and new surged in him as *her* touch, so light in its gentleness, caressed and loved and soothed. He could stand it no longer, and his eyes opened. Her face was right over his, and the wide, lake-blue eyes were filled with an emotion he had not seen before.

"MacKenzie," she said, and the sound was full of magic for him, so caring, so wistful.

He tried to answer, but no words came. He was confused, his world whirling around him. There was something in him that warred with his natural caution, with the protective walls he had constructed over the years. He tried to move, and once more pain and weakness stopped him. Baffled by his own feelings, by a vulnerability that appalled him, he retreated behind his old facade of detachment.

"How do you feel?" April asked, sensing his silent struggle for control. It had been a day and a half, and his color was better, and she knew now he would live. She felt his intense gaze, and she wanted to shrivel up inside as she thought how

she must look. She had seen something in his face when he first
woke, when his eyes opened, but it had quickly faded. Now his
eyes were assessing, questioning, with no hint of anything
more.

He tried to lift himself with one arm, but fell back.

"I'm so damned weak," he said, almost in condemnation of
himself. He looked at the wound on his side. It was red and
puckered and raw but already beginning the healing process.
"You did well," he said, and the words restored her pride as
nothing else could.

"I was so afraid," she admitted slowly. "I was so afraid you
were going to die."

There was a bare, painful shadow of a smile on his lips. "I
think I would have without you... I remember..." He stopped.
What did he remember? Bits and pieces of images, a will
stronger even than his own. Once again, he tried to move, suc-
ceeding only a little before waves of nausea and pain forced him
down again.

"The boy?"

"He's been helping. Getting water. Getting firewood." April
hesitated, then added, "Praying."

MacKenzie's eyes closed. There was a sweet hurt at her
words. And guilt. A terrible, stabbing guilt. He had placed
them, both of them, in terrible danger. They should feel anger, hate even, and yet they had given him loyalty and care and
even affection. He didn't understand. He didn't understand at
all.

And that made him angry. When he opened his eyes, they
were fierce and forbidding, the tenuous bond between him and
the woman sliced coldly...at least he thought so. But April saw
the brief confusion and, with new awareness, understood his
fear. Just as she understood there was now something between
them that could never be broken—no matter how hard he tried.
And that he *would* try, she knew and accepted. It would be, she
knew, a battle of wills. And with determination forged from a
strength she was just beginning to realize, April Wakefield
Manning decided it was a battle she would win.

Chapter Ten

General Ira Wakefield's voice was deceptively gentle.

Only his adjutant, Bob Morris, suspected the fury behind it and felt a fleeting sympathy for the young lieutenant who, he knew, would be on his knees before he left this office.

"Tell me again," Wakefield said. "Tell me everything. From the beginning. From the time MacKenzie reached Chaco."

Wakefield didn't have to be told. He already knew everything, or almost everything. Every damning, mismanaged thing. He had personally interviewed each man on Pickering's detail from Chaco, and had had an earlier session with Pickering himself. Even then, he knew the lieutenant was conveniently omitting important details.

He knew because it was entirely incomprehensible that MacKenzie was responsible for the crimes he was charged with. Except for his flight—given reason enough. Wakefield was fully aware of the scout's distrust of the military. He had been burned once before. And if half of what was finally wormed out of Pickering's men was true, Wakefield could well understand MacKenzie's escape. But he couldn't accept the rest of it: the accused rape, the murder, the kidnapping of his daughter and grandson. MacKenzie had always steered clear of trouble, even, at times, at the cost of his very strong pride. The scout had something stronger driving him. The only time Wakefield had known MacKenzie to react violently was when an army detachment had massacred an Indian village of mainly women and children. Despite the scout's aloofness and almost fanatical independence, Wakefield had always felt he harbored a deep, unspoken compassion for the weak and victimized.

Rape? Impossible. Murder? Also impossible...unless it was to save his own life. Kidnapping? A woman and child? Unlikely. Unless he felt forced, and even then Wakefield doubted it. At least he had until he heard how MacKenzie had been chained to a wagon and dragged across desert lands. Wakefield's hands balled up in quiet rage as he listened to Pickering's faltering explanation.

"Let me understand," he asked in the same quiet tone. "My scout told you Apaches were massing, and you ignored it."

"Sergeant Peters said he was lying, sir."

"And you, in your youthful wisdom, thought I would employ a scout who wasn't to be trusted?"

Pickering felt the sword point in his gut. "No...no sir, but..."

"And so instead of heeding his warning, you saw fit to drag *my* scout across the desert without food or water...in front of women and a child."

"He raped..."

"He was accused, Lieutenant," Wakefield interrupted. "Accused. But even if he was guilty, we don't treat prisoners that way. Especially my men, my scouts."

Pickering was white now. "But Sergeant Terrell..."

"Tell me, Lieutenant, was Sergeant Terrell in command?"

"I...I..."

"I understand," Wakefield added, "that MacKenzie was never meant to arrive here. Alive, anyway."

"That's not true. I gave strict orders..."

"So it *was* by your orders that MacKenzie was treated as he was."

"No, sir."

"No? Make up your mind, Lieutenant. Because I damn well want to know what fool caused ten of my men to be slaughtered by Apaches and allowed this whole territory to go up in flames because he was too goddamned arrogant to listen.

"And," he added, his voice deadly quiet, "I want to know how my daughter and grandson disappeared from your camp. And why."

"MacKenzie..."

Wakefield visibly had to control himself. He had never wanted to hit a man so badly in his career. "You fool...you stupid, bumbling fool. I'm going to see you're assigned to the worst hellhole in this army. Now get out of here before I do something I regret."

Pickering needed no urging. His hand, when he saluted, was shaking. Wakefield did not return the salute but merely glared at him.

When the door closed behind him, Captain Morris turned to Wakefield. "What now, sir?"

"The girl and Terrell have already pressed charges. I don't have any choice but to file them. And send a detail after MacKenzie . . . and my daughter and Davon."

"Why do you think MacKenzie took them? It doesn't make sense."

"You're right, Bob. It doesn't. I think I know him better than anyone. Or as well as he'll allow anyone to know him. I just can't believe he would hurt April in any way."

"Unless he's turned completely loco."

"MacKenzie? Never."

"But if he was goaded enough . . . ?"

Wakefield turned toward the window and stared at the desert that stretched endlessly before him. His voice was tortured when he finally spoke again.

"He didn't want to return to the army, but I convinced him things would be different, that Elbow Creek wouldn't be repeated. Damn, I need him. Especially now with this new outbreak." He paused. "Bob, I know it's not your job, but you know him. Maybe you can talk to him. Take a company. Try to find him. Try the cabin in that valley of his. I doubt if he goes there . . . he knows we're aware of it, but it's a beginning. Find April and Davon. And take MacKenzie alive!"

"If I can't?"

"Just do it, Bob. Do it."

"If he's guilty . . . or even if he's not . . . he may not give me a choice."

"The girl's lying. I can see it in her eyes. And Terrell's lying. And while you're gone, I'm damn well going to prove it. Tell him that."

Morris studied his commanding officer carefully. Wakefield had been a different person since hearing that April and Davon were coming. There had been a new spring to his step, a

happy gleam in his eyes. Now they were gone, and there was
only a deep weariness. "Yes, sir," he said. "I'll try my
damndest."

Wakefield acknowledged the words with a brief salute, then
turned back to the window. "Bring them back, Bob. The three
of them."

April swallowed, trying to keep back the bile that kept rising in her throat. Her fist clutched the knife.

There is no choice, she told herself. The bear was lying there,
and they needed food. The salt pork was gone, and only hardtack remained, scarcely the best diet for one who had lost so
much blood.

MacKenzie had tried to rise again this morning, but could
manage only several steps before paling to a pasty white and
falling. April had scolded him, asking if he was going to complete what the bear had failed to. She used the only argument
that had ever worked with him. "We need you too badly."

MacKenzie tried to argue. They needed food. But when he
tried once more to move, his legs collapsed under him, and he
went tumbling down, wincing at the new pain in his side. His
eyes smoldered with frustration, and April once more felt the
now familiar ache inside her. He was not a man used to helplessness, nor one to depend on another. But he was forced by
his own body to do so. And he despised himself for it. She
wanted to tell him it was nothing to be ashamed of. God knows,
he had done far more than any other man could have when he
attacked the bear. But she knew that meant little to him.

The bear! As much as the thought appalled her, she knew it
offered what they needed most at the moment: meat.

She waited until he went to sleep, found the knife and went
the nearly half mile to the bear.

She reluctantly approached the dead beast. It smelled even
worse than it had three days ago. She had been told no animal
smelled quite like a bear, and now she believed it.

It was not only the bear smell, but the added odor of dried
blood. MacKenzie's and the bear's. She swallowed again.

Davey was with MacKenzie. Thank God for that, anyway.
She finally reached the animal and stooped. She still remem-

bered how it had twitched, and she halfway expected that it would come to life and take a swipe at her.

Where to start? The fur was thick and matted. For a moment, she wished she knew how to skin and cure it for it looked enormously warm, but that was out of the question. She would be doing very well if she could just carve a piece of meat from it. Something already had, she noticed, shivering with horror and distaste as she noticed rips in its body. She wondered if she was truly grateful that something was left.

The haunch. She knew about that. If only she could reach it. The stench would have emptied her stomach had there been anything in it. She wondered if she could, indeed, force herself to eat any bear meat at all. But perhaps it wouldn't be so bad cooked.

The bear was half on its side, and there was a part that looked untouched. She moved the knife, closing her eyes as it entered in flesh. She hacked and cut, not knowing quite what she was getting, until she freed a chunk of meat. She went deeper, trying to get some without fur attached, her stomach rebelling at every additional slice. At one point, she had to retreat to the trees where she kneeled over and retched what little there was inside her. Then she started to work again. It seemed like hours before she had three relatively large pieces of meat.

She cut them in smaller chunks and put them in the old jar that MacKenzie had found in the cave days earlier. She would add some water and wild onions and let it cook on the fire. She knew from watching MacKenzie how to build a little platform over the flames.

April retreated from the bear, hoping she would never have to see it again. It was far enough away from the camp that predators could feast without fear of humans. She hoped that this meat would be edible, but the Lord knew it wouldn't be in several more days. If she had to, she would go hunting. She wasn't quite sure how desperate she would have to be to kill something. More desperate, certainly, than she had to be to carve on a dead bear. As revolting as that was. Or perhaps she could fish. Except she didn't know how to clean fish. It couldn't be any worse than butchering the bear.

She couldn't ignore the sense of accomplishment. She had done the unthinkable. And she had done other things in the past three days, things she never thought herself capable of. In addition to searing MacKenzie's wound, she had washed the man nearly from head to toe, neglecting only his most private parts. Severe injury had shut many of his systems down, and there had been no need yet for anything horribly personal. But she had washed the sweat from his body and had made him a sort of rough shirt.

MacKenzie, she had told him with a small smile, was very hard on shirts. The last one had been torn to shreds by the bear.

And April did know how to sew. Even if she had no needle to sew with. She painstakingly used a knife to make laces from the torn shirt, and cut a new covering for MacKenzie from one of the blankets, using the remainder to make a coat for Davey. She punched holes in the heavy, rough material and fastened the material with the laces. The garments were not very attractive and definitely not stylish, but they accomplished their purpose: they provided warmth.

MacKenzie had, predictably enough, protested. They would need the blankets. But she ignored him, knowing he was too weak to fight her on this. He had to have some kind of covering on his upper body.

She had done other things. She had found the yarrow plant MacKenzie described and, following his instructions, made a salve, which she smoothed on his wounds and on her own blistered hands. The Utes had used it for years, he told her.

And she had kept the fire going, even through the cold nights, and washed the blood from her clothes and from MacKenzie's deerskin trousers. He had protested again, but she insisted, turning her head as Davey helped him pull off his knee-high moccasins and then the trousers stiff with dried blood. When she turned back to him, his lower body was covered by a blanket, his eyes once more full of confusion...

She understood his confusion, for she was full of it herself. If anyone had told her a month ago she would be hacking her own dinner from a dead animal, or bathing a man wanted for rape and murder, she would have thought them entirely insane. She wasn't aware of the soft smile on her face as she thought of MacKenzie's hard, bronzed chest. She had washed it, wiping the blood from the many cuts and scratches while he was unconscious. It had given her time to admire his body without his knowledge. Even with its numerous wounds and the blackened, raw burn, it had been quite magnificent . . . broad, strong shoulders and upper chest corded with muscles before tapering to a lean, rock-hard waist. Her eyes had wandered further down, to the tight deerskin that molded the strong legs, the lean hips.

April felt the heat rise in her again as she recalled every contour of his body. They were well set in her mind, even as she chastised herself for such thoughts. Think about the bear meat, she told herself. But still she couldn't control the sweet wild blaze within her as she triumphantly approached him with her offering.

MacKenzie, who had awakened while she was gone, couldn't help but smile when he saw her. She looked like a lioness bringing its family dinner, her chestnut hair sparkling in the sunlight like a tawny mane. Davey looked at the jar quizzically.

"Bear meat," she announced in reply to both their unspoken questions.

She watched as the disbelief in his eyes turned to appreciation, then pride. His face gentled. "That must have been very difficult for you."

"I wasn't very good at it," she admitted shyly. "But it should make some soup. I thought about trying to shoot a rabbit, but . . ."

"It's never easy to kill," he said, in the same gentle, almost tender voice. "Especially the first time. In fact, for some, it's always hard—even when there's no choice. It's not weakness . . . it's respect."

April knew from the fleeting cloud in his eyes that he meant himself as well as her, and those few words told her more about him than a book. That he had said them to *her* meant even more. He was telling her he *trusted* her to understand, and that, she knew, was a rare gift indeed. Her heart twisted and melted like wax over a flame. A peculiar tingling numbness paralyzed her body as her eyes met his and the now familiar electric currents flowed and flamed between them.

She finally forced herself away from him and made a little platform over the fire. She felt his constant appraisal as she divided the meat, keeping some in the jar for her broth and placing the rest on a spit over the fire. When she looked up, her eyes locked with his, and she felt they could almost consume each other in the blast of heat that exploded between them.

"MacKenzie?" April's voice hung in the air like the soft song of a hummingbird, and it was full of questions he couldn't answer.

"MacKenzie," she repeated. "What are we going to do? Where are we going to go?"

He didn't miss the implication of her words. It was no longer "you" but "we." He felt an infinite sadness growing within him, a tender yearning for something that was being offered but that could never be. He tore his eyes from her, and turned to Davey, who was, self-importantly, gathering pine needles and small twigs for the fire.

"Mrs. Manning," MacKenzie started.

"April," she insisted.

"Mrs. Manning..." It was a test of wills, and they both knew it...just as they knew the unspoken reasons behind it.

"It won't work, you know that. It doesn't change anything...whatever name you call me."

"I don't know what you mean," he lied, a muscle throbbing in his cheek.

He flinched inwardly at her look of disbelief. He had never been a coward before, nor had he consciously lied to anyone or, more importantly, to himself. MacKenzie turned away from the challenge in her probing eyes.

"I need...we need...to leave tomorrow," MacKenzie said, trying to reestablish the old lines of captor and captive, trying to stoke the resentment he knew she had had in the beginning, even as he knew they were far beyond that now. How had it ever gotten so turned around?

That she knew what he was doing was obvious. That he was failing miserably was equally obvious. It was in the lovely eyes that made him weaker than any loss of blood. They were more dangerous than all the Apaches, all the troops they had left behind.

Davey's small voice piped up. "I'm hungry," he complained, and MacKenzie blessed the interruption. His voice struggled for balance as he watched April take a piece of meat from the fire, smiling as Davey grimaced when he took the first taste. But he ate it. They all ate the rancid but nourishing meat, each quiet as they struggled to keep it down.

April said no more, but the determined tilt of her chin as she sat stubbornly chewing the terrible meat told MacKenzie it was only a momentary surrender.

There was no chance to speak later. The pile of firewood was rapidly disappearing, and the wind, howling now through the top of the trees, signaled another cold night. They had no ax and were completely reliant on fallen branches and pieces of decaying trees that had fallen to disease or lightning. April and Davey struggled during most of the afternoon to pile bits and pieces, knowing they would disappear rapidly in the greedy flames.

Later in the afternoon, they all had some of April's soup. It was a little better than the roasted meat, because some of the bitter taste was disguised by sweet wild onions. Restored slightly by the food, MacKenzie, leaning on April for support, managed to reach the stream where a pool promised fish. With a hook he had fashioned from a piece of metal on his saddle, he fished while the Mannings sought wood. Davey had, quite efficiently, found him some fat worms at the base of a cottonwood. He leaned against a tree trunk, willing strength into his body. The blanket shirt itched, but its warmth felt good in the increasingly cold air.

He turned his attention toward the pool. It was vital that they have more food. If he could catch enough fish, they could smoke some and carry them for the next several days. But where? They couldn't stay here much longer. He wondered if Pickering had reached Defiance yet and, if so, whether Wakefield had taken to the trail himself. He doubted it. If nothing else, Wakefield was a very competent commander, and with the territory aflame with Apache raids, his first duty would be to quiet the frontier. Even his daughter and grandson would come second, as painful as that might be. But he would send someone; of that, MacKenzie had no doubt. Probably Morris. Morris had visited MacKenzie's valley once with Wakefield. That would be the first place they would look. The thought did not comfort him. Morris was a damned good officer, which was why he was Wakefield's adjutant. Wakefield did not tolerate inefficiency or failure.

MacKenzie knew they did not know about his father's cabin. He had never talked of it, nor had he ever mentioned his father to Wakefield. It had been an omission made partly because of his father's obsession for privacy, and partly because it was something MacKenzie did not care to remember or divulge. His origins were no one's business but his own. Out of duty, he had made the journey to the cabin twice a year, bringing flour, coffee, sugar and oats for the one horse his father kept. His father had been old, too old for the kind of life required of him on his mountaintop. The last time MacKenzie had climbed the mountain, he had found his father dead, an ax in his hand.

The line in his hand jerked, and MacKenzie was startled back to the present. He slowly pulled in the string, feeling the heavy weight fighting the hook. It was a game fish, he thought, wishing he had the choice of letting it go. He knew how it felt to be trapped, to be pulled inexorably against one's will. He knew why he had never taken up trapping, like his father. He felt too strongly about life, about its value, to kill wild things for coin.

There was something inherently satisfying about a morning frost glistening like pearls in the rays of an early sun, MacKenzie reflected as he baited the hook and returned it to the water. The smell and taste and sound of a cold clear mountain stream, the beauty of a canyon wall struck by the rosy glow of twilight. The images once more stirred regret. Nowhere were they more lovely than in his valley.

Instantly, his decision was made. They had time. He would visit the valley once more. There was more than one reason, more than his need to see it again. There were blankets there, and tools, and clothing. And they were in need of all three. Perhaps he could even leave April and Davey there, knowing that someone would be along soon. But the thought fled instantly. He could never leave them without protection, even for a few hours. And he was just guessing about Wakefield's moves. What if he didn't send anyone, what if he couldn't? Or what if the Apaches killed the detachment? No, he could not leave them alone.

But neither could he keep them with him. It was too dangerous for them—and for himself. He was much too susceptible to
his emotions when they were around. He was already afraid
they were dulling his instincts, clouding his judgment.

Amos! Perhaps the answer was Amos Smith, an old despera-
do who had been his father's only friend. Like many mountain men, the old man worshiped women and children. Amos
had fled some deep trouble in the past, but he never spoke of
it. When MacKenzie had left his father's cabin, Amos had become Rob MacKenzie's one link to the outside world, trading
his furs for occasional food staples and other goods. Amos
frequently traded with the Utes, and from his cabin word about
April could be passed to General Wakefield. He would never
reveal the whereabouts of Rob MacKenzie's cabin, and the
woman and boy would be safe with him. Safer than with himself, MacKenzie thought, as he remembered the passion that
had flared earlier between April and himself.

When April and Davey returned, MacKenzie was exhausted, but he had eight cleaned fish beside him. April could
feel the gnawing hunger rumbling in her stomach. Proud as she
had been of the bear meat, it had been truly awful, and she had
not looked forward to finishing it.

The smell of sizzling fish made April's mouth water. She
sniffed appreciatively as the bite of the wind caused her and
Davey to move closer to the fire.

After resting for a little while, MacKenzie insisted on taking
over care of the fire despite April's protests, and he was keeping it low while the fish cooked. In one corner, he had spread
the ashes, covering them with the extra fish, wrapped in water-
soaked leaves, to smoke.

The sunset was even more spectacular than usual this evening, April observed with delight, as a host of clouds diffused
the light into layers of brilliant color. Billowy puffs of white
moved with purpose across the vast expanse as the daylight
faded into the indigo gloom of the pines that covered the
mountains rising to the north.

The stream next to them was almost alive, with flashes of
gold and silver shimmering over its surface, and its bank on the

opposite side was scarlet with patches of poison oak and Virginia creeper.

April felt humble in the midst of so much natural beauty and knew a hardly bearable joy at being here . . . sharing such magnificent riches with her son. And MacKenzie. She looked at the silent, intent man next to her. As their eyes met, she knew he was sharing the same tender anguish. It was evident he loved these hills and canyons and mountains. Her heart swelled with the knowledge, with his closeness, with the warmth she felt radiate from him.

All her senses were so alive. The air was pure and clean, and pungent with the smell of smoke and the surrounding pine. The silence was interrupted only by the sizzle of their dinner and the chirping sounds of grasshoppers. April knew at that moment there was no place she would rather be, no other person she would ever need. MacKenzie. He was so different from any man she had ever met: so quiet, so sure of himself, so at home in this world of color and challenge. So very alone.

April felt a shiver of fear. She had vowed never to give her heart again, and now it was offered quite openly and without shame to a man who had given no indication that he wanted it. To a man whose future was dubious at best. Was she willing to risk not only her own life but Davey's future as well? Was she willing to risk more years of fear and hurt and waiting?

Davey crawled into the crook of MacKenzie's left arm, and his dark head settled on MacKenzie's shirt as the small face looked up at the scout and asked a question. April saw pain flash across the man's face as the boy accidentally touched his wound, but it was gone instantly, as he bent down to answer. April watched the two together, Davey boyishly eager and MacKenzie murmuring softly in his ear. Her heart seemed to explode with sweet pain, and she knew she would risk anything, everything, to stay with this man.

In the next several days MacKenzie's strength slowly returned, though the wound remained ugly and raw. April would see it when he applied the yarrow salve; he would not let her do it. He would, in fact, let her do very little although he showed her how to clean fish, and she took over that small chore. She hadn't been able to make him rest nearly as much as she thought he should; he fished in the morning and had even gone hunting, bringing back two rabbits. He had been his usual reticent self, and any attempt at conversation on her part met mostly with a yes or no.

But his mere presence and the chance to watch him grow stronger were enough for the time being. April's eyes rarely left him when he was in camp, and Davey was his shadow.

The nights were growing colder, and the three of them usually stretched, like wagon spokes, from the fire, feet closest to its warmth. Davey and she shared two blankets, and MacKenzie took one and that only at her threat that if he didn't, she wouldn't use her two.

April seldom slept well. She was constantly tormented by her need for MacKenzie. She was at a loss about how to cope with it, particularly when he was so careful to keep his distance.

It was the fifth night since the bear attack when she first heard the wolf. Its lonely, long howl woke her from her usual troubled sleep. Davey was lying next to her, and they were both wrapped together in blankets against the cold. April blessed the pine boughs that made a fine mattress and kept them from the cold ground.

The howl came once more, joined by another. She was grateful Davey slept through the fearsome sound, amazed once more at the child's ability to sleep through almost anything.

Her slight movement alerted MacKenzie, who was once more piling wood on the fire. "There's naught to worry," he assured her with a soft burr. "They won't come near a fire."

"I haven't heard them before..."

"It's the weather...they feel winter coming."

"Winter? It's only September." Or was it October? She had lost all track of time.

"It often comes early in these mountains," he said with his usual brevity.

"When...?"

"Soon," he said. "I can almost smell it." He hesitated. "I want to see you safe...before it comes. We'll leave in the morning."

"Where?"

"There's a cabin in a...valley one day's ride from here."

April caught the momentary hesitation in his voice before he said "valley," and she wondered what it meant, but she had no time to think about it, for he was continuing.

"We can get some supplies there, some warmer clothes."

"And then?" April held her breath.

"There's a man in the mountains...you will be safe with him, and he can get word to your father."

April gently unwrapped herself from the blanket, careful not to disturb her son. She sat up and huddled near the fire. "I want to stay with you." She kept her face averted from his. She hadn't meant to say the words, not yet. They were muffled as she bit her lips against them. But she could withhold them no longer.

There was a long silence, and April was both afraid that he had understood her words . . . and that he hadn't.

She heard his deep sigh and then the infinite sadness in his voice as he answered her with regret.

"It cannot be."

"You don't want us?" Once more, April hadn't meant to say the words, but the hurt was suddenly too deep.

Again the silence seemed to stretch into hours, and she didn't think he would respond.

She couldn't miss the pain in his voice when he finally replied, and it sent ripples of anguish through her body.

"I will be hunted... I'll not have you and the boy hunted with me."

There was finality in the words, but April couldn't stop. She had already gone too far. "I don't care."

"But I do... I'll not have anything happen to you."

"Davey loves you." It was her last weapon.

Again there was a silence, and his jaw hardened with purpose. His words, when they finally came, were obviously painful. "He'll ha' no chance wi' me."

The Scottish pronunciation told her something about how much the statement cost him. She had discovered it only surfaced when he was deeply disturbed about something. She had kept her head down, avoiding his eyes as she'd so clumsily declared herself, but now she looked directly at him. His face, lean and handsome in the flickering firelight, was tormented, and his eyes, when the light hit them, seemed to hold a need as vast as her own.

Her hand went to his, partially covering its hard leatherlike surface. Her fingers stroked his, seeking their warmth, compulsively needing to touch some part of him. She turned his hand over until his palm was toward her and studied its callused strength with her fingers. Bringing it to her face, she pressed it against her cheek in a gesture of complete surrender, of infinite tenderness, and felt the wild desire rushing through her veins.

MacKenzie grew rigid as her soft caress ignited blazes more painful than that of the knife days earlier. The gentleness of her touch and all it represented filled him with a desolation larger than the barrenness of the great desert. He knew he should take his hand away before he was lost, but the velvet feel of her cheek transfixed him. He had no will as she moved his hand to her lips and he felt their soft touch. Without words, she was proclaiming her love for him, offering him everything she had without condition or expectation.

MacKenzie felt he was drowning in their combined need, and his body coiled like a tight spring as he struggled for restraint. But still he left his hand in hers, unable to tear it from her. Her touch was hypnotizing. Her lips were incredibly sweet as they spoke silently of a heaven he'd never suspected existed.

Both were barely aware of the fire, which crackled and flamed against the midnight-blue sky. The moon was laced by clouds, and only a slight streak of silver was visible. But April and MacKenzie were oblivious. Nothing mattered except each other, and the sensuous cry of their bodies, the silent scream of fettered emotions.

With a tremor that shook his entire being, MacKenzie turned her hand with his captured one and gently guided it to his side. Unable to help himself as he searched her wistful, longing eyes, he pulled her close, cupping her face with his free hand.

"If it were otherwise . . ." But what he was about to say was stopped, for her lips were near his, and he could no longer resist their promise. His mouth met hers with a gentleness that was almost ethereal as he savored the first taste of her. Their lips explored, teased, caressed until they both felt maddened, and the gentleness turned to hunger...insatiable hunger as each sought more and more of the other. More to hold. More to keep. More to remember.

MacKenzie's tongue entered the delectably soft mouth, feeling sensations he had never known before, feeling his heart swelling with tenderness. He had never made love before, had only taken—quickly—relief for his body. He had never touched like this, or been touched, had never known the millions of pinpricks of fierce desire that could torture a body with exquisite pain. And the soul.

He felt the limits of his knowledge fall away, and the ground become a large pit in which he was falling in great spiraling circles. He reached for safety, but found none, only a bottomless vortex that he was powerless to fight. His hands tightened on her, and his lips moved to her cheeks, her eyes, her hair, her throat. They moved greedily, wanting to capture all of her, to taste all there was to taste, to know all there was to know. That she *wanted* him to know was obvious. She met caress with caress, hunger with hunger, her body straining toward his with primal need.

The long, mournful howl of the wolf came once more, joined by others, the chorus swelling with echoes in the cold black night. The woeful, lonely cries jerked MacKenzie back to reality, and to thoughts of a night a year earlier when he had said farewell to his father, to who he was and where he was going, and why. And to the plain undeniable fact that, for everyone's sake, he had to go alone.

A piece of molten lead seemed to lodge in his chest as his lips slowed their avaricious journey. A moan tore from his throat as he forced himself to pull away.

"MacKenzie...?" April's voice was like a whisper of a summer breeze. "Your... wound...? Did I hurt it?"

Better to let her think that. "It's... still tender."

He saw the guilt in her face and wanted to reassure her, but he couldn't. "I think," he said stiffly, "that we both need some rest."

Consumed by guilt, April could only nod. She touched his arm again, this time for reassurance that he was all right, but his face was once more closed and shuttered against her. The distance between them suddenly yawned enormously, and she wondered for a moment if she had only dreamed those won-

derful caring moments. She saw him flinch under her hand and
she took it away, staring at him with tear-misted eyes. It was
almost as though she now repulsed him.

She drew back, confused and wretched, her face so full of
hurt that MacKenzie wanted to reach for her, comfort her. But
with all the will remaining to him, he turned instead and refueled the fire, his shoulders denying her the smallest solace.

"MacKenzie...?" she tried again.

He faced her, but his eyes were empty. "Get some rest, Mrs.
Manning. We leave for the valley at dawn."

Chapter Eleven

The night was the longest April had ever spent.

She was unable to sleep as she recounted, over and over, each word that had been said during those few moments with MacKenzie. She puzzled over his consistent withdrawal from her whenever she thought she was lowering the barriers, and relived the pleasure of his touch and the taste of his lips. But then her stomach would knot and churn with hurt at his rejection. Each minute seemed an hour and each hour an eternity, knowing as she did that he lay within feet of her, a distance that now seemed like miles. She could hear his own restless movements, and she wondered if they resulted from the continuing pain of the wound or regret over those few seconds of reluctant surrender.

Regret? She bitterly doubted whether he regretted anything or even, at this moment, whether he felt anything. She had offered everything she could, and he had rejected it. Rejected her. Rejected Davey.

She heard him move again and hid her face in the blanket, pretending a sleep that eluded her. She could hear him feeding the fire again, and then there was silence. She sensed his presence above her, and once more she was bewildered. A warmth encompassed her, even now in her despair, and she could almost see his eyes on her. They were engraved indelibly in her mind, like everything else about him. Only their mood escaped her. Indifference? Impatience? Curiosity?

Her heart pounded harder as she realized he was drawing closer, and she felt his hand, warm and tender, touch her hair and the back of her neck with feather lightness. It lingered there, and her heart seemed to stop as his fingers moved ever so gently against her skin. April tingled all over, and she was sure he must know she was awake, that he could feel the great waves of desire that he created with the slightest touch. The fingers stopped, and she intuitively knew he hesitated, that he didn't want to abandon contact. She felt the blanket being rearranged, as if he wanted to do something for her... even if it wasn't needed. And finally—as if their spirits were melded together by some invisible cord—she silently felt the regret and weariness that flowed from him, and thought her heart might break. He wasn't indifferent or impatient or angry. He was afraid, and the knowledge gave her even greater pain. Strong, indomitable MacKenzie, the man who attacked a bear without hesitation, was tortured by fear.

He stayed there for several moments and then the warmth disappeared, and April knew he was gone, although his moccasins made no sound in the still night. There was an emptiness and chill where he had been, and she curled up in a tight ball of misery and dug deeper in her blanket.

In the morning, April rose to gray skies. MacKenzie's eyes were the same bleak color, and his tone was once more cool and emotionless as he parceled out duties. April wondered once again whether she had dreamed everything that had happened last night. She saw MacKenzie wince several times as he leaned down, and she knew his injury was still painful. He should not be riding this soon, but she guessed from the hard jut of his jaw that he would not change his plans.

Her own anger grew at his obstinacy, obstinacy about his wound and about her. Even about Davey, because this morning he was cool to the boy, and she could scarcely bear the sight of her son's hurt puzzlement.

They ate the last of the hardtack taken from Pickering's troops, along with smoked fish and bear berries they had picked the day before. MacKenzie ate hurriedly and alone, then saddled and packed the horses, pacing restlessly as April and Davey finished the sparse meal and took a few moments to attend to their private needs.

His hard, piercing eyes gentled only when Davey approached and asked if he could ride with him on the Appaloosa. April could see refusal in MacKenzie's face, but then his mouth seemed to relax as if giving in to something he really wanted anyway, and he lifted Davey to his saddle with a small wry twist of his lips.

It was as if there were two MacKenzies, April thought wistfully, each battling the other for supremacy. She pondered the sheer contradictions of the man...and the outcome of the war within him.

Mounting her own horse, she silently followed his lead from the clearing where she knew she had lost her heart. She looked back to the place where the fire had been, but even that was now bare. MacKenzie had taken great care to eliminate any sign of their presence. Once they were gone, the great bear carcass would soon be devoured by wolves. A sense of sadness encompassed her as she turned her head toward MacKenzie's stiff back. Despite the raw violence of the bear attack, she had known moments of unprecedented joy here. She wondered if she would experience them again. He seemed so determined she would not.

They climbed steadily, in silence, into the mountains, and by late afternoon April's mood was lifted by the sheer enchantment of the beauty that surrounded her. The threatening clouds had disappeared, leaving the sky a brilliant blue. Giant snow-covered peaks rose in sharp contrast to the sky, and a bright sun intensified their pristine cloaks and warmed the earth. They passed through gates of rock and alongside red-tinged canyon walls that fell sharply to dells of bright green grass. Crested blue jays darted through the dark pines, and scores of squirrels chattered merrily among the branches. A lone eagle soared gracefully overhead, reminding April of MacKenzie. Solitary, splendid and dangerous...and every bit at home in this wild untamed country.

They stopped beside a small lake and once more dined on smoked fish and berries they found. The water was cold and wonderfully refreshing after the tepid remainders of the canteens. Davey, eager to stretch his legs after so long on horseback, started his usual exploring, but after the bear attack he was careful to stay within sight of both his mother and MacKenzie, glancing at them frequently for reassurance.

MacKenzie was unnaturally stiff, and April knew he must be hurting. His normally clear gray eyes were fogged with pain, and he moved slowly, watering the horses and hobbling them so they could feed on the rich grass before he took any rest of his own. He finally sat and leaned against a cottonwood tree, unconsciously releasing a long, grateful sigh.

"You can't go any farther today," April said with combined concern and exasperation.

"We can." The reply was terse. "And we will. I just need a little rest."

"You need more than that," she said sharply, surprised that he'd admitted any need at all. She went over to him and knelt. Without waiting for his consent, she pushed up the blanket shirt, revealing the bandage she had made from her pantalets. It was stained through with both salve and secretions from the wound.

He winced as she carefully untied the bandage and gently pried the soft cloth from the puckered burned skin, studying the discolored areas that surrounded it. MacKenzie was uncharacteristically docile, and the unique attitude worried her more than any other symptom. She looked with dismay at the purple bruises that still covered so much of his body. The last hours must have been torture.

"You are not going any farther today," she pronounced, "not if you want to be able to move tomorrow." Surprisingly, MacKenzie didn't protest. She wondered how long such acquiescence would last.

"We need food," he observed mildly, his eyes never leaving her face as she studied his burn.

"I think I might be able to find something," she said.

"You've done enough," he said, his jaw tightening as her fingers soothed the skin around the burn.

The wound was secreting a watery yellow substance, but April didn't think it was infected. It didn't have the smell or look of the gangrene she had seen in the prison hospital. But it did look angry and painful.

"This wouldn't have happened if Davey and I hadn't wandered off," April replied.

"It could have happened just as easily in the clearing," he replied. "The bear was heading for it. There was something wrong...perhaps it had lost its cub or been wounded by an arrow earlier. It was nothing you did."

"Perhaps not, but you're still hurt because of us."

He flinched once more, not because of the physical pain but at the fear he remembered, the fear for the two of them when he had seen the bear. He had almost been too late, and he had realized only too well in the past several days that his actions in taking Davey in the beginning had almost killed them both. "You are not here by choice," he finally said.

"I am now," she answered softly.

"No...you're here because I kidnapped your son. And I put you both in great danger. Don't forget that, Mrs. Manning, because I can't."

"April," she said patiently.

He stared at her with chilly remote eyes that thawed gradually as he puzzled over her persistence. Then the side of his mouth twitched. She was a glorious woman. Maddening. Stubborn. Resourceful. Proud.

"I'll make some more of the salve and wash the bandage while you rest," she said, hating to leave him for even a moment, particularly when she saw the warmth in his eyes. She wanted to touch him again, like she had last night, but then she remembered how he had drawn away. She forced herself up.

MacKenzie had packed some of the yarrow plant, and now she made the salve with water. She spread it over the burn, all the time feeling the almost intimate touch of his eyes on her. She let her fingers linger on his skin after the chore was done. She knew the process had been painful, although he had said nothing, had not indicated his discomfort by even the slightest move or expression. April finally compelled herself to leave him and took his bandage to the lake where she scrubbed it and set it on a rock to dry. She sent Davey to look for firewood, warning him to keep within sight, and she started a fire.

April Manning learned fast, MacKenzie thought, as he watched her build the fire like an experienced woodsman. He felt its first blast of heat with something akin to gratitude. The air was cooling again, now that the sun was withdrawing toward the west. It would be even colder tonight, and tomorrow. He could almost smell snow. He knew they should be moving on; he had wanted to get to his cabin tonight, but his strength was gone, and he felt as weak as a newborn cub. Once he had sat down, his body had rebelled, and he couldn't seem to force himself up. The woman was right. He could go no farther today. He would only endanger them all even more. But it galled him that he could do so little now for April and her son, could not even provide them with a decent meal. He closed his eyes, willing his strength to return, but total exhaustion from pushing his body far beyond its endurance nudged him into a heavy sleep not far removed from unconsciousness.

April made a neat pile of firewood and searched the bedroll and saddlebags, taking inventory of the food supply. With the fish MacKenzie had smoked, and berries, they had enough for perhaps two days. But MacKenzie needed something more substantial. He was a large man, despite his rangy frame, and he had lost a great deal of blood.

She looked at him. The past few days had taken their toll. His face, even in sleep, was creased with pain and weariness. Lines of worry extended from his eyes now, incongruously sheltered by long black eyelashes. She sat down beside him, content for the moment to be near him, to hear his soft breathing and study the strong face covered by black stubble. Each severely chiseled feature had, in the past few days, become very dear to her. Sleep had softened the face only a little.

April felt a crippling weakness of her own. She had never known love could be so formidable, could affect every thought and every action. Each time she looked at him she seemed to turn into a puddle of wax, every sense melting with her need for him, a need that went far beyond physical touch although she ached and yearned for that, too, she thought ruefully. She came alive in his presence. The sky was bluer, the stars brighter, the sunsets more vivid. She also hurt more, but even that had an aching beauty to it. Her insides seemed to turn into a knot as she thought what he had brought her: a wonder she hadn't known existed, a joy that came with just being with him. She hungered to know everything about him, to know his pleasures, to share his pain. She had tasted his passion, however briefly; had seen his gentleness with Davey; had sensed his compassion for all living creatures; had felt his deep protectiveness toward her and her son.

As he had the night before, she leaned toward him, unable to keep from touching him any longer. His cheeks were bronze from the sun and weathered by the elements. The usual lock of midnight-black hair fell boyishly over his forehead, and she pushed it back, relishing its thick texture. In sleep, his mouth had lost its harsh tight line, and her fingers touched it, remembering its tender exploration just hours earlier. *MacKenzie. Whether you want it or not, I'm not going to let you go. Not ever.* He moved slightly, and she reluctantly moved her hand away. He needed as much rest as he could get. With one last long, searching gaze, she rose. There was much to do before nightfall.

When MacKenzie woke, the sun had disappeared behind the mountains, but its afterglow remained, coloring the horizon. Ribbons of gold and crimson framed the rugged canyon walls. The dark pines were mirrored in the silent lake, and as he watched, the entire sky turned a muted violet, which seemed to blend heaven and earth. MacKenzie knew the same reverence he always did when confronted with God's craftsmanship in his beloved mountains. He had been away for too long. He thought of the hangman's noose that awaited him...or, at the very least, prison. And he knew the latter would be for him far worse than the cessation of life. To be caged like an animal. Never to see the sun rise or set or smell the fresh clean scent of the forest. Never to feel the serenity and purity of a world untouched by man-inspired violence or hate. He felt a coldness inside, and it steeled his determination to make good his escape.

The bitter thoughts contrasted with the calm, silent tranquility of the evening. The world seemed stilled now. It was a time of profound silence, when the day creatures had retreated and the night ones had not yet emerged. It was a time of expectancy and change, and MacKenzie felt its old elemental pull. It was the time he had always loved best.

The silence was pierced by a sharp crack as a large piece of wood fell farther into the fire. He was now aware of the tart smell of smoke and the savory aroma of cooking fish. He turned his head and watched as April, unaware that he was awake, bent over the fire, her long braid caught against the red flames. He could see her profile, like a fine sculpture, in the sun's afterglow. There was a smudge on her nose, and her lips were pressed tightly together in concentration.

He wondered briefly how the fish had been obtained. He didn't think Davey had yet mastered the art of fishing, and he had gained the impression that April had never fished. She was full of surprises, an endless spring of ingenuity and resourcefulness. He was awed at the deep, warm pride he felt in that discovery.

MacKenzie tried to rise, but his body did not cooperate. It was stiff and painful, every movement agony. He had tried to go too far too early, but he was determined to reach his valley before the army; then he would go to Amos's cabin, where he could safely leave April and Davey. Another kind of anguish attacked him at the thought. The woman and child had become a part of his life, a wonderful, joyful part that warmed and delighted him as nothing else in his experience. The exquisite pain of tenderness, the trusting touch of Davey's hand, the light in April's eyes and the gentle touch of her fingers on his face were all gifts of such great magnitude that he didn't know if he could bear them . . . or their loss. He thought of the years of loneliness that stretched before him, years when the only warmth would be the memories. And his heart hurt far worse than his body.

April heard the slight movement and turned, her lips flashing a brilliant smile, which seemed to embrace him in its radiance. Her blue eyes touched him with such concerned gentleness that he once more felt himself falling into a pit of hopeless yearning. He felt blood in his mouth where his teeth bit into his lip, and he struggled to rise again, to escape the trap of that smile, of that look, of the love he wanted so badly but could not take. Because now, he realized, he loved her, too much to ruin her life—and Davey's.

MacKenzie rose slowly, awkwardly, welcoming the waves of pain that flooded him...anything to distract him, to jar his eyes from April's face. He did not want to turn from the love written there, or the bright seductive promise of her lips, the eager expectation in her eyes.

"You shouldn't move," she said. "You should let your body rest more."

A wry smile twisted his lips. How he longed to touch her. He hoped that wish wasn't in his eyes, but he was afraid it might be. He could no longer control them. His voice was very low, the burr heavy. "We cannot stay here...and I cannot let my side get too stiff. We must leave on the morrow."

Some of the brightness left her eyes, and she turned back to the fire, turning the fish on a makeshift spit much like the one he had designed several days earlier.

"You caught those?"

April looked at Davey, who was sitting cross-legged near the fire. "Davey helped...he found the worms." She grinned. "And put them on the hook."

Her quick, self-deprecating smile touched him. She had done so much more than he thought possible of a woman of her background.

"You're a very unpredictable woman..."

"April," she prompted.

"April," he surrendered, and April's heart did a quiet little dance.

Their eyes locked on one other, and it was as if a cyclone had snatched them up, sending them spiralling to its eye and holding them there in a deceptive calm charged with electricity.

The enchantment was such that MacKenzie was almost unaware as his hands went to her shoulders and hovered there. She glided into him, and his hands moved to her back, holding her tightly against him, taking comfort in the soft yielding body and the sheer pleasure of having it pressing close to his. He could feel her shiver, and knew she must be hearing the pounding of his heart as her head lay so trustingly against his chest. Nothing else was necessary at the moment, only this gentle embrace. MacKenzie felt his heart expand, and when April looked at him with unabashed love, he knew there was no greater heaven.

Neither knew how long they stood there, oblivious to the fire and Davey who sat with fascinated wonder at the utter intensity binding his two favorite people in all the world. He didn't understand what he was seeing or feeling, but he sensed the currents and somehow felt a new security. He had been afraid they did not like each other, that MacKenzie would leave them. He didn't want MacKenzie to leave, not ever.

Neither did April. She told him so silently, and only the raw anguish in his eyes answered her. It was so agonized that she stepped back, and as his hands fell from her she grabbed one, refusing to release it.

"Never," she whispered. "I'm not going to let you go."

MacKenzie could do nothing but stare into the bottomless blue eyes that asked him only to love. The silence was pregnant with thoughts unsaid, with needs unmet.

His free hand touched her face. "You're beautiful ... beautiful and strong." He buried his lips in her hair. He had wanted to continue, to say that she would meet a man who could give her and Davey a home, but he couldn't force the words. The very thought cut to the bone, so he just stood there, unable to relinquish her, although he knew he was making everything worse. For everyone.

"Whither thou goest . . ." she started.

"You cannot go," he interrupted. The few words from the Bible shattered the illusion he had momentarily permitted. He took a step backward, his hand falling from her face to her shoulder, holding her away. "If you don't think about yourself, think about Davey."

"He loves you," she said. "He needs you."

"He needs a father who can give him safety, and a home, and education."

"We can do that . . ."

"Not safety . . . not ever safety. Not now. I'll not have a bullet meant for me destroy him . . . or you."

"We can solve this ... together. Some way. Father will help."

"I could not stand a cage, April. Not for a moment. I'll never again let anyone do what they did in Chaco." He hesitated, then added softly, "Not even for you." His strong proud face tensed, and she knew for the first time the full extent of what that terrible journey had cost him in dignity and pride.

"I love you," she whispered.

He could not answer, could not offer the words he wished he could return. He had not the right. Instead, his mouth quirked in a self-mocking smile and his grave gray eyes fastened on something beyond her, as if he could no longer bear her gaze. April felt the tears well up in her eyes and brim over. It shamed her that such was the case, but she couldn't prevent them. And then she felt his eyes on her again, and she blinked under their intent stare. Surprisingly, his hand went up and wiped the tears from her face with gentleness.

"Don't cry, April. I don't think I can stand remembering your tears." He smiled, a real smile, and it was breathtaking. "I want to remember you bringing in the bear meat so proudly, and bullying me and . . . defying Terrell. You're strong enough for anything. Always remember that, because I will. Your strength."

The tears were coming faster now despite, or perhaps because of, his words. She turned away, not wanting him to see them. Her voice was shaking with emotion, but she tried to regain some measure of dignity. "I won't change my mind."

"Neither will I," he said in a low voice. "I'll not risk your lives."

Her teeth bit into her lower lip. "You'd best eat," she said finally. "You need to build your strength." Her voice told him she would never surrender.

"Yes, ma'am," he said, trying in some way to lessen the tension that stood between them, like a living thing. He started to lean down to take the spit, but the pain in his side at the sudden movement was so great he couldn't withhold a small groan.

"Go sit down," she ordered, and like an obedient child he did. He knew he needed his strength, now more than ever. He had to get the Mannings to safety. And for his sanity it had to be as soon as possible. April Manning was as debilitating to him as his wound. And every day it grew worse.

The three ate in silence. Davey crept over to MacKenzie's side, realizing that the closeness he had sensed between MacKenzie and his mother had turned into something else. He had not heard all the words, but he had seen his mother's tears and the pain on MacKenzie's face.

"Are we going with you?" he asked.

"For a little while," his friend answered slowly.

"Why not forever?"

"Because," MacKenzie tried to explain, "we're going in different directions. You want to see your grandfather, don't you?"

"I want to stay with you," Davey said stubbornly, his lips in a rare pout.

"And I would like that...very much," MacKenzie said, "but you must go with your mother to Defiance, and go to school and meet other boys. I think I know how much your grandfather wants you with him. You don't want to disappoint him."

"I don't know him," Davey said belligerently, and there was a little fear in his voice. "I want to stay with you, both Mama and I. Please. Please."

Once more, MacKenzie felt mortally wounded. How could he comfort Davey when there was no comfort for himself?

This time it was April who assisted him. She had gone to the lake for some water and heard only the last of the conversation, but could tell from MacKenzie's face some of the ache he was feeling.

She held out her hand to Davey. "Come on, Davey, we need some more wood for tonight. Will you help me?"

Davey's eyes went from one to the other. Neither smiled, although his mother tried. Something was very wrong. But he saw the plea in her eyes, and he slowly consented. He looked back at MacKenzie who, with a nod, urged him on. He took his mother's hand, and together they faded into darkness.

MacKenzie watched them go, knowing they would not venture beyond the flames. He moved closer to the fire for warmth and closed his eyes, willing himself to sleep once more. It was, he reasoned, to build his strength, not simply because he couldn't bear to watch April and Davey, to know that they wanted him and he could not have them.

But no matter how hard he tried, he couldn't block out the sight of soft tears falling from April's eyes or Davey's pleading face. He did not realize when a tear of his own trickled down his hard bronze cheek.

Chapter Twelve

The valley lay below like a polished emerald.

April had moved her horse up beside MacKenzie's and gazed down at the wonder below. Beneath the steep cliff was a plain of blue-green grass fed by a stream that fell from a high cliff into a pool at its base, then meandered gently through the tall grass. There were hundreds of aspens, their white bark and slender trunks contrasting with the vivid colors they held—ruby to topaz—moving slightly in the breeze so that each tree seemed to be magically shimmering in the bright sunlight. It was splendid in its perfection, as tranquil a picture as April could envision.

She glanced at MacKenzie and knew that he was lost in the same enchantment that had overwhelmed her. Yet there was something more. It was as if the sight enveloped every part of him. His eyes drank it in hungrily, and his mouth softened. A muscle throbbed in his cheek as he stared intently at every piece that composed the whole, like a person who had painstakingly put a puzzle together and now rejoiced in its completion. It was a look of love, of ownership.

"This is the valley you mentioned? The one with the cabin?" She asked hesitantly, timid to interrupt such deep emotions. But her curiosity could not be stilled. This valley was obviously very important to MacKenzie, and she wanted to know everything about him.

He looked at April, his eyes naked for a change. There was love and pain and a certain despair in them. And pride.

"It's mine," he said softly with a kind of reverence.

"But I thought the Utes owned all this . . . by treaty."

"They do...except for this valley," he said slowly. "And legally I suppose they own this, too. But I won use of it in a contest with a Ute chief...for me, for my children, for my children's children."

"What kind of contest?" April asked, fascinated.

MacKenzie smiled, and the smile lit his face in a way she hadn't seen before. The angular planes eased and the mouth became vulnerable...approachable.

"A horse race."

"Just a horse race?" From the unexpected mischief in his eyes, she knew there was more to it. Much more.

"A very different kind of horse race," he said, but then his face closed again, and the reserve, which had been there since daybreak, was back.

"Can we get down there?"

He nodded, but his attention was once again focused on the scene below. In his mind, he saw the future he had intended: a valley of a new strain of horses—a cross between the hardy, surefooted mountain horses like his Appaloosa and swift-blooded eastern stock. He saw them now in his mind: young fillies and colts frolicking beside their dams; stallions, their heads tossing with freedom, asserting their dominance among the mares and yearlings. It was a dream that had inspired him for more than ten years, that had spurred him to do many things he detested. The softness left his face, and his mouth pressed in a grim line. It did no good to think of it now. And he couldn't waste time. General Wakefield was only too aware of this valley and its importance to him. It would be the first place he would look. Which was part of MacKenzie's plan.

He turned to April, who was riding with Davey to prevent any more hurt to MacKenzie's wounded side. "I'll take the boy," he said curtly. "It's a steep ride. You have to be careful." He did not worry about her safety. She was a fine rider, but he knew it would be easier for her without worrying about Davey.

After taking the boy, MacKenzie turned his horse toward some pines hovering over the cliff. As they entered the trees April was startled to see a path that led downward. She noted that it was not visible unless you knew exactly where to look. MacKenzie had not exaggerated. It was a difficult passage, but the sturdy horses nimbly picked their way through the rocks and branches. The path was wide enough for two horses, but they went single file to avoid coming close to the edge of the precipice. April said a brief prayer as she leaned over and looked down the sheer cliff, and was humiliated when Mac-Kenzie picked that time to look back and see her apprehensive expression.

Once more that day, his eyes softened. "Don't look down," he said. "You're doing very well."

The words restored her courage, and she took his advice, keeping her eyes on the trail in front, seldom moving them to MacKenzie's back. His usual easy grace was missing, and she knew he was once more pushing himself unmercifully.

April was grateful when they reached the bottom, and the majestic plain lay before them like a magic carpet. "It's beautiful," she whispered with no little awe.

"Aye," he said. "It is that." He turned his horse and they rode to a corner of the valley that could not be seen from overhead. A small, neat cabin stood with its back to the rock of the canyon wall.

MacKenzie placed Davey on the ground and dismounted slowly, as if in pain. He went to assist April, but she was only too aware of his injury and she slipped down easily without any assistance. MacKenzie took both pairs of reins and tied them to the branch of a nearby tree.

April watched and waited, her eyes following his every move as he went from the horses to the door of the cabin and opened it, nodding for her and Davey to enter before him.

She didn't know what she expected but certainly not the interior that met her gaze.

It was whimsical. No other word could quite describe it, and the cabin said more about MacKenzie than anything he had revealed in the past two weeks or more. She had expected its neatness, for he was meticulous in everything he did. But in addition, it had color and character and charm. Blankets woven with intricate designs and bright colors decorated the walls and bed. A woven rug of various shades of blue covered the wood floor. A mantel over a huge fireplace held several wooden carvings of horses. In addition to the bed, the furniture included a finely carved chest, and a table with two chairs. The overall feeling was one of warmth.

April turned and looked at MacKenzie's half-expectant, half-wary expression. "It's wonderful," she said, and was rewarded with a brief smile. She went over to the carvings and fingered them with appreciation. They were roughly carved, almost primitive, yet each had its own charm. It was almost as if they were alive, so well did the creator capture the fluid movement of a horse in motion. She turned to MacKenzie. "Did you do these?"

He nodded. "When I was a boy."

"The blankets?"

"Navahos." His mouth became grim again. They had come from the small band massacred by the Apaches.

April looked around again, taking in everything. How much it revealed of him. How much it belied the stoic, harsh exterior he seemed to have mastered. But she didn't have time to ponder the discovery because he was moving around, reaching for tins on shelves and selecting several food items.

"Can we stay here?" April asked, wanting very much for the answer to be affirmative.

A muscle throbbed in his cheek before he answered. "No." The answer was abrupt, and April sensed the reluctance behind it.

"We'll eat," he continued, "then pack some of these blankets. We need them. And clothes. There're some in the chest. See if there's anything warm you can cut down for Davey and yourself. We have two more days' ride, straight up, and it will be cold.

"But why can't we stay here?"

MacKenzie looked at her carefully. "Your father knows of this cabin and how to reach it. He'll send someone here. But I can't leave you. Not alone. With the Apaches on the move, he may not be able to send anyone right away or, if he does, they might be slowed by Indians." Or massacred, he thought to himself. Damn. He was running out of alternatives, and the very thought of April's presence for additional days was pure torture, almost as great as the thought of losing her.

April bit her lip, wishing she hadn't asked as she realized he believed he was giving up this place he loved, possibly forever.

NO COST! NO OBLIGATION TO BUY! NO PURCHASE NECESSARY!

PLAY ''LUCKY 7''
AND GET AS MANY AS SIX FREE GIFTS . . .

HOW TO PLAY:

1. With a coin, carefully scratch off the silver box at the right. This makes you eligible to receive one or more free books, and possibly other gifts, depending on what is revealed beneath the scratch-off area.

2. You'll receive brand-new Harlequin Historical™ novels. When you return this card, we'll send you the books and gifts you qualify for *absolutely free!*

3. If we don't hear from you, every other month we'll send you 4 additional novels to read and enjoy. You can return them and owe nothing, but if you decide to keep them, you'll pay only $2.89* per book, a savings of 36¢ each off the cover price! There is *no* extra charge for postage and handling. There are no hidden extras.

4. When you join the Harlequin Reader Service®, you'll also get our members' only newsletter with each of your shipments, as well as additional free gifts from time to time.

5. You must be completely satisfied. You may cancel at any time simply by sending us a note or a shipping statement marked ''cancel'' or by returning any unopened shipment to us by parcel post at our expense.

*In the future, prices and terms may change, but you always have the opportunity to cancel your subscription. Sales taxes applicable in N.Y. and Iowa.

*You'll love your elegant bracelet watch—
this classic LCD Quartz Watch is a perfect
expression of your style and good taste—
and it is yours FREE as an added thanks for
giving our Reader Service a try.*

DETACH AND MAIL CARD TODAY

BUSINESS REPLY CARD

First Class   Permit No. 717   Buffalo, NY

Postage will be paid by addressee

Harlequin Reader Service®
901 Fuhrmann Blvd.,
P.O. Box 1867
Buffalo, NY 14240-9952

NO POSTAGE
NECESSARY
IF MAILED
IN THE
UNITED STATES

"Where are we going?" April pleaded. "Where are *you* going?"

"I'm going to leave a note for your father and tell him I'm leaving you and Davey with Amos Smith. He's an old mountain man. You will be safe with him."

"And you?" she whispered.

"I'll be going on, up into the high country where I can get lost," he said frankly.

"We'll go with you," she offered once more, forsaking her pride completely.

"I know," he replied. "I know you would, but I can give you nothing. Less than nothing. Only hardship and danger, constant danger, and running. Always running."

"I don't care."

"You must . . . for Davey, if not yourself."

She knew he was right, although she had been avoiding the fact. She had to think about Davey. But Davey loved MacKenzie.

MacKenzie saw the flickering emotions cross her face. He gave her his last argument. "And it would be dangerous to me," he said. "A man alone can lose himself, but a half-breed with a white woman and child. Even in the mountains, whispers travel." April's eyes clouded, and he knew he was, at last, winning. It gave him no satisfaction.

"Eat," he ordered as he opened some tinned peaches with his knife.

If April's stomach wasn't in her throat, she might have enjoyed the treat. Especially after so many days of fish, hardtack and dried beef. But all she could do was move the morsels around in her mouth. Davey, who didn't quite understand everything, had no such reservations and in minutes the tin was empty, and another was opened, and another.

MacKenzie was, as usual, impatient, and as April and Davey ate, he busied himself. Not bothering with false modesty, he discarded his awkward blanket jacket and found a clean buckskin shirt in the chest. He knew April had already seen him in several states of undress. He then packed another shirt and pair of cotton pants in saddlebags, and pulled out some clothes he thought April and Davey might be able to adapt. He scooped flour from a barrel and tied it in a bag, grateful that he always left supplies in the cabin; he never knew when he would return, and the supplies had been safe there. Only the Utes and a few acquaintances knew of the cabin and how to reach the valley floor. He added the colorful blankets to the bedrolls, along with several cooking utensils. When he'd completed packing, the cabin looked bare. He handed one of the carved horses to Davey, whose face lit at the gift as his hands fondled it possessively.

MacKenzie urged April to select the clothing she needed, then sat down to write a note. It was short and abrupt, saying only that April and Davey were safe and could be found at Amos Smith's cabin. He offered no excuses or explanations. For, in his opinion, he had none. Although he had not committed the crimes of murder and rape, he was responsible for equally unforgivable ones, including the kidnapping of a woman and child. He did not expect General Wakefield to forgive or forget.

When he finished, he found April watching him, her dark blue eyes steady.

"May I write my father?"

MacKenzie winced at the question. She didn't need permission for anything. That had ceased days ago. But he merely nodded at the several sheets of paper he had taken from the chest. He purposely moved away so that she wouldn't think he didn't trust her.

April hesitated. She knew what she wanted to say, but not quite how to say it. She wanted her father to know she and Davey were well, but mostly that MacKenzie was innocent and should not be hunted. She finally dipped a pen in ink Mac-Kenzie supplied, and carefully wrote:

Please don't blame MacKenzie. We went with him willingly to keep Sergeant Terrell from killing him. He saved Davey's life with grave injury to himself. If anything happens to me, please know he's innocent and has done everything possible to protect us.

Your Loving Daughter

She looked at MacKenzie. "Do you want to read it?"
MacKenzie shook his head. "It's time we left."

April sighed. She wished they could stay here a day or two, at least until MacKenzie had healed a bit more, but she had not missed the tenseness in his body or the forbidding set of his jaw.

He gave her a sheepskin coat that had been in the chest and took a lighter one for himself. He made sure Davey was wrapped in several layers of heavy clothes and gave April a giant pair of leather gloves obviously meant to fit himself. Her fingers were lost in them, but she suspected she would be grateful for them later.

The sun was halfway down the horizon when they re-mounted their horses. MacKenzie believed they would have at least four hours of daylight. He wouldn't hide their tracks, not until after he left Amos's. It would be then he would become the fox.

Captain Bob Morris, twenty men riding behind him, pushed his horse as hard as he could in the rocky terrain. He recognized several of the natural landmarks, and he knew he was only hours from MacKenzie's valley. He was tired, dog-tired, and he guessed each of his troopers shared the same affliction, for they had stopped only for brief rests in the past four days.

He also knew his only chance was to find MacKenzie at the valley. The damned scout could be a wisp of wind when he wanted, and the only hope they had was that the woman and child might have slowed him down.

Morris had been astonished at Pickering's and Terrell's tale. He himself had never cared much for MacKenzie, not because he was half-breed, but more because of MacKenzie's own distant attitude. His take-it-or-leave-it arrogance did not make things easy for those who employed him. It had not bothered General Wakefield, however, whom Morris suspected harbored a deep affection for the scout, as well as respect. It was, all personalities aside, a respect Morris shared. He knew his life had been saved more than once by MacKenzie's instinct and knowledge. And he had never doubted MacKenzie's intelligence and loyalty once he undertook an assignment. Morris agreed with his commanding officer that Pickering was a fool, and his rage grew as he saw burned-out ranches and farms along his way. Some of it could have been avoided had Mac-Kenzie's warning been heeded immediately. His detail had already been weaned by the necessity of sending escorts back with the fleeing settlers.

He wondered about April Manning and the boy...and how they were faring in this rough country. It was no place for women and children, especially when they had been east for so long. He had seen April's portrait frequently since he had been assigned to General Wakefield two years earlier, and he had looked forward to her arrival. More than a little, he admitted. There were few women at Defiance, and most of them were married. The others were mainly laundresses and whores. Which reminded him of Ellen Peters.

Wakefield had been unable to shake her story, despite several interviews. She clung to her tale of rape and murder, and insisted on charges being pressed and MacKenzie apprehended. But she certainly seemed to have no sorrow over her father's death or even the slightest fear of men. Because she was a material witness and because Wakefield wasn't through with her by any means, Ellen had been allowed to stay as a laundress, a very unpleasant job in the sweltering Arizona heat. But she apparently had no other place to go. What Ellen didn't know was that Wakefield wanted her to stay, to watch her...and break her.

But that was not Morris's problem. His was to find Mac-Kenzie and April and the boy. He knew MacKenzie had a substantial head start, but the scout would have to take roundabout ways where he was taking the most direct route. And Mac-Kenzie had the woman and boy to slow him. Like his commanding officer, Morris was sure of one thing: MacKenzie would see they would not come to harm. If it were possible! In this hard country, nothing was certain, nothing was safe...even with MacKenzie's bloody competence. Morris saw a level stretch of country, and spurred his horse into a gallop.

Morris and his men reached the rim of MacKenzie's valley just as the sun was setting. The captain had visited it previously with Wakefield when the general had sought once more to obtain MacKenzie's rare talents. He had sent for Mac-Kenzie to no avail and decided to take matters into his own hands. Wakefield had known of MacKenzie's valley, although he did not know its exact location. He had employed a Ute to guide him, and both Wakefield and Morris had been astounded by the beauty of the valley and the comfort of MacKenzie's cabin. They had not, Morris remembered, been exactly welcomed—either by a big gray wolf that bared its teeth and never took its eyes from them, or by MacKenzie, whose whole demeanor told them he resented their intrusion—but after a day's discussion, Wakefield's persuasion finally won...

Like MacKenzie and April not many hours earlier, Morris gazed down at the valley with something akin to awe. In the faltering light, it was indescribably lovely. The various hues of the sunset seem to inflame the falling water on the opposite cliff wall, and silver and gold danced in the pool below. The color of the grass seemed even richer in the muted light. He could find no sign of activity. It seemed an empty painting...too beautiful, too peaceful to be real.

He sighed, sensing he was too late, but gave the order to descend. He could only hope there was some kind of sign, some indication of where MacKenzie was heading.

The cabin was much as Morris recalled, although it seemed emptier than before. He had remembered more color. His eyes immediately saw the paper on the table and in three easy strides he was fingering the notes. He quickly read MacKenzie's note, swearing as he did. Smith's cabin was a good two day's ride. His men and horses were exhausted, as was he. And the territory MacKenzie was entering was even more treacherous than this. It was no place for a lady and boy. Morris wondered how long ago MacKenzie had been here. He saw an empty tin in a corner and took it, smelling the residue. It hadn't been long. No more than a day if that long. God damn it. If only they had arrived a little sooner, MacKenzie would have been trapped. The man was as elusive as a damned ghost.

Morris took the second note and scanned it. He wondered briefly if the woman had been forced to write it, but he quickly discarded the idea. MacKenzie wouldn't have bothered. Two words particularly caught his attention. "Grave injury." So that was why he had almost caught up with the scout. He wondered how badly injured. How much it was slowing him? How much it would continue to slow him? Perhaps he could find April and Davon Manning. And maybe, just maybe, he would bring in MacKenzie as well.

Captain Morris gave the order to dismount and make camp. He could not risk going up the steep trail at night, and they all needed rest. In these mountains, MacKenzie would also have to stop at night, particularly with a serious injury. Tomorrow his men would be fresh and able to move fast. He wanted to catch up with MacKenzie before he reached Smith's cabin . . . while he was still slowed by the woman and child and before he could erase his tracks. Morris knew once MacKenzie was alone, he would be impossible to find.

April, Davey and MacKenzie dined on dried fish, berries and another can of sweetened peaches. MacKenzie had located a deep cave just as twilight surrendered to darkness, and they had settled in for the night. The moon was now almost full but MacKenzie couldn't risk April's and Davey's lives by continuing after dark. The steep trails fell to deep canyons; bushes blocked the paths, and the footing was often treacherous. Several times they had had to dismount and lead their nervous mounts through cramped passages or across narrow ledges.

Davey helped MacKenzie take care of the horses, and then both fell to the cave floor in exhaustion, Davey after a full day of fresh air and activity, and MacKenzie because of his continuing weakness and lingering pain. With the addition of extra blankets, MacKenzie decided not to build a fire. He did not know how far behind any pursuers were; he had risked a great deal by stopping at the valley but had deemed it necessary—both to obtain warmer clothing and to provide for April's safe return. But he did not care to offer Wakefield any additional help by providing a beacon if anyone were determined enough to travel at night. The moonlight would permit it, dangerous as movement might be, and were it not for his wound and his two charges he would have attempted it himself. He stood and walked outside the cave, watching the moon play over mountaintops dressed in white. The stars seemed incredibly bright against the blue-black sky, and the cold pure air of the mountains invigorated him. He lifted his head toward the sky, trying to toss aside the melancholy that had plagued him since leaving the valley. He used to take pleasure from such a scene, but now there was only a deep loneliness. He had discovered the joy of sharing such gifts. And soon the sharing would be over.

He sensed April's presence before seeing her. She, too, had been quiet during the past hours. He wondered whether she felt the same bittersweet emptiness, and knew she did as she slipped a hand in his. Despite his best intentions, he turned to face her, and he felt his heart contract at the love that was so openly expressed in her face. How hard it would be to leave her.

"Tell me more about the valley," April probed gently.

And suddenly he wanted to, needed to.

He guided her, and they both sat in the moonlight, staring at the infinity above, which seem to make them very small indeed. But what flowed between them was strong as steel and, April knew, as enduring. "Tell me," she said again.

MacKenzie started slowly. He was unused to revealing anything about himself. It was a habit difficult to break, even with April. "I had planned to raise horses." Each word was carefully spoken as if difficult to extract. And April knew each was a victory for her. "There was a major I knew...Bennett Morgan. One of the few really good officers, the only one to take the time or trouble to learn to track, to learn Indian ways. He had a blooded horse that could outrun any on the post. Even," he added wryly, "my own mountain pony, which had always won races before. But it didn't have my horse's endurance. I thought then, and so did Major Morgan, that a cross between the two would be unbeatable. It was a dream for a long time, but I didn't think there was any hope for it. I didn't have the money to buy stock or land, and I doubted I would be welcome anyplace." His words were bitter, more bitter than any she had heard. "I didn't care what anyone thought," he continued slowly, "but I didn't want to have to fight all my life."

The words faded in the night air, and April felt the stillness. But the peace was gone. His anger simmered below the surface. It was several minutes before he continued.

"It was always there...the idea...in the back of my mind...and then it became possible. I was challenged to a horse race by a Ute chief. He had never lost and thought he never would...not to a half white anyway." There was a small, rueful smile on MacKenzie's face as he remembered the chief's chagrin and fury when he lost his favorite horse—the Appaloosa. The chief threw out a second challenge, this time a more difficult one. They would race bareback with a weapon to be picked up from the ground. MacKenzie would never forget that race, leaning down to grab a tomahawk, his face close to the horse's hooves, his balance maintained only by a handful of mane. But the prize was a great one—the valley; and he had won. There was also a fight, a bloody one, and again MacKenzie had triumphed. He had won the respect, if not friendship, of the Utes. They had honored the wager.

But he said little of this to April, only that he had won both the horse and the valley. And it had given him the start he needed. He'd continued scouting to earn enough money to buy the blooded stock he wanted. He had figured he would have enough after this last assignment with the army.

MacKenzie paused. "I had planned to go to Texas, ask Bennett Morgan to help select stock and bring them to the valley. It's a natural corral, and the grass is rich. It's protected from the wind by the canyon walls. I could easily round up wild mountain horses for breeding. It all seemed so possible . . . just a few more months."

April let several seconds go by. She could feel his anguish, the loss of something vitally important to him. She was startled he had let her see it. Startled and pleased and infinitely sad. There had to be some way she could help.

"This Major Morgan . . . he is a friend?"

MacKenzie hesitated. "Not a friend . . . I think he was as cautious about trusting as I was . . . but I think we respected each other. There's not many I feel that way about . . . perhaps your father . . ." His voice trailed off as he remembered exactly what he had done to her father, how worried he must be about his daughter and grandson.

And April knew she couldn't offer any comfort. She, too, thought about her father, knew how much he had looked forward to her coming, to seeing his grandson for the first time. She had tried not to think about it, but it had been there, in the back of her mind, since the beginning. She had considered it when she asked to go with MacKenzie, had battled with her loyalties.

A shooting star flamed its way across the sky, and both MacKenzie and April watched it silently, each wondering whether it was an omen, and if so, what it portended. April laid her head against his chest, and it was enough, just then, to be together.

Chapter Thirteen

Long before they reached Amos Smith's cabin, MacKenzie knew it had been another futile effort.

Amos's dog, as faithful as his own wolf, always sounded an early warning of strangers. There was nothing now but silence. And MacKenzie didn't know whether he was blessed or damned. He did know he would have to make a decision immediately. He had insured that by leaving the note in his cabin. He could not linger here, not unless he wanted to be taken back to Defiance in chains, and that he had sworn would not happen. Yet he had promised Wakefield his daughter and grandson would be waiting here.

He was unaware that his face reflected his dismay and that his back had stiffened even more rigidly. Somewhere in the past few days his protective shields had ceased to work. He heard April draw abreast of him and saw her puzzled face. It was full of questions.

He could only shake his head and shrug in reply. He pushed his horse into a trot and within minutes they saw the dried mud roof of a rough cabin. There was an air of desertion about it.

April watched while MacKenzie slung a leg over the saddle and slid easily to the ground. He dropped the reins, knowing the Appaloosa would stand quiet for the few minutes he needed. He unhitched the latch holding the door closed and entered the cabin, his eyes immediately assessing the interior.

The dust was not heavy, and MacKenzie knew Amos had not been gone long, perhaps not more than a week or so. He could only surmise that Amos had headed for Denver to trade furs for winter supplies. Of all the damned bad luck! His had to be the worst. He left the cabin and strode to the side of April's horse, first taking Davey down, then offering a hand to her. The touch was like fire to both of them, burning like a brand through their skin, the heat racing through their blood like fast-flowing lava.

MacKenzie looked at their hands, still entangled together, hesitating to relinquish the brief contact even as the heat magnified. His gray eyes became smoldering coal, and hers were the color of an inviting mountain pool. Both probed and queried and explored, finally locking in an understanding and knowledge that shook them with their strength.

There was some satisfaction in April's voice when at last she spoke, piercing the tense silence. "He's not here," she said, stating the obvious. "You'll have to take us on with you now."

The words jerked MacKenzie back to reality and the terrible dilemma facing him. He could take April and the boy higher into the mountains and hope he could find someone to whom he could entrust their safety. Or he could stay here with them and allow himself to be captured.

April read the indecision in his face. "No," she said. "I will not stay and let you be taken."

Despite his worry, MacKenzie had to smile slightly at the fierceness in her voice. "I thought," he reminded her wryly, "that's what you were urging me to do."

It had been, April admitted to herself, but that was before she knew MacKenzie so well. She was no longer willing to take even the slightest chance with his life . . . or freedom. The latter, she had discovered, meant more to him than breathing. She had seen it in every restless movement and every loving look he cast on his mountains. And she wanted to be with him. Oh, how she wanted that! Every moment she could borrow or steal. She tore her eyes from his face and looked down at Davey. Did she have the right to make this decision? But then she saw the look of trust and worship in Davey's face as her son looked at MacKenzie, and she knew no more doubts. Only her father gave her pause. She was being so unfair to him. Yet she had no choice. Her heart was giving her none. It was as if MacKenzie, in the space of three weeks, had become her life. And she would be a hollow, empty thing without him.

"I will not stay and let you be taken," she repeated, this time even stronger. "Davey and I go with you."

MacKenzie fought himself. She had never been so beautiful. Her eyes sparked with the light of battle; her chin jutted defiantly. The thought of losing her and the boy was excruciating; yet what could he offer them? Once more he weighed his alternatives. They were so damned few.

He could not leave them here alone, any more than he could have left them in the valley. He believed with all the instincts that kept him alive this long that there were troops behind him—and not long behind. But he could not be sure, and he could not gamble April's and Davey's lives on it. The second choice—the mountains ahead—was what his heart was arguing. More days, more time with April and Davey. Time to explore these new feelings that gave grace to a life previously untouched by love, or trust, or giving. But didn't that also mean sacrificing? Sacrificing his happiness, even his life, for their safety?

But they would be safe with him . . . for a while . . . until he could find a haven for them. No one knew of his father's mountaintop cabin. He could readily supply them with the food, shelter and clothing they needed until he found a way to get them home. And he could collect memories, store them and treasure them for when he was, once more, alone. Need and greed—need for belonging, greed for love—swamped him, drowning his reservations and his usual calm, dispassionate judgment.

Ignoring the warning sick feeling in his stomach, he made his decision.

His hand touched her cheek, and he gave her a rare smile. "I think the Fates are making the decisions for us," he said softly. "We'll go on together."

Spontaneously, she reached up and kissed him, and Mac-Kenzie was swept up in it. The kiss was at first hard, then sweet and lingering as neither wanted to let go. It was MacKenzie who remembered Davey, and pulled back, reluctantly releasing her.

"I really didn't want to leave you," he admitted wryly as he watched her face light with happiness. Suddenly, he felt like the boy he had never had a chance to be, and his smile broadened, reminding April of the brilliance of a rainbow after a storm. The hard lines smoothed out, and his eyes flashed silver with an openness and anticipation she had never seen before.

Elation filled April, chasing any specters that remained. Love filled her so thoroughly she thought she might explode of it. "We should hurry," she said, afraid now that something or someone would alter his decision.

MacKenzie nodded. Now the decision, for better or for worse, was made, he was caught up in an urgency of his own. But first there was something that must be done. He could not leave Wakefield with no word or explanation; he had put the general through enough already. There was no pen or paper in Amos's cabin; the mountain man could not read or write. And MacKenzie had taken no writing materials with him. With all he needed, that seemed the most useless. Asking April and Davey to stay outside, he went back into the cabin. With his knife, he cut a small trail in his wrist, and let drops of blood fall on the table. With a finger, he wrote the words which he hoped would explain, if not excuse.

When he returned outside, he saw April eye his bloody wrist, but he shook his head as if it were no matter. He helped her mount once more, then mounted himself, leaning down and lifting Davey in front of him.

Without looking back, they trotted away.

Captain Morris eyed the vacated cabin with frustration. He had pushed his men until they were ready to drop, but still they had not been able to overtake MacKenzie. His growing anger, spawned of one disappointment after another, increased tenfold when he failed to find the general's daughter and grandson at Smith's cabin as promised. The rough table caught his attention, and he strode over to it. His fingers traced the bloody letters. Only MacKenzie, he thought, would communicate in quite this fashion. He read, with difficulty, the brief message: "Amos gone. Couldn't leave Mannings alone. Safe."

"Damn the man's eyes," Morris whispered under his breath. "Damn his soul."

He strode outside, carefully observing the manure that lay just outside the cabin. He leaned down and touched it. Fresh. He had missed them by hours.

Morris looked up at the lemon-colored sky. There was something about it that alarmed him. The wind had increased and now was making low moaning sounds as it swept through the trees. He pulled his greatcoat tighter, shivering. He thought of the woman and child caught in one of the furious snowstorms that sometimes isolated entire mountain areas for weeks and even months at a time.

"Damn MacKenzie," he cursed once more. He had been entrapped in one of these storms before, and he didn't want to repeat the experience. He and a small detail had watched their horses freeze and had almost starved to death before eating horseflesh. Morris had come close to dying that time, closer than he wanted to remember. He knew MacKenzie came from these mountains and that probably no one was better equipped to survive a hard winter, but what about Mrs. Manning and her son? He dreaded returning to Defiance without them... and without MacKenzie. His right fist, gloved in warm leather, balled and unballed before he made his decision. "Get mounted," he told his sergeant. "We're going after them."

MacKenzie's eyes searched the sky warily. In the past few hours great gray-black clouds had swept across the sky, blocking the sun and shrouding the mountain peaks. Although only midday, it was growing so dark it looked like dusk.

The wind was rising rapidly and there was an electric tension in the air that always foreshadowed a mountain storm. He considered returning to Amos's cabin, and then thought about his father's place just a day and a half ahead. It was straight up, and the trail split at several places, the last segment so rarely traveled as to be practically invisible if one didn't know it well. If he eliminated any sign of their presence, there would be no way to find him. And if it did snow heavily, the passage would be blocked as thoroughly as if by an iron gate.

MacKenzie did not worry about the storm once they made it to his destination. Rob MacKenzie's cabin was sturdy, like the man who had built it, and as in his own cabin, there should be tinned goods and flour to keep them until he could hunt. There had been plenty a year ago and he doubted whether anyone had been there since. It was simply too isolated. The question was whether he could reach the cabin before snow made travel too dangerous. He was avoiding the other nagging problem. How could he live closely in a cabin with April and Davey without becoming further ensnared in a web that had no escape? The thought both alarmed and elated him.

He looked at April who was riding abreast of him and was also anxiously scanning the sky. He answered her unspoken question. "It's another day away..."

They were even beginning to think alike now, April thought. They were so in tune with each other that spoken words were almost unnecessary.

"We can't go back," she said, dismissing the very idea. She was not going to give him up now.

"It could be dangerous...Davey..."

She shook her head. Her faith in him was absolute. Nothing would happen to them with MacKenzie.

He read her expression and once more smiled, though it did not ease the worry lines around his eyes. He might have hesitated, if he did not know these mountains so well. But he knew every rock and cranny, every hiding place and every trail in the area. He had roamed it incessantly as a boy and young man. He knew he could find the cabin even with the snow...if they reached Devil's Fall first. He would not even attempt the treacherous pass with April and Davey if they did not outrace the snow. It was dangerous enough without ice.

MacKenzie tightened his hold on Davey and spurred his Appaloosa forward with new urgency.

An icy rain began to fall as the three reached Devil's Fall. April gazed with trepidation at the steep winding path that fell sharply off on one side. It made the descent into MacKenzie's valley look like a cow path.

MacKenzie dismounted and eyed the trail dubiously. It had never looked quite as dangerous as it did now. It was a short passage, to be sure, and they would be well over it before the rain froze, but still....

April shivered from both cold and fear, but she had come too far to falter now. She looked at MacKenzie's grim visage. "I'm not giving up," she said, trying to keep the tremor out of her voice.

MacKenzie knew he could not hesitate. Each second counted. In an hour, the trail would be impassable. To him or to anyone following. It was that knowledge that decided him. He could get the Mannings over safely...now. He had no doubt of that ... but he loathed the fear he saw in April's eyes, fear he knew would worsen when they continued.

Her chin lifted as if she could read his mind. "We can't stay here," she said, her voice stronger.

"You'll have to trust me completely ... do whatever I say when I say it ..."

She nodded, her hands tightening on the reins.

His mouth relaxed. He reached up and took Davey from his saddle. He quickly unrolled his bedroll and took out a blanket, wrapping it around the boy. He then lifted Davey up and placed him at the front of April's saddle.

April watched as MacKenzie tied the reins of his horse to his saddle horn, taking just a second to run a hand down the horse's neck in reassurance. He then took the reins to April's horse and started walking, knowing the sure-footed Appaloosa would follow behind them.

The path narrowed even more, and April felt the icy rain pelting down, soaking the sheepskin jacket that until now had kept her warm. She knew MacKenzie, with his lighter coat and moccasins, must be freezing, and she shivered uncontrollably. Remembering the brief fear she felt descending into the valley, she forced her eyes away from the sheer drop on her right side and hugged Davey closer.

The climb seemed to go on forever. April wanted to close her eyes, but couldn't. Instead, she fastened them on MacKenzie who moved surely but cautiously along the path, seemingly unaware of any discomfort or fear. She felt her horse stumble, and froze, but MacKenzie merely turned, his hand quieting the horse as he whispered soothing words. And then they were going on again. This time she shut her eyes tightly, listening to the cadence of her horse's iron shoes against the rock. It was a comforting sound among the other noises—the wailing of wind and the cold beat of rain against the canyon walls. Davey seemed to try to burrow himself further into her, and her hands, now nearly lost in MacKenzie's large leather gloves, found Davey's, which had been wrapped in the blanket. She helped them wriggle inside her gloves, and held them tightly as he arms continued to wrap around him, sharing warmth and courage.

The horse stopped, and April opened her eyes. MacKenzie's eyes were on her, a victorious smile on a face dripping with rain. She looked around. The path had leveled and widened, and trees now rose where previously there had been only dark yawning space.

"It's over?" she whispered, hating the fear that lingered in her voice.

He nodded. "There's a cave not far... I'll try to build a fire." He looked back at the pass. In an hour, it would be sheer ice. If there were pursuers, they would come no further. Not for days. The trail from here on was rough but passable, unless the coming snow was unusually heavy. Approaching snow or not, they couldn't travel much longer; what little light remained of day was fading fast, and he was freezing.

Captain Morris and his scout stared at the fork in the trail. They had left Smith's cabin two hours earlier, and MacKenzie's path had been easy to follow until now. At this point, there was no indication as to which way the half-breed and his two prisoners had gone. The ground was rocky, and there were no hoof marks. In fact, there was nothing. Morris's scout had tried both directions and found no evidence of passage. It was as if their quarry had simply vanished into thin air. A rain was falling now, rain mixed with sleet, and Morris knew everything would soon be washed away... if MacKenzie was careless enough to leave any trace at all. Morris doubted it. But he had come this far, and he was not ready to stop. He called his sergeant over.

"Take ten men and try the left trail. I'll take the right. We'll both go about two miles. If you don't find anything, come back here and wait an hour. If I'm not back by then, follow me. I'll follow the same procedure. Look for the smallest thing... a piece of cloth, a broken branch. You won't find anything else... not with MacKenzie."

The sergeant nodded, wishing he were anyplace but in these mountains. He, too, knew MacKenzie and felt the whole thing was an exercise in futility. Yet he also understood a woman and child were at risk. He would do his best. He hunkered down in his coat, and signaled the other men, cursing under his breath. What damned miserable weather!

It was Morris's detail that reached Devil's Fall.

He had found nothing, not the slightest clue when he reached the steep trail upward. Rain had turned to sleet, and his horse was already having difficulty keeping its balance. He looked at the icy trail and knew it was hopeless to go any farther. He also sincerely doubted whether MacKenzie had gone this way. It would take a mountain goat. And while MacKenzie might attempt it alone, he doubted if even the scout would try it with a woman and child. Morris sunk his chin in the collar of his heavy coat and turned around. He hoped like hell his sergeant had found something. Otherwise they had no choice but to start back to Defiance. They couldn't wander around these mountains blind in a snowstorm, and he knew one was right behind the sleet. He shook his head. How in bloody Hades would he ever explain his failure to General Wakefield? One eloquent curse followed another as he turned his horse around and started back.

He wasn't surprised when his sergeant had no more luck than he had. With heavy hearts, the twenty men made for Smith's cabin. They would warm themselves, and eat, before turning back toward the fort.

It took MacKenzie more than an hour to kindle a fire. He had sought dry wood under heavily laden trees where there would have been some protection, but all of it was at least damp and resisted his attempt to light it. He finally urged a spark from some juniper needles and the wood began to smoke reluctantly, igniting into flames.

April couldn't stop trembling . . . from both the cold and a delayed reaction to the fear. She wondered if she would ever be warm again, yet most of her concern was for MacKenzie. Davey was already wrapped in layers of blankets and was drowsily nodding. But MacKenzie! His clothes were soaked through and his black hair was still wet with icy moisture. His face was red from the wind and cold, and his lips had turned blue. His eyebrows seemed like tiny silvery icicles in the cave's dark interior. He had worked ceaselessly since they'd arrived, bringing the horses in from the now howling wind and braving the stinging sleet to find wood. Now she knew it was catching up with him. His entire body was shaking with cold and exhaustion.

April took one of the least wet blankets and drew it around him tightly, her hands going around his wide shoulders. She hugged him with her arms, trying to share some of her warmth. She felt him shuddering under her touch and lay her head against the iciness of his hair. One of his hands reached for hers, and she felt its chill. It was so large and hers so small, she doubted what little body heat she had was doing him any good. His head turned and in the slight glow of the struggling fire his eyes were enigmatic silver. Her arms tightened around him once more and she felt the hard tense muscles in his arms and chest. "I love you, MacKenzie," she whispered under her breath so he wouldn't hear. She knew he didn't want to hear it again, that he was fighting it, but she couldn't stop the words. The feeling was too deep. She felt him react, felt his body stiffen and saw something new in his eyes when once more they met hers.

"You mustn't," he rasped, his gray eyes now steely with determination.

Now it was out, April decided she would not retreat, not any more. "I'm afraid you can't do anything about it," she said. "It's done." Her tone held finality, and he could only stare at her with a kind of hopelessness.

April did not give him time to ponder her words or to speak. She took her arms away and searched in the saddlebags for something dry. When she found a shirt she had taken from his cabin, she returned to his side and used it to towel his hair and try to at least take some of the freezing moisture from it. He was unexpectedly still under her ministrations, and she didn't know whether it was acceptance of her pronouncement or simply fatigue.

The fire was catching now, finally offering some heat and light. The flames danced merrily against the dark walls of the cave, and April felt the shivering of MacKenzie's body gradually abate. She slipped down beside him and, without words, he opened the blanket and included April in its warmth. Side by side, silently, they shared the blanket and the fire, listening to the howl of the wind and the sound of sleet pounding a tattoo on the side of the mountain. The words were gone now; none were needed. Both felt comfort at the simple pleasure of being close to one other while the elements warred outside. They disregarded the nervous stamping of the horses and the quiet breathing of the sleeping boy. For those few moments, only the two of them existed in a world made exceptional by the depth of their emotions. The simple touch of their bodies spoke of love, so strong was the electricity that sparked and burned and illuminated.

April snuggled closer to him, feeling as if she belonged there in his warm curves and protective arm. Her hand wandered to his shirt and inside the still damp cloth to his chest. She rubbed its cold hardness until it strained and trembled under her touch. She looked up at his face, and his eyes were now like molten steel, fiery and impassioned. April melted under the gaze, her body almost uncontrollable as it seemed to reach of its own volition toward his, her lips inviting, then demanding with their expectancy.

MacKenzie groaned and surrendered.

He could no longer deny himself, any more than he could stop breathing. He wanted April Manning more than he ever wanted anything in his life, and he was tired of fighting. Of fighting the world; of the exquisite agony of fighting her...and the feelings she aroused in him. At this moment the only thing that existed was the fierce, heated passion that raged between them.

His lips reached down and touched hers with a barely restrained hunger that stoked her own. They seemed to question at first and, finding the answer, sought more. His mouth played with her lips and, feeling them open to him, his tongue reached out and explored greedily. Her tongue met his, and they teased each other in a dance that sent all their senses reeling and crying for more...

MacKenzie knew a craving he had never felt before...and so many other complicated feelings. He had never felt so alive as he did this minute, so completely enveloped in waves of sensation as he felt April's body press against him with a need as elemental as the storm outside and the warmth of a summer sun. The combination was irresistible. As if, he thought wryly, he had any will left to resist.

His lips kissed and caressed with a possessiveness that jolted him, and he drew away for a moment, his eyes assessing. God, how he wanted her. In so many ways. Even while he knew it meant disaster. But at this particular moment, he didn't care. He knew somewhere deep inside that he had been waiting for this all his life. This caring. This gentle, aching link to another person, a puzzling mixture of sweetness and ferocity, of the need to give and take at the same time. Suddenly, nothing existed except this moment. And it had to continue.

MacKenzie saw the question in April's face, and in response he shook his head in defeat and saw the joy leap in her eyes, unaware that it was reflected in his own. He only knew the exultation of feelings acknowledged and returned and treasured.

He felt her hand on his face, exploring its planes, and his hand captured it, bringing it to his mouth. He kissed it simply, first on the palm, then on the back, and he was plunged into waves of longing, longing that could no more be suppressed.

April knew the moment it happened. It was as if a shade had been lifted from his eyes, and he had finally decided to reach out. She felt his hands, both tender and urgent as they reached for her clothes, resting for a moment on her breasts before continuing.

Don't stop, she willed him as she sensed the momentary hesitation.

She felt his hands moving once more to remove the clothing, and she wanted to help as her innermost part quivered and quaked with the need to join with him, to become one, to feel his strength and innate gentleness in the deepest core of her body.

April touched her lips to his cheek, then nuzzled his ear, rejoicing in the rushing momentum of passion that she felt rising in him...and in her. She could barely lay still under his hands, but she was afraid to move, afraid that he might once more distance himself. She didn't think she could stand that, not now when her body was afire and her heart drowning in love for him...and the need to express it in the most intimate and elemental way.

Somehow he had taken his coat off as well as hers, and they lay wrapped in the blanket, skin searing skin. For the moment April wondered how she could have been so cold earlier. For now she felt like rivers of fire as his lips found her breasts and fondled them as waves of pleasure swept through her. She felt him trembling as he moved closer to her, and she could hear the pounding of his heart. Through her torn riding skirt, she felt the throbbing of his need as he pressed even closer to her, igniting wildfires throughout her body, each feeding a giant conflagration, which greedily demanded more and more sensation, more and more touch, more and more everything. She had never known such raging need, or understood how powerful, how all-consuming it could be.

She could not suppress a small moan of desire, of urgency and she felt him stiffen with a passion as deep and compelling as her own. His lips touched her skin, and caressed it, then licked it, leaving trails of liquid fire as he went from one breast to another, the sensations multiplying until April thought she would die if he did not enter her and fulfill the promises he was making with every touch. Her hand went to the mound between his legs, a mound straining against the buckskin, hot and pulsating and full of the same imperative demand that so tormented her, with the necessity to become one, to explore the full eruption of colors and sounds and feelings each teased and awoke in the other. Most of all, she wanted the comfort of his body connected and bound to the deepest essence of her own, for then, and only then, would she truly feel she would know him, would become a part of him, and his life. And this she wanted more than she had ever wanted anything before.

She untied the rawhide thongs on his trousers and felt them giving way, releasing his straining manhood. It seemed so natural to caress him, her fingers touching and exploring, feeling the power and strength . . . and raw need. Almost from a distance, she heard him moan and shudder with desire barely held in check, and his lips hungrily attacked her mouth as his hands now searched to free her intimate entrance, as *she* had released him.

He groaned once more in frustration as his fingers swept away her riding skirt, only to find pantalets barring his way. Finally, he found the tie, and then he felt her sleek bare stomach. His hands wandered softly down her curved hips to a patch of hair, and he tangled his fingers in it, feeling her body rise and arch in response to his touch . . .

MacKenzie felt a kind of fear he had never experienced before. He knew there was a magic between them, and he was deathly afraid that he would do something to destroy it, to hurt her, to break the spell that wove them in its golden threads. Every fiber of his being was tingling with anticipation and a sweet gnawing hunger. He had always taken his pleasure quickly, without preliminaries; his partners having had little more interest than he did in anything but the quick physical act, whether it was done for money or lust. But now he ached to prolong each moment, to savor the waves of tenderness that swept him just by touching, to give April the same unconditional love and joy she was now offering him with such complete trust. *He loved her.* He knew it now, without question. And for these few priceless moments he wanted to tell her in every way possible.

His body lowered to hers with a control that required all his massive will to maintain. He let his manhood touch the most sensitive and tender part of her, and he felt her tremble under him. Her hands went around his shoulders, trying to draw him closer, but still he hesitated, wanting to prolong every second, every minute until the fire within them would brook no more delay. His lips once more touched her face, moving with a reverent tenderness from her eyes to her lips as he gently allowed his manhood to probe and caress and finally enter the soft velvet opening that was so irresistibly welcoming. MacKenzie tried to go slowly, to extract every exquisite rush of pleasure as their bodies came together in a symphony of sweet giving, then a burning passion that knew no limits. He thrust deeper and deeper as her body arched upward for more and more, each knowing they had not yet reached the limits of the comet that streaked across their consciousness with such great brilliance. The crescendo built, their bodies moving in tandem, exploring and filling hollows in their lives and knowledge and feelings. They were reaching for the moon, and the stars, and they carried ecstasy with them. With one final, wild, desperate plunge that reached into the core of April's being, they were flooded with billows of fulfillment, one great surge after another, and their world exploded with millions of lights falling around them, trapping them in a radiant glory that shook them both with its grandeur. And love. And belonging. And peace.

They lay together, MacKenzie still warm within her. April felt every after quake as her body quivered at his slightest movement, as her womanhood contracted and moved, seeking every sensation he offered, refusing to relinquish the joy of her body fused with his.

MacKenzie was equally reluctant to move. His tranquillity was like a drug ... her possession of that most sensitive part of him a priceless gift. He felt his shaft growing hard again within April's pulsating core, and he felt her own renewed awareness and hunger. Once more, they came together with a tender ferocity, in a primal rhythm that became a song as they reached new summits of pure, uncomplicated bliss ...

April and MacKenzie remained locked together until he felt her shiver and knew the fire was dying. Reluctantly, he finally moved, gently disengaging her and pulling on his buckskin britches. He looked at Davey, wondering how the boy could have slept through the howling storm outside and the intense one inside the cave ... but grateful that he had.

He quickly refueled the fire, his eyes rarely leaving April. He piled on enough to keep them until morning and regarded April with quizzical eyes. The invitation was too great to resist. He gathered another blanket, now almost dry, and draped it around her. Without a word, he dropped next to her and held out his arms. She rolled into them and nestled deep into his body, her mouth kissing the arm that held her. She knew he would not be there in the morning, but she was grateful for these minutes and hours. It was strange, she thought. She was in the mountains in the midst of a winter storm, and she had never felt safer. She snuggled even deeper into his curves and closed her eyes.

Chapter Fourteen

MacKenzie woke to an unfamiliar warmth. His arms were still wound tightly around April, and he felt both tenderness and desire rising within him. He did not welcome either of them this morning, but neither did he have regret. It had been too incredible an experience, too miraculous, to regret. But he did know it could not happen again. He could not risk leaving April with child, a quarter-breed bastard of an outlaw. Some of the old bitterness chewed at him as he remembered the few times he had encountered civilization as a child. Civilization! He had felt the hatred. He hadn't understood at first but it was soon made clear to him. He had the scars to remember. And because of all that had happened in the past weeks, a child of his would have a greater burden . . . a father labeled a rapist and a murderer.

He lay there quietly for minutes, relishing the feel of April in his arms. He wished he could tell her he loved her, but he could not. That would only make things more difficult. For both of them. Instead, his mouth gently touched the curly hair that had escaped the braid. He listened to her quiet breathing, and forced himself to keep from tightening his hold on her. Sweet Jesus, he wanted to keep her there forever.

MacKenzie could hear the wind outside, and he felt the growing chill in the cave. The fire was once more fading, and he needed to stoke it. It was, he judged, near dawn. A faint gray light was snaking its way into the cave. They needed to leave early if they were to reach his father's cabin before dark. His eyes fastened on the cave entrance, and he saw the snow flurries and knew they could not delay.

He carefully unraveled himself from April and the blankets, covering her up. He pulled his shirt on quickly as the cold hit him with a frigid blast. He found his coat, now dry from the fire, and slipped it on. After feeding the fire and watching it roar with new vigor, he walked to the cave entrance and stood there in lonely solitude.

Gray was spreading over a sky churning with rapidly moving clouds. They were threatening-looking lumps this morning, purple and black and fat with moisture...moisture he knew would become snow and ice and freezing rain. The first few flakes of snow were already settling on the earth, like sugar on a cake, but not nearly as benevolent. It would not be an easy journey today. But then, he reminded himself, none of it had been easy. For any of them.

He didn't know exactly how long he stood there, watching the snow's lazy pattern, knowing from experience it could soon change into a blizzard. He felt a strange lassitude. He did not want to leave this place where he had found such warmth and happiness and all-consuming pleasure. He did not want to leave because it must end here. And, God help him, he didn't want it to end, didn't know if he could make it end. Not with the days ahead when they would be forced together by weather and circumstance.

MacKenzie felt April next to him, felt her head leaning on his shoulder. He looked down, thinking how right it felt, having her there. She had the blanket wrapped around her, and his mind disobediently reminded him there was nothing under it. He stiffened with the knowledge, feeling his manhood swell once more within the confining britches.

"It's beautiful," she whispered, looking out at the softly falling snow.

"And dangerous," he replied grimly.

"Like you."

Damn. She could make him feel like a trembling child. His lips pressed tightly together. He wondered how he could keep from touching her.

But April had no such compunctions, and while one hand clutched the blanket, the other reached out and touched his hand. She wasn't ready to relinquish the MacKenzie who had introduced her to such dazzling feelings and emotions.

MacKenzie tried to keep his gaze from her, but the black velvet eyelashes banked her challenging blue eyes, and her mouth was swollen with the passion they had shared...and that both remembered. In every vivid detail.

He jerked away as if touched by a burning brand. And he was. His whole being was on fire. Once more, he felt himself tremble, felt the shudders that ripped through his body at her nearness.

"We must go," he said, self-anger making his voice harsh. "Get the boy." He stalked out of the cave, into the frozen world he knew and understood. *What in hell was happening to him?*

The horses struggled against a howling wind and snow that was becoming denser by the minute. They had been on the trail nearly eight hours, and MacKenzie knew they would be hard put to reach the cabin. Wrapping a blanket tighter around Davey, he kneed his horse, stepping up the pace despite the treacherous footing. It was becoming a race, and MacKenzie didn't intend to lose. There was too much at stake. The weather was worsening faster than he had ever seen it, and for the first time he knew a real fear of the mountains. He could no longer make out the trail that, in the best of times, was only slightly visible. He used landmarks instead . . . the cliff shaped like the bow of a ship, the knotted, gnarled trunk of an ancient juniper, but even those were disappearing in the swirling snow. He was moving by instinct more than anything else . . . and prayer, as unfamiliar as it was to him after years of rejecting it completely. It had been his father's refuge...as much as the mountains had been...but his father's religion had been cold and harsh, as merciless as the mountains and their many moods. Retribution had been its keystone. MacKenzie could still hear the echo of his father's curses of damnation against those who had sinned against his family and taken that which should have been his.

MacKenzie had heard the story often enough.

His father's family, an old clan with a wild and proud history, was proscribed in the 1700s...outlawed by the British for their constant attempts to restore the Stuarts to the British throne. Their lands were taken and their leaders beheaded or sold as slaves. It was called transportation, but the title made

no difference. It was still slavery, which was worse than death
to the proud Scots . . . to be auctioned off and forced to labor
in another man's fields or home. The clan members who escaped such a fate became outlaws and remained outlaws when
other clans submitted to British rule.

MacKenzie's grandfather had been publicly hanged by the
family that usurped the MacKenzie lands, and Rob Mac-
Kenzie had fled Scotland for France, then America, with little
more than his pipes and kilts. He retreated to the Kentucky
mountains, then moved farther west where, he heard, the
mountains resembled the craggy Scotland highlands. But he
never forgot the injustices he felt had been inflicted on his
family, or the tales of old days when clans raided one another
for sport. His background was thievery when he and his father
had robbed for their needs, and it was a practice he continued
in America until he was caught and almost hung like his father. He had escaped and climbed to a place where no white
man would ever find him . . . unless he wanted them to. He had
found refuge for a short time with an Indian tribe where he
learned many of the skills he needed in return for teaching them
to use the white man's rifles they had stolen. It was 1834, and
Rob MacKenzie became one of the first of the mountain men,
following Jeremiah Smith by only a few years. Now the men
were spotted throughout the Rocky Mountains, nearly all of
them hiding or running from something. MacKenzie had always understood them, but had not felt a part of their suspicious brotherhood . . . until now.

MacKenzie brushed away the bitter thoughts as he sought
familiar sights. He felt Davey wriggle with cold in his arms, and
he wrapped his arms tighter around the boy. And prayed.

April was numb. The cold had seeped through every layer of
her clothes and into her bones. Her hands, in the heavy leather
gloves, could hardly cling to the reins as her horse wearily followed MacKenzie's Appaloosa. Her eyes fastened on Mac-
Kenzie's back but now, more often than not, it disappeared in
the snow and she depended upon the horse to follow. She knew
MacKenzie was breaking the trail, which was now high with
snow. He frequently looked behind, but still she was seized by
numbing fear. What if she got lost? She scolded herself.

MacKenzie would never let it happen, but still...it was so cold. So very, very cold. She looked around, wondering how MacKenzie knew where he was going. Everything looked the same to her, like an icy blanket, white and pale and deadly. *Dear God, how much longer?* She felt her horse stumble, then sidestep as it tried to regain its balance. She grabbed for the saddle as she felt herself falling. She screamed.

Everything was fuzzy. Why was it so fuzzy? April tried to lift her head, but it wouldn't cooperate. She heard the thrashing horse next to her, and she tried to reach out and touch it but she felt as if someone had tied her down. *MacKenzie.* Where was MacKenzie? And then he was beside her, his hands, wrapped in torn cloth to keep them warm, fondling her face and running expertly over her body. MacKenzie. She felt a warmth flood her. He was here. He would take care of her. She felt his lips on her face, saw what looked like tears before they froze on his cheek like scars, she thought, as she tried to respond. She finally struggled half upright with supreme effort. She had to help him. She couldn't bear to see his ravaged face.

"April." How nice her name sounded on his lips, she thought sleepily. But just as she savored the sound, she felt pain on cheeks she thought numb, and she realized he had slapped her. She looked at him with astonishment.

"April," he said again, urgency in his voice. "You have to help me."

"Help...?"

"Can you stand?"

She would have died for him, but she didn't know if she could stand. She took his hand and, using his strength, slowly rose, feeling her legs quake under her. She saw the horse thrashing in the snow, and her gloved hand tightened against MacKenzie's as she stared at him questioningly.

"His leg's broken," MacKenzie said, his voice oddly restrained. His hand reached out and stroked the horse's neck, and it quieted under his touch. He stayed there a moment, still rubbing the horse gently. With bleak eyes, he turned to April.

"You take my horse," he said as he moved away from the horse that lay quiet now. He made her walk, knowing she needed the movement to revive her legs, her body. When they reached the patiently waiting Appaloosa, he lifted her into the saddle behind Davey. He walked the horse several feet, then tied the reins to a tree.

His face etched in gravity, he turned back to her. "I won't be long," he said, and the words seemed forced from his throat.

April sat on the horse, clutching Davey, knowing what was coming. She wasn't quite prepared, however, for the sound of gunfire, which echoed through the cold, frozen forest like thunder. Nor was she prepared for MacKenzie's expression when he materialized next to her. It was harder than she had ever seen it. She hadn't thought it possible. Even as thick, driving snowflakes clouded her vision, she could see the agony in his eyes. He took the reins in his hands and started walking. He didn't look back.

MacKenzie led the Appaloosa through drifts two and three feet high. He stumbled and fell but still he kept going, his feet like burning embers under the layers of cloth he had added to the moccasins. He had stopped only once, to cut a blanket and wrap pieces around the inadequate footwear. Ice coated his cheeks and made icicles of his eyelashes. As he had done in the desert, MacKenzie put one foot in front of the other, hoping they would support him a little longer . . . just a little longer. Where in God's name was the cabin?

April saw it first . . . a shadow in the distance. At first she thought it a mirage in the graying light, and then the outlines became clearer and clearer. She didn't even try to think how MacKenzie had found it. It was enough that it was here. She looked at MacKenzie, and slowly realized, even in her own cold and tired daze, that he was plodding on as before, completely unaware that they had found safety.

"MacKenzie," she called, but there was no answer, nor did he slow. It seemed as if he would lead them straight past the shelter. She jerked the reins, nearly spilling Davey, and finally MacKenzie responded, turning to her with a puzzled face. She stretched out her arm toward the cabin, and saw realization grow on his face. Without a word, he changed direction and moved toward the cabin, his face grimly shuttered as he released the reins and worked the latch on the door. It didn't want to open under the fumbling of his frozen fingers. April, now unmindful of her own cold agony, lifted Davey from the horse and slipped down, making her own way laboriously through the heavy snow. She took off one of the huge gloves and awkwardly unlatched the door.

April fetched Davey, who had sat down in the snow, too tired and cold to do anything else, and pushed him into the cabin. She watched as MacKenzie entered slowly behind her, every movement impossibly slow and deliberate, and she knew he must be in great pain. Frostbite? Please, no!

Her own immense discomfort meant nothing. Davey and MacKenzie needed her help.

She looked around the cabin, noting its neat, spartan nature, looking for anything that she could use. Thank God, firewood was piled neatly in one corner.

The matches. Where were the matches? Out of one eye, she saw Davey crawl into MacKenzie's lap and saw MacKenzie's arms, almost unconsciously, wrap around the boy. But both were so cold and wet, there was no warmth in either of them.

Matches, April reminded herself. Where . . . ? MacKenzie's coat. She searched frantically, feeling his shivers through material never meant for such intense temperatures. He tried to stand, to help her, but he simply couldn't move again. His legs collapsed under him and he stumbled as she reached to catch him and, with strength she didn't know she had, lowered him onto the rope bed. She tried his pockets again, finally triumphantly coming up with several long matches. She piled wood in the fireplace and tried to light it. The flame sputtered and died, and she tried again. This time a tiny spark hit the dry wood, and she watched as a small red glow inched along a juniper log. She stood there for a moment, incredibly grateful as the thick gum on the log sizzled and sparked and flamed, spreading golden light and the first surge of warmth into the cabin's icy interior.

Disregarding her own overwhelming need to stay close to the fire and soak up a little of its heat, she once more studied the cabin and its meager furnishings. It had been deserted for longer than a little while. Dust and dirt clung to the otherwise flawlessly neat interior. The smell of mold and disuse was heavy. Her eyes finally settled on several worn blankets piled at the end of the bed, and her indecision ended immediately. She pushed aside the enervation caused by cold and weariness, which threatened to paralyze her.

Lifting Davey from MacKenzie's lap, she placed him in front of the fire, as close as she could safely set him. Then she turned to the man who had once more risked his life for theirs. She carefully unwrapped the freezing wet cloth from around his moccasins, and with great difficulty loosened the frozen thongs, finally pulling the leather from his legs. She looked at them with worried eyes; they were blue and purple, and altogether unnatural looking. April looked up, and saw MacKenzie's eyes on her face. His whole body was shaking with cold, and she was seized by a terrible urgency. She took one of the dry blankets at the end of the rough cot and wrapped it around him, then took the second and wrapped it tightly around his feet and legs. She wanted to rub them, but knew she could not. She had learned that much from a surgeon when her father had been posted in the cold northwest. The frozen limbs would have to warm gradually. MacKenzie silently endured her efforts, not even a facial muscle reflecting the burning pain she knew he must be feeling. His eyes were as hooded and unfathomable as the first time she had seen him.

The first time! It seemed like years ago, now he was so much a part of her life. Her life and soul. Tears gathered at the corners of her eyes as love and tenderness and desperation flooded her. He had to be all right. He had to. Her hands increased the pressure on the blanket, pressing it against his feet, trying to speed the warmth.

MacKenzie watched her helplessly. He knew the danger of frostbite, of subsequent gangrene, but he couldn't move if he wanted to. Every part of him seemed frozen stiff, and his fatigue rendered him powerless. But she should be seeing to Davey, and herself. He tried to tell her that, but she ignored his half-frozen muttering. He didn't know how long she stayed beside him, keeping the blankets tight against his legs, his feet, but finally he felt a tiny warmth creep into them, and the burning sensation diminished in intensity.

Heat from the now roaring fire seeped through the room, gradually replacing some of the fierce icy cold. The cabin, he knew, was tightly built and once warmed would stay that way as long as the fire was continually fed and tended. His father had been nothing if not meticulous. Still, MacKenzie could hear the wild howl of the wind outside, and knew they were not yet safe. Their food supply was low, and they would be in real peril if he could not soon hunt. And the wood...it, too, was in short supply. His expression grew even grimmer as he realized the extreme danger in which he had placed April and Davey. He silently cursed himself for not staying with them at Amos's cabin...to wait for troops, which could guarantee their safety. But he had let his own selfish desires rule his judgment, allowed his compelling need for April to place her in intolerable danger. He had, he knew, almost killed them once more, and he hated himself for it. He had always had a certain pride in himself, he realized ruefully, in his own skills and detachment. It was what had made him a good scout and kept him alive these past years. But that often arrogant objectivity was gone now...destroyed within a matter of weeks until he no longer knew who or what he was.

April's head was leaning over his legs, her chestnut hair glowing in the firelight. Her tenacity and strength astounded him, though he knew by now it should not. She had surprised him over and over again. Surprised and amused and delighted him, and frustrated him. He had never met anyone like her. She must be tired beyond reason, and yet she had not stopped moving since they reached the cabin. Just then she looked up, and he caught the triumph in her eyes and the smile on her lips, and he felt his heart ache. He could never mean anything but death and misery to her. He wanted to give her happiness, but had brought her nothing but hardship and trouble. If he had not fully realized it before, he did now. He moved slightly, retreating from her touch.

"Look after the boy," he said shortly. "And yourself. My legs will be fine now." He hesitated. "Thank you," he added stiffly.

The formal words were like a blow to April. She knew he was once again moving away from her. She had hoped, believed, they were beyond that now, that their common danger had bonded them even tighter. But it was the opposite, and she thought she knew why. He was blaming himself for what had nearly happened. She would not let him.

"I begged to come," she said. "And I don't regret it."

"You should," MacKenzie rasped. "If not for yourself, for the boy. You don't belong here. You never did. You never will." The words were purposely cruel. He had to break this link between them, had to make her understand there was no future together. Even a short one.

April's face grew taut with stubbornness. "You're wrong. I belong with you. We belong with you. I don't care what you say," she said. "You can't change how I feel." She turned away from him and went closer to the fire, her face easing as she saw Davey asleep on the floor. She wanted to join him, Lord, how she wanted to join him. She was so tired. But the cabin creaked with the force of the blizzard outside, and she remembered the horse. She looked at MacKenzie and knew he had the same thought. He tried to stand but stumbled, and April knew he could not walk yet. Firming her shoulders, she tucked her chin into MacKenzie's heavy sheepskin jacket and started for the door. "I'll take care of the horse."

"Like hell you will," he replied and tried again. But once more his body failed him, and he fell back on the cot, his grizzled face now savage with frustration. He watched with rage as she ignored his words and unbolted the door, disappearing into the gray evening.

April had seen the small shed when they rode in, and now she took the Appaloosa's reins and led him into the stall of what was little more than a lean-to. At least he would have some shelter from the snow and wind. She angrily berated herself for not bringing MacKenzie's gloves, but then she probably wouldn't have been able to do anything anyway. They were altogether too large and bulky. But still . . . her hands were getting colder by the moment, slowing down each of her motions. She awkwardly unclenched the saddle, and was barely able to catch it as it fell, precious saddlebags, bedrolls and all. She took just an extra second to unwrap a blanket and settle it on the horse. After all, she and Davey and MacKenzie had a fire. April put her face against his muzzle in comfort, wishing she had some oats or an apple or anything. He had done well today. His breath looked like smoke in the air, and she hoped he would be all right. MacKenzie should be better in the morning and he would know what to do. He always did. With that comforting thought, she headed back to the cabin, bedrolls tucked under her arm while cold red hands buried themselves in Mac-Kenzie's sheepskin jacket. She sniffed it appreciatively. It smelled like him. Leathery and masculine and woodsy.

April hesitated before going in despite the cold. She knew he would still be angry. He was always angry when he allowed any emotion to show. Almost always, she amended with a small smile as she thought of the previous night.

She pushed open the door, allowing a blast of cold air to enter with her before she could push it shut again and drop the bar across it. Davey was still asleep, and MacKenzie was sitting up, his back against the wall as he eyed the door impatiently, his lips compressed in their usual tight line. He had obviously not mellowed in the few minutes she was gone; he seemed, in fact, even more frustrated. From the mess of blankets on the floor, it was obvious that he had tried to walk again—and failed.

April dropped her burdens on the floor and unwrapped them, placing the wet things near the fire and drawing a dry blanket around Davey. She then handed a blanket to Mac-Kenzie. "You need some rest," she said, and braced herself for the sparks she knew she would see.

She was not disappointed. "You expect me to sleep here like a wee babe while you and the boy sleep on the floor?"

"Davey's content," she answered, "and I don't want to disturb him, and as for me...I thought..." She looked at one side of the bed longingly. She wanted to sit, to lie down. The weariness was catching up with her now...the fatigue and the fear and the cold. She knew she would always remember the bone-aching cold. And more than anything she wanted the comfort of his presence, of his body. She wanted to share her warmth with him and know they were safe. Her legs almost gave under her, and she took a step toward him before they gave way completely and she felt herself falling. Her eyes closed before she saw him quickly lean forward and catch her in his arms, but she felt their power...and gentleness. She barely heard his soft, crooning voice. "Such a brave girl." She felt his lips on her brow, and she didn't want to open her eyes. Not ever.

She fell asleep there, finally captured by complete exhaustion and by the comfort of his closeness. She didn't know he held her there for minutes that turned into hours, unmindful of anything but the light, courageous bundle in his arms and the strange feeling of contentment that spread within him. He waited until her breathing deepened and he knew she would not wake easily.

MacKenzie finally shifted his burden, lying her flat on the bed and covering her with blankets. He used the side of the bed to help him rise, feeling once more the sharp pain in his feet and the exhaustion that had numbed his body and made it useless. He stumbled, more than walked, to the fireplace, piling new logs on the still blazing fire. He then took one of the drying blankets, wrapped it around himself and lay down next to Davey. He thought of April on the bed and hungered for the feel of her. It was a hunger he would tame. He had to. But Lord, at what price? He didn't know how long they would be here; they could be snowed in for days, weeks, even months. The very thought was torture. Despite his complete exhaustion, MacKenzie lay awake for hours...wondering what in the hell he would do. He listened to the lonely wail of the wind and a faraway coyote and the crackle of burning wood, and he wondered . . .

Chapter Fifteen

The next two days were among the most miserable April had ever spent.

The blizzard continued unabated, and they were forced to remain together in the small cabin but, as far as MacKenzie and April were concerned, they might have been hundreds of miles apart.

No matter what April tried, MacKenzie seemed to withdraw further and further. Neither she nor Davey seemed able to coax even the smallest smile from him, although in the evenings, MacKenzie would spend hours with Davey, telling of Scottish adventures and legends and history. They constituted most of the stories he knew, stories that he thought would distract an active young boy confined to a small cabin. But he never smiled. Never.

Once in a while, April would catch his eyes fastened on her, but they were always hooded, and she couldn't tell what he was thinking. Or feeling. Then he would slowly turn away, not quickly as if caught unexpectedly, but slowly, deliberately. It hurt, but then she suspected that in some way it was meant to. That he was warning her in the only way he thought she might understand. Words certainly hadn't done it.

The morning after their arrival, April had awakened cold and alone, her hands stretched out for someone who wasn't there. In her half-awake state, she was seized by fear and emptiness...such a great emptiness. Her eyes flew open, but the room was dark, lit only by the flickering flames of the fire. Her eyes adjusted to the dim light as her heart pounded with a sudden panic. Where was Davey? MacKenzie?

It slowed only slightly as she saw the two forms on the floor, one small and one large, each sleeping peacefully. Why had he left her? She remembered his arms around her last night, the comforting warmth of his body, the tender feel of his lips on her forehead. Why had he left? There was room for both of them. She drew her blankets closer around her as she felt the chill. She wasn't quite sure whether it was from the cold that was once more invading the cabin or from the loneliness she instantly felt at MacKenzie's abandonment. She huddled on the bed, wondering what was happening outside. Was it still night or had dawn come? Was it still snowing or had it stopped? It was impossible to tell with the two windows shuttered and barred, but she no longer heard the battering of the wind against wood. There was only complete quiet except for the occasional tiny explosion from the fire as it found a pocket of sap in the wood.

She knew she should get up and put new logs on the fire, but she felt an unusual languor, created, she thought, from a combination of leftover weariness and disappointment at finding herself alone on the bed. She wanted MacKenzie next to her. She yearned to fit into his hard, muscled body and feel his arms protectively around her. *Get up, April. Don't torture yourself.*

April moved slowly, trying to infuse herself with the old energy. Somehow, MacKenzie had taken her coat off, but all her other clothes remained and she felt heavy and burdensome, even while grateful for the warmth they provided. How could he be attracted to her? She knew her hair must be tangled despite the ugly practical braid, and strands had come loose, matting around her face. She had not had a bath in days and suspected her face was smudged and dirty. She felt woefully lacking in every way. She buried her head in the blanket like a child, trying to escape the reality of a misdeed.

Another need cropped up, one that wouldn't be denied. She would have to get up and make a trip outdoors. She dreaded it. If she opened the door, she would wake MacKenzie, and she wasn't quite sure if she wanted to face him at the moment. And she shivered at the thought of baring even a part of herself in the frigid temperatures.

But it had to be done.

She finally struggled to her feet, feeling the chill in the cabin that even the fire couldn't alleviate completely. Reluctantly she moved to the diminishing pile of logs and added two to the blaze. She found the sheepskin coat next to the bed and pulled it on. When she reached the door, she looked at MacKenzie before unbarring it and saw that his eyes were open and steady on her.

She went over to him, stooping down. "How are you?"

He gave her only an almost imperceptible nod in answer as he cautiously sat up. His face had settled into its old, grim, implacable lines. "You're not to go out alone," he said, rougher than he intended. Then his voice gentled as he tried to explain. "You don't know this area…there could be crevices just barely covered over, or you could easily get lost." He hadn't lost that terrible fear from yesterday when he was afraid April and Davey might die in the storm. He didn't want to take any more chances.

"You can't go with me," she replied, a small, embarrassed smile on her lips, and he immediately understood.

He used a corner of a chair to help himself stand, then limped painfully to the door. He took the bar down and opened the door. The snow was still falling in huge thick flakes. April could barely see the shed.

He closed it again, then fetched his coat, shrugging it on before reopening the door. He took her arm protectively and headed toward the shed, then nodded for her to go to its side. April flushed, remembering that first morning after they had been taken by MacKenzie. She had been mortified when he so nonchalantly acknowledged bodily functions. After so many years of pretending they really didn't exist, particularly in the presence of men, she found it awkward, if not difficult, to understand his casual acceptance of such needs even while she knew it was an absurd social custom not to do so. Without another word, she did what she was told. For the sake of her chilled flesh and her mental discomfort, she quickly took care of her physical needs, straightened her clothes and, with as much dignity as she could muster, returned to MacKenzie, who was looking after his horse.

His veiled eyes might have held a second of amusement at her obviously wounded modesty despite their weeks together, but the severity of his facial expression did not change, and she wondered if she'd imagined it.

"Why did you leave me last night?" she asked bluntly, deciding to attack.

"Because it's best," he replied with a deep frown.

"I needed you," she said, throwing her pride to the winds. She found it meant little compared to her overwhelming need for him.

"You don't need anyone, April," he said, his eyes fierce, blazing with something April couldn't identify. "Much less me or the trouble I carry."

"You didn't do anything..."

"Damn it, April. I have led you into one danger after another. You and Davey have nearly died several times because of my selfishness, because I took him when I had no right. Because I didn't stay with you at Amos's cabin. Do you know how close you both came to freezing to death yesterday?" She flinched at the bitter self-condemnation in his voice as he continued slowly, painfully. "I wanted you...wanted you both...just a little longer, and I almost killed you." A muscle flexed in his jaw. "We have to forget what happened...back there at the cave. And when it's clear enough, I'm taking you back."

She stared at him. "But you can't..."

His voice was harsh. "I can and I will...and I'll not leave you with a bastard child, a part-Indian bastard." He turned to her, his expression fierce. "Do you understand, April? It can never happen again."

"No," she said defiantly. "You can't change the way I feel, no matter how hard you try."

She could barely hear his words, but she knew they were a long, frustrated curse. "It won't happen again," he repeated with finality.

He took her arm and, ignoring a brief moment of resistance, led her back to the cabin.

He was as good as his words in the next few days as the snow continued to fall heavily. Confined to the cabin, they ate the remaining food, and any conversation was between Davey and MacKenzie, who was unfailingly gentle with the boy. He virtually ignored April except for a few polite words. On his occasional short trips to get wood and see to the horse, he had found a place under a stand of trees where the snow was not as thick and the animal could dig for grass under the snow with his hoofs. There were also oats and a little fodder in the shed from his father's time.

But even MacKenzie was reluctant to venture far in the blinding snow, and tension in the small cabin continued to grow.

On the third day, April rose after a sleepless, lonely night and opened the cabin door to find that the snow had finally stopped falling. Instead, there seemed an unearthly peace this morning. Fresh snow glistened and sparkled in the first glimmers of a rising sun. The sky, frothy yesterday with dark clouds, was now pink and gold and the palest pristine blue. The pines were wreathed with crowns of white, tinted by the gentle colors of dawn, and their branches dipped with silver ornaments. It seemed a fairyland. Pure and untouched and lovely. April almost forgave the blast of freezing air that accompanied it.

She stood in awe, unable to say meaningless words. And then she felt MacKenzie's presence.

MacKenzie understood her silence. Only too well. The scene seemed entirely too perfect to be real. But he also knew the beauty disguised the dangers: drifts that covered chasms, hunger that lured the predators; the blanket of white that hid landmarks and could easily deceive; a numbing cold that could kill silently. "You're not to go alone," MacKenzie reminded April. His voice was harsh, without tenderness.

Davey was just waking when they reentered the cabin, eyes crusted with sleep, and April knew she would have to make a trip outside, but MacKenzie moved quicker, putting his lighter coat on and bundling Davey up. April eyed him speculatively, then gave him, instead, the sheepskin coat. "You'll need this," she said, meeting his direct gaze with one of her own, refusing to back down. MacKenzie shrugged and took it.

MacKenzie's scarcity of words continued for the rest of the morning. After he and Davey returned, he distributed what little food they had to Davey and April despite her protests that he had kept nothing for himself.

"I'll find some game," he said shortly. "Stay inside the cabin until I return." His tone permitted no argument, and April nodded, any rebellion quelled by the hungry rumbling of her stomach. She watched him disappear out the door without further words.

The day seemed endless. Occasionally April would unbar the door and look out, but each time a blast of cold air would blow in, and it would take hours for the fire to reheat the cabin. She would have been frightened if she had not, by now, known MacKenzie so well. Despite his pronounced limp, she knew he would bring food back.

April used part of the time to take some snow from outside the cabin and heat it in a large pot she found in the corner. She poured some of it in a pitcher for drinking water and used the remainder to wash both herself and Davey. He still looked like a chimney sweep, and she knew she didn't look much better, despite a similar attempt to wash clean the day before. She had felt self-conscious then, trying to wash in front of MacKenzie, and had just rearranged the dirt. April found the mirror MacKenzie had used earlier to shave. There had been a strange intimacy in watching him perform such a personal task. She had tried to avert her eyes, but couldn't, and she knew he was watching her through the mirror. Now she looked in it, and promptly wished she hadn't.

Her face was red and raw, first, she supposed, from exposure from the sun, then the cold. Her hair, which she usually kept washed and tamed in a neat knot at her neck, had escaped much of the braid and went in all sorts of odd directions. It had lost its reddish shine and looked dark and heavy and ugly. Her hands were likewise far from the soft white skin she had previously pampered. They, too, were raw-looking and covered with calluses. April regarded herself sorrowfully, wishing for the luxury of sitting down to cry, but there was Davey, restless Davey, to think about. *How could MacKenzie care for her at all?*

She steeled herself against self-pity. MacKenzie certainly hadn't asked her to fall in love with him. She had all but thrown herself at him. And if she was completely honest with herself, which she was loath to be, she could delete the words "all but."

April didn't understand how quickly she had fallen in love with a man who didn't want to be loved. After David's death, after four years of complete purgatory, of waiting, she had vowed never to subject herself to such agony again. And now she was in love with a man whose life expectancy was probably even lower than her husband's had been.

And yet, she would do anything, sacrifice anything, to be with him. Anything but Davey. Deep in her soul, she knew MacKenzie would never allow anything to happen to her son. Which was why she was so ready to give her heart, to journey with him anyplace, under any conditions. But despite that night before the storm, he had given no further indication he felt the same. He had never, ever mentioned the word "love." He had merely taken what was offered.

She missed him even now, even that glowering presence that held her at arm's length. She missed the masculine scent of him, the way he dominated the cabin, the catlike grace with which he moved. She missed everything about him. And she always would, no matter where she was, or where he might go.

April played absentmindedly with Davey. He had brought out MacKenzie's carved horse and they discussed, most solemnly, a name for it.

"Horse," Davey finally said.

"That's no name," April scoffed. She thought she had offered some much better ones.

"That's what MacKenzie calls his horse," Davey insisted.

"He does?" April said. Come to think of it, she had never heard him call his horse much of anything. She wrinkled her nose. "Horse?"

"Well, he says that's what it is. No sense putting fancy names on it, he said. It'll do the same no matter what you call him."

April sighed. MacKenzie didn't even want to get familiar with his damned horse. What chance had she? She supposed she was lucky that he called her April. When he wasn't calling her Mrs. Manning. Thank God that, at least, had stopped.

"I still think," she insisted, "that *this* horse would like a name. Devil take MacKenzie."

"That's it," Davey grinned like a pleased gremlin. "I'll call him Devil."

It wasn't exactly what April had had in mind, but her son looked so pleased with himself she didn't protest.

"I can't wait to tell MacKenzie," Davey ran on. "When do you think he'll be back?"

April flinched. It would be just like Davey to explain exactly how Devil had been named. "It shouldn't be long ... let's look outside." She sincerely hoped it wouldn't be long for many reasons. She could hear her stomach growl and churn with hunger, and she knew Davey must be feeling the same empty feeling. They still had some flour, but without lard or fat or meat she didn't know quite what to do with it.

She and Davey bundled in their heavy clothes and opened the door, going out quickly and closing it behind them to keep the cold air from snaking its way inside. Once again, she thought how beautiful it was as the snow glistened in the sun. Davey was silent. He had seen snow in Boston, but never like this, never so purely white.

"Let's build a fort," he said suddenly, his face aglow with excitement. He had never been allowed to play in the snow in Boston, not unless he and April sneaked out. Even then they had faced disapproving stares when they returned ... which had spoiled everything.

April remembered MacKenzie's warning, but at the moment she decided not to heed it. *He* had gone out, and had been away for nearly half a day, and she, as well as Davey, already had cabin fever. It wasn't fair that he could roam the woods while she and Davey stayed penned in the sparse cabin. Besides, she reasoned, they were almost at the door of the cabin. The eagerness on Davey's face precluded any additional caution. She caught her son's excitement, and together they started building their own peculiar version of a fortification.

Busy packing the walls with the same diligence her five-year-old had, April didn't realize that Davey had moved farther and farther afield in his search for branches to use as cannons. She heard his frightened voice before she even noticed he was not at her side.

"Mama."

April looked up, and her body turned numb as she saw a wolf approach from the woods, its fangs bared and a small growl coming from deep in its throat.

Oh, God, not again. Why had she not heeded MacKenzie's words?

The wolf was approaching cautiously, all menacing, lean grace. Davey was between her and the animal. April very carefully stood and took one slow step after another toward her son, afraid any quick movement might bring a similar response from the wolf. Perhaps her size might frighten the animal...she knew they usually went after smaller game. Like her son.

The wolf stopped but didn't retreat. April continued, one terrified step after another, all the time whispering to Davey to keep him still, keep him calm. She saw the wolf's fierce dark eyes follow every step and almost felt the lithe power of the beast when it seemed to tense as if ready to spring. Still she continued, fearful her legs would buckle under her. It seemed like hours but she finally reached Davey and very deliberately picked him up. She took one step backward, then another, and her throat caught when she saw the wolf stalking them like a rabbit or a young deer. If only she could get to the door. She heard the growl again. It came from deep within the animal, and she shuddered at its vicious sound. Why hadn't she at least brought the pistol? She imagined it was still in the shed where she had left it last night. Only ten more feet, then eight, then six. The wolf poised for attack, and April knew she wouldn't make it in time. She could only hope to divert the animal until Davey escaped inside.

She whispered to Davey, "When I put you down, go inside and bar the door, no matter what. Wait until MacKenzie gets back before you open it. Do you understand?"

Davey didn't. Not exactly. But his mother's tone was more grim than he had ever heard it. He nodded.

He was halfway to the door when April heard a low whistle and saw the wolf pause, then turn in the direction of the sound. In numb amazement, April saw the beast bound toward MacKenzie who stood at the edge of the clearing. For a moment, her heart stopped as she expected the wolf to lunge at MacKenzie. But the scout's rifle was at his side and he stood there unconcerned, a rare smile on his face.

The wolf stopped at MacKenzie's feet and sat, his previously lethal-looking teeth bared in what could be nothing but a grin. April's eyes went from animal to man, almost feeling the affection flowing between the two, although MacKenzie made no move to touch the beast.

April felt herself trembling almost uncontrollably. She felt Davey's hand snake itself into her glove, and knew he was also suffering from the aftermath of fear.

MacKenzie faced them both, the slight smile still on his face, his eyes warm. She had done it again, risking her life for her son's. He thought he had seldom seen such courage as he came into the clearing. April Manning had been willing to be torn apart for Davey's safety. He had thought her beautiful before but never quite so much as now.

"You need not worry," he said gently now. "The wolf will not hurt you . . . he was just guarding the cabin. He would not have attacked unless someone attacked me." He took a step toward Davey, and the wolf rose and followed at MacKenzie's heel. Davey stepped back, but MacKenzie stretched out his hand toward the boy, and Davey hesitantly, fearfully, took a trusting step toward him.

MacKenzie's hand reached Davey's and took the small one, urging him even closer, until boy and wolf were almost together. He could feel the trembling of Davey's grasp, and he felt brief pleasure that the boy so trusted him. He stooped until the three of them were all at the same height. "Let him sniff you," MacKenzie told Davey quietly, and Davey bravely withstood the animal's inspection. "Now you," he said, looking at April who stood, still mute and almost in shock. When she didn't react, he reached out his other hand for her, and she took it, following his example and stooping. She tried to hide her fear as the huge, lean animal sniffed her, its tongue flopping out of the side of its fierce-looking mouth.

MacKenzie stood, pulling her up. "He'll protect both of you now . . . with his life if necessary."

April couldn't rid herself of fear quite that easily. "I don't understand."

"I raised him from a cub . . . his mother had been killed," MacKenzie said slowly. "I take him when I go to the valley, but when I'm scouting I bring him here . . . to his old home. I think he's safer here. People . . . hunters . . . wouldn't understand a tame wolf."

"Tame?" April finally managed. The wolf had seemed anything but tame to her.

"He's not afraid of men, not like other wolves. He would be easy prey. Sometimes I wonder if I shouldn't have taken him back to the wilds sooner. There's no place for a wild thing in civilization."

April wondered for a brief moment if MacKenzie was thinking only of the wolf. She looked at the animal and sensed why MacKenzie and the wolf appeared so well matched. They were alike, these two. Both creatures of the forest: lean, graceful and cautious.

She felt Davey move next to her, and she saw his small hand touch the wolf, who now tolerated it with an air of complete indifference.

"Does he have a name?" April asked, feeling foolish as MacKenzie raised his eyebrows quizzically.

"Name?" he questioned.

April remembered Davey's earlier revelation about the horse. Her mouth turned up in a sudden smile. "Wolf, I suppose?" she said mischievously.

MacKenzie's throat constricted. He liked her more every day. Liked? Loved! He longed to reach out and touch her, to place his fingers at the corner of her smiling lips and taste her sweetness again. His hand started to reach out, then fell back to his side. He nodded curtly and forced anger into his voice. "I thought I told you to stay inside."

April's smile faded, and MacKenzie felt he had just tortured a young live thing. But there was no help for it. He had to keep a distance. He had to... for both their sakes. He had to keep control, and he had to make sure she obeyed his commands... for her own safety.

"I...I...thought...we were just outside the cabin door."

"Damn it," he exploded. "Anything could happen just outside. You didn't even bring the gun with you."

"And if I had, your...pet...would be dead," she retorted, her anger growing at his sudden arrogance.

MacKenzie had no easy answer to that. He did not doubt it for a moment. April handled herself well in emergencies, and he knew by now she had not boasted when she had said she could use a pistol.

He looked at Davey. The boy's eyes were going from MacKenzie's face to his mother's. He sensed the sudden hostility and didn't understand it. His hand went to the wolf and buried itself in the deep, thick fur, his eyes clouded.

"We won't discuss it in front of the boy," MacKenzie said abruptly and turned away.

"Damn you, MacKenzie. You won't discuss anything. Ever. You just order."

He whirled around, astounded at the sudden fury in April's voice. Even the night of his escape, he had not heard such angry depths. He winced as she cautioned.

"You can't keep running from everything forever..."

"I'm not..." he started to say, then stopped. He *was* running away from her...as much as he was running from those who would take him to Defiance. Even if it was for her sake and Davey's, it was still running. Despite her words, he was not used to it. Yet it seemed all he was doing now. Running from the army. From his own tumultuous emotions. From April. Retreating. He was suddenly uncertain.

His right hand knotted in frustration. "I'm trying to keep you alive, damn it," he growled. "And you don't make it easy."

April's indignant face relaxed. That soft, telling burr was back in his voice, and she saw the shadow of pain flit across his eyes. She sought to break the tense silence. "Did you find some game?"

"Aye," he said. "An elk. I brought back what I could. I hung up the rest...to keep it from the wolves."

"Does that include your wolf?"

"He roams with them at times...when I'm not here. He'll stay close now to the cabin." He looked at her. "I meant what I said. Davey will be as safe with Wolf as with me. He's very protective..."

"I noticed," April said wryly. "I was sure he was going to attack." She shuddered, remembering those few horrible moments.

"I should have warned you," MacKenzie said. "But I thought I would see him before you did. If you had stayed in the cabin..."

April bit her lip in exasperation. "I know," she said. "But you can't expect us to remain locked up inside forever."

He nodded, knowing she was right. He should have realized how difficult it would be for an active young woman and child to stay inside, particularly when the outside was so inviting in the sunlight. It had been his fault, not hers. He was not used to women and children, and it had not occurred to him that their restlessness might override their obedience. It was just another example of why he needed to see them safely home. He couldn't protect them here, no matter how hard he tried.

MacKenzie, the wolf at his heels, turned and limped to where the Appaloosa was standing at the fringe of the clearing. He had been walking most of the morning, and each step worsened the pain in one of his feet. It still had not quite healed. He remembered the moment he had approached the clearing and had seen April's terrified face as she had whispered to Davey and turned to face the wolf alone...

Now he lifted two haunches of meat from the saddle. He set one on the ground while he took a knife to the other, cutting two large pieces of meat. He deliberated over what to do with the remaining carcass, finally deciding to hang it from a tree just outside the clearing. He wanted it no place near the shed where the Appaloosa stayed, in case it attracted wolves.

He looked up and saw April standing there, ready to take the meat. "I can cook it," she said. She looked at his feet, still clad in the knee-high moccasins. "You need to sit down, or lie down, or..."

April was a bit surprised when he handed her his bounty without comment. "I'll take care of the meat and horse first," he said. "Davey should get inside. The cold is deceptive."

"For you, too," she warned and was rewarded with a small, rueful smile and a nod.

"Soon," he agreed, and her heart caught at how the small smile relieved the harsh, uncompromising lines of his face. It was such a strong face, and yet it could be gentle and compassionate. When he would let it. With an effort, she forced herself to turn toward the cabin, ushering a reluctant Davey inside. Now that Davey's fear of the wolf was gone, he wanted to stay with the huge beast.

Compared to the food of the past few days, dinner was wonderful. April had roasted a large piece of elk on a spit, and had already started a soup, which she thought would be just right in the morning. There were no spices other than some salt that MacKenzie had brought from his own cabin in the valley, but she could thicken the soup with some flour and it would be warm and hearty. They all ate well, including MacKenzie, who had finally appeared and agreed to sit while she tended the fire. He said little, but April could feel his eyes on her.

She thought of the wolf. That a wolf should be his sole friend and companion seemed tragic to her. And yet, as she thought of them together there was a rightness about it. They *were* alike: fierce yet unexpectedly gentle, wild yet protective. She wondered how long it had taken MacKenzie to tame the wolf, and how long it would take her to gentle MacKenzie? Or even if she wanted to. Perhaps that was what attracted her so . . . that wild free spirit. And she wondered if it could ever, completely, be done? And whether some day either one—MacKenzie or the wolf—would turn on the one that limited their freedom?

Chapter Sixteen

The tension between April and MacKenzie was always there, live and sizzling, as October turned into November and November into December. Although there was no additional snow, except for an occasional flurry, the temperatures froze what was on the ground, and MacKenzie knew there was no way through the passes that led to his mountain hideout.

For him, it was a time of supreme joy and supreme agony.

He treasured every moment during the day with the boy and April, but each night was a long, hellish torment as he warred with himself. So far his iron determination to stay away from April had won, but just barely. And the open, wanting invitation in her eyes had not helped matters.

At his insistence, April slept in the bed with Davey, and he continued to use the floor. It did not bother him. He was used to sleeping on the ground, and the floor next to a fire was almost a luxury in itself. At least it would have been had April not been inches away.

He would often rise in the middle of the night and sit, watching her sleep and feeling himself grow rigid with need and desire. Her black lashes swept the eyes he could never dismiss from his thoughts, and her mouth beckoned him. What was always so agonizing was that he knew she was there for him...waiting, willing, needing. It was only his own willpower that kept him from the bed.

After minutes, even hours, of thus torturing himself, he would sometimes get up and go inside, letting the cold air douse a body nearly ready for explosion. Wolf would join him, and he would stare at the myriad stars haloing the white-clad mountains and wonder what had happened to him...to the man who had never needed or wanted anyone. One part of him longed to lose himself in the old protective isolation, but another knew he had been immeasurably enriched. He had been given unqualified love and trust by both April and Davey, and it had made him whole for the first time in his life.

Although the days had settled into a routine of activity, they were routine in no other way. So many moments were joyful treasures to be hoarded and remembered. All but the persistent ache in his loins that wouldn't go away. It was a constant reminder of the barrier between April and himself, of the potential disaster if he weakened in his resolve. A child. At times he would fantasize about having a child with April, and he would briefly allow his heart to soar. And then it would come plummeting down as he considered the consequences, the uncertain future such a child would have, the danger to April. And he would place the thought aside in some secret place within him and berate himself for his foolishness.

In the meantime, there were times of great sweetness and a belonging he had never known. Realizing the stark truth of April's accusing words the afternoon Wolf appeared, he started taking Davey and April for long walks every morning. With Wolf beside them, MacKenzie and Davey would explore fresh tracks in the snow, search for patches of grass for the Appaloosa and even indulge in occasional moments of snowball pelting.

April would usually stand back and watch, content with the sight of boy and man enjoying each other so completely, feeling the joy bubbling inside her that such was so. She had never seen MacKenzie so relaxed or Davey so happy. The scout even smiled on occasion, sometimes forgetting to catch himself, she thought impishly. Her only misery was his continued insistence that they stay apart at night. He recoiled from her slightest touch, shying as if burned when their fingers accidentally met at mealtimes. She would have been hurt and angered were it not for the fierce hunger his eyes could no longer hide, or the nights she woke and sensed his gaze on her and heard the frustrated closing of the door as he went outside.

She knew him well enough to realize that the only thing holding him back was pride, that deep, fierce pride that demanded he keep her and Davey safe. He mistakenly thought the danger lay within himself. It was a belief April intended to dissolve; to make him see that happiness also lay there. But she had decided to move slowly, to let him learn bit by bit what it meant to love. She had the time, she thought, as she looked at the icy cliffs and ravines still filled with snow, although the sun had washed some patches of earth clear. And the reward would be worth it. The future would take care of itself. She had to believe that . . . for she could no longer think of a life without MacKenzie.

MacKenzie continued to hunt alone in the afternoons, leaving Wolf with April and Davey. He thought they were safe enough from predators when guarded by the huge, protective beast. But he still warned them not to venture out of sight of the cabin. They had plenty of elk meat remaining, but MacKenzie didn't know how long they would be here, or whether they might be victim to another blizzard. He wanted skins for warmth and a sure supply of food. He brought back rabbit and venison, and he and April and Davey would smoke some, as well as dry strips of meat.

There was a warm intimacy about these days despite MacKenzie's grave reserve. April saw new sides of him daily: a sly sense of humor as he recited some Burns verse; a curiosity about everything that matched Davey's own; a tender playfulness as he wrestled with Davey on the cabin floor.

But she was restless, and MacKenzie recognized it. She was intrigued when one day he brought home something that would have appalled her months earlier: a bloody animal skin.

He cautiously watched her expression, a combination of interest and horror, and he gave her that rare slight smile. "I thought you might learn to dress a skin."

April eyed the bloody mess dubiously, wondering how it could ever become anything useful, especially under her hands. But she had been complaining she had little to do, and she could hardly decline. Besides, she had done much worse. She shuddered as she thought of the bear so many months ago, and how she had butchered it.

So she nodded and was immediately pleased she had. His eyes warmed to a rich charcoal, and the twist of his mouth grew a trace wider.

"What do I do first?" she said.

"I think we'll wash it first," he said, his eyes conveying a small twinkle as she continued to eye his prize dubiously.

April accompanied him to the stream near the cabin. It was iced over, but MacKenzie had chopped a hole on the first day and kept it open by breaking the ice every morning. It was here he fished and drew their water. He filled a pail, and they rinsed the skin together, their hands tingling with the cold before they finished.

Strangely enough in this new world of hers, April particularly cherished the next step, for she and MacKenzie worked in tandem, and even Davey helped. The three of them laid the skin on the floor of the cabin, and she and Davey spread ashes over the hair side of the hide, which lay stretched on the floor. They then poured water over the ashes, according to MacKenzie's instructions, and in three or four days they were easily able to pull the hair from the skin.

Davey found the process a game, piling his hair in a neat lump and challenging April and MacKenzie to match his growing pile. Before long they were all speeding along, laughing as they sought to outdo each other. MacKenzie was uncharacteristically clumsy; and April grinned inside at his obvious attempt to give Davey a victory.

Their hands met occasionally, and for once MacKenzie didn't pull away, but let his hand rest against hers for a fraction of a second as his eyes glinted in a way she had not seen before. She swallowed, forcing the breath through the thick lump that settled in her throat so frequently now. She loved these rare moments when he relaxed and the angular planes in his face smoothed out in a smile. It was dazzling to her, like the first rays of sun striking the ice-covered stream and sending paths of gold and silver skittering over it. Or the rainbow over a rain-washed forest.

She wondered, but only for seconds, how a chore so inherently distasteful as this could be such a joy. But then almost everything accomplished with MacKenzie was a pleasure.

Davey won the hair-pulling race, and he swaggered with no little pride, MacKenzie's amused eyes on him as he sought a reward. They finally settled on one: a song, one of Davey's favorites, about a frog courting a mouse.

"How could a frog speak to a mouse?" Davey asked after the song. "They wouldn't speak the same way, would they?"

"He croaks and she squeaks," MacKenzie answered with the mischief worthy of a small boy. "I guess they just gradually learn to understand each other."

"But how?"

MacKenzie cast a pleading look at April. He was still not completely used to little-boy questions.

"When you love someone," April said with mischief of her own sparking in her eyes, "you just naturally understand." The message was aimed at MacKenzie as much as at Davey.

"But . . ." Davey persisted.

"There are ways you understand," April said. "The look in an eye, the touch of a hand. Like when you touched Wolf. You didn't speak the same language, but you knew when you became friends."

Davey smiled, finally satisfied. Wolf and he *did* talk in their own peculiar fashion.

April looked at MacKenzie, who wore an expression of part admiration, part wry understanding.

"I think," he said slowly to Davey, obviously trying to change the subject, "that you might like to learn to speak like a Scot."

Davey's eagerness was only too apparent. He hadn't understood some of MacKenzie's stories before, but he had known from his tone whether it was funny or sad. Now he soaked up his first Gaelic words, and laughed as MacKenzie rolled off some that he had heard before, taking heed of what his mother had told him.

He listened carefully as MacKenzie explained that "rantin" meant merry, and "hae" meant "have," and "warl'" meant world. And then MacKenzie's wonderful deep voice enriched the room as he recited with a lilt in his voice:

"O Willie, come sell your fiddle,
O sell your fiddle sae fine
O Willie, come sell your fiddle,
And buy a pint of wine;

If I should sell my fiddle,
The warl' would think I was mad,
For many a rantin day
My fiddle and I hae had."

It was an exquisite evening for April, and she hugged it to herself, afraid it might flee along with MacKenzie's rare mood. There was a light in his eyes, and she could tell he was thor-

oughly enjoying himself. Once she caught his eye and he even
smiled, as if, for this evening anyway, he had cast aside all his
devils.

She had hoped, in some part of her, that he would join her
in bed, but though he didn't hide the longing in his face, he
placed a sleepy, happy Davey on the bed and, without a final
word, rolled up in his blanket beside the fire.

But April had something to keep her warm. MacKenzie was
changing, slowly. He was letting himself relax, feel, smile. It
was no little progress, she thought, and she went to sleep, still
hearing his "Froggy Went A'Courtin'" song.

The deerskin continued to keep them occupied over the next
several days.

Once the hair was removed, MacKenzie placed the skin in a
large pail of water and animal fat and let it cure for a few days.
After that he showed her how to work it and beat it over a
stump or log until it dried. The whole process, messy though it
was, gave April a tremendous sense of accomplishment. She
blushed under MacKenzie's sparse praise and watched with
satisfaction as the skin emerged as something beautiful and
useful. In three months, there were several such skins, and they
used them for additional covering.

One evening after a skin was completely dried, April sat in
the one chair near the fire, fingering the soft, supple leather,
which she was stitching into new moccasins for MacKenzie.
MacKenzie was on the floor with Davey, the two dark heads
bent together as MacKenzie recited another poem. She had
ceased to wonder about his uncanny ability to remember so
many and the expressive way he relayed them. She listened
closely as his soft burr once more deepened into the taste of the
Scottish tongue. She could make out a few words, "The Twa
Dogs," but not much more, and she doubted whether Davey
could, either, but MacKenzie's deep voice was mesmerizing,
and she felt shivers as it rose and fell according to the content
of the poem.

His voice was humorous and wistful by turns, and April felt
herself melting at the complete delight of it. MacKenzie was
such a strange man, so full of contradictions and unexpected
depths and riches. Each day she discovered a new facet, and she
fell deeper in love until she thought her love could be no greater.

But then something else would happen...he would whistle with a bird, or tempt a squirrel to his hand, or wrestle ever so gently with Davey, and she knew what she felt would grow every day of her life, and the thought made her eyes mist. More than anything else in the world, she wanted to bring him joy and laughter and love. Gifts that he continued to reject.

When he finished his poem, he glanced at April, his lips smiling. Like the night they had pulled hair from the first deer hide, his eyes were completely unguarded, and the wistfulness so recently in his voice was in his eyes for her to see.

"Bobbie Burns," he said with a slight abashed smile that looked like one Davey frequently had. "I grew up with him...and the Bible. I think I can recite from memory every word he wrote. He became a very good friend." April's heart raced. It was one of his longest speeches, and one of the few that revealed anything.

"Your father taught you to read?"

MacKenzie's smile disappeared, and April wanted to kick herself for sending it away, even if she didn't know why. She wished again she knew more about him.

"Aye," he said shortly, then turned back to Davey.

"He lived here long?" she probed gently.

"I was born here," MacKenzie said, not entirely answering her question.

"And your mother?" April ignored the growing frostiness in his eyes. She had to know. Perhaps then she could better understand him...and his iron determination not to care, not to love.

"She died when I was Davey's age," he said shortly, then sprung up. "I'll see about some wood," he muttered, all the time knowing that it was obvious they needed none. Logs were piled high on both sides of the fireplace.

"MacKenzie?" April pleaded.

He hesitated. "Get your coat," he ordered suddenly, and April hurried to comply. Davey also stirred, but MacKenzie shook his head, and Davey, already half asleep, nodded.

The night was clear and pure, the midnight-blue sky a perfect backdrop for the brightly shining stars and the moon, which rode full and high. April tucked her hand in MacKenzie's and was surprised when he didn't pull away. But neither did he encourage her any further.

They walked to the edge of the trees, and MacKenzie stood there, the creases that stretched outward from his eyes deeper than she had ever seen them. Still and silent in the moonlight, he seemed completely lost in thought, removed from her in so many ways she didn't understand. Looking up at the strong, solemn profile, she felt a knife twist deep inside her with longing, with the need to erase some of the gravity that was always so much a part of him.

Had she ever been carefree? Had he laughed as a boy, and teased and loved as little boys should? She doubted it. He often seemed seized with wonder at Davey's delighted grin. He wasn't aware that not many weeks ago, Davey had some of that same solemnity. He didn't realize it was he who had given Davey that laughter and childhood, nor how much April wanted to gift him with it in return.

"I'm sorry," she said. "I shouldn't have pried."

He withdrew his hand from hers and clasped both his hands behind his back as if to bind them there. His now silvery eyes pierced her. She saw both desolation and determination in them. It was time that she realized the full extent of the differences between them, he thought.

"My father," he said slowly, "was a very bitter man. He came from Scotland, from a famous clan, which had lost everything in their support of the Stuarts. He was an outlaw there, fighting fruitlessly to regain something that had been gone for a hundred years. When he was forced to flee to America he became an outlaw here. He disappeared in these mountains to escape the law…and, I think, to recapture a part of Scotland that obsessed him to the day he died."

MacKenzie studied April's rapt face. "He was so full of bitterness for what he felt was taken from him that he had no room for anything else. Certainly not love."

"Your mother?"

She could feel his bitterness when he replied.

"A Shoshone stolen from her people and made a slave by the Comanches. After they had used her, they sold her to my father for a horse. One horse. Which showed her value to both! She was nothing more than a slave to my father, a concubine to use and ignore. There was nothing left in her when I was born. I don't remember her ever speaking one word. She did as my father commanded. Nothing more. I think she willed herself to die when I was Davey's age."

April ached for the child, and for the man who still carried the burden of those years. It must have been a horribly lonely life for a small boy and later...

Her hand crept to his arm, and even through his coat he could feel its warmth. She still didn't understand. He continued:

"My father taught me to read and write, mainly because he needed me. I did the trading for him, and he didn't want to be cheated. And he taught me the pipes." His eyes fastened on hers. "Can you imagine anything more senseless? He would sit there and listen, and he would be back in Scotland, the laird of a great clan." This time the bitterness was thick in his voice. "But he did teach me the mountains... and how to survive... and how to be alone."

MacKenzie's face was suddenly blazoned with determination. "Do you understand, April? Do you understand any of this? I thought I could break the circle of hatred and bitterness. I thought I had a chance with the valley, but I don't, and I'll end up just like him... living with dead hopes and bitter dreams... running from the law, unable to ever meet a man without wondering whether he brings death. I will *not* give that kind of life to Davey. Or you."

His voice broke, and April could feel a hot tear running down her cheek. She had never realized the depth of his loneliness. How could she? What he was saying was so foreign to her. Not to have had any love at all.

"You're not like that," she whispered. "You're not like your father at all. You have so much love to give... I've seen it with Davey... Don't give it up."

"Do you think I want to?" His voice was more a groan than anything else. "But I could never live with myself if I hurt..."

April's hand moved up to his face, as she thought once more how strong and beautiful it was. "I love you, MacKenzie. I love you more than I thought it possible to love another person. I hurt all the time because of it, but it would be far worse if I lost you. I don't know if I could stand that."

His next words were purposely cruel. "Your husband... you survived that..." Could he never make her understand that he could bring her and the boy nothing but pain? Either way. If he went back, he would hang. It was that simple. And she would be there to see it. That was the course he had already chosen. He had made his decision. He had to see them to safety, back to her father, Davey's grandfather. The more she became involved with him, the more terrible it would be...for all three of them. The other way, the way he had already weighed and discarded, would be to give her the same life he had, to constantly subject the only two people he had ever loved to constant danger and isolation.

Love. He had never thought anything could give so much joy, so much pain. April's face, lifted to his, was now dotted with tears, and he shivered at the glowing love that shone so unashamedly from it.

Unable to resist despite his fierce will, his lips reached down and his tongue tasted the tears from her face before moving to her mouth and claiming it. In one violent movement, his arms seized her and pulled her body tight against his with a need so desperate that, at the moment, nothing else mattered. Time seemed to stop as he hungrily sought to bind her to him, to capture a moment in time and hold it forever.

April melted into his arms, feeling his strength and his weakness, understanding him as she never had before, loving him even more, if that were possible. She met his passion with one every bit as fierce, every bit as uncontrollable. Her body strained to feel him, to know once more the hard feel of his manhood, which had swept her to such sublime heights. More than anything else, she wanted him to become one with her again, to relive that fervent ecstasy, to taste his lips as he thrust deeper and deeper inside...

"Oh, God," he whispered, and April could merely cling tighter to him. "We can't stay here...and Davey..."

"Davey will probably be asleep...it won't be long..."

MacKenzie shook himself, as if from a dream. He felt his heart in a vise. His body was trembling with need, his arousal full and demanding. His breath caught somewhere in his throat, and he shuddered as caution warred with need, responsibility with desire. "We cannot risk a child," he said finally, but his hands still kept their hold on her.

"I want your child," April said.

Those words, lovingly said, stunned him. And made him drop his hands as nothing else could have done. "No," he growled. "No, damn it." Raw agony was in his face, and his eyes blazed with silver fire.

April watched as his jaw set and he turned away, striding from her and the cabin, and she wanted to kick herself. One step at a time. She watched him disappear among the trees and knew she should not follow. He had to fight his own demons. As she had to fight hers, for she had never known her body to ache so painfully, to cry so for release.

She slowly walked to the cabin, damning MacKenzie's father with every step.

Ellen Peters lowered her eyes in a way meant to be both innocent and seductive, but they no longer had the power they once had over Phillip Downs.

Sitting on the ground behind some outbuildings where there was a semblance of privacy at Fort Defiance, at least during this time in early evening, Lieutenant Downs just felt disgust. Disgust with himself, disgust with the clinging woman next to him.

My God, but he had been a fool. He had found out just how much of one the night before, when he had heard other officers snickering. Apparently, everyone had known about Ellen but him.

He had thought her a victim, a girl raped against her will who had then watched her father die at the hands of the half-breed rapist. He had been kind and gentle and had refrained from seeking much more than a kiss. He had treated her as a lady, though he was puzzled at times with the strange, bright light in her eyes. He had even, at her not so subtle hints, considered marriage. Marriage!

Phillip shied away from her hand, and she glanced at him with surprise. He had arrived at Fort Defiance several weeks earlier, and she had met him when he brought his uniform to be washed. He had been gallant and sympathetic when she had poured out her story. She thought she had played her role of despoiled maiden well, for he had sought her out and asked to court her, stating awkwardly that he would give her time to recover from her most terrible experience.

In the next several weeks, Ellen displayed acting talents that had been honed well. Between tears and feigned bravery she went after the young lieutenant with a campaign that would have done a general proud. More than anything else in the world she wanted to be an officer's wife, and she would do anything to accomplish that. To her, that was the greatest prize a woman could earn. After being an enlisted man's brat, she was obsessed both with improving her station and with men in uniform. She loved army posts, despite the heat and discomfort. She knew nothing else, wanted nothing else than to be among so many men, men who carried an aura of violence and danger with them. It excited her, made her body tingle and shiver with anticipation. It was why she had become a laundress, one of the nastiest and hardest jobs on any post. She knew she would eventually find a husband. Women were at a premium here, and many men wanted a lusty woman. She had, in fact, had several offers. But never from an officer.

And then Phillip Downs appeared. He had known nothing of her reputation, and his standoffish personality kept him from mingling with the other officers and hearing the gossip. If only she could get him to marry her before he did.

So she had played the innocent, trembling when he neared as if still frightened from the rape. It had produced a protectiveness in young Downs that kept him from seeing her as she really was. Until he had taken a walk last night after leaving her in a barracks reserved for the laundresses.

As he had turned a corner, he heard three officers laughing.

"Did you see old Downs...actually courting Ellen Peters?"

"Serves him right...thinks he's too good for the rest of us and here he's treating the biggest whore on the post like a princess. I hope he does marry her...make him the laughingstock of the army."

"I think he actually believes she was raped...as if anyone would need to rape her, even that damned half-breed. Never believe that part of the tale, not after she'd been here two weeks. No woman who'd been raped would jump that fast into someone's bed."

"You, too?"

"Are you surprised? Anyone among us ain't been in her bed?"

There was laughter. Then another voice. "She's easy and hot, all right."

"But trouble. I stopped going. Kept remembering MacKenzie. I can't say I ever liked him, but damn if I don't think he got one hell of a raw deal. She probably egged him on, and then cried rape when her father found them."

"That's what Bob Morris says the general believes."

"What about Morris?"

"Don't know. He doesn't say. He was mad as hell when he came back without the general's daughter."

There was a more thoughtful voice. "I'm with you, Sam. I didn't like MacKenzie, either, but damn it, when he rode scout you knew what was going to be there. Not like now. Carter's detail...the one that bungled into an ambush just a week ago...that wouldn't have happened with MacKenzie."

"Have you heard what the general's going to do?"

"Can't do anything now...that whole mountain area's impassable. Probably stay that way most of the winter."

"Damn if I don't feel sorry for him. He sure was looking forward to seeing that daughter of his."

"So was I." The words came with the amused chuckle of one of the men. "Haven't seen a good-looking available lady in more months than I want to count. I think every unmarried officer in Fort Defiance would like to go after the half-breed for stealing her away."

"Don't let General Wakefield hear you call him that," came the thoughtful voice again. "He dressed me down well for using it."

"That attitude might well have changed since then."

"I doubt it," the voice continued. "I heard him and Sergeant Terrell having a go at it. I think he blames the sergeant more than MacKenzie..."

"I wonder where he's gone...Terrell? He sure was angry when he resigned...I heard he had a choice of that or a court-martial. And after seeing General Wakefield's fury, I think he was damned lucky to get off that light. Losing the general's daughter and grandson, for God's sake." There was a note of thanks in his voice that he had not been attached to the ill-fated patrol.

"Pickering might as well resign. He was assigned to that prison island off Florida...where they're holding that doctor who was in the conspiracy to kill Lincoln. I hear it's a hell-hole."

There was another laugh. "Another of Ellen's victims. I wonder if Downs will actually marry her. You think he's that big a fool?"

"Aye," said one voice to general laughter.

"I'll make a small wager..."

Phillip Downs had cringed against the side of the building as he heard the wagers being made. How could he have been so foolish? He was also hurt, by Ellen's deception and by the general contempt in which he was apparently held. His aloofness came not from arrogance but from insecurity and shyness. Which, he thought, probably made him so susceptible to Miss Peters. Starting tomorrow, he vowed, he would disengage himself from her, and try to establish a rapport with his fellow officers. If the damage hadn't already been done...

Now, as he looked at Ellen, he wondered how he had missed all the signs, how he had misinterpreted that too bright gleam in her eyes, the touches that he had believed accidental...

Had she really falsely accused someone of rape? Was she responsible for her father's death? He shuddered. As he thought of it he realized she had never shown any indication of grief over her parent.

"What's the matter, honey?" she said. "You seem different tonight."

"Perhaps I am," he answered cryptically.

She snuggled closer. "When are we going to get married?"

Downs jerked away. "I don't think marriage is something to jump into," he replied cautiously.

"But you said you wanted to take care of me..."

Raw anger tinged Downs's words. "Like others have?" he said softly.

Ellen blinked. "I don't know what you mean."

"I think you do."

Ellen Peters, unfortunately, did. Somehow he had heard things. She started to defend herself. "You've heard talk...because I was raped." Somehow, in Ellen's mind, her claim of attempted rape had turned into the actual thing. "No one will ever forget I was raped by a dirty half-breed; they all think I should kill myself or something. Is that it? Because I didn't have any choice but to lie with an Indian? They say all sorts of things because of that...that I'm loose. I'm not, Phillip, I was raped, and it wasn't my fault." There was a note of panic in her voice. She was losing everything.

"Were you, Ellen? Were you, really? That's not what I hear."

"I don't know what you heard, but it's a lie. It's all lies. I was a virgin until I was raped. I swear it." A dangerous gleam came into her eye. Just as it had with MacKenzie, an uncontrollable fury was working up within her. She was being rejected again...just as she thought she was reaching her goal. Reason fled, and she would do anything, anything, to hold onto her dream.

Her face became almost feral as Downs watched in horror. Her eyes were calculating and cruel, all of their feigned innocence gone. "You promised to marry me," she said flatly.

"I promised nothing. We simply discussed the possibility, but surely you see now it's impossible."

"Impossible?" she said in a tone that almost made Downs shudder with its malignancy. My God, what had he gotten into?

"Impossible," he confirmed.

"No, it isn't," she said, all reason gone. She only remembered what had worked before. Her hands suddenly started tearing at her clothes.

He watched in horror, too startled to react physically.

"If you don't keep your promise, I'll scream and say you raped me. That you said if a half-breed was good enough, you were, too. I'll ruin your career, see you hang. Not good enough for you?" she spit. "I'll make sure *you'll* not be good enough for anyone else." Her rising voice calmed slightly. "But if you keep your promise..."

"You're crazy," Downs sputtered without thinking, wondering whatever happened to that sweet brave girl he thought he was courting. He *had* been a fool. All of a sudden, he felt a surge of sympathy for the Indian scout he had been hating.

Her face tightened, but she persisted. "Will you marry me?"

"When hell freezes," he answered coldly.

He was not quite prepared for the scream that followed, or the crowd of soldiers that appeared, or Ellen's panicked accusations. A superior officer, a captain, came, and a stunned Phillip Downs was confined to quarters until an investigation could be conducted. As he was led to his spartan officer's quarters, he turned to his escort and asked that General Wakefield be informed that Downs had information of importance to the general.

The next morning a sullen Ellen Peters was ushered into Wakefield's office. With Captain Morris as a witness and a sergeant to take down the words, Ira Wakefield offered her a chair and started gently. "I'm sorry for all your trouble with my command, Miss Peters."

Ellen eyed him suspiciously. He had, she knew, doubted her story about the half-breed.

"Two attempted rapes, Miss Peters?" His eyebrow rose in disbelief. "One perhaps, but two? I would think you'd be a little wary of being alone with any of my men."

"I thought Lieutenant Downs was a gentleman, an officer," Ellen replied. "I was wrong."

Wakefield pulled his chair over to where she sat, and folded himself into it, his eyes now level with hers. "I was rather surprised at the charge," he said. "Lieutenant Downs has an estimable record. This will probably destroy his career, if not send him to prison." He watched her carefully. "Is that what you want?"

"Yes," she said vindictively. "He attacked me."

"Did he, Miss Peters? He says not."

Ellen's face blushed. "Of course he would deny it."

"Did MacKenzie also deny it?" He didn't miss the further heightening of her color or the guilt that flashed across her face.

"No," she said triumphantly. "He never did."

Wakefield's face moved closer to her own. "But then he never had a chance...because you and Sergeant Terrell planned not to give him a chance."

"He killed my father..."

"Why did he kill your father? Because your father was trying to kill him?"

"Yes...no... he was trying to protect me."

"Protect you from what, Miss Peters?"

"That half-breed raped me...he did..."

"Did he rape you ... or did he try? Make up your mind, Ellen." His voice softened as he used her first name, and Captain Morris knew his general was getting ready to strike.

"He raped me..."

"Like Phillip Downs?"

"Yes, like Lieutenant Downs," she said defensively.

He sat back in his chair and half closed his eyes. "You've been a busy little lady," he said.

"I don't know what you mean!"

Wakefield rose and went to his desk, where he picked up several sheets of paper. "I have a few statements here," he said. "There are Lieutenants Canfield, Harding and Davie, Sergeant Edwards, Corporal Brown. Among others. Do you know any of these men?"

Ellen's face had gone from red to white in seconds. She started to answer, then thought better of it.

"Each," Wakefield said, "said they had intimate relations with you." He leaned forward. "Do you know the penalty for perjury, Miss Peters? Do you? You can go to prison, and I don't think you would like it there."

"I didn't do anything," Ellen protested.

"No?" Wakefield said. "Your accusation killed your father, caused my daughter and grandson to be lost, cost the lives of at least ten men and God knows what else. Now you're trying to ruin another soldier. You are a very dangerous young woman."

Ellen started to fold as she kept glancing at the papers in Wakefield's hands. She thought about everything she had heard about prison and shivered in fear. "Not prison," she whispered. "Please don't send me to prison."

"Then tell me what happened that night at Chaco, and last night. The truth...if you know how...and perhaps I can do something."

"I wasn't lying about MacKenzie. He was going to rape me. I know he was!"

"Going to?"

Ellen burst into tears.

General Wakefield looked at her without sympathy. My God, the damage she had done to good men. "Why were you in the bathhouse?"

"I was bringing some clean towels."

"And yet when you saw it was occupied you didn't leave...you went inside."

Ellen Peters looked around helplessly. "I...didn't think anyone would be there...it was mess time."

"And where was MacKenzie?"

She hung her head. They had been over this before...when they had first arrived. Why in heaven's name had she accused Phillip Downs? What a fool she had been. Now she knew General Wakefield wouldn't stop.

Patiently, as if talking to a child, Wakefield drilled her. Over and over again until she no longer knew what she was saying.

"All right," he said finally. "So MacKenzie didn't touch you. You just thought he would. And your father came in. Did he draw on MacKenzie first? The truth, Ellen, or I'll make sure you go to prison."

"Yes, damn you." She almost spit the words out.

With no satisfaction, Wakefield leaned back again. "So it was self-defense."

"He's a dirty Indian," she said. "He doesn't have the right to kill a white man, no matter what."

"Just what did he do to you, Ellen? Turn you down?"

It was so softly said, Ellen just sat there, the truth written all over her face.

"And Lieutenant Downs . . . did he turn you down, too?"

Her expression confirmed his charge.

Wakefield sighed. "You will sign the statement Sergeant Evans took down. Captain Morris and I will witness it. And then you will leave Fort Defiance. God help you if I ever hear of you on an army post again, for I will make very sure you pay for all the damned misery you've caused." He stood and left the room as if he could no longer bear the odor of it.

Captain Morris was right behind him, and once they reached fresh air both men stopped.

"You were right, General."

"That gives me damned little pleasure at the moment."

"Where does this leave MacKenzie?"

General Wakefield's mouth was rueful as he considered the question. "Only with a few capital charges like horse theft and kidnapping."

"The letter your daughter left . . ."

"He shouldn't have taken them . . . he knew the dangers."

"Then why did you go after Ellen Peters?"

"I don't want him for what he didn't do. But God knows I want him for what he did do!"

"I thought you wanted him back as a scout."

"It's been three months, Bob. Three months without word." Wakefield's voice was strained. "I never thought MacKenzie would go this far. I thought he would find a way to send them home. His fists clenched as he thought of April and Davey in the mountains. "I want him," Wakefield repeated through clenched teeth. "I want him very, very badly."

Chapter Seventeen

April peered out the door with dismay.

The sky was lemony, just as it had been the day before the blizzard that had almost killed them all.

MacKenzie had left minutes earlier. She had seen his tense, tight face when he had returned from a short walk. His words had been even more clipped than usual. "It looks like another bad storm. I'm going after some fresh meat. I'm taking Wolf so you and Davey stay inside. All the way inside. Do you understand?"

April felt a rush of resentment at being treated like a child. Then she remembered the last time she'd disobeyed him. "Yes," she consented, although there was a defiant note in her voice, which he ignored with a half smile at her truculent tone. He had left, and April knew it was partly because he wanted to be away from her. He had, since that evening several days earlier, avoided her as much as possible and cautiously spared his words when he could not.

It had hurt at first, but then she realized that she should have expected it. MacKenzie obviously didn't find sharing thoughts or feelings easy. She knew he wanted her as much as she wanted him, and there would be another opportunity. She was sure of it, and she waited, not willing to push. Not yet.

She watched him disappear through the trees, wearing the Colt in a gun belt around his waist and carrying a rifle. With Wolf at his side, he appeared untamed and savage, and April smiled softly. Only she and Davey knew the gentleness that was so abundant under that proud and free exterior. She had closed the door against the cold and worked with Davey on his numbers.

But as the wind increased and the temperature inside the cabin grew colder despite a roaring fire, she occasionally looked out. Snow flurries started and grew in intensity until they became as large as pebbles and the trees on the other side of the clearing disappeared in a white shower. She watched anxiously for MacKenzie, but her view was becoming more and more limited.

April glanced at the wood piled on both sides of the fireplace. MacKenzie had left plenty, but perhaps she should bring in a few more logs while she still could. It would keep him from having to do it later; he still hadn't totally regained his strength, partly, she thought, because he kept pushing himself. He never seemed to rest. At night, his face was creased with deep lines of exhaustion and even pain.

In her desire to make things a little easier for MacKenzie, she conveniently forgot her promise to him. The woodpile, after all, was less than a hundred feet away. Nothing could happen in that distance.

She put on MacKenzie's lighter coat; he had taken the sheepskin jacket and gloves. Extracting her own promise from Davey that he stay before the fire until she returned, April opened the door a crack and darted out, fastening the bar on the outside so it wouldn't blow open. She shivered. It was freezing. She buried her hands in pockets in the jacket and started toward the woodpile, stumbling several times in the howling wind. She could barely see the woodpile. The wind and cold and snow almost blinded her, forcing tears from her eyes, that immediately froze on her face.

April didn't know how long it took her to reach the woodpile . . . forever, it seemed. This storm was even worse than the one on the way here. How could the snow envelop everything so quickly? MacKenzie. Where was he? Anyone could get lost in this white cloud. Even him, she feared. She filled her arms with wood and looked the way she had come. Her footprints were already gone, and the cabin . . . where was the cabin? All she could see was snow. But she knew the direction . . . it was straight back from the woodpile . . . she remembered that. But she had moved around the pile, trying to find logs easy to handle. It had to be in front of her . . . or was it to the left? Why didn't the snow slow a moment, just long enough for her to get her bearings? Her hands grew colder as they clutched the precious pieces of wood, and snow covered her chestnut hair. She would have to guess. After all, if she went in the wrong direction, she would run into some trees, and all she would have to do was go in the other direction. She would be all right if she kept moving. But it was cold, so terribly cold.

Still holding the wood, she struggled against the wind that was already creating drifts. She took one step, and her foot kept going down. She stumbled, and the wood went flying from her hands. As she sprawled on the ground, her head struck one of the fallen logs. White turned into black as the blow whirled her into a spinning void.

The storm's fury came even faster than MacKenzie had anticipated. He had had little luck, only two rabbits. The other animals, sensing the storm, seemed to have disappeared from the earth, each finding its own shelter. He was nearly back when the snow became blinding, and he blessed the fact he had taken Wolf. The animal unerringly moved ahead, and MacKenzie knew his companion would get him to the cabin. April and Davey should both be safe there. She had promised not to leave it.

God, he was cold. He thought about the roaring fire awaiting him, Davey's welcome and April's bright blue eyes. He tried to push back the wild joy that always welled inside when he returned to the cabin, to home. Strange to think he never thought of it as home before. Inside the leather gloves, his fingers reached and stretched and clenched in anticipation. His heart was speaking a new language, and he was just beginning to understand its complexities. He had tried not to, had tried deliberately to ignore its call, but little by little he felt his barriers breached. He smiled, thinking of April, of the long chestnut braid and the warmth of the blue eyes. "Come on, Wolf," he said. "Let's hurry," and the animal seemed to catch his urgency, quickening the pace through the deepening snow.

As he moved steadily behind the wolf, he wondered whether April was still angry. She had been this morning when he had been so short with her. But he had needed to leave, and he wanted to know she would be safe. The atmosphere between them in the past few days had been uneasy at best. He had not returned until late that night he had revealed much. She was on the bed and appeared asleep, but his instinct told him she was as wide awake as he was. He nonetheless had settled before the fire without a word, and spent a sleepless night. *If only he didn't want her so badly.*

But he had survived the night and the next days with a minimum of words, and was grateful that she didn't mention that night or what they had discussed. She seemed, in fact, preoccupied with something else altogether. While part of him was thankful, another incomprehensible part was strangely wounded. It didn't make any sense. The only cure, he knew, was to get her and the boy back home. And before this storm, he had thought it might be possible in the next few days. He had stopped thinking about himself weeks ago. The only important thing, his driving force, was to return April and Davey safely.

While he still walked with Davey and April in the mornings, he would disappear in the afternoons without so much as a word. He had not told April he had been checking the passes every several days. The sun's rays were slowly melting the icy surface, despite the freezing temperatures. He thought it might be safe enough within days. But he had said nothing to April, sensing she would protest or attempt something foolish. What, he didn't know. But he had in the past weeks learned something about her determination and stubbornness.

Now it seemed his plans were once more being thwarted by outside forces, and he couldn't bridle the feeling of elation that swept through him. He had never before felt such delight at failing to accomplish something he had set out to do. More hours, more days with April and Davey.

Wolf stopped, and MacKenzie could barely make out the outline of the cabin just inches away. The snow was that dense. His hand sought the door and his heart stilled as he saw the bar across it. How could it be barred unless someone was outside? But she had promised!

His hands fumbled with the bar, and he pushed the door open. Davey was alone, his face white and terrified.

"Mama," he whispered.

"Where did she go?"

"To get some wood."

MacKenzie cursed under his breath. "How long ago, Davey? How long?"

Davey shook his head, but MacKenzie saw the dried tears on his face, and knew it must have been a while. Damn. Why did he leave this morning? He should have realized she still didn't understand all the dangers of these mountains, how quickly a storm could cover everything, how deadly the snow was. She wouldn't have thought the woodpile so far. What could have happened?

His hand went down to Davey's shoulders and he stooped to the boy's height. "Don't worry," he whispered. "Wolf and I will find her. You stay right in front of the fire. We can't lose you, too. A bargain?"

Davey nodded.

"You promise?"

Again, the boy nodded, his anguished eyes pleading with MacKenzie.

"I'll find her," MacKenzie said again. He grabbed a piece of clothing and opened the door again.

Wolf was still there, seemingly waiting to be invited inside. MacKenzie once more stooped down. "Find her, Wolf, find April."

The wolf sniffed the garment and looked questioningly at MacKenzie.

"Find her," MacKenzie urged again, and felt hope mix with fear as the animal moved away from the cabin. After endless steps he spotted the woodpile at his immediate left, but the wolf continued on. MacKenzie's foot kicked against a log and then Wolf stopped and he heard the animal's soft whine. He leaned down, brushed snow off a mound and felt April's body. She was completely covered, and her face and hands were like blocks of ice. He took off his jacket and wrapped it around her, burying her hands in its folds. He picked her up. "Take me back," he ordered the wolf, and the animal turned and headed back, MacKenzie no more than inches behind.

When they reached the cabin, MacKenzie placed April on the bed. She was unconscious but still breathing. Davey approached, his eyes full of fear. "Is she . . . is Mama going to be all right?"

"I think so, Davey, but we have to warm her as quickly as possible."

MacKenzie took the cold jacket from her and carefully stripped off the other wet and frozen clothes, wrapping her in blankets while allowing Davey to wrap her hands with one of his shirts. The boy needed to do something, and the faster he could get warmth back into her hands and feet, the better chance she would have to escape without permanent harm.

When he had dried and wrapped her to his satisfaction, he picked her up and took her to a chair next to the fire, where he sat, holding her tightly against him, sharing his own warmth.

One hand gently rubbed her frozen cheeks, and his fingers found a large bump on her head, and some dry blood. He knew it was important that she wake and move around, but he was loathe to let her go. She was so impossibly light that he felt as if he were holding a spirit in his arms. She had lost weight during this journey, and he felt desolated, knowing that he was responsible. Like he was responsible for all the other discomforts and dangers. He loved her, and he had almost killed her. Not once but over and over again. He hugged her even closer to him, as if he could transfer his strength and warmth to her, but her body kept shivering, sometimes in spasms. "Fight, April. Fight," he whispered, his mouth burying itself in her hair, still wet from snow.

When another series of spasms hit her body, he lifted her and carried her to the bed. As Davey watched, MacKenzie covered her with everything he could find, then told Davey to snuggle up in front of her. MacKenzie also reclined on the bed, pulling her into his arms and bringing her to him as tightly as possible until April was like a piece of meat between two pieces of bread, soaking up the warmth of both.

MacKenzie didn't know how long they stayed like that. Davey eventually went to sleep, but he could not. He could feel her body gradually relax and the shivers decrease in intensity, but her skin still felt cold, and she had not yet gained full consciousness, although she seemed to try to move a little. His hands stroked her, and he felt new tremors and wondered if they came from the lingering cold or from some other unconscious response. His own hands shook. He loved her so much, and if he had been just minutes later . . .

He didn't move until he felt her harsh breathing soften and felt her mold herself securely into the curves of his body. He rejoiced when he heard her whisper, "I love you," and he clutched her even tighter as he felt her body relax and knew she had fallen into an easy sleep.

For those few moments when he thought he might lose her, he had felt an emptiness as vast as the mountains. He didn't think now he could ever let her go.

* * *

It took three days before April was back to normal. She continued to shiver the next day, and her head hurt from the blow. When she tried to rise, she felt dizzy, and MacKenzie finally decreed she lay still.

The snow continued to fall hard, though not as densely as the first day. MacKenzie, who kept the area around the door clear, said it was as high as the roof in some places. He strung a blanket up to give April a little privacy and though he did not join her in bed again, he frequently touched her...as if she might be a miracle he didn't quite believe.

In fact, April couldn't quite believe he had been there in bed before, anyway. She thought it must have been a dream...those arms around her so possessively. She remembered bits and pieces of that day...the walk, her fall, then, perhaps, his arms. But he said nothing about it, and she and Davey were alone on the bed when she woke the next morning. MacKenzie was feeding the fire and had a broth bubbling in a big kettle.

Nothing had ever tasted so good as that rabbit broth. Perhaps it was because she remembered how cold she had been and thought she would never be warm again. Or perhaps it was because MacKenzie had made it.

Whether or not he had been in bed with her, something in him had changed. He no longer hid his concern or his tenderness under the blank mask. He had even smiled at her when she complimented his soup.

"I wonder," he said with a small twinkle, "if you are ever going to do as I ask?"

"I truly thought it was safe...it was such a little way...and I didn't want you to have to do it when you got back."

MacKenzie grimaced and shook his head. "Mrs. Manning, your father should have taken a switch to you long ago." His eyes and their tender expression belied his words, and April's heart did funny little flip-flops. He was regarding her so fondly, even after all the trouble she had caused. It seemed she was always doing that to him. The bear. Her horse falling. The snowstorm. She had been nothing but trouble from the beginning.

"I'm sorry," she said. "I am. And thank you for finding me."

"You can thank Wolf for that."

"I can thank him for finding me, and I can thank you for taking such good care of me."

"As you did me...twice," he said softly. His voice broke. "I am so sorry, April. I'm so damned sorry for everything I've put you through, you and Davey."

April was stunned. There was a stiffness in his voice that told her the apology was rare indeed. Her hand crept over to his and found its way into its hard calloused interior. Instinctively, his hand closed around hers with a tenderness that would have surprised her if she hadn't seen it with Davey. She would never really understand how his gentleness had taken root and survived during his childhood. But he was the most exceptional man she had ever met.

"Don't," she said. "Don't say that. You've given us both something special. You've shared your world with us, and you gave Davey wonder...something that I allowed to be stolen from him," she said. "Almost since the beginning, we came because we wanted to. And you've protected us over and over again. We're alive because of you."

"But if I didn't take him in the beginning..."

"Our lives would be empty...even with my father. Don't you understand, MacKenzie? You gave us both love. You may not have planned to, or even wanted to, but you did." Tears glazed her eyes. She wanted so badly for him to understand, to believe, to accept.

A muscle throbbed in his cheek. "I have...nothing..."

"You have more than any man I know...you just won't accept it."

"You...and the boy will be in danger."

"We can go away...where no one can find us. I don't care where...not as long as we're with you. Mexico, perhaps."

There was a glimmer of hope in his eyes. "It's impossible," he said but for the first time there was a hint of indecision in his voice. "It's impossible," he repeated.

"It's impossible to kill a bear with a knife, and to find your way in these mountains during a blizzard. But you did it, MacKenzie. You did it." She was fighting for her life now, for hers and Davey's.

"Your father..."

"I can write him. He'll understand. He loved my mother very much. He knows what it's like."

For the first time, his eyes were completely naked. She saw hope struggling with fear, love with his sense of duty. They were so perfectly beautiful to her, the silver streaks mixed with such deep gray wells.

"A child . . . would be part Indian. He would never be accepted."

"By those who count, he would. Tell me truly, MacKenzie, my father accepted you . . . the major you mentioned . . . there must have been more. Do you really care about the others . . . like Lieutenant Pickering and Sergeant Terrell?"

For the first time, MacKenzie grinned. "I can't say I do, little wise one."

"Then . . ." she said triumphantly.

"You forget," he reminded her gently. "I'm wanted. There will be an army of bounty hunters. There will never be any peace, any security."

"You are all the security I want."

He turned away from her, and April was immediately glad there was a blizzard outside. Otherwise, she knew, he would be out the door. It was a victory that his hand continued to grasp hers. "Do something for me?" she requested.

His face turned back to hers in question.

"That first day on the trail. You sang to Davey. It was so beautiful, so haunting. What was it?"

MacKenzie's face relaxed slightly. "An old Scottish song . . . about a bonnie young prince who had to flee Scotland . . ." His face tensed again as he recognized some similarities.

"Will you sing it for me?" she said, refusing to give up.

MacKenzie hesitated, but it was a small thing after what she had gone through. She had never asked anything, not really, and at least he could give her a song. But in doing so, he knew, deep inside, he would be giving her something else. A piece of himself. But he could no more refuse her than he could stop breathing.

April had almost thought he was refusing until she heard the first light hum. It grew until it filled the room with the haunting melody, and April listened to the wonderful, soft, sad voice as it told of a ship carrying a young prince from his home. Davey came over and crawled up on the bed with her, his eyes rapt. When MacKenzie finished the song hovered in the cabin, and April felt the tears in her eyes.

MacKenzie suddenly smiled, and his face crinkled in a way she had not seen before. His voice took on a lilt and he sang an enchanting little song about a squirrel, a partridge and a possum. There was so much humor and affection for his subjects that April and Davey regarded him with awe. They could almost hear the squirrel's chattering, see the speckle-breasted partridge who steals the farmer's corn and sympathize with the possum who isn't afraid of anything till he hears the hound dog's bark.

They begged once more for the frog and mouse tale, and they both giggled as he trilled the mouse's part, and Davey clapped his hands in delight.

MacKenzie looked very pleased with himself when he finished.

"Where," April asked with fascinated laughter, "did you learn all that?"

"I listen," he said. "There's a lot of musicians in the army."

"Ah, MacKenzie. How many other surprises do you have for us?"

"Sing another," chimed Davey.

He did, and April was completely charmed by his thoroughly unusual mood. For the first time since she had known him, he seemed totally relaxed. And happy. Perhaps that was it. She lay down and reveled in the spell he was weaving.

All too soon he stopped, and some of the severity returned to his face, but there was something else now, too. Something lighter.

And so the next two days went. They were locked in together, and MacKenzie seemed determined to make it as pleasant as possible for both Davey and April. It had been his fault, all of it, and he was trying in some small way to make amends. For despite those few moments of hope, he doubted it would ever work. He was still determined to take her back. He would probably die for it. But for now, he was taking what he could and giving what little he had.

Christmas came to the small cabin tucked in the heart of the mountains.

For MacKenzie, it was a singularly new experience.

He had never observed Christmas. It had always just been another day, although he had sometimes curiously watched the often elaborate preparations at some of the army posts to which he was attached. It was a quiet time with fewer details, and he generally used the opportunity to ride out and enjoy the solitude. He was never invited to any of the celebrations, nor would he have attended if he had been. Crowds held no interest or pleasure for him. And, to him, religion was empty words. Good will toward man was a philosophy that seemed to last one day.

But where he had always regarded Christmas with indifference, April was the opposite. She loved Christmas. When she was a child, Christmas had been a wonderful, magical time, full of love and surprises. She wanted it to mean the same to Davey. And to MacKenzie. Whether he wanted it or not.

But how? They had little but the necessities of life, and not too many of those. And she had lost track of time. She could only guess the correct date. But that she did. And she announced to MacKenzie that Christmas would be held in the cabin in ten days.

He could only eye her warily, wondering what was expected of him. He was damned if he knew.

But he couldn't help but be affected by her enthusiasm and Davey's anticipation. And he would try . . . for them.

The days since the second blizzard had been the best he had ever known. Having made the choice, he decided to enjoy it, and time passed in a haze of belonging and love. There was no more talk of the future, and though a tiny voice in the back of his mind nagged at him to be careful he pushed it away. There was not even the slightest possibility now of getting through the mountains, not with the snow piled in drifts of ten and twelve feet and higher in some places. And there probably wouldn't be until spring.

MacKenzie took every moment as a gift. The only blemish was the unrelieved tension of his body. For although he relaxed with April, he remained adamant that they would not join together again. He would not leave her with a child. Davey's constant presence made the vow easier to keep, but it did nothing to cool his body, which constantly ached to merge once more with April's. He couldn't forget that one night when he felt so vividly, wonderfully alive, when every sense had exploded with such total fulfillment. He often lay awake at night, feeling his manhood swell with memory and desire.

When April mentioned Christmas, he at first wondered how and why she would observe it, but he was soon caught up in her enthusiasm. He found himself seeking a small tree and picking berries and watching as she carefully used her needle to string them together with a piece of yarn she'd unraveled from a blanket.

He would return from a hunting trip and find April and Davey giggling together and hiding things, and was astounded at his own excitement. Soon he was sneaking off by himself to carve a small boy for April, and a wolf for Davey. He had not carved anything since he was a child, but a rough skill was still there and he was not unproud of his efforts. He wanted to please as he had never wanted anything before.

So did Davey and April.

"What can I give MacKenzie?" Davey asked one day when they were alone.

"I don't think you need to give him anything at all, love," April said. "Just yourself."

Davey made a face. "That's nothing..."

"It's a great deal, Davey," she assured him, but he looked anything but comforted.

She finally came up with an idea and presented it to Davey, who grinned with delight. She had bits and pieces of her riding skirt left, and Davey could make MacKenzie a scarf with it. She showed him how to turn the edges and sew them, and while the stitches were not particularly even, Davey spent hours and hours trying to make it as perfect as possible. When his mother wasn't looking, he used his new, albeit somewhat unperfected, skill to make a ribbon for her hair.

April's Christmas dawned bright and clear. As usual, MacKenzie had woken earlier than anyone else and stoked the fire before leaving to attend to his personal needs. On his way back he stopped at the small stable and took the two carved figures he had hidden there. He touched them, wishing they were better. Almost shyly, he hid them in his large hands and returned to the cabin. He put them under the tree, and watched April and Davey as they continued to sleep.

His heart swelled with an aching tenderness. Both looked so young, so vulnerable in their sleep. Davey's hair was mussed and his long, dark eyelashes swept over an expectant face. And April. How beautiful she was with her arms around her son, her chestnut hair framing her exquisite face. She was his, no matter how temporarily. She was his. He watched as her eyelashe finally fluttered open, her eyes caught and held his and a slow, sleepy smile bid him a good morning.

"It's Christmas," she said unnecessarily.

"Aye . . . I guess it is, and there's two lazy shakes still abed."

She grinned at him, delighted. He had recently started to tease her, and she loved the mischievous light that lit his eyes when he did. That and the soft affection that always accompanied it.

"I suppose," she replied, snuggling deeper under the blankets, "you want me to do something about that."

"'Tis no matter. I enjoy watching you just like that. It's *your* Christmas!" But April didn't miss a certain anticipation in his voice, as though he might have a few secrets of his own. But it couldn't be. He had been dragged, somewhat reluctantly, along with her plans.

Her hand tousled Davey's hair, and he wriggled, and then his eyes sprang open as he remembered what day it was.

MacKenzie turned away to give April some privacy as she slowly unwound herself from the blankets. He knew she was wearing one of his father's old shirts and a pair of trousers held up by a piece of rope. Her own clothes had disintegrated weeks ago, not long after she was caught in the blizzard. He knew she despaired of the garments, but he thought she would be beautiful in sackcloth.

MacKenzie tried to look unconcerned as April and Davey rose, but Davey's eyes caught the small tree in the corner and then the two little figures, and he squealed with joy as he picked up the one that looked like Wolf. MacKenzie felt April's hand on his arm, and he heard her whisper, "Thank you, MacKenzie." There was such quiet amazement in her voice he almost smiled.

"The other one's for you," he said.

April looked under the tree and saw the tiny carved boy. It had Davey's smile and stance. She had never understood crying with happiness before, but now she did. A tear welled up in her eyes and splashed down her face. Nothing in the world spoke more eloquently of MacKenzie's feeling than the two small, imperfectly carved figures.

When she could finally bear it, she looked up at him, finding his face crestfallen, like Davey's when he had disappointed her.

"I know they're not very good..." he started, then turned toward the door, ready to escape.

"It's the most beautiful thing I have ever seen," she said slowly. "It's the most wonderful present in the world." Another tear formed.

"But..." MacKenzie stopped, and his hand wiped away the tear.

"Oh, MacKenzie, I love you. By all the saints, I love you." She flung herself into MacKenzie's arms, and after a second's hesitation they closed around her. She savored his gentle warmth, felt his lips touch her lightly on the lips and his hand tangle itself in her hair. They stood there like that, silently exchanging feelings too strong to utter. She lay her head against his heart and heard its strong beat and felt the heat of his body. The tears made hot paths down her cheeks even as she tried to halt them, for she knew MacKenzie didn't understand. He backed away, just a little, to study her tear-stained face.

"This Christmas of yours," he teased, "does it always make you so sad?"

"Happy sad," she answered. "Oh, so very happy..."

MacKenzie saw the bright light in her eyes and thought he understood, for he, too, felt an agonizing, bittersweet torment, which apparently came with loving.

April left the comfort of his arms to present her own surprises. MacKenzie knew she had sewn a deerskin shirt for Davey...she had done it at night when the boy was asleep. And Davey had known she was sewing one for MacKenzie. But neither knew they were receiving one of their own...each identical except for size. She had unraveled more yarn from the blanket to bind them together, and they were handsome. April had always been able to sew well, and these were labors of love.

And then it was Davey's turn, and with great pride he presented his treasures to April and an astonished MacKenzie, who could only stand there, completely silent. Only the possessive workings of his fingers over the new garments showed his emotion. But it was enough for April and Davey, who now knew him and understood.

As for MacKenzie, they were the first presents he had ever received, and he looked at the shirt and crooked scarf with disbelief mixed with a sharp anguish as he now understood April's recent tears. "Thank you," he said quietly and, sure that he could not withhold the bubbling emotions within him, he turned around and went out the door. He stood there, leaning against the wood, his hands still wrapped tight in the shirt as tears glistened in deep gray eyes.

Chapter Eighteen

Spring came unexpectedly early. Too early for April. In fact, never would have been too early.

The winter in the small cabin had been a time of happiness, of joys small and large, marred only by MacKenzie's refusal to join with her physically. But he had showed his love in so many other ways. She laughed as she pulled at a soft blade of new grass.

After that wonderful Christmas day, MacKenzie no longer fled from her. It was as if he had made a bargain with himself. She didn't know exactly what that bargain was, and she feared its ultimate outcome, but in the meantime MacKenzie had shed his cloak of solitude and severity and had joined wondrously in their lives. He made no mention of the past or the future, and the three of them simply took each moment for its own sake and squeezed it to extract as much from the precious time as possible.

April's laughter floated over the hill, catching in the soft, chilly breeze that rustled through the pines. MacKenzie and Davey and Wolf had gone out early this morning. She had stayed behind, intending to wash their clothes, and herself, in the stream under a warming sun. And she wanted Davey to have this time alone with MacKenzie. He loved the man so. As did she.

She lay in the new grass, studying the clear cerulean sky. Was the sun's new warmth, its golden promise, going to take MacKenzie away? Already his smile was fading, and the glow in his eyes was waning. It seemed several times in the past few days as if he were trying to say something, but couldn't quite force the words.

MacKenzie. How she loved the name. How she loved everything about him: his strength and determination, his courage and gentleness, and the quiet vulnerability within him that touched her heart and made it ache. And that unique ability to communicate with almost every living thing except his fellow humans.

Her smile disappeared. She had learned much about him in the past months, probably more than he had ever intended. But once he had opened his heart and mind to her, bits and pieces had come out, albeit slowly.

She recalled one afternoon when Davey was sleeping. She and MacKenzie had taken a short walk, leaving Wolf guarding the cabin. The earth then had been a mixture of snow shining brilliant in the sun and patches of emerald-colored new grass, and the trees stood proudly like sentinels guarding treasure. Everything was always brighter with MacKenzie. Brighter and shimmering with life.

April had tried to extract information from him, asking about the man Bennett Morgan he had mentioned weeks earlier. She wanted to know more about the one man MacKenzie considered a friend. Perhaps he could help in some way. MacKenzie, she had learned well, did not give his trust easily, or fleetingly. But there had always been something else there, too, when he mentioned the army officer. A deep bitterness and an undercurrent of sadness.

And so she had probed, even as she saw a strange haunted look drain his eyes. And when he finally spoke, the old bitterness was thick in his voice. "I was a scout in the northern plains," he said finally. "Your father was in Washington, and Ben Morgan was temporarily in command. He sent me out on a patrol commanded by a young lieutenant with an itch for glory. Like Pickering he was, without an ounce of sense in his head. There had been several attacks on supply trains, and we were sent to see if we could find any sign of those responsible. I found the tracks and stupidly led them to an Indian village." He stopped, and his jaw tensed as he remembered the horror that followed. The hostile Indians apparently had stopped there and then traveled on, for there were only women and children and a few old men. He had watched for several hours before reporting to the lieutenant.

"There were naught but women and children," he said, "and I told the lieutenant that. But he ordered an attack, saying they had sheltered the renegades. I tried to stop it, but he ordered me under arrest, and I was bound.'' He didn't tell her he was tied to a tree where he could see and hear everything. He didn't tell her about the screams of women as their children were skewered with bayonets before they themselves fell. He had watched the killing and the burning and wondered exactly who were the savages as he fought the ropes until his blood ran freely.

"They were all killed," he said in a toneless voice, "and I was charged with interfering with an officer, dereliction of duty, cowardice..."

April had winced at the last. She knew MacKenzie's pride. Only too well.

MacKenzie hesitated, before continuing slowly. "Major Morgan was probably the best officer I have ever known...along with your father. He wanted to learn everything he could about the tribes in the area, and he learned to track...the only officer who ever took the trouble. They relied on us...their Indian scouts...though they didn't trust us." Once more his grim mouth twitched with bitter irony.

"When we returned, Morgan was out on patrol himself, and the lieutenant lied to the second in command. He said the village harbored the fugitives and that they had killed many braves. I was branded a liar and renegade and thrown in the stockade." His whole body was rigid with tension. "I learned then," he said, "not to trust white justice or to contest the word of whites, not when it was theirs against mine. And I swore I would never be caged again...never."

April bit her lip. She now thoroughly understood his single-minded determination to escape Terrell. But there was more to this story; there had to be. He had spoken of Morgan with respect. "What happened?"

"I was there a week before Morgan returned." MacKenzie's face relaxed slightly, and there was almost a note of disbelief in his voice. "He believed me...questioned all the men on the detail until one finally broke and told the truth. He ordered me released and the lieutenant court-martialed. He asked me to stay, but I couldn't forget those children. I still can't. I left and remained in the mountains until your father found me two years ago. By then I had the valley and I wanted to stock it. So I went back." There was a pause. "Nothing changes, April. I should have known that. I saw them destroy the Navaho, and I was a part of it." There was self-loathing in his voice now. "But I wanted to build something, something of my own."

April's hand crept into his. "It would have happened anyway. You know it. The Navaho wouldn't stop fighting."

"No," MacKenzie agreed. "They had too much pride..."

April knew he wasn't just talking about the Navaho. She leaned her head against his chest, trying to give him comfort from the pain simmering inside him...

But that had been weeks ago, and the black mood had passed. Only infrequently after that had it returned until the last several days, and then it was only a shadow that clouded MacKenzie's face when he thought he was going unnoticed. She knew he continued to worry about their safety, but he had said no more about taking them back. And she, afraid of the answer, had not asked.

She had tread lightly, never requesting more than she thought he could give. But she sensed the time was growing short, and she wasn't going to let him go without a fight. She yearned deep inside for a child who would, perhaps, bind him to her, but they had been together only that one time, and she had not conceived...

April washed the clothes, then her hair in water she heated over the fire. She still wasn't quite brave enough to use the water icy cold from the stream, although she enjoyed basking on the bank. She knew MacKenzie was taking his baths in the stream, and she shivered at the thought.

She leaned against the bank, where the sun blessed the earth with its warmth, and combed her thick chestnut hair, allowing it to flow down her back instead of twisting it into the braid. There was little she could do with her clothes...other than wash them. She wondered if she would ever be comfortable in a dress again after a winter of wearing trousers, large and baggy as they were. It was wonderful not being squeezed tight in stays and petticoats. But she thought it would be nice to look pretty for MacKenzie. He had seen her in a dress but once, and that was the night at Chaco when he had stumbled in front of her. She doubted very much if he had noticed then. After that she had worn the practical riding clothes. Had it been only six months ago? It seemed a lifetime.

The sun reached its zenith before MacKenzie and Davey returned, the boy happy and tired.

"We saw a deer and its baby, and we got nearly close enough to touch," he exclaimed with excitement, his words running into each other. "And there's flowers...almost next to the snow." His voice was full of wonder and his eyes bright with enchantment at the miracles.

He was still so excited, he missed the glance that passed between MacKenzie and his mother...a guarded look that asked and answered. It would no longer be safe here.

"The ice is all gone?" April questioned.

MacKenzie nodded, his expression unfathomable.

"The pass?"

"Clear."

"They still can't find us, can they? You said no one knew about this cabin."

"I don't think they ever had reason enough to really look," he replied. "Your father will turn these mountains inside out now."

"Then we'll leave...go someplace else."

MacKenzie looked at Davey, who was listening intently. "I think this young cub needs some sleep. Then he can help me catch some fish. All right, Davey?"

Davey nodded his head in assent. Fishing had become his greatest joy in the past few days. While he dearly loved his mother, he treasured the hours alone with MacKenzie, and their grown-up talks. And besides, he was indeed sleepy. "Can Wolf stay inside with me?"

"I was just going to suggest that," MacKenzie said as they walked to the cabin. "You two take good care of each other."

"We do, don't we?" Davey agreed seriously, and Mac-Kenzie could barely restrain a smile despite the confrontation he knew was coming with April.

"Yep," he agreed and watched as Davey downed a bowl of simmering soup and then climbed on the bed while Wolf settled on the floor next to him. His wild wolf had become like a puppy with Davey. What would become of the animal now? He didn't wander as he once did, disappearing for days at a time, but stayed close to the cabin and close to Davey.

MacKenzie waited until the boy's eyes closed and his body relaxed. He put his hand on April's shoulder and guided her out. They no longer needed coats, but April wore two shirts against the nip in the air. MacKenzie wore only his buckskins. They walked to the stream, to where it started its meandering path through the trees. Finally freed of the ice, it now seemed to rejoice in its freedom and babbled happily among the rocks.

MacKenzie's fist knotted, and April felt the tension reflected in the straining muscles of his arm. "It's time to leave, April," he said, his voice harsh.

"Where?"

There was a long silence. His voice was a whisper when he finally spoke. "To where you belong."

"That's with you."

"No."

"Damn you, MacKenzie," April said. "I'm not a child to simply say no to. It's my decision, too, and I won't go."

"You will, if I have to hogtie you up."

April pushed out of his arm's reach. "I love you, MacKenzie."

"You'll forget about me. You're a beautiful woman; there will be many men eager to wed you."

April went white. "After they hang you, you mean. I'm to watch you go meekly to your death, then pick a substitute. Like a cherry pie when the apple pie is stolen. Is that it?" She was enraged, and her hand went flying toward his cheek, and she heard the impact as from a distance. "Is that what you think of me?"

Tears rushed from her eyes and she sank to the ground, her arms going around her knees and clutching them to stop the waves of pain that assaulted her.

Hopelessly, MacKenzie looked at her. God, he had been clumsy. How could he let her know he wanted only the best for her? For the boy? He knew he should leave her, *now,* but he couldn't.

Instead, he knelt next to her and took her in his arms, holding her tightly against him and trying to kiss the tears away. He might as well have tried to stop a waterfall from flowing, as all her withheld fears and uncertainty and wild desperate longing for him poured out. Her body was heaving with great spasms of grief, and her arms dug into his back. At that moment he was completely defenseless. He wrapped his arms tighter around her, and crooned to her as he had once done to Davey. She smelled like flowers, and his lips tasted the newly washed silk of her hair. He was lost. Completely. His hand found her chin and gently brought it upward so his mouth could meet hers, and it did, eagerly and greedily. All the months of denial had built in him a colossal demand, and now it exploded.

"April," he said in the ragged, desperate whisper of a man no longer able to prevent himself from doing what he considered a great wrong. His lips met hers with a fierce tenderness, and he was scarcely able to keep from ravaging them, so great was his need for her.

Her mouth opened to him, and his tongue explored its sweetness. He would never be able to get enough of her, he knew, and he tried to curb his raw, hungry desire, but he could not. He felt the throbbing, aching arousal of his manhood, and once more thought how different it was now from the other times when he had merely taken relief. He was consumed with the compulsion to give pleasure, to make April feel the same soaring elation, the exquisite torment that made his body a miracle of blinding sensations.

Somewhere, a warning pounded at him, but he was beyond that now. He could no more stop than he could hold back the sun.

His lips slipped from her mouth, and his tongue played up and down her neck, savoring the nectar of her taste, the light, soft flavor of her skin. He felt her react to the slow sensuous movement, felt her body tense and move under his touch, then arch toward his in an agony of her own repressed need. For the moment there was only the two of them, and nothing else mattered, not the past, not the future...only the fierce, sweet love they exchanged in each touch, in each look, in each soft caress that turned deliciously savage as they sought to become one in every possible way.

Somehow their clothes were removed; neither exactly knew how, nor did they care. It was enough that their bodies were touching, searing each other to their very souls, sending ripples of ecstasy through every nerve. They moved together, his maleness gently probing her before moving, with incredible restraint, into the warmth he craved with all his being. He moved within her, like a sensual dancer, awakening and teasing every tingling nerve end until April thought she could bear no more and her body arched up in a desperate plea. He plunged deeper and deeper, filling her with the most glorious wonder even while she ached for more. He moved rhythmically within her, each time exploring even farther, sweeping both of them into a frenzied, whirling world pierced by bursts of supreme pleasure that spread like sun rays to every part of their physical and emotional being.

But still April reached, unwilling to release him even as rushes of ecstasy flooded her and exhausted her body; even then she craved the feel of him inside her, the wonderful, gentle yet irresistibly probing intensity of his body merged so deeply with hers. She felt his maleness quiver inside her with renewed strength, and once more she was transported on a journey that held new and miraculous surprises at every sensuous movement. When she thought there could be no greater pleasure, he moved with deliberate, savage grace within her until her body was a roaring inferno. She felt the tiny explosions building until it seemed her whole body erupted with sensations so great, so rapturous that she thought she would drown in them. Her body filled with his seed, and she felt its warmth mingle with her own, and she exulted in it.

April felt his soft stroke on her face, the whisper-light caress of his lips as he told her he loved her in ways more meaningful than words . . .

Afraid he might hurt her with his weight, MacKenzie rolled over, keeping her at his side, still joined to her in the most intimate way. He was loath to let her go, to relinquish the delight and peace . . . and utter blissful lust that had done such peculiarly wonderful things with his body and spirit. His heart sang with such joyous music it engulfed the ominous warnings of his mind. She was like the rain to his thirst-ravaged soul, like the sun to newly planted seeds. She gave him life.

And he couldn't let her go. God help him, he couldn't let her go.

Ex-Sergeant Terrell jerked his reins, unmindful of the hurt to the horse's mouth. His spurs dug into the animal's side as he raced out of the Ute village. It had taken him all winter, but at last he had what he wanted: the probable location of the goddamn 'Breed.

The man had eluded him for months, despite his intensive search. He had a score to settle and, if it took the remainder of his life, he would see it done.

Terrell had lost everything.

Since he was eighteen, the army had been his life. He had joined in the fifties and fought Indians on the plains where he

forged a deep hatred for any of their kind. He had seen men he
had served with massacred and mutilated in the most horrible
ways, and he felt, no, knew, that none of the damned redskins
were any more than animals. Including the children. "Nits grow
into lice," he had frequently said, echoing a widely held belief
among soldiers. He had been transferred to the Army of the
Potomac during the War Between the States, and if any compassion had remained in his soul it had been trampled in the
four years of slaughter. His life had been complete when he was
promoted to sergeant, a position of respect, and he relished the
company of men like him, men who enjoyed the camaraderie
of a life spiced by hardship and danger.

MacKenzie had robbed him of that by killing one of his
closest friends and getting Terrell himself thrown out of the
army. A damned redskin who paraded as a white man. Hate
festered in the bitter man as he remembered his meeting with
General Wakefield. He could recall every word, and it spurred
the rage inside him.

The damned turncoat general had taken the 'Breed's part.
Terrell had stood there in disbelief as the general told him he
was a disgrace to the army. *That* after serving loyally and
faithfully for more than fifteen years. A court-martial, the
general had threatened. Humiliation in front of men he had led.
Or he could resign.

Terrell knew a court-martial panel would include Wakefield's handpicked men. He had no desire to go to prison for
perjury or to be publicly drummed out of the service, his but-
tons and sergeant's stripes ripped from his uniform in front of
the assembled troops. So he had resigned, vowing to get both
Wakefield and the 'Breed. But the 'Breed came first, and then
perhaps he would get Wakefield through his daughter, the In-
dian-loving bitch. It had been all her fault. If she hadn't inter-
fered in the beginning, if she hadn't showed up, MacKenzie
would be dead, hung by the trail and left for the buzzards.
Terrell smiled tightly at the thought. It was his one pleasure
now, thinking of what he would do to the 'Breed. Cripple him
first, perhaps. Watch him crawl. Terrell had little doubt that he
could do it. As good as the 'Breed might be at fighting, Terrell
was confident in his own skills. He was a born killer, and few
were his equal with the rifle. It was just a matter of finding
MacKenzie. Finding him and waiting for the right moment to
ambush him.

Finding him had been the obstacle. After his resignation, Terrell had followed Captain Morris's detail until the trail narrowed and he could not continue undetected. So he had waited and watched as Captain Morris returned without MacKenzie or the girl. After the captain started toward Amos Smith's cabin, Terrell followed the trail Morris had abandoned and reached the same fork that had so concerned the army captain. With snow falling in great clumps, he realized it was senseless to go any farther.

The snow kept him out of the mountains, but it didn't deter his search. Tossing aside his hatred of Indians, he searched them out. The Utes knew this area better than anyone; he suspected if anyone knew MacKenzie's whereabouts, they would. And they were at peace, so he could easily enter their camp. He hid his hatred and purchased gallons of cheap whiskey, which he took by packhorse into one Ute camp after another. The Utes were nomads, and he spent his winter going from the plains to the hills to the mountains. Family groups formed small bands, and he learned about one from another. Finally he found one that was familiar with MacKenzie.

The braves were, at first, reluctant to talk to a white man. But whiskey loosened the tongue of one who remembered the horse race between his chief and a white man. The chief was humiliated when the white man won both his horse and his land. The fact that the man was half Indian meant little. The Ute was only too eager to win favor—and Terrell's whiskey—by betraying the man who bested his leader.

He told of the valley, but Terrell already knew about that. There had to be another place. The brave said he had heard rumors of a place high in the mountains where few traveled.

"Can you draw me a map?"

In response, the Indian took a stick and drew a rough map, nodding his head at various questions. Terrell felt a malignant satisfaction. He knew he could find his quarry, and the weather was no longer a deterrent. The ice and snow had melted, and most of the passes were safe to travel. MacKenzie was his. He would bring him back dead, and prove his worth to Wakefield. He would say the half-breed killed the general's daughter and grandson. It was, he thought, a fitting revenge all the way around.

* * *

Captain Bob Morris supervised the packing of provisions. It was usually a job left to his sergeant, but he was determined to go as long as necessary to find MacKenzie and the general's daughter. The man was not going to elude him again.

General Wakefield had been uncommonly understanding when he had returned months ago empty-handed. It was almost as if he had expected Morris to fail, which, in retrospect, did nothing to soothe Morris's raw anger or pride. It was bad enough to fail; it was worse to know that he only fulfilled expectations.

But this time he would not stop until he found April and Davon Manning.

He had chafed as the winter wore on, and he and General Wakefield knew any attempt to penetrate the mountains would be useless. But after thinking about it for months, Morris had become more and more convinced that MacKenzie had taken the steep path he had earlier discarded as a possible route.

He had studied the few available maps of the mountains. The maps were incomplete and fragmented, and sometimes nearly indecipherable. But he persevered and finally reached the conclusion that MacKenzie had taken the high route. Everything he knew, or had heard, of MacKenzie told him the scout had gone higher. And while Morris knew he could not breach the mountains in winter, neither could MacKenzie move. Morris knew he had to reach the fugitive while the scout still felt safe, which was, he suspected, only as long as he thought the range impassable.

Morris had, in the past few months, become obsessed with MacKenzie and the liberation of April Manning. Not a night went by that he didn't dream of her, that the picture on his general's desk didn't haunt him. He didn't share Wakefield's rather paradoxical opinion of MacKenzie. While his commanding officer was undeniably enraged about his daughter's disappearance, he still seemed to feel in some way that she and his grandson were safe.

But Morris didn't have the same confidence. A man who would take a woman and child up into the mountains in the height of winter was capable of anything. Including rape. The two of them were, after all, alone for months and months, except for the boy. His stomach tightened into a ball every time he thought about it.

Finally satisfied with the provisions, Bob Morris gave the order to mount. A troop of thirty men followed him out of a gate that consisted of nothing more than two posts and a crossbar. Impatiently, his hand went up and forward, and the riders pressed their horses into a trot.

MacKenzie, his arm around April, watched as Davey and Wolf wrestled in the meadow among the wildflowers. The wolf growled menacingly, but none of them took it seriously. Not when the great tongue lolled happily out one side of his mouth. MacKenzie looked down at April's laughing face and wondered at his good fortune. He was still fascinated that his life had changed so radically, that there was so much easy joy and quiet pleasure in it. He no longer fought it. His surrender had been unconditional. He knew he should probably move on, and he had decided to take April and Davey with him, but he was caught by an unusual languor. This was where he'd discovered a happiness he had never expected, and he was reluctant to leave. The cabin, he convinced himself, was safe . . . at least for a while.

"You're worrying again," April said as she put an arm around him and pulled him closer. "Do you think we should leave?"

His lips touched the top of her head. She tasted so wonderfully delicious. He didn't know if he could wait until tonight to pull her tight against him, kiss her breasts, her neck, feel her strain toward him with a passion that equaled his own.

It had been delicately suggested to Davey that he might like his own bed, and the three of them had designed a bed of boughs, cushioned by skins and blankets. Davey felt very grown-up because of it. He barely noticed that MacKenzie took his place beside his mother, and since he had always slept very soundly, he never woke during the muffled happy sounds coming from the bed. The days passed with frightening speed, and April watched as the last vestiges of snow disappeared and wildflowers grew in number . . .

MacKenzie pondered her question. They should leave. He knew it. But there was something he had to do first. His mouth twisted into a crooked grin.

April couldn't suppress a smile of her own. He could look more like a small boy than Davey at times. She had discovered in him a talent for mischief that never failed to delight her. It was as if all that had been suppressed for so long was now welling forth.

"What are you plotting?" she asked.

His gray eyes twinkled. "Stay here," he ordered. "I'll be back soon. Don't move."

April had never seen expectation in him before, but, unless she was very wrong, that was what was in his face.

She watched him disappear through the woods, his long legs consuming the distance with graceful speed. She smiled with elation, thinking about the changes in him in the past months. His hand often touched her lingeringly, and his eyes were soft when she found them on her. Like him, she refused to consider the future.

April sat down, her back against the tree, and closed her eyes. Wolf, she knew, would watch Davey as well as she could. Perhaps even better. What a peculiar circumstance! Trusting a wolf to guard one's son. But then everything was topsy-turvy since she'd encountered MacKenzie. Up was down, and down was up. And she would have it no other way.

Suddenly tired of waiting and curious beyond tolerance, she traced MacKenzie's footsteps toward the cabin and leaned against a tree as she watched him dig.

The ground was still hard, and sweat dripped from his face. She heard a grunt of satisfaction, and he stooped on the ground, bringing up a hide crusted in dirt. Still unaware that April was watching, he carefully unwrapped it.

April approached, and MacKenzie swung around. But there was no frown on his face at her disobedience, only triumph. He held a book in his hand, and April immediately saw it was an old worn Bible. There were other items lying on the hide, but she noticed none of it, only the intensity on his face.

He took her hand. "April . . ." He hesitated.

She looked up at him, her clear blue eyes meeting his now cloudy mysterious gray ones. "MacKenzie?" It was a love word. It was always a love word.

"We need to leave in the next several days," he tried again. April nodded.

"We could . . . I mean it's possible . . ." Again he stopped.

"What's possible?" April asked, her eyes now sparkling with amusement. She had never seen him quite as uncertain.

"A baby," he finally blurted.

She tried to repress a grin. "Yes," she admitted with a slight smile. "I think it's entirely possible, considering..."

"I don't want him to be a bastard." The words seemed forced out by pure determination.

"Or her," April said, her mouth now twitching with amusement at his difficulty.

He scowled as if he hadn't considered the possibility. It was bad enough to raise a boy if they were fugitives, but a girl... He wondered why he had not thought of that. A girl. Like April. With the same honest blue eyes and impish smile and stubborn set of the chin. His heart contracted.

"I thought...I mean...that is, if you will..."

She looked at the Bible in his hand and suddenly understood. But the mischievous side of her was not going to make it easy for him. He had avoided words of love.

"It would be a mountain marriage...it's legal if there's no authority around...no one will have to know...that is, if there's no child..."

April's amusement fled. "You mean I can deny it on whim. Damn you, MacKenzie. Won't you ever understand? I love you. I would never be ashamed of you, or your child, or the time we have together."

Her fierce look pierced him. He knew she was hurt by his words, but he had had to say them. Their future was too uncertain.

"You'll do it then?"

"MacKenzie," she sighed. "That is probably the worst proposal in history, but let's go tell Davey."

He took her arm. "Are you sure, April?"

Her hand touched the worry lines in his face. "I have never been so sure of anything in my life."

MacKenzie smiled then, a slow, sad smile that almost broke her heart, and his lips touched hers with a soft, sweet poignancy.

Davey was, as predicted, delighted, and felt very important as MacKenzie and his mother stood in the meadow, their hands jointly on the worn MacKenzie Bible, and exchanged short vows.

April thought there couldn't be a more perfect chapel. The sky was the purest blue and the mountains were majestic with their robes of white. The sun had never shone so brightly, nor had the choir of birds trilled quite as sweetly. Only their tightly clasped hands indicated the fear behind the words, the terror of potential loss.

But the undertones escaped Davey, who shivered with excitement. "You're really and truly my daddy now," Davey said immediately.

"Really and truly," agreed MacKenzie.

"What should I call you then?"

"I think I'm used to MacKenzie," he replied.

Davey gave him a brilliant smile. "Me, too," he said. "And Wolf . . . he's my family, too?"

"Oh, I think he adopted you long ago," MacKenzie said, leaning down and picking up the boy.

"I suppose," Davey said with a considering look, "that I'm the happiest boy anywhere."

Only April saw the sudden misery and apprehension on MacKenzie's face, and she couldn't repress her own premonition. She would be relieved when they left.

It was only later that night, after they had made love with a frantic, needful urgency and MacKenzie lay sleeping beside her, that April realized that he had never mentioned the word love.

Chapter Nineteen

April looked around the cabin helplessly. She didn't know what to pack.

They had only the one horse now, and they were limited in what they could take. She had made several bundles, each of which she knew was too cumbersome. She wanted to sit down and cry.

Part of the problem, she knew, was that she really didn't want to leave this austere cabin with all its memories. It would be like leaving part of her heart. Despite its plainness, she had been happier here than any place in her life. MacKenzie had filled it with his own peculiar brand of enchantment.

Now she didn't know where they were going or what would become home.

She dismissed her sudden misgivings. Nothing was important as long as MacKenzie was beside her.

She tried again, sighing as she attempted to roll three blankets and two hides together along with several pieces of clothing. And then there were the pot and the cups and the dried beef and...the bagpipes. MacKenzie had unearthed them along with the Bible, and she had pleaded with him to play them. He had acquiesced without pleasure, but once he put them to his mouth, they made wonderful music...full and majestic and hauntingly lovely. She could tell from his eyes that he both loved and hated them.

And then there were the guns. MacKenzie had taken one rifle with him and left the other rifle and Colt with her; both were hanging on hooks out of Davey's reach. MacKenzie had already mentioned teaching Davey about them, but April wanted to wait. It was soon, much too soon for her son to learn about death. Davey. Where had Davey gone? He was six now and feeling all too confident and grown up. Wolf had gone with MacKenzie to dismantle the snares he had set, and April had been keeping half an eye on her son. Through the open door, she heard his happy chatter as he conversed with MacKenzie's horse. April shook her head. He was growing more like MacKenzie every day, with the same love and instinct for animals.

April gave up. She would let MacKenzie do it. He knew better than she what they would need. Instead she would take these last few hours of sun and play with Davey. Tomorrow, at dawn, they would leave.

Humming the irresistible lonely melody she had learned from MacKenzie, she walked over to Davey. Perhaps they would make up some stories while they waited for his return.

Terrell moved cautiously through the underbrush. There had been one false lead after another, but he finally found a faint trail...if it could be called that. He felt as if he had been going around in circles, but then he saw the twisted tree that had been drawn by the Ute and he was heartened.

He knew MacKenzie well enough to be very careful. The only way he would take the man was by ambush, and at a distance. When he reached another point described by the Indian, he tied his horse and moved stealthily by foot. Minutes went by, then, he reckoned by the sun, an hour before he saw an opening in the trees. He got down on his knees and crawled forward until he saw a small, neat cabin. Above it were some rocks; they were the perfect place for an ambush.

Terrell circled, every instinct alert. He moved low and slowly, his rifle clasped tightly in his hands. Where was MacKenzie? He finally reached the rocks and spread out behind their protective covering, releasing one long breath. He stayed there several seconds, trying to calm his jangled nerves, then he peered between two boulders.

He still didn't see MacKenzie, but he did see the woman. She and the boy were sitting in the grass, their faces rapt as they talked. He sighted the rifle, judging the range. The barrel of his seven-shot Spencer found April's breast, then the boy's heart, then wandered back to the woman. He thought about firing; he had already decided he had to kill both of them, but then he hesitated. The sound of gunfire might warn MacKenzie, and *he* was the greatest danger. No, he would wait. Then after wounding MacKenzie he might take the woman while the 'Breed watched. Terrell remembered how the girl had slapped him on behalf of the damned Indian, and his finger tightened once more on the trigger. It took all his control not to pull it.

The sun was behind him, and he hoped MacKenzie would hurry. If his first shot missed, MacKenzie would be blinded by the blazing sun, and he would have a chance for another shot before the bastard could find his position. Impatiently, he awaited his quarry.

MacKenzie dismantled the last snare. There had been one rabbit, and that they would have for dinner. He took his time in returning, he and Wolf. This might be the last time he would wander these woods he knew so well. He studied them without regret. April and Davey were his future now and somehow, somewhere, they would find peace. He knew it. He could not allow himself to think otherwise, for there was no way he could turn back. He realized he had a stupidly happy grin on his face. It seemed to be there quite often these days. It had quite stunned him that anyone could be this happy, this content . . . even with the problems that faced them. But April had made him believe . . .

He pointed the rifle at the ground, his fingers away from the trigger as he hurried his pace. April would be waiting, and in his mind's eye he could already see the welcoming sparkle she always had for him. He knew he would never understand his miracle, his great luck in finding her and Davey.

The grin turned wry. It was well they were leaving this place. He knew his normal caution had been dulled, that his feelings for April had blinded him to everything else. But it was difficult to think of danger after the bliss of April's arms. He turned his mind to tomorrow's journey. It would be a difficult trip with only the one horse for three of them. But he had the gold he had saved, and he hoped they would find two other mounts on some isolated ranch. He had thought about going to Denver but quickly dismissed the idea. He was known there, and surely word would have traveled. All of a sudden, guilt attacked him. They would have to avoid all settlements from now on. It was so damned unfair to April and Davey . . . and yet she swore it was

what she wanted. And after the last miraculous weeks he was
too selfish to say nay. Just thinking about them brought the
smile back to his face, and a whistle to his lips. His eagerness
to reach April blinded him to the flash of the sun on a rifle
barrel. As he left the shelter of the trees, he had eyes only for
April, who stood at the cabin door. The sun had turned her
chestnut hair to flaming gold, and her eyes were so blue . . . so
very blue . . . and dancing with delight at seeing him.

The noise and the pain came together. MacKenzie felt his leg
crumble as agony flooded him, and the rifle went skittering
from his hands. He tried to look toward the direction of the
shot but the sun blinded him, and he knew complete helplessness. Somewhere his mind registered the low growl of the wolf
as the animal sought to find the danger, and he saw Davey
running toward him.

"No," he yelled to the boy. "Go back," but Davey kept
coming. He heard another shot and saw the boy go down, and
suddenly the wolf was streaking toward the rocks above the
cabin. MacKenzie tried to crawl to Davey, to protect him with
his body. April. Where was she? He looked up and saw a man
standing up against the sun, his rifle pointed toward the animal hurtling at him. He heard another shot and saw the man
fall just as the wolf sprang. There was a terrible scream, then
silence. He tried to locate his rifle. Was there just the one man?
Or more? Davey or the gun? He had to protect the boy . . . the
boy and April. *What a fool he had been to think he could take
care of them.* He sacrificed the gun to crawl to Davey, noticing
the blood pouring from a wound on the boy's scalp. *Oh, God,
please let him be all right.* And then he saw April kneeling beside him, a rifle still in her hand and tears snaking down her
fear-stunned face.

"Davey?" It was a whisper.

"Get him inside," MacKenzie grimaced. "Give me the rifle."

"But . . ."

"Get him inside, there may be others." The pained desperation in his voice convinced her. And there was another gun in
the cabin. She gathered Davey in her arms and ran toward the
cabin.

The rifle clutched in his hands, MacKenzie rolled over, the
pain momentarily dulled by his fear for April and the boy. His
eyes searched the rocks, the woods. He whistled and Wolf ap-

peared, his muzzle covered in blood. "Any more, boy?" he asked, and the wolf's ears perked upward, but the animal showed only wariness, not a warning.

Finally convinced the danger was over, MacKenzie checked his wound. It was bleeding profusely and hurt like Hades. The shot had ripped into muscle and tissue but he was thankful that it had gone through his leg without shattering a bone. He took the bandanna from around his neck and tied it tightly around the upper part of his leg to staunch the flow of blood. Using the rifle, he tried to stand. God, but it hurt. Only determination brought him to his feet. He stumbled across the rocks, then crawled up until he came to the body.

It was hard to tell anything. There was a bullet hole in the man's shoulder, and his throat was ripped. There was so much blood that, at first, MacKenzie didn't recognize him. But the burly build struck a memory, and he leaned down and wiped some of the blood from the man's face.

Terrell!

Why was he alone? Where were the others? Then he saw the civilian clothes. What had happened?

He heard the low growl of wolf.

"It's all right," MacKenzie said. "He's dead." There was no doubt of that. No one could survive that kind of wound or the loss of so much blood. MacKenzie's jaw tightened. The man had purposely shot a small boy. May he roast in hell.

Davey!

He would have to do something about Terrell's body, but that could wait. He had to see about the boy. Using the rifle as a crutch, he climbed down and limped painfully to the cabin.

The pistol lay on the table where April had left it after realizing the danger was gone. Now she was bent over Davey, her hands wiping away the blood with a wet cloth.

MacKenzie's voice was ragged. "How is he?"

"Stunned, I think," April whispered. "And the bullet . . . I don't think it's dangerous but . . ." Her voice faltered. "Oh, MacKenzie, there's so much blood."

"It's my fault," MacKenzie rasped and April could scarcely stand the agony in his voice. "Damn, but it's all my fault. I was a fool. A damned stupid fool." He took a step and fell, and April whirled around, her eyes going to his bloody trousers.

"MacKenzie," she whispered, her desperate eyes going from him to Davey.

"Stay with the boy," MacKenzie ordered harshly, and April obeyed. The sooner she finished with Davey, the quicker she could care for MacKenzie. She knew he would not let her touch him until then. Thank God, Davey was still unconscious. His breathing, however, was deep and even. She threaded a needle and tried to keep her hands from trembling as she sewed his wound together.

When she was finished, she turned to MacKenzie. "Who was it?"

"Sergeant Terrell," MacKenzie said through clenched teeth.

"Dead?" Her voice was surprisingly calm.

"Yes."

"Was it my shot?" Her face was tense as she waited for the answer. He had tried to kill her son, and MacKenzie, but she shuddered inwardly at the thought of actually killing someone.

MacKenzie heard revulsion in her voice, and understood, and it did nothing to ease his self-hatred. Christ, what had he done to her? "No," he said in a voice meant to be gentle but which, instead, was raw with guilt and rage. "Wolf," he explained shortly.

April's eyes closed as she remembered the scream, and MacKenzie felt his heart shatter. If there had been even a small part left intact, it was destroyed at her next words. "We have to leave quickly. If Sergeant Terrell found you..." Her words died, their meaning hanging thickly between them. If Terrell found them, then others would.

"Do you think you can travel soon?" she asked dispassionately as her hands busied themselves, cutting his trousers with a knife, eyeing the two holes in his leg cautiously.

The silence was deafening. When MacKenzie finally spoke his words were like those of a dead man. "I'm taking you back."

April looked up from the wound. MacKenzie's jaw was set...and not just with physical pain. His eyes were as they used to be. Hooded. Secret. Unyielding.

"No." It was a desperate cry. And she knew it would do no good."

"Mama."

April spun around at Davey's cry.

"I hurt, Mama," the boy said, and her eyes quickly went to MacKenzie's face. He couldn't curtain it fast enough, and it was filled with such raw, naked emotion that she felt herself turn to stone. She knew from his anguished expression that this time he would not change his mind.

"See to him," he said in a choked voice. "I can take care of these myself." He wanted to feel the pain. He deserved every second of it. He deserved to die. He deserved anything they did to him. His fingers angrily jerked the bandanna from his leg, and he wiped the wounds with it. He didn't really care if he bled to death or not. Except for one thing. He had to get April and Davey home. And nothing, and no one, was going to stop him from doing that.

April looked at him hopelessly. She wanted to soothe his hurts, ease his pain, but she knew now that it would only increase his suffering. With an instinct born of loving him, she knew he needed, at this moment, to do exactly what he said, to take care of himself. He would accept no help from her, and if she tried, she would only make things worse for him. She turned away as he patched himself together, wincing at his sometimes awkward efforts, which she caught in sideways glances. And she died a little from wanting to help. Wanting so very much to help. And knowing she could not.

It was as if the last few months had never happened, April thought the next day. MacKenzie was as detached and cold as he had been the day he had taken Davey. Perhaps even more so, if that were possible.

He was also drinking.

April had not realized there was any liquor around the cabin, but after Terrell's attack MacKenzie had limped to the shed that sheltered his Appaloosa and returned with a jug. After pouring a goodly portion on his wound, he sat on the floor morosely and drank.

She did not say anything because she knew he must be in a great deal of pain. He had not let her touch his wound but had sewn it himself after washing it with the raw liquor. She knew the agony must have been terrible, but he didn't flinch once. Indeed, he seemed to take grim satisfaction in the pain, and when the cabin fell dark he did not return to her bed but simply lay on the floor, leaving her lonely and aching and frightened.

The next day was no better. She had hoped that he would at least talk to her, but he didn't. He was gone when she woke and when she looked outside, he was sitting motionless on a boulder, a shovel at his side. She immediately sensed he had buried Terrell. She wondered how he had done it with his injured leg, but then nothing he did surprised her anymore. He had a will unlike any other.

She remembered the last time he had used the shovel, and how happy they had been. Would they ever be happy again?

Despite his shadowed look, she went over to him. "Davey's better," she offered, and he merely nodded.

"He was not that badly hurt," she tried again.

MacKenzie didn't look at her. Neither did he answer. There was nothing to say.

April wanted to scream at him, to climb the barrier that he had resurrected, but it was higher than ever. "Don't do this, MacKenzie," she pleaded. "Davey's ever so much better, and he's asking for you."

MacKenzie looked at her then, the mask firmly locked in place. His expression didn't change. "He's better off not seeing me. You, too. I'll be sleeping out here until I think we're both fit enough to travel. I'll not risk you again."

"You *can't* go back. They will hang you."

He shrugged with indifference.

"Damn you. Don't do this to us."

He whirled on her. "I've already *done* everything to you except get you killed, and I've come damned close to that several times. Do you want to see that boy dead? Two inches. Just two inches, and he would have been. God knows what could have happened to you, to the boy, if Terrell had aimed a little better and killed me straightaway. Even if Wolf did kill him, do you really think you and Davey could survive in the mountains...or find your way out? We've all been dreaming fools. It's no good, April. And if you care for me at all, you'll leave me alone. When we get to Fort Defiance, I don't want to see you again...neither you nor Davey." His hand caught her chin, forcing her to look in his cold, determined eyes. "Do you understand, April? Do you?"

April jerked away, unable to continue looking at the icy eyes, so different from yesterday morning when they had twinkled and laughed with her, when hope and happiness had turned his mouth into such wonderful shapes.

"No," she whispered defiantly. "I won't let you go. I won't ever let you go. I will go wherever you go, be with you no matter what happens. I'm your wife. Do *you* understand?"

MacKenzie groaned. He had tried to forget those moments. How could he have done this to her? "It is easily remedied," he said, forcing a coldness into his voice. "It's not been sanctioned by legal authorities. I will deny it."

April was furious now. "Deny all you want, MacKenzie, but it's done and everyone will know it if you're stubborn enough to commit suicide by going back." Too angry to continue, she stood and stalked to the cabin.

She didn't know where he went after that, but he took the Appaloosa and didn't return until dusk. He had another horse with him. Terrell's, she surmised joylessly. It would make it only that much easier for MacKenzie to take them back. Back to what? She would be as lifeless as MacKenzie without him.

When he finally entered the cabin, he took some dried meat and lifted the jug. His limp was much more pronounced than it had been in the morning, and he couldn't hide the tiny lines of pain in his face. His face gentled only momentarily when his hand touched Davey's hair and then, jug in hand, he painfully left the cabin. He didn't return, and April could only believe he had settled in the shed. Soundlessly, so as not to disturb Davey, she cried herself to sleep. MacKenzie had filled her life, and now he was draining it, leaving her hollow and aching. She could only go with him now and do what she could to save him. He obviously had no intentions of trying to save himself.

MacKenzie settled himself down in the corner of the shed and took a long draw from the jug. His father had made the liquor, probably not long before he died. Rob MacKenzie had liked whiskey and often drunk himself into a stupor. When he hadn't turned mean, that was...which had happened frequently. Both MacKenzie and his mother had felt his father's hand in a drunken rage. Because of that, MacKenzie had never had a taste for drink. He knew it clouded his judgment, and that was something he could not afford. Until now, he thought bitterly. Now he didn't have anything to lose. But April did, a voice inside him said. She depended on him. He buried his head in his hands. What in the hell was he doing? He had never wallowed in self-pity before. April and Davey would need his strength in the coming days. It was the least he could do after everything, see them safely home even if it broke his heart to do so.

He cast the jug aside, watching the last remnants of alcohol seep out, and stretched lengthwise in the shed. The horses were hobbled outside, but the wind was still cold at night and the walls of the rough structure gave him some protection. He needed to sleep, to regain his strength. He planned to leave the day after tomorrow. He figured his leg would be well enough then to tolerate the endless ride back. How could he bear being alone with April and Davey for so many miles, so many nights? And how would he ever be able to see those nights end?

And, in God's name, how could he ever make April let him go when he didn't know how he could do so himself?

Plagued by physical and mental pain, he stayed awake much of the night until finally his will triumphed and he fell into a short, troubled sleep.

Captain Morris stopped at Amos Smith's cabin for a short rest. He had been delayed repeatedly along his journey. General Wakefield's troops had captured a number of hostiles during the winter, but there were still a few roaming bands. Morris and his men had found the tracks of one band near two ranches, and he detoured to warn the settlers, only to find them under siege. He had ordered an attack and then sent his men after the escaping Apaches. It had taken the better part of a week to find them, and then he had had to divide his force to take his captives to Fort Defiance. He was down to ten men now. His fear was not of MacKenzie, if he could ever find the damned elusive renegade, but of the trip back through Indian territory with the woman and boy. But he was not turning back, not this time.

Smith was at his cabin, but he was silent and unfriendly. He didn't like the army. He didn't like authority and, most of all, didn't like anyone who was going after MacKenzie. Rob MacKenzie had been his friend, and he had always admired his independent son who asked nothing of anyone. Smith didn't believe a damn word Morris said . . . not about MacKenzie.

Bob Morris found his questions answered with a blank stare.

When asked about MacKenzie's possible destination, Amos Smith eyed him with contempt. "I don't know nothin' and even if I did I ain't tellin' you little blue boys."

Captain Morris knew complete frustration. "He took a woman and child . . . doesn't that mean anything to you? They could be in danger."

"Not with MacKenzie," the old man said calmly. "Now git out of here. You ain't welcome."

Morris wasn't ready to give up. "There's a pass not far from here, real steep. Is that where they would go?"

There was a flicker in the old man's eyes. "That ain't no pass. It falls off. Sheer drop."

Morris allowed himself a small smile. The man was lying. He had been right. That was the trail MacKenzie had taken. "Thank you," he said with ironic courtesy. He turned to his sergeant. "Tell the men to mount. I know MacKenzie's direction."

Amos cursed himself as he watched the blue boys wearily throw themselves back into the saddle and take the trail toward Devil's Fall. Then he shrugged. MacKenzie could take care of himself. He was probably a hundred miles away by now. A woman and child, huh? MacKenzie must have finally taken a wife, or else he would have had nothing to do with such a thing. The boy had always been too damned honorable for his own good. Not like his pa or even himself. Well, it was none of his business. Nonetheless, he felt a certain apprehension for one of the few men he called friend. "God speed," he whispered to the wind.

MacKenzie packed with the silent efficiency April remembered from their first few days together. If he felt any regret at leaving he didn't show it. His limp was better, except when he didn't know she was watching. Then he would sag wearily against a wall or tree, and she knew the pain must be great. But he would not let her near him, much less look at his wound. She didn't know when he tended it, or even if he bothered. It worried her constantly, but after two or three attempts to help she gave up.

Davey was much better. His wound had not been deep, and while it would leave a small scar on the side of his head, there was no sign of infection. Even the pain seemed to disappear completely, except when he rolled on it in his sleep. Then April would hear a small whimper, and she would take him in her arms and hold tightly. He, too, was feeling the hurt of Mac-

Kenzie's rejection, although it was not as obvious as her own. MacKenzie would tousle his hair or smile faintly, almost distantly, at him, but there were no more walks, no more songs, no more private talks. Davey would look at him with hurt confusion, and if her heart hadn't already broken, that look would have done it. However was she going to explain everything to Davey? What if MacKenzie was executed? How would she and Davey survive? They were questions she couldn't answer.

MacKenzie had decreed they would leave in the morning. April thought about trying to take one of the horses and Davey and run away, forcing him to come after them. But MacKenzie, almost as if he sensed such a plan, seemed to appear every time she went near the animals. Besides, she knew deep inside she could never get far enough to do any good. He would find her within hours, and nothing would be accomplished. Damn. She felt so completely helpless. This afternoon, she would make one last attempt to talk to him, to change his mind. She had to. She just had to.

MacKenzie was at the stream when she found him. Wolf was with Davey at the cabin, and she had made him promise he would not leave.

When MacKenzie sensed her presence, he turned and faced her, and instinct told April he had expected her. But his eyes were unfathomable, his face held firmly in control. She wished that she had the same ability. She knew her heart was in her face, and she could already feel the hot rush of tears in her eyes. She had never cried much before she met MacKenzie, she realized with a sort of detached observation. He must think her weak and emotional. The thought hurt, but did nothing to alleviate the trail of tears.

His hands remained at his side, and something flickered in his eyes. "Don't, April," he finally said. "Please, don't cry. I can take anything but that." His voice broke on the last word, but April heard every excruciating syllable. She saw his strong jaw tremble with effort and a muscle throb in his cheek. His whole body was tense with the steely determination that controlled his life.

"I will have nothing without you," she said simply.

"You have Davey. You have your father. You have your life."

"Not at the expense of yours. I may go on living...I have to because of Davey, but it will not be life. It will be existence."

MacKenzie knew about existence, and probably nothing else she said could have made the impact that word did. He opened his arms, and April went into them. They held each other closely, each seeking strength from the other, for both knew MacKenzie had not changed his mind, nor would he. It was Davey's life as well as their own.

"Once more, MacKenzie," April whispered. "Fill me with glory once more, and I will do what you say." She knew she had no other choice.

His large hand tenderly pushed a curl from her face and his lips touched her forehead, then the eyes awash with tears. His hands had never been so gentle as when they cupped her face and lifted it so he could memorize everything as it was this moment. There was so much brave love shining from it. And neither for her sake nor his own could he deny the deep aching need to join once more, to feel hearts and blood and sorrow flow together for one last time. There was no urgency, only a measured poignancy that demanded that every touch, every movement be treasured and remembered.

When at last he entered her, he did so with a slow magic that enraptured and enslaved her. He moved deliberately, teasing every sense and reveling in the sweet agonizing pain of his core melding with hers, of going deeper until they were both lost in the depths of a bittersweet mixture of joy and fear, of rhapsody and discord...until the sensations became so thunderous, so fiery, so brilliant that everything else was forgotten...and they were left with exploding stars, bits and pieces slowly floating to earth...

Like broken pieces of a heart, April thought as MacKenzie slowly withdrew from her, leaving her still throbbing with fulfillment, still hungry for more. She would always be hungry for him, for his touch. Forever.

They said nothing as they dressed. There was nothing more to say.

It was gray the next morning. The usual subtle pastel colors of dawn were lost in dullness. It fitted April's mood.

Without a will of her own, she watched MacKenzie's preparations as through a haze. It was as if she had known but it hadn't really become real. Now it did. They were leaving. They were returning to Fort Defiance.

She watched with deep hurt as Davey said goodbye to Wolf, his face streaked with tears. He didn't know where they were going or suspect what would happen. She had said only that he would see his grandpa, and her words were accepted. As long as MacKenzie was going...

But his departure from the animal who had become his friend, his protector, was almost more than April could stand. She knew that MacKenzie had planned to take the animal earlier, when they thought they would find another place in the mountains. But there was no way he could take Wolf to the fort. It would be a death sentence for the animal as well as... *Don't think, April. Don't think of it.*

Finally they were ready. Davey had asked to ride with MacKenzie and with that sad wry smile, he agreed. MacKenzie told Wolf to stay, and they rode out of the clearing, Davey looking back to see the animal sitting there, as told, anxiety in every tense muscle.

This time, April didn't even care as the tears poured down her face.

The trail was narrow, and branches slapped at her, scratching her flesh and tearing her clothes. She was still wearing Rob MacKenzie's old worn-out trousers and shirt. There was nothing else. She looked ahead at MacKenzie. He was just as disreputable. He wore the deerskin shirt she had made, but his trousers were of coarse cotton. His buckskin ones had been ruined by Terrell's shot and the subsequent blood. He had also neglected shaving for the past couple of days, and his face was covered with black stubble that made him look more dangerous than usual.

He sat on his horse with his usual grace, but his shoulders were uncharacteristically slumped. His eyes were wary, but his face, when he turned toward her, was lined and hollow. She knew he hated what he was doing... giving up without a fight... but she also knew he felt he had no other choice. What had she done to him?

MacKenzie's hands still burned with Davey's tears as they left Wolf. Now the boy's head rested against his chest, and he could feel the bulky bandage still covering the boy's head. He had turned around once, after a particularly difficult part of the trail, and watched April struggling against the branches that stung her body. Her expression was lifeless, unlike any he had seen on her face before. All the laughter was gone. The determined courage. Oh, God, what had he done to her? To her and Davey. No matter what happened, he would never forgive himself for the misery and pain he had caused them.

He was so lost in regret, in guilt, that he didn't see the first patch of blue against the brown of the brush as they rode directly into Captain Bob Morris and his small command.

Chapter Twenty

It was difficult to determine who was more surprised.

But it took only seconds for Bob Morris's men to surround them, and MacKenzie found several guns pointed directly at him. He leaned back in the saddle, one hand still on Davey, the other relaxing with the reins on the saddle horn.

"Morris," he observed with a crooked, ironic twist of his mouth. "If you had waited a few days, I would have saved you a ride."

Bob Morris felt ire flooding his face and fought to control it. MacKenzie never had paid any attention to rank, except perhaps for Wakefield. And the scout's cool insolence now didn't mollify the anger that had been quietly building within Morris during the past six months of frustration.

"Hand the boy over to the sergeant," Morris said, his voice sharp. He turned his head to indicate the intended recipient. "Take him, Sergeant."

The sergeant moved his horse with difficulty along the narrow trail and leaned over to obey, but the boy tried to squirm away. "No," he insisted. "I want to stay with MacKenzie."

Morris saw MacKenzie whisper something to the boy, and the child stopped protesting. Reluctantly, Davon Manning let MacKenzie pass him over.

"Now you, MacKenzie. Give me your pistol and rifle . . . and do it slowly."

MacKenzie obeyed without comment. In some secret part of him, he felt a measure of unexpected relief. It was over! There was no longer a choice; he was no longer waging a war between what he wanted to do and what he had to do, a war that had tormented and crippled his defenses. The fact that he had wandered unawares on Morris showed exactly how much. Or perhaps it had not been entirely unawares. Somewhere in his mind, he had heard the faint hoofbeats, had seen the fragments of blue through the trees, but he had disregarded them. Perhaps part of him had welcomed them. Davey and April would be safe now. He knew Morris was a competent officer.

"Keep both hands on the reins," Morris said, "and move slowly until we get to a clearing."

Receiving no reply, he added sharply, "MacKenzie, I want an answer."

"I didn't think it was a question," MacKenzie said, his jaw locking with sudden anger. He hadn't wanted Davey to see this. The boy, sitting stiffly with the sergeant, was regarding the captain with wide, rebellious eyes.

"Damn you," Morris said. "You make the slightest move to escape, and my men have orders to shoot you."

MacKenzie again didn't answer, but his thighs pressed the sides of his horse, and he moved into line in back of a trooper, leaving Morris to fume silently. Morris moved his horse to the side of the trail, enabling the others to pass until the young woman came abreast of him.

Even dressed in a man's clothes, she was a beauty. Perhaps it was the defiant sparkle in her eyes, or the proud tilt of her head, or the way the sun caught the red-gold flame in her hair. Perhaps it was his obsession with finding her, with the picture in Wakefield's office, with all the fears he had harbored for her for so long. He had, he supposed, expected gratitude, but what he found was anger. She was glowering at him. Nothing less. Instead of thanks, there was a deep, simmering antagonism that scorched him with its contempt. He almost flinched under her gaze.

He sought to reassure her. "Mrs. Manning...are you all right? We've been trying to find you, you and your son. Your father's been very worried."

She looked at him coldly. He had taken away time during which she might have changed MacKenzie's mind. She hated him at that moment. "Why?" she asked frankly. "My father knew I was with MacKenzie."

"For God's sake, Mrs...." He stopped when he realized what he had said, and his face went red. "Beg your pardon, Mrs. Manning, but he kidnapped you."

She had already decided on her defense. "He did nothing of the kind," she said. "I knew Sergeant Terrell was going to kill him, and I went with him willingly. And he didn't try to rape that girl, or kill anyone except in self-defense. Didn't my father get my note?"

"Yes . . . but he could have forced you . . ."

"Do I look forced, Captain?" she said, permitting only a trace of amused irritation in her voice. She wanted to tell him that she and MacKenzie were married, at least in the sight of God, but she decided she owed it to her father to tell him first. It would also, she knew, be her greatest ammunition, and she wanted to use it in her own way.

Morris didn't reply. MacKenzie had obviously influenced the woman in his behalf . . . along with the boy, if those first few minutes meant anything. He would have to keep them apart during the trip back, and hope she would see MacKenzie for what he was: a half wild renegade who had used her.

They finally rode into a small clearing, and Morris ordered MacKenzie to dismount. "Search him," he snapped despite April's protest, and a grim smile appeared when MacKenzie's knife was found in his boot.

"Put the handcuffs on," Morris told the sergeant as April and Davey looked on, Davey with bewilderment, April with vivid anger.

"No," she protested. "He was giving himself up."

It was as if Morris hadn't heard. He nodded to the sergeant to continue and watched as MacKenzie held out his hands and the iron bands were locked around his wrists. April started toward him, but MacKenzie glared, stopping her as effectively as any hand. "Stay away from me, Mrs. Manning." He whirled toward Morris. "Are we going on?"

Morris nodded, feeling as if his command had just been taken away from him by his own prisoner. "But you take that black horse over there. The sergeant will ride your Appaloosa."

MacKenzie's eyes sparked icy fire, but he understood the reasoning. He could ride his Appaloosa with the mere touch of his legs, and everyone knew it. Morris wasn't taking any chances. Without another word, he limped to the designated horse and mounted, watching carefully as the reins were taken by a trooper. He stared straight ahead until everyone had remounted. His back straightened, and he focused his attention on the trooper who led his horse. He was damned if he would give them any satisfaction.

They rode until the sun set and the going became too difficult to manage in semidarkness. The horses were secured in a picket line and a fire was started. MacKenzie was allowed a few minutes of privacy before being chained to a slender pine. The left cuff was unlocked and circled around the pine to clasp the chain near his right wrist. It left one hand free to eat, but made escape impossible. He saw April trying to approach him, but she was stopped by Morris. They spoke for a few moments, then Morris approached him with a plate of beans and bacon and a cup of coffee. He set it down and stared at MacKenzie.

"I saw your limp...and the boy's head...what happened?"

"Your Sergeant Terrell. He tried to ambush us."

"And..."

"I killed him," MacKenzie said flatly. He didn't think it a lie. His wolf did it, and if he hadn't, MacKenzie would have. He wouldn't bring April into it. "Another charge you can add," he said with seeming indifference.

"Were you really bringing them back...Mrs. Manning and the boy?"

"What difference does it make?"

"Maybe a lot..."

"I don't think so," MacKenzie said. There was no bitterness in his voice, only a calm acceptance, and Morris wondered at it. It certainly wasn't what he expected, but then he had never known the scout well. The man had never let anyone know him well.

Morris's thoughts were interrupted once more by MacKenzie. "You will never know now anyway, will you?" It was almost a taunt.

"Mrs. Manning wants to talk to you," Morris said, trying to hold his anger.

"No," MacKenzie said sharply.

"And the boy?"

The cold mockery left MacKenzie's face and for the first time Morris saw real suffering. It surprised him to realize it was for the boy. Damn, could Wakefield have been right? And was it true that MacKenzie was coming in on his own? He thought for a moment of telling the scout about Ellen Peters, but felt it wasn't his place. The rape charge had been dismissed, but the death of her father was still active. It would be Wakefield's decision, not his, and he didn't want to feed false hope. He knew Wakefield's anger had increased over the endless winter months.

"I would be obliged if you kept him away, too. It's better for him." It was probably the first time, Morris thought, that anyone had heard MacKenzie ask a favor.

Morris nodded. He asked one of his men to get some blankets for the prisoner, and the army captain spent much of the rest of the night staring thoughtfully into the fire.

Morris paced his horse next to April's in the morning. He could actually feel the hostility brimming from her. Every time he attempted a pleasantry, he was pierced by daggers in her eyes. It hadn't helped when he told her she couldn't talk to MacKenzie and had placed several soldiers between them to make sure she didn't.

"The boy seems fond of MacKenzie," he finally said.

"Of course," she said, as if he were not very intelligent. "MacKenzie saved his life several times, was almost killed when he jumped a bear to protect Davey. My son wouldn't be here, nor would I, if it wasn't for him." She turned to him. "Captain, let him go. Let *us* go."

So much for rescues and gratitude, Morris thought bitterly. "I'm sorry, Mrs. Manning. I can't do that."

"Then let me talk to him, be with him," she said desperately.

"It's his decision, not mine," Morris said stiffly.

"At least take those handcuffs off him."

"You ask the impossible, Mrs. Manning. If you're right, if he was coming in, what's to stop him from changing his mind now you're safe? Your father wants him."

"My father wouldn't chain him."

"Your father gave me my orders."

"Because my father didn't know what happened."

Morris's voice softened. "We know what Terrell tried to do. We know about Ellen Peters..." He hadn't meant to say the last, but the suffering in her face prompted the words.

"You know..."

"We know part of it. Your father kept expecting you and Davon to appear..."

"He tried. MacKenzie tried. Over and over again, he tried to find someplace safe for us. But there were Apaches every-where, and the Ute village was deserted, and then Amos was gone, and . . ."

"The storm came . . ."

April stared at him. "How did you know?"

"I was right behind you. Mad as hell, beg your pardon."

"Then you know he tried . . ."

"Do you have any idea how old your father has grown in the past months? At first, he was sure MacKenzie would get you back, and then months went by, and he didn't know if you and his grandson were dead or alive."

April grew quiet. She had known but had tried to push the knowledge away from her.

"I love him, Captain," she said finally.

Morris pushed his dreams away and sighed. "I know," he said. "And I wish I could help you, but I can't." He put his finger to his campaign hat and pressed his horse into a gallop.

The next few days were misery for everyone, except perhaps for MacKenzie, who had locked himself tight in a shell of his own. He rode with the familiar easy grace. His eyes were al-ways hooded now, and he stared straight ahead day after day. Several times, April had managed to ease next to him, but he didn't acknowledge her existence with either words or looks. Davey was different. He couldn't lock the boy out, not when the green eyes were so beseeching. Davey would often elude Morris's guard and find his way to MacKenzie's side, resisting any attempt to stop him. MacKenzie would reach out to touch, to reassure, his jaw tightening as the handcuffs restricted his movements. He had never wanted Davey to see him like this.

Bob Morris watched it all. He saw MacKenzie's eyes on April when he thought no one was observing. And April's open, un-ashamed ones on MacKenzie. He saw the boy's adoration of the half-breed, and MacKenzie's rather futile attempt to hide his own love for the boy. And he knew a fierce envy despite MacKenzie's precarious position. No one had ever looked at him like that.

Nights were worse, he thought. He supervised securing MacKenzie to whatever was available, all the time feeling the condemning eyes of April and Davey hard upon him. Mac-

Kenzie was the only one who didn't seem to object, and Morris had to admit to a growing fascination with the man. Most of the arrogance he remembered was gone, although Mac-Kenzie's disregard for rank or authority still seemed firmly in place.

More often than not, Morris took his meals with the prisoner, who was less hostile than Mrs. Manning and the boy. At first, MacKenzie was silent, regarding Morris with open indifference. But Morris prodded him with carefully phrased questions, focusing on MacKenzie's knowledge of the area tribes. At first, MacKenzie answered in monosyllables when he answered at all, and then his own curiosity was provoked by the captain, and his answers became more detailed. He wanted to know what had happened in the six months of winter isolation. What of the Apache?

"We caught the ones who killed your Navahos," Morris said. "They're on a reservation." He shrugged. "I don't know how long they will stay there."

"The children?" Again Morris was struck by MacKenzie's inconsistencies. Prior to this assignment, he had never seen this side of the scout. He knew, as did everyone who had been on the post for several years, that MacKenzie had fought for one particular family of Navahos, but no one knew the reason.

"I'm sorry," he said, and meant it as he saw MacKenzie's tense expression. "We didn't find them. They had probably been sold already."

Morris saw the brief interest fade from his prisoner's eyes, replaced by bleakness as MacKenzie leaned against the tree to which he was attached. The man's face was dark with stubble, and his black hair was falling on his forehead. He looked savage, but Morris was finding, day by day, sides to the man he never thought existed. What he didn't understand was Mac-Kenzie's inexplicable passivity. He was wary of it. Even while he discovered, to his amazement, he was beginning to like the man.

MacKenzie was, indeed, biding his time. Now that Davey and April were reasonably safe, he started thinking of escape. He wanted to wait, though, until they were through Apache country. He had to be sure, absolutely sure, that the two would reach Fort Defiance safely.

And he had to be sure April, along with Davey, wouldn't try to follow him, that Morris could prevent it. He had been studying and testing Morris, just as he knew Morris had been studying him. The thought amused him in a cold, wry way.

He had shaken the lethargy the second day, but he had not allowed it to show. He was not going to let anyone hang him. Or imprison him. Though he may not be able to have April and Davey, he would, by God, have his freedom, what freedom there was now. He wondered how much it would mean without them, and his throat choked with emptiness when he thought of it, but he would not leave them with the image of him defeated.

He would wait until they reached the great massive towers called Ship Rock because of its resemblance to a sailing ship. Once past there, they would move into the Arizona territory where there would be more patrols, more safety for April. And then, somehow, he would make good his escape. And disappear. He already knew how.

April clutched Davey like a lifeline. They had been six days on the trail, and MacKenzie had not spoken a word to her. It was almost as if she ceased existing for him. The forest had turned from twisted pines and brush to thick oak and mahogany, and finally to cactus and brush. It seemed as though the trip into the mountains, when she had fallen so deeply in love with MacKenzie, was being kaleidoscoped in rapidly moving, mocking images. The hours of watching him ahead, his broad shoulders straining against the shirt, his head still held proud, were miserably slow, and yet they went too fast, for she couldn't bear to think of their end, of what might await them at Fort Defiance.

She thought constantly about helping him escape, even knowing he would probably refuse any help. During the long hours on horseback, she schemed. Possibly sensing her intentions, Morris had taken the rifle from her saddle, and she knew she was watched. Discreetly, yes, but undeniably. She would somehow have to steal a gun. MacKenzie would never survive without one. But how, without alerting someone? Perhaps Morris. Her initial repugnance to the captain had faded in the past several days. It was difficult to hate someone who was so unfailingly kind to her and her son and, though she disliked admitting it, fair to MacKenzie, despite the fact he wouldn't change his mind about the handcuffs. She had seen the two men talking, almost as if they were friends, and she felt an ache deep inside that MacKenzie would lock her out while opening himself to someone else.

She knew it was that damned stubbornness. He had, once more, convinced himself he was dangerous to her and Davey, and he had withdrawn, as he had so many other times. And, she knew, it was also pride. How many times had he vowed to her he wouldn't be taken again? She sensed it was excruciating to him to be a prisoner before her and Davey. But was he really so helpless? The thought suddenly struck her. He was being a little too cooperative. Even after the events of the past week, he was being very unlike any of the MacKenzies she knew. Hope suddenly seeded, grew and blossomed inside her. He was planning something. She knew it. There was a momentary agony when she realized she was probably no part of his plans. She couldn't restrain a small smile. She would make herself a part of them . . . she and Davey.

Her campaign started immediately. She started by pulling up alongside Captain Morris and, disregarding his inquisitive look, graced him with the first smile he had seen in the days they had been together. It was tentative, to be sure, but April was afraid to offer more. She didn't want to make him too suspicious. Even then, there was a slight wary look in his eyes as he returned it.

"Tell me about my father, Captain," she said, hoping the innocence rang true. It should. She did care. Desperately. But she had been too hostile earlier to voice her concern to Morris. He was, after all, the man who was taking MacKenzie from her, and she had hated him desperately. Even Davey had picked up the hostile vibrations and had been unusually cold to Morris, despite the captain's many attempts to make friends.

An eyebrow raised, and she saw his skepticism.

Go slow, April, she told herself. Don't arouse his suspicions. She felt Davey stiffen in her arms, and knew he felt her own tension, though he didn't understand why. She forced herself to relax.

"Captain?" she said, pretending not to notice his hesitation.

"General Wakefield is fine . . . though worried . . . as I mentioned. I know how he was looking forward to meeting his grandson." Morris's eyes went to Davey and he wished he could do something to remove the dislike in the boy's eyes.

April saw the regret, and part of her mellowed. Morris, after all, was only doing his duty. But that did not sway her from her plans. It merely made her smile a little more sincere, and Morris, despite his inner caution, responded.

"I'm sorry, Captain," she said slowly. "I've been rude and difficult. MacKenzie has been . . . he's risked his life numerous times for us . . . and I hope you understand that . . ."

"I know you must feel gratitude, Mrs. Manning," Morris broke in. "There's no need to apologize."

He was making it altogether too easy for her. April suffered under his warm smile. Deception did not come easily to her. Even for MacKenzie.

"Truce?" she said.

"Truce," he confirmed. But he was far too experienced not to notice the flicker in her eye. He knew he should be angry, but he wasn't. He suddenly realized he would be disappointed with anything else. Yet . . . it was his duty to bring in MacKenzie. It was proving, he thought, to be a much more complex, and unpleasant, task then he had first thought.

Ship Rock stood majestically against the blue sky and silvery sand floor. The small group of riders was dwarfed by its size and the barrenness of the landscape. While the cool wind still ruffled the highlands, an early summer had hit the desert floor, and the heat made the riders miserable.

Except, possibly, for MacKenzie. He relished it. He knew it was draining the others, making them careless. Only Morris seemed alert.

Unlike his experience during the earlier trip through the desert, this time he was being kept well supplied with food and water. And he didn't have any of the duties Morris's small group was saddled with . . . tending the horses, scouting, sentry details. He found himself growing stronger as his guards grew weaker. His eyes occasionally found April, and he felt a sharp knife twist in his gut when he saw her with Morris. He could envision the smile in her eyes, the smile that had been reserved for him. He tried to tell himself that Morris would be good for her, for Davey, but reason couldn't stop the fire within him, the longing. He knew he would have to tame it to survive.

That night...the first evening past Ship Rock...they stopped at dusk. There was not so much as a cactus to secure Mac-Kenzie, and Morris, after allowing his prisoner dinner and a short walk, almost apologetically had MacKenzie's hands handcuffed behind him, and his feet tied.

It was exactly what MacKenzie had been waiting for.

April, with the instinct that came with love, knew it.

Bob Morris could smell it.

The sound of a harmonica in the night broke the almost leaden silence of the desert. April moved closer to Bob Morris and shuddered with the loneliness inherent in the plaintive music.

"Davey?" the captain asked.

"Asleep...at last. He misses MacKenzie's singing."

"Singing?"

"He's a half-breed...he doesn't know songs...he can't be kind to a boy...is that it, Captain?"

"No," Morris said softly. "That's not it, Mrs. Manning...April. I think you've condemned me without a hearing. Tell me about him."

April squeezed her eyes shut. She could stand anything but his kindness. She didn't know what would be required of her this night, but she knew she would do anything necessary to be with MacKenzie.

"I'm tired," she said, dismissing him, and he gave her a long, measuring look.

Morris watched as she took several blankets and wrapped them around herself and her son. She was so pretty. So blamed pretty. And so unreachable. He strode over to MacKenzie, who lay quietly under a blanket, and checked the bonds. He had the key to the handcuffs tucked securely in his boot, and the ropes around the ankles were firm. Why then did he feel such damned disquiet? He remembered Pickering's carelessness. And the lieutenant's fate.

He posted guards, one more than usual although he knew all his men to be immensely tired, then finally settled down in his own bedroll. The harmonica was silent, the night very still. He knew the slightest noise would awaken him, especially tonight. But he was spooked, and it took hours before he went to sleep.

MacKenzie waited until the deep of the night. Only a sliver of a moon showed itself in a partly cloudy sky. His careful eyes studied the guard set to watch him, and he could see the man's head nodding. There was another on the edge of the camp. Cautiously he strained under the blanket, twisting his body to slide his handcuffed hands down under his buttocks and up under his legs until they were in front of him. He quickly untied his ankles. He lay there for minutes, hoping no one had noticed the strange contortions under the blanket. But all was silent.

His tameness in the past days had apparently disarmed at least some of the patrol. He didn't think he had entirely fooled Morris, but the man couldn't stay awake all the time. MacKenzie eyed the captain's sleeping form. He had waited hours for the man to sleep, and even now knew it would take little to wake him. April was not far. He looked at her... for the last time...knowing he was leaving his heart here. She and the boy would be better off without him.

Tearing his eyes away, he discarded the blanket and crept toward the guard. He had to reach him before the man heard a sound. It would be awkward to take him with the handcuffs, but he had no choice but to try it. He could rid himself of the shackles later; there was no way of getting the key from Morris without waking the whole camp.

Deftly, his hands slid over the picket's head, clasping the mouth shut. He had just enough chain between the iron bands to deliver a short but potent blow to the side of the head. The man would live, but he would have a whopping headache the next morning.

MacKenzie snaked his way over to the other sentry. This one was more alert and turned just in time to receive a blow to his head. The man's intended cry never reached his mouth. MacKenzie went to the horses and untied his Appaloosa. He didn't want the sound of hoofbeats in the deep silence of night...not yet...and he led the horse a distance from the camp before leaping to its back and pressing his knees in its side.

April had watched it all, and now she woke Davey. If they were lucky she and Davey could follow without waking the camp. She moved carefully, pressing a finger on Davey's lip and smiling when he nodded with understanding. She saw Morris's revolver lying next to him and knew she and MacKenzie would need all the guns they could get. She imagined Mac-

Kenzie had relieved the guards of theirs. Her hand slipped into
Morris's holster, hoping she would not disturb him. She had
just freed it, and it lay in her hand, when Morris woke, jerking
fully awake.

The captain took only a moment to adjust his eyes and see
MacKenzie, low on the neck of his horse, streaking across the
desert. He reached for his pistol, and instead found its barrel in
his side.

April shook her head. "No, Captain," she said softly.

"You won't shoot." His voice was low and level.

She regarded him sadly. She had lost MacKenzie now. She
could not follow. But she would make sure he made good his
escape. "Not to kill, perhaps, Captain," she said slowly but in
a very determined voice. "But I would put a bullet in your
leg . . . it would give him enough time to get away."

Morris looked at her tense face and believed her.

He stood carefully, keeping his eyes on the steadily held gun.
"We will get him, you know."

She smiled slightly. It was a wistful smile, but there was also
a hint of elation in it as MacKenzie and his Appaloosa disappeared in the black night.

He was free!

Chapter Twenty-One

MacKenzie raced his horse, feeling the cool breeze ruffle his hair and tease his skin. He had hoped to regain that old sense of exhilaration he had always had when he and his horse were one, running like the wind across the plains.

But it wasn't there, not any more. There was only a tightening in his gut, the feeling that nothing would ever be the same again.

He felt the Appaloosa's muscles straining under his legs. He had taken no saddle, but he was riding as he had always liked to ride, unfettered by leather and bulk, the communication between him and his horse direct and easy. He had not even taken the time to place the bit and reins in the horse's mouth, and his fingers wound themselves in the horse's mane while his knees issued directions.

He cursed the handcuffs, hating the limiting of freedom, but he would break the chain with his pistol handle when he reached the hills. The sentry's pistol and ammunition belt were slung around his neck; he had no way of buckling it on with the chain binding his wrists. He had to leave the rifle, having no way of carrying it. Later he would find a way to rid himself of the iron bands. One hand fingered the chain. It was the last time, by God. The last time anyone would bind him again.

Knowing he was too far away now to be caught, MacKenzie threw back his head and a savage yell, half elation, half anguish, echoed through the silent desert, its sound just barely reaching April and Morris, who still stood there silently with a pistol between them.

The sound woke the troopers, and they were on their feet almost instantly, weapons drawn, only to find their captain disarmed and held at pistol point by the general's daughter.

"Sir?" said the sergeant, not quite sure what to make of the situation and even less sure of what to do.

Morris, his mouth crooked into a rueful smile, looked at April. "The young lady says she'll shoot me. I believe her."

April's hand wavered for a moment at Morris's almost gentle tone, but then it steadied again, and Morris's expression grew grim. "May the sergeant check the sentries?" He nodded toward the silent forms.

April nodded. "After he drops his gun...along with the rest of them."

Morris's eyes pierced her, his jaw tightening. Then he shrugged. It was too late now, anyway. MacKenzie had a long lead, and the Appaloosa, he knew, could outrun any of their horses. At least he had the woman and boy. He would go after MacKenzie later. He wondered briefly if she would try to go after the scout, but realized instantly she could not. She would only lead them to him. She had made her choice when she held him at gunpoint. Morris couldn't help but admire her, even as he swallowed his chagrin. He would probably never live this episode down, his command shanghaied by a woman. And how in the devil would he explain it to Wakefield?

He nodded at his men, and they dropped their weapons. The sergeant carefully approached the fallen guards who were now returning to consciousness and wondering what in the hell had happened. At April's orders, the ten men sat while she carefully kept her gun aimed directly at Bob Morris until the first glimmers of dawn appeared in the east. She then, quite simply and without words, handed it back to him.

MacKenzie barely saw the flash of light in the gray haze of dawn. He squinted his eyes, wondering whether he had merely caught a ray of sun against the mesa, but no...there it was again. Soldiers or Indians? The Indians had easily picked up the art of signals, much to the army's discomfort. They had even used signaling once to lure a detail into ambush.

He put one leg over the horse's neck, resting for a moment as he pondered the meaning of the flashes. Morris had told him a number of the Apache renegades had been captured, and their attempt to mass had been foiled by their own internal feuds, but there were still roving bands that eluded capture. And, MacKenzie knew, they would like nothing more than sleek army horses. Damn. How long had Morris's little group been under surveillance? And why, for God's sake, had MacKenzie not noticed it?

But he sure as hell had been noticed, and he realized instantly they knew that he had seen something, that he suspected their ambush in the arroyo ahead. He saw the mounted figures sweep down toward him. He could race for the mountains...and freedom. Or return and warn Morris. He looked at his chained wrists and, longingly, at the distant peaks.

And turned his horse back, leaning low on its neck. "Go, boy," he whispered, and felt the valiant power beneath him as the horse raced back to the handful of army troopers...and April and Davey.

Morris's small detail was preparing to mount when Davey saw MacKenzie, and he yelled and pointed. He had not understood anything earlier, except, perhaps, that MacKenzie had left him. There had been tears, then little-boy bravery.

But now he saw the Appaloosa rushing toward him, and a trail of dust behind, and he tugged at April with a wide grin on his face.

His smile was the only one. April, fear filling her with dread, saw the troopers grab their rifles, and one was preparing to shoot when Morris told them to hold their fire as he saw additional clouds of dust whirling behind MacKenzie.

Almost before April could breathe again, MacKenzie was in their midst, sliding off his horse while yelling to Morris. "Thirty Apaches, at least...behind me...they were waiting in ambush."

Morris nodded, giving orders immediately. One man was told to hold the reins of the horses; the others to spread out on the sand. MacKenzie shouted at April and Davey to get behind him, and he, too, lay nearly flat on the sand as his hand jerked the pistol from the holster on his shoulder.

April had no time to think. None of them did. Screaming painted Apaches were bearing down on them, and bullets were already peppering the oncoming riders. The troopers had the seven-shot rifles and were deadly accurate. Morris had selected only the best for this detail, and each made every shot count. MacKenzie didn't have the range with his pistol, but he, too, brought several men down as some of the most daring of the Apaches were able to approach the perimeter of Morris's circle. Almost as soon as it started, it was over. The Apaches had thought the small group easy prey, and had no appetite for the type of punishment they'd received. A third of their number lay dead on the ground.

When Morris was sure there wouldn't be a second attack, he stood and inventoried his small command. Two were dead, two wounded. His eyes wandered over to MacKenzie, who also stood slowly. His wrists were still cuffed together, and his pistol hung from one hand. He looked at Morris with a crooked smile on his lips, and eyes full of self-mockery. He offered the gun to Morris. "I'm afraid it's empty."

"If it wasn't?"

MacKenzie shrugged.

"You didn't have to come back."

MacKenzie looked toward April and Davey. "Didn't I?"

Morris sat down and pulled off his boot, tipping it upside down to retrieve the key to MacKenzie's handcuffs. He stood and unlocked them, watching as MacKenzie, his gray eyes questioning, rubbed his wrists.

"Get the hell out of here, MacKenzie," Morris said.

MacKenzie turned to April, who was holding Davey tightly. Her eyes hadn't left him.

"They stay with us," Morris said, correctly interpreting MacKenzie's look.

MacKenzie surveyed Morris's diminished force before locking eyes with the captain in a contest of wills. "You can't make it with what you have," he said finally. "Especially without a scout."

He looked out to where the dust was still settling. "They haven't given up; they'll just look for a better spot."

"I'm all out of scouts at the moment," Morris replied.

"Maybe not."

"I can't promise you anything."

"I know," MacKenzie said softly. "But I'm damned tired of running."

Morris let a small whistle pass his lips. "You should know...Wakefield's mad as hell."

"I would guess as much."

"But he knows you didn't rape the Peters girl, and Sergeant Peters...well, the general sort of figured that out, too."

MacKenzie lifted an eyebrow.

"But there are still a number of charges..." He looked at April and her boy. "You could still go to prison or...even hang."

MacKenzie's mouth straightened in the old grim line. "I know. But I can't leave them...or you...out here now, God damn it. Now will you get ready before those Apaches change their minds?"

Morris nodded and quickly gave orders. April helped tend the wounded while the two dead men were buried. It was mid-morning when the small group mounted and headed west. MacKenzie had left an hour earlier to scout the trail.

Morris, who rode next to April, couldn't help but question his own actions. He had risked his bars when he'd offered to let MacKenzie go, and now he was trusting his small command to a renegade half-breed who was wanted for any number of criminal acts. He shook his head as he realized he had seldom felt in better hands.

April and Davey saw little of MacKenzie in the next several days. He was out scouting most of the time and only rarely rode in, and then only to confer briefly with Morris. They were taking a zigzag path, and whenever they seemed low on water, MacKenzie would almost magically find a muddy hole. The water was never very appetizing, but at least it kept thirst at bay.

They saw no more Indians, although there were sometimes tracks. And then, they stopped, and April knew they were approaching Fort Defiance. She had tried to talk to MacKenzie the few times they had stopped to make camp, but he had avoided her.

It was a pattern that continued until the night before she was told they would reach the fort. Much to her surprise, MacKenzie sought her out. His eyes dark and hooded, he spoke briefly to Morris, then approached her.

"I want to talk to you," he said without preamble, his face harsh.

Vacillating between hope and fear, April could only nod, and she followed him out of camp, beyond hearing range.

"I want to say goodbye," he said abruptly. "Now. I'll be arrested tomorrow, and I want your promise you won't try to see me."

"You can leave tonight . . . we can leave tonight," she said. "Captain Morris won't try to stop you."

"It would just be someone else then," he said tiredly. "Make it easy for me, April."

"Captain Morris will help you . . . I'll help you. And I know Father will help . . . when he knows everything . . ."

"Stay out of it, April. Please."

"Do you always have to be so damned independent, so damned alone?" she cried in frustration, a hot tear forming in her eye.

"You don't understand . . . your name can't be linked to mine . . . it will brand you . . . you and Davey."

"You are my husband," she said, her fury mounting as she saw him wince at the reminder. "Do you think I can just walk away? It may not have meant anything to you, but . . ." His rejection hurt more than anything in her life, and she turned so he couldn't see the aching pain and misery she knew must be plain in her face.

He didn't have to see her face. It was in the slumped shoulders and the head bent low, the proud courageous head, which should always be held high. He had brought her to this . . . and it could only worsen . . . if he couldn't make her let go. He wondered if anyone could ever invent a torture more agonizing than this. It was as if his heart had been lifted from his chest as it still beat and was being shredded piece by piece. "You must forget it, April. If not for yourself, then for Davey."

She whirled around, her voice ragged with emotion. "No, I love you. I'll always love you . . . and I'll yell it to the world."

His arms caught her, and his hand cupped her chin, forcing her to look up. "If you love me, if you really love me, you will do as I ask."

"You can't do that to me," she cried rebelliously. "I won't accept that."

Tears glistened in the moonlight, and he put his head down on hers to hide his own agony. She must not know how much this was costing him.

"Even," he said slowly, letting every hurting word be understood, "if I don't go to prison, you can't be with me.

There's no room in my life for a wife and child. I want to be free...free...in every way..."

"I don't believe you."

"Damn it, April. I don't want you. Can't you understand that?"

"The marriage..."

"Was a mistake. I thought it would make you happy...but now it's over. All of it."

It was the cold emptiness of his voice that finally made an impact on her. The voice and the hostile eyes. There was no trace of the familiar warmth, of the tender protectiveness. He was a stranger. A cold, antagonistic stranger, and she believed none of it. The voice, the words, the eyes were all made liars by the gentleness of the hands. There were some things he could hide, but others he could not. She hadn't imagined the pain in his earlier words.

She straightened, her eyes filling with secrets of her own. She realized there was no way she could tell him he was wrong, not now. He had decided he had to do this for her, and she would let him think he had convinced her, even though it sent a dagger through her heart to do so.

April cried inside for him, for all the wounds he was afraid to show, for everything that made him feel his love was a hurtful thing rather than the bright and warming glow it really was. He was trying to give her the only gift he thought he had, and she knew, because she knew him, that it was tearing him apart to do so.

The only thing she could do, at this moment, was to make it easier for him...until she could talk to her father, until she could, in some way, making things right, make it possible for him to accept that they could live together in happiness and peace, that there were more men like her father, and Bob Morris and Ben Morgan, that they all weren't like Peters and Terrell. And she had to do it. As she looked into the gray eyes struggling to remain cold, into the face creased with lines that shouldn't be there, she felt her heart swell and expand until she thought it would crush the flimsy shell that held it. She wanted to touch him, to love him, to share her faith.

And she could not. Not now, not tonight. For it would make his pain unbearable. Her hand trembled as she sought the courage to make him believe she accepted his words.

Her chin went up proudly and her eyes sparked. "And you want me just to forget everything?"

It was all he could do to nod.

"And Davey?"

"He's young . . . he'll forget soon enough."

"Forgive abandonment . . . I doubt it." In her own churning confusion, the words escaped before she could stop them and she immediately knew the depth of the blow she'd delivered.

She saw the hurt he couldn't hide this time, the agonized twist of his mouth as he recognized the truth of her words.

The tears in her eyes had dried. She needed the same strength he had to continue the fable.

For him.

She turned her back and walked away, every step a feat of extraordinary struggle between her needs and his.

For him, she told herself, she could do anything.

April didn't sleep at all, and she knew from MacKenzie's too still form that neither did he.

Even then, morning came too soon with its seductively soft golden light that promised so much and offered so little.

She tried to keep Davey from MacKenzie, but he slipped away. MacKenzie had been gone most of the last several days. He had left early and seldom returned until Davey was asleep. But he wasn't going to get away from the boy today. Davey had been waiting to pounce. He delivered himself at MacKenzie's side as the scout prepared to mount. With six-year-old determination, he spread his legs with all the belligerence of a young bull.

"I want to ride with you," he pronounced, his confidence belied only by the trembling of his lips.

It would have been easier for MacKenzie to shoot a puppy than refuse. His hands reached down and picked Davey up, holding him close for an infinitesimal time before settling him in the saddle and swinging up behind him. Without any words, he moved away from the rest of the group, once more placing an invisible wall between him and others. Only a small hand on his arm said anything different.

When they were within hailing distance of the fort at midday, MacKenzie rode to April and, his face hard and unyielding, handed Davey to her.

"Morris and I are going ahead," he said curtly. "Stay here with the other soldiers."

Her arms tightened around Davey, and her hands squeezed the leather reins so tight she thought the horse would spook. But it was as tired and exhausted as she and merely stamped in protest. She nodded, and he turned.

"MacKenzie..." She couldn't prevent uttering his name.

He turned, his eyes swirling with something she couldn't identify.

"Thank you for taking Davey."

His jaw worked for a second, then he turned and pressed his horse into a gallop. He and Morris disappeared behind a churning cloud of dust.

General Ira Wakefield was waiting at the gate for his daughter and grandson.

He had been in his office when Morris and MacKenzie rode in. Despite Morris's objections, the officer of the day had immediately ordered MacKenzie confined in the guardhouse. There were standing orders for his arrest.

Morris angrily strode over to Wakefield's office to have those orders changed. If nothing else, he wanted MacKenzie to share his own quarters... under house arrest if there was no alternative. MacKenzie, he felt, had saved his patrol when he could have made good his escape. In the past few days, his initial grudging acceptance of the half-breed had turned into a somewhat wary friendship.

But he had no chance. Wakefield's concerns at the moment were his daughter and grandson. Before Morris could utter a word, Wakefield had left his desk and was glowering at him.

"April and Davon?"

"We found them, sir, or," he admitted wryly, "they found us. MacKenzie was bringing them back. They're following us by just a few minutes."

It was enough for Wakefield. He was buttoning his coat and out the door before Morris could say any more.

"General Wakefield!" The general turned at Morris's unusually sharp voice.

"Yes?" He said impatiently.

"About MacKenzie...he's been taken to the guardhouse..."

"Good," Wakefield said with satisfaction. His anger had grown throughout the long months of uncertainty. It was, in fact, explosive. At the moment, he would have cheerfully pulled the man apart with his own hands.

"General Wakefield . . . he was bringing them back, and he saved my patrol from Indians . . . I think . . ."

"Later, Captain . . . I'll deal with MacKenzie later. Now I just want to see my daughter. And I'll want a full report in three hours. In the meantime, MacKenzie stays where he is."

"Yes, sir, but . . ."

"Captain!"

Morris was effectively gagged, and he knew it.

"I would suggest," Wakefield continued, "that you get yourself cleaned up. You're dismissed."

"Yes, sir," Morris conceded, and saluted. He started planning his defense of MacKenzie as Wakefield hurriedly left the room.

Despite April's deep fear for MacKenzie, she couldn't restrain a wide grin when she saw her father standing stiffly beside the gate. She would always see him this way, tall and straight. But his face was older, worn-looking, and the twinkle in his eye was not as bright as she'd remembered.

She brought her horse to a stop before him and handed Davey down to him. "Your grandson, sir."

Wakefield took the boy, and held him out for a moment, studying every feature. How he had longed to hold the boy. But it was, he sensed, too soon. The boy was stiff, and his look suspicious. Wakefield set him on the ground, and kneeled to the boy's height. "I'm glad to make your acquaintance, Davon," he said formally, and the words brought a slight smile to the boy's face, and he relaxed a little.

"Is MacKenzie here?" the boy asked, his eyes searching the parade ground.

Wakefield stiffened, then looked at April, who had just dismounted. She had the same question in her eye.

Wakefield held his tongue and opened his arms, taking April into them and holding her tighter than he ever had before. There had been days and weeks and even months when he wondered whether he would ever see her again.

"MacKenzie," Davey insisted, his concern for his friend overpowering his awe of the tall authority in blue.

"He's resting," Wakefield replied gently as he noted April's similarly questing eyes. He looked at his daughter. Her coarse clothes had been designed for a man substantially larger than her, and they were coated with layers of grime and dust. Her face was smudged, and her chestnut hair dull and messy in a braid hanging down the back. But her eyes were bright and her skin healthy and glowing. It had been more than six years since he had seen her last, and he had expected change, but not quite the strength and maturity now facing him.

She had left him a girl, and returned a woman. A beautiful, glowing woman. And a determined one, if he was right about the stubborn jut of her jaw whenever Davey mentioned MacKenzie.

"Come to my quarters," he said, placing one hand on her shoulder and the other on Davey's. "I've waited for this moment for a long, long time."

His house was fairly plain, but large. Large clay jars hung both inside and outside. They were filled with water, which evaporated rapidly in the heat to provide some cooling, but still the air was stifling at this time of day. April and Davey were greeted by the general's striker, a soldier who served as cook and housekeeper.

He, like everyone by now, had heard that the general's daughter and grandson had arrived, and he had already prepared some lemonade. He grinned happily, hoping that the general's dour moods would disappear.

But Wakefield's joy was dimmed by Davey's quiet reservation and April's reticence.

April finally got Davey to take a nap, and she and her father sat in the parlor together.

"Tell me what happened," Wakefield said gently. "Everything. Did MacKenzie hurt you in any way?"

April started slowly, telling him about the first night she had seen the scout, the terrible day in the desert as MacKenzie was dragged without food or water.

"He didn't have a choice, Papa. He truly didn't have a choice, and he thought it would just be a matter of hours, or a day at most, before he could...get rid of us safely." She told him about the Navahos, and the bear attack, and the blizzard when he had saved her life, and finally Terrell's attack.

"He saved our lives over and over again," she said, "and then when he could have gone free he did it again...on the way here. Even then, he could have gotten away, but something... wouldn't let him."

"He may have saved your lives," Wakefield said, "but he put them in danger in the beginning. I don't know if I can forgive that."

"Neither can he, Papa. I think that's why he came back. I offered to go with him. Anyplace." She saw her father wince at the words. "I love him. There are so many sides to him, so many gentle places he tries to hide."

"He's part Indian," Wakefield said. "You know what that means in the west. Some people will never understand."

"I don't care about them!"

"You must... if not for yourself, for your children."

"He's the most decent man I have ever met, the most compassionate, the most caring," April said, tears misting her eyes. "And Davey loves him."

"I've noticed," her father said dryly. As for the rest... were they talking about the same MacKenzie?

"What are you going to do with him?"

He studied her anguished face. "I don't know, April. Ellen Peters confessed to lying, and admitted MacKenzie killed her father in self-defense. If he hadn't escaped, we could have straightened it all out. Now there's horse theft and kidnapping, theft of government property and any number of other things. When I sent Bob Morris after you, I couldn't keep it quiet. It's gone farther now than this post."

"Sergeant Terrell never meant for him to arrive here alive," she countered. "And it was his own horse."

"Two were missing."

"I stole one," she said defiantly. "And I wasn't kidnapped, and I would testify to that."

Wakefield shook his head in defeat. "I don't suppose it would look very good for a general's daughter to admit to stealing a horse." He took her hand. "I'm not promising anything, April. Not until I talk to him. Even then I don't know what I can do."

"Father... there's something else..."

He looked at her with some wariness.

"We were married... in the mountains... according to mountain law. Davey was a witness."

There was a long silence. "I'm not sure how legal that is."

"I don't care whether it's legal. I'm his wife in my heart. And that will never change."

"And MacKenzie?"

"He's afraid Davey and I will be hurt."

"Not an altogether unreasonable assumption."

"Not if he's cleared of charges, not if we can go to his valley..."

He sighed wearily. "I love you, April. I want you and Davey to be happy more than anything in the world. I know how terrible those years were... when you waited for news of David. I don't want to see you hurt again."

"Nothing will ever change the way I feel. MacKenzie is my life. He's Davey's life. They adore each other, and he's been so good for my son. It will break Davey's heart if he's taken away."

"Are you sure about the way MacKenzie feels?"

"He's afraid right now," April said. "He's afraid of caring, afraid of hoping, afraid of hurting... but yes, I think I know how he feels."

Wakefield looked at his daughter. Her love and compassion and understanding were quite beyond him. They filled him with a certain awe that he had helped produce her.

But still he hesitated. Some of his anger had seeped from him during April's recital of events, but nothing could really block out the months of agony, of not knowing what had happened to the only two people he had in the world. He understood most of MacKenzie's moves, but not the one at Amos Smith's cabin, not the one in which the scout had consciously taken his daughter and grandson up into the mountains. But then he realized why he didn't understand. It had been a human decision, a humanly selfish decision, one he had not expected MacKenzie to make. He had long ago stopped expecting weaknesses in the man, but apparently his daughter and grandson had wreaked havoc with his iron reserve. Wakefield could almost smile. Almost. MacKenzie must have gone through hell.

It was a different aspect of MacKenzie. But a husband for his daughter and a father for his grandson? The notion was too new for him to readily accept. April had said he was gentle and tender, but those were sides he had never seen in his scout, though he had observed a sometimes contradictory streak of stubborn defense of those weaker than MacKenzie.

"I'll talk to Morris, then to MacKenzie," he said. "We'll discuss it again later. In the meantime, Mrs. Forbes, one of my officers' wives, will help find you some dresses, and I think you probably want a bath." He took her hand. "I love you, April. I'll do what I can. I promise."

Morris was anything but objective during the interview, and Wakefield wondered at his captain's heated defense of a man he had never previously liked. It was, in a sense, gratifying to find his own judgment so resoundingly echoed, but Wakefield still had his reservations and wasn't sure he wanted to forgive MacKenzie quite so easily. The charges would be easy enough to dismiss; they had stayed within the military system thus far, and Wakefield's influence was considerable. But a part deep inside, a part he wasn't particularly proud of, wanted the scout to suffer just a little of what he had been suffering these past months. It was also difficult to reconcile April's description and Davey's hero-worship with the cold, aloof and arrogant traits of the scout he had so valued for his objective ruthlessness.

After dismissing Morris without comment, Wakefield made his way to the guardhouse.

Without being told, he would have known which of the two cells held MacKenzie by the restless stalking within. A guard hovered near him and, with an impatient wave of the hand, Wakefield banished him.

With a trace of ironic humor, Wakefield regarded MacKenzie carefully. "If you're going to stay here long, it seems we'll have to replace the boards."

MacKenzie stopped his pacing. "Am I?" He had wondered if and when he would be turned over to civilian authorities. The sooner the better. He did not want to be this close to April and Davey. It hurt too damned much.

"Going to stay here long? I haven't decided." After months of agony, he wasn't going to make this interview easy for the scout. Besides, he wanted to make his own judgment on April's choice of a husband.

MacKenzie met his direct stare. He had surrendered his freedom but not his pride, not his spirit. He dominated the small cell.

"I could easily, and quite happily at the moment, shred your skin for the worry and trouble you've caused," Wakefield said slowly, emphasizing every word.

MacKenzie's gaze didn't waver. "I'm sorry," he said, and somehow Wakefield knew it was a unique announcement. "I'm sorry for that," MacKenzie repeated. "You didn't deserve it."

"Humility, MacKenzie?"

A small smile lit the scout's face as he considered the question. "Perhaps."

"Well, maybe the past months did accomplish something, then," Wakefield observed. MacKenzie's face *was* different. Only a hint of the old arrogance remained, and there was a sort of puzzled humanity that Wakefield had sensed but had never actually seen there before.

"Most of the charges have been dismissed," Wakefield continued abruptly. "The Peters girl finally told the truth. April says she went with you willingly. There remain the small matters of stolen property, assault on army personnel, escape . . . I could continue."

MacKenzie, feeling his gut tighten into a knot, acknowledged the words with a grim set of his mouth. "I suppose you could," he conceded.

The two men stood there in tense silence. Weighing each other carefully.

It was several minutes before Wakefield began again. "My daughter says she stole one of the horses . . . not a very good admission for a general's daughter, do you think?"

A muscle throbbed in MacKenzie's cheek. "She did not, and I will say she did not. I forced her through the boy. She is guilty of nothing except . . ."

"Except what?"

MacKenzie's voice shook just a little. "Of being too kind, too caring."

"Strange," Wakefield said. "That's what she says about you. Somehow I never expected it."

MacKenzie strode to the bars, and his hands clasped them desperately. "Send me away from here . . . I don't care where. Just get me away. It's better for them."

"Is it?" Wakefield said coldly. "Or is it better for you, MacKenzie?"

Only the raw agony in the scout's face answered him.

"My daughter says she married you. She considers it binding. Apparently you don't," Wakefield added with ice still glinting in his eyes.

MacKenzie's hands were white as they strained against the bars. "She . . . shouldn't have . . ."

"I am finding my daughter every bit as stubborn as you, MacKenzie. I don't think I envy either one of you."

MacKenzie slowly absorbed the words, a seed of hope growing within. "I don't . . . understand . . ."

"Do you want my daughter and grandson?" The words were purposely blunt.

MacKenzie's eyes closed with sudden wild, elated confusion. It couldn't be happening. When he opened them, Wakefield had his answer. Longing and love were so very obvious in his face. It was, indeed . . . tender.

"I'll see that all the charges are dropped," Wakefield said, somewhat more softly than he meant to. "I do expect a more . . . traditional ceremony . . ."

"General . . . ?"

"Of course," Wakefield continued, halfway enjoying the rare confusion in MacKenzie's face, "I will probably be losing a good scout . . ."

"Not so good anymore," MacKenzie commented wryly. "I stumbled right into Morris."

"Distracted?"

"A little," the scout admitted. "Your daughter has a tendency to do that to me."

The bantering tone left Wakefield's voice, and it became harsh. "Can you make her happy?"

"I don't know," MacKenzie said with some of the old doubt. "I just know I would try like hell."

"You're not exactly the son-in-law I would pick."

This time, MacKenzie's mouth spread in a wide arc. The sunbeam inside had spread to a miraculous sunrise . . . a blinding glow of light and promise. "I can understand that," he said in a voice that Wakefield thought came close to sounding humble. MacKenzie?

"I love her, MacKenzie. And she loves you. And so, obviously, does Davey. I trust her judgment. But by God, if you cause her one more moment of unhappiness . . ."

MacKenzie's eyes were haunted. "I don't know . . ."

"More humility. I think I could learn to like that in you."
Wakefield grinned. "Morris has offered to share his quarters
with you. I take it I can accept your word that you'll stay at
Fort Defiance until I can work everything out."

"I still don't understand . . . why you're doing this . . ."

"Because I don't want to be tarred and feathered by my own
family. And, believe it or not, MacKenzie, I've always sort of
liked you."

MacKenzie was released several hours later, and April was
waiting for him in the guardhouse office. She had taken a bath
and changed to a borrowed pink dress. She had always been
beautiful to MacKenzie, even in the worst of times, but now her
happiness gave her a special radiance. He was still a bit disbe-
lieving at his sudden change of fortune, but holding April
helped make it real. He wondered how she could abide him. His
whiskers were thick on his face, and his clothes were the same
ones he had worn for the past several weeks. Still, she drew as
close to him as possible while she looked at him with such naked love that he thought his heart would burst. They stayed like
that, as the guard self-consciously found other duties to attend to, until General Wakefield entered. Only his lifted eyebrows commented, and MacKenzie and April separated a little,
their hands still tightly intertwined.

"I've taken the liberty of talking to the post chaplain," he
announced. "You can marry tomorrow if you're both still of
the inclination." He sighed as he saw, very obviously, that they
were. "He did say he needed MacKenzie's full name."

There was complete silence. Wakefield had never known it.
April had never heard it. MacKenzie was not pleased about
sharing it.

"MacKenzie?" Wakefield questioned.

MacKenzie hesitated, his mouth twitching. Finally, he admitted wryly, "Burns MacKenzie," as he eyed April for a hint
of distaste.

Her hand cupped in his, April could barely restrain a giggle.
She looked up at him, laughter and love and joy lighting her
face. "I think it's perfect," she whispered. "Just like you."

MacKenzie felt a flood of warmth and belonging and tenderness he had thought he would never know. "It's you, my
love," he replied quietly. "You gave me a miracle."

* * *

The miracle continued. MacKenzie first went to Wakefield's home where he was reunited with Davey. After bounding into MacKenzie's arms and receiving a bear hug unlike any MacKenzie had previously offered, Davey stepped back, a very serious expression on his face. "Are you all right now, MacKenzie? Are you really all right?"

April and MacKenzie stared at each other. Apparently everything they had been trying to keep from Davey had communicated itself, in some way, to the boy.

MacKenzie slowly smiled, a wide smile full of joy. April trembled from its impact. It *needed* to be used sparingly, she suddenly thought, or she would remain in a state of perpetual idiocy. She could barely stand now, so weak were her legs, so trembling her body.

But it was nothing compared to the next few moments. MacKenzie got down on his knees and regarded Davey solemnly. "I have a request to make," he said in his wonderfully soft burred voice.

Davey looked at him with his head tipped, curiosity in every feature.

"I want your permission to marry your mother again..."

If heaven was ever in a little boy's face, it was in Davey's that moment, and now April's heart joined the quaking and general disability of her body. She struggled to keep back the tears as Davey whispered, "Yes...oh, yes."

The rest of the evening went by in a blur... every moment a wonder in itself, until MacKenzie finally left for Morris's quarters. Lost in a happy daze, April prepared for bed and, for the first time in days, slipped easily into a sleep no longer dominated by fear but by a soft happy contentment.

Some of MacKenzie's reserve returned as he approached Morris's quarters. He had, more or less, been ordered to stay there by Wakefield, but he felt awkward and uncomfortable in doing so. He would have preferred a piece of ground some place, he thought, where he could be alone and consider the last few hours. He wanted, with all his heart, to marry April, but he couldn't dismiss all his fears about what it meant for her, of the misery it might bring.

He didn't exactly know how he felt about Morris. Their relationship thus far had been wary, that of captor and prisoner, then scout and officer. He had to admit a grudging respect for the man, and Wakefield had told him Morris had been almost insubordinate in his defense of MacKenzie. But MacKenzie still couldn't quite dismiss that warning voice inside, the one that told him not to trust.

Morris was reading, a glass of whiskey at his side. Any doubts MacKenzie had about his welcome were quickly dispelled by the wide smile.

"I hear congratulations are in order."

"Thanks to you, I'm told," MacKenzie said hesitantly. "I understand you . . ."

"To hell with that. The old man had already made up his mind. He's always liked you." Morris grinned disarmingly. "I could never quite understand why." He offered MacKenzie a glass. "Until recently, that is. I've found children are seldom wrong." He held out his hand, and MacKenzie took it firmly, and both men knew, somehow, it would be a lasting friendship.

MacKenzie, still new to the idea, hesitated, then very slowly, very carefully asked, "I don't suppose . . . I mean I think I need someone to stand with me tomorrow . . ."

Morris's grin extended even farther. "I would be delighted."

MacKenzie didn't sleep nearly as well as April. A thought nagged at him throughout the night, and it continued to nag him the next day.

The wedding was set for the post chapel, and he was tense and wary, not for himself but for April and Davey. He knew Wakefield had invited some people, and he feared they would snub her. It simply was not acceptable for a white woman and a half-breed to marry.

But the chapel was respectably filled and the faces, far from malicious, were sympathetic and warming. There were even tears. Everyone, by now, had learned much of the story, and it had touched their romantic souls. The image of MacKenzie attacking a bear with a knife to save the general's grandson did what little else could do. That and the fact that the scout had sacrificed his own freedom to save some of their own. The obvious love in the eyes of all three participants did the rest.

And MacKenzie looked devilishly handsome. There were even a few sighs from the women in the chapel when he entered. He had borrowed dress clothes from Morris, and their black starkness emphasized his gray eyes and black hair. But it was the look in his face and eyes when he visually caressed his bride that affected everyone. The hard, austere face had softened in some mysterious way, and the mouth folded into a shy smile that held a wealth of charm. Hearts fluttered and eyes teared. The men wondered if this was the same arrogant scout they had served with. And April ... April was beautiful in her borrowed blue dress, her eyes glowing like a lake shimmering with the rays of the sun.

Afterward, MacKenzie accepted their congratulations awkwardly, amazed at their apparent sincerity. He clutched April's hand like a lifeline, and his eyes laughed only when they touched April or Davey.

April kept looking at him, and not only with fascination. There was something bothering him, something that was beyond the things she already knew. There was a strange light in his eyes that had not been there before. She could feel the tension in his body.

As soon as she thought it polite, she made excuses, and she and MacKenzie left, leaving Davey in his grandfather's proud care. They would use the general's house tonight, while he stayed in one of the vacant officer's quarters. Tomorrow they would switch, until all of MacKenzie's legal problems were put to rest. And then they planned to leave for MacKenzie's valley.

It was twilight, and the first stars were blinking above while the earth was bathed in muted gold and pink. For a land that could be so savage and unforgiving, it was incredibly peaceful, April thought. Her hand tightened around MacKenzie's as a sweet pain struck her.

"It wasn't so bad, was it?" she said teasingly.

"I think I would rather had fought that bear again," he answered, and April smiled inwardly at the wry self-mockery in his voice. But it held none of the old bitterness, and there was a new note in it. Something light and hopeful.

She looked up at him. "MacKenzie?"

There was a painful self-searching in his face. "I've been wrong all these years, haven't I?" It hurt him to say the words, to admit that so much of his life had been based on a lie.

April's hand squeezed his, sensing the wounds and uncertainty.

"My father... he taught me, made me believe, all men were like Terrell and Peters and Pickering. I never gave anyone a chance to prove otherwise... not even your father, or Ben Morgan. I was always so afraid of being betrayed that I betrayed myself." Each word was hesitant, like the steps of a man walking in the dark. "I wouldn't let myself see people like Morris... or those today."

April thought her heart would break, and she was heedless of the tears snaking down her face. But she could say nothing. He had to do it. He had to do it all.

"April." He released her hand and cupped her face in his hands. "I didn't know what I missed until I met you, until Davey put his hand in mine, until Bob Morris risked his career for me."

Now there were tears in his eyes. "Teach me, April. Teach me to trust." There was such anguished yearning in his eyes that April couldn't, at first, speak.

But she knew she didn't have to. He had already started to learn, and while she knew it might be slow, the seed was well planted. "Ah, my love," she said, "you've already started. So well. So very well."

His eyes were searching as he sought reassurance, as he sought her own confidence. He found it in her face, and he knew that no matter what happened, what their future might hold, he would never be alone again. He would have her. He would have her love. And because of it, he would have so much more.

MacKenzie's lips turned upward in the first untroubled smile they had known. And they touched April's.

Oh, so gently.

Oh, so hopefully.

And oh, so completely!

Epilogue

The sun was setting as MacKenzie and April reached the path to his valley.

Without speaking, they stopped and dismounted and went to the place they had stood once before so many months ago. MacKenzie put his arm around her shoulders, and together they watched the huge red ball dip slowly behind the golden cliffs. Its lingering, caressing rays painted the blue-green valley floor with rich strokes of rose and gold and coral, mixing with the thin column of smoke that came from the cabin. Davey was down there. Davey and her father.

April leaned against MacKenzie's lean, hard body, a body she had gotten to know well in the past month. And yet there was always something new about it, and the incredible responses it brought forth from her own. It had been a month of discovery and supreme happiness. A time of loving without fear, without doubts, without ghosts. It had been a time of gentleness, of fierce splendor, of incredible sweetness.

April looked up at MacKenzie's face, hardly crediting the changes in it. His mouth smiled easily now, and his eyes were alive with eagerness and anticipation. They had relished this time alone, but now both were eager to see Davey again, to begin a life that held so much promise . . .

Wolf whined anxiously. He had been waiting at the mountain cabin when MacKenzie and April had arrived, his onyx eyes full of welcome.

It had been partly for Wolf that April and MacKenzie had retraced their steps. And partly, April thought, to rid MacKenzie of the last vestige of a haunted childhood, a sort of cleansing. He had gathered the last of the items he had unearthed several months earlier and stared at them for a long time before reburying all but the Bible. This time, they would stay there. He had taken the money with him to Fort Defiance, intending to see that April and Davey received it. It had now been sent to Ben Morgan in Texas, to purchase some blooded stock. The horses would be here soon. Here in his valley.

April and MacKenzie had needed this time alone, to learn about each other without the fear that had haunted them earlier. It had been a time of golden treasures for both ... every shared sunrise and sunset, the carefree swims in mountain brooks, the teasing times before they united in fiery, loving embraces and the aftermaths when they lay contented on the sweet-smelling pine needles.

Davey had stayed with his grandfather. Once he had learned that the stern man in blue meant no harm to MacKenzie, he had readily succumbed to Wakefield's rough affection, and Wakefield had hungered for the chance to get to know his grandson.

The sun disappeared completely behind the craggy mountain peaks, and only a misty pink glow remained. The waterfall seemed to beckon them down, and Wolf whined once more with eagerness.

MacKenzie looked down at April, his face bathed in the soft twilight, and his hand tightened around her shoulder. He wondered how anyone could be this happy, this content.

"Come, love," he said finally as the music welling up inside him threatened to erupt and overwhelm him. "Let's go home."

* * * * *

COMING NEXT MONTH

#27 SILVER SWORDS—Caryn Cameron

Proud Louisiana beauty Melanie McVey had always done
things her way—until barbarous Gulf pirates turned her
life into a wretched nightmare. The dashing pirate Silver
Swords vowed to protect the stubborn spitfire who'd
ignited his soul, but could Melanie let herself love a man
who lived by his sword?

#28 WIND RIVER—Elizabeth Lane

A woman alone in rough Wyoming Territory, Stella
Brannon was asking for trouble. She'd shot a boy,
accidentally or not, and the town's restless mob threatened
to have its fun and then lynch her. Cade Garrison wanted
justice, but his plans for a fair trial were jeopardized when
he found himself falling in love with his brother's killer.

AVAILABLE NOW:

#25 SO SWEET A SIN
Brooke Hastings

#26 SEIZE THE FIRE
Patricia Potter